Healers of Big Butte is a light-l
inner struggles during a little knov
Butte, Montana Territory, 1875-18.
the once pristine mile-high bowl on the Continental Divide, where
miners and cattlemen come into conflict, and tensions lead up to the
Nez Perce War.

*"I am reading Jan Elpel's first book, Berrigan's Ride, which I am quite en-
joying, first for her writing style and second the careful threading together of
history, geography, and fictitious life stories."*
— Mitzi Rossillon, Consulting Archaeologist, LLC

*"Healers of Big Butte is another significant story from one of Montana's
historical writers. The attention to detail and accuracy in Jan's latest novel, set
in and around Butte, one of the most historically important places in Montana,
cannot be overstated. The Healers are intertwined with each other in caring
for the people of the Territory, albeit their opinions and practices are very different. It truly helps us understand life in the 1870s in the mining cities of
Montana Territory."*
— Margie Peterson, Editor and Oral Historian

"Tex wanted to dispose of the horse right away...I couldn't do it,
but I suppose if his mind isn't right, we will have to do it sometime."

"If this is a case of weed poisoning, I have seen them go either
way—but he is entirely worth the effort to save him." Carrie had already
fallen in love with the Connemara for his will to fight for his life."

I thought I was your love," Mac muttered, nudging her cheek much
like Love did. Sometimes with your healing obligations I wonder if I
have a wife at all. If you start healing sick horses I'll be a lonely man."

In Idaho Territory, Jonathan Duprés exercised his utmost skill in
interpretation to no avail... since Non-Treaty Nez Perce grievances
failed to be addressed.

A fiercely painted warrior beat upon the ground and said, "What
does the ground say? Can we divide the Great Mother?"
—From *Healers of Big Butte*

"Wisdom comes to us in dreams."
—Smohalla, Shahaptian medicine man of the Dreamers

HEALERS OF
BIG BUTTE

JAN ELPEL

Silver Sage Studio & Press, LLC

Healers of Big Butte

Cover Art and Illustrations by Jan Elpel
Cover Design by GRIFFUI

Publisher's Cataloging-in-Publication Data
Elpel, Jan 1937–

Healers of Big Butte / By (Author), Jan Elpel

    ISBN: 978-1-892784-39-1 $16.00 Pbk. (alk. paper)
    1. Historical Fiction. 2. Montana Territory. 3. Butte
    Silver Mining. 4. Nez Perce War. 5. Nineteenth Century
    Medicine.
    I. Elpel, Jan. II. Title.

Silver Sage Studio & Press, LLC

Published by
HOPS Press, LLC
12 Quartz Street
Pony, MT 59747-0697
www.hopspress.com

Author's Notes

Healers of Big Butte, 1875–1877, explores the period of silver mining in Big Butte, Montana Territory, between the gold rush and the Copper Kings. This novel is a work of fiction portraying attitudes, relationships, and medical practices of Butte's diverse population. In an often light-hearted vein, the story exposes weaknesses, prejudices, tempers, charity, humanness, and magnanimity of these individuals who lived and interacted in close, competitive ethnic communities. The characters represent a diversity of healers in an often humorous or tragic study of modern medicine in mid-1870s.

From the journals of Lewis and Clark to history of the United States' intersection with western tribes, research establishes a panoramic view of rapid if not always judicious expansion of the country and its wealth. I found this larger picture, and the benefit of hindsight, shed light on the short but significant period of silver mining in Big Butte and tensions leading up to the Nez Perce War.

All the cities, towns and geographical locations in this novel are factual. All characters are imaginary, while legendary figures such as Doc Beal, Marcus Daly, William Clark and Conrad Kohrs are cited in the historical background. The Continental Hotel and other buildings and their locations in Big Butte are fictitious, though streets generally conform to present day maps. County and Territorial Commissions are used loosely to convey issues and attitudes of the day. An effort has been made to otherwise fairly represent the times and events in historical perspective.

I attribute what may appear to be irreverent views and characterizations to reflections of the attitudes and culture of the times. For any and all errors and untoward portrayals, my apology. Reader comments are welcome.

—Jan Elpel

1

Big Butte, Montana Territory, 1875

There is nothing standing still in nature; if it were, creation would languish and die. Nature will not be trifled with; these are her laws... and we cannot infringe them with impunity.

Prudence B. Saur, M.D.

Carrie Tarynton and Jackson Colter tied their horses away from the corrals to avoid startling the sick horse—if he was still alive. They edged towards the new stable around barking dogs that set off howls from hunting hounds kenneled to the rear of the barn. Carrie wanted a chance to see the stallion prior to Mr. Huckins coming from the house. A beat-up dapple gray in a side pen, alive and swaying unsteadily, appeared unaware of the presence of visitors.

"Blind," Carrie whispered, "or almost with all that blood and damage." On closer inspection, she saw the horse's left eye was swollen shut beneath a huge purple bruise. Lacerations above and below his eye oozed red over dirty caked blood down the sides of his jaw. Chunks of hide and hair scraped from his hindquarters left jagged raw wounds. Mucus and pus dripped from his torn nose.

"Hold on, hold on, aye." Huckins hastened up behind them. "This morning I thought this horse was dead, but I see he's up. He's been running into the pole fence and throwing himself over backwards for three days. I'm surprised he has lived through it."

He paused to catch his breath, his chest heaving under a wide tight vest and gold chain.

"I am glad to see you, Mrs. Tarynton. Ian Huckins here." He extended a hand to Carrie, known by reputation as Mountain Woman, the healer. He nodded at Jackson. "My thanks to you for bringing her." His voice was thick, choked.

"I'll get Tex to rope the darn fool for you. I don't want to lose this horse, you understand."

"Let's think a moment," Carrie said quietly. "What did this horse have to eat and when?"

"Nothing. He has not eaten for three days nor drank any water that I know of." Huckins checked the water tank and found it untouched.

"No, no, I mean before that. When did you get him?"

"He was delivered two weeks ago, an import from the Isles, but he was in the corral for about ten days until I turned him out with the mares. He has a job to do, you know, that's why I brought a stud all the ways from Clifden in County Galway."

The dapple raised his head at the sound of Huckins' voice and backed up. Breathing hard and listing to the side he retreated to the far pole fence. With his head turned, Carrie could see the right eye probably had partial sight though it was bulging and battered.

"When he started moving unsteadily and wandered aimlessly, Tex brought him in. Locoweed, Tex says, or bluebonnet, though I don't know what he's talking about. Makes them go crazy, he says."

"Yes, I would say so," Carrie agreed. "Possibly locoweed or hound's tongue here in autumn. He's not used to either and shouldn't be eating them anyway with all the good feed. I would consider other causes. Ticks, snakebite, or an illness from the long trip among other horses. We don't know, but the harm is done. Let's see if he has a chance of recovery."

She unfastened chaps strapped over her split riding skirt and set them aside with her coat. "We need to avoid frightening the horse with anything that might rustle or flap in the breeze."

In her everyday work clothes and boots Carrie was taller than many men and very thin. Striking, some said. Her wide shoulders set off an angular frame softened by shoulder length brown hair unencumbered by pins under a man's hat.

"He is a beautiful horse, Mr. Huckins. What do you call him?"

"His registered name is Royal Magic O'Shannon, but I call him King. He is a Connemara from a long line of wild horses that roam the mountains of Ireland. He is taller than the ponies and has an excellent disposition that I want in my breeding line. And of course he reminds me of home, the Old Country. I think highly of this horse, Mrs. Tarynton. I hope you can do something."

"I hope so, too. I'll spend some time with him and see. You folks go on and take the dogs away. King needs peace and quiet. Jackson, you can go home, too. Thank you for fetching me. This is a critical time for the horse. He'll survive physically--if he will drink some water—but it is equally critical that he gets his mind back." She eased into the pen as Huckins and Jackson reluctantly left her alone with the unstable stallion.

Little reaction remained in King, whose mouth gaped open, dripping a thick slime of saliva that he tried to lick from his chin and nose. Carrie circled to examine his eye with sight and remained still, talking to him for a long time. Tex came with a rope but she motioned him away. He draped himself over the fence to watch. Her hands were at her sides, eyes downcast to present nothing threatening to this animal that had been pulled away from everything familiar to him. He had spent a grueling month-long journey onboard ship, perhaps longer, across the Atlantic, and traveled by rail to St. Louis. From there Carrie guessed he went by steam freighter up the Missouri to Fort Benton, then trekked three hundred miles cross country to Big Butte.

Images flowed effortlessly through Carrie's mind as she felt the accumulation of terror, sea sickness, and finally trust that must be placed in humans for King to endure the strange and daunting experiences. It was the trust that Carrie replayed in her mind in order to connect with this now deranged stallion whose eye flickered scant recognition of a person. Slowly she turned towards the horse and waited. His unsteadiness was worrisome. He could fall to either side but he held his ground with outspread legs. She moved next to him while her hands smoothed the torn coat and mimicked nuzzling motions that his mother might have made years ago. King snorted, blowing great gobs of mucus on the ground and opening cuts around his nostrils.

When he lowered his head Carrie took the opportunity to place her palm between his ears, allowing her calmness to settle into his body. Carrie found trembling flesh and muscle along his shoulder with her other hand and stood fully connected in spirit if not in mind with the horse. She pictured him well, free and happy in a beautiful green pasture, her breath deeply in tune with King's own inhales and exhales. The heaving of his sides gradually slowed. Tex left, impatient with the inactivity, but came back a half hour later to find Carrie sloshing cool water from a bucket over King's nose and chest, encouraging him to drink. The wild look in the pulpy right eye appeared calmer now, and the stallion took a few faltering steps forward.

"I will come back in an hour and work with him some more," Carrie said to Tex. "Now if I can get some coffee and a bite to eat that would make up for missing breakfast. Jackson and I were up at 4:30 to ride back from the Tarynton cattle drive up Bison Creek." Carrie felt her legs weak and wavering, her work with the stallion having drawn down her reserves.

Tex nodded and sent her to the house, an imposing new two-story log home set next to the mountains where Blacktail Creek emerges from a winding canyon below the Continental Divide in Montana Territory. Tex's attitude clearly conveyed that he was not inspired to commend her work with King. Huckins was not much more confident in a favorable outcome.

"Tex wanted to dispose of the horse right away—before it hurt anybody, or the mares. I couldn't do it, but I suppose if his mind isn't right, we'll have to do it sometime."

"I wish I could tell you that he will be all right, Mr. Huckins, but time will tell. If this is a case of weed poisoning, I have seen them go either way. We might consider other causes for this sudden severe reaction, but be assured he is entirely worth the effort to save him." Already Carrie had fallen in love with the Connemara for his will to endure, to fight for his life.

When she returned to the pen King was down on his right side. His left legs and hooves hung awkwardly in the air, his head thrown back amid his disheveled thick, gray mane. Stricken, Carrie plunged to his side and knelt at his back, her hands running from neck to sides to belly, which now heaved unevenly. Breathe, she told herself, first calming her own frightened response to the collapse of Huckins' prized horse. She focused all the healing energy she could muster, sending it into the heaving body. Eyes closed, she fell into a familiar trance state, one hand now circling counter-clockwise on the horse's belly to relieve his agitation and increase his trust.

Moments later she looked up to see Tex approaching the pen with his Winchester. She slowly rose and straightened to her full five-foot, ten-inch height between Tex and the horse.

"Get some saddle blankets. Hurry."

At the command the hired hand halted as if he had hit a stone wall. Flashing a look of disgust, he set the rifle down by a post, opened the tack room and grabbed an armload of new wool saddle pads and blankets, which he tossed on the fence rail. Carrie pulled out what she could carry and indicated that Tex bring the rest. The two of them covered the prone animal from head to hindquarters with layers of blankets.

"That's the last time I'll see this horse alive." Tex's high-crowned hat, stained by countless years of sweat, branded him as an old school cowhand, along with his short temper and ready solution.

"Bring some linseed oil or melted lard in case we need it," Carrie fumed, knowing men get calloused after years of dealing with thousands of horses and cows, and just get on with it. She refused to brood; the outcome would be what it would be. She doused cold water from the trough over the top of the stallion's head, then her own face and arms. The chill running down her front struck a powerful current within and renewed her strength.

"If I hadn't been successful in dealing with colic and seizures and convulsions, I would not be doing this right now. Could you please go fetch Mr. Huckins for me?" Carrie felt King would not be safe with Tex if she left them in the corral. Huckins soon came barreling down the walk to the stables.

"So he is gone? Or good as gone?"

"I think he is turning a corner for the better. He is resting."

"I'll be damned if he is," Tex blurted. "Them legs sticking out is a sure sign of a fit. He's dead as hell or should be." He spit a long stream of tobacco for emphasis.

Huckins looked helplessly at both the hired hand and Mountain Woman. "In any case I cannot use a half-dead horse with a twisted mind. You take him," he signaled to Carrie, "or Tex will shoot him in the morning."

Tex and Carrie glared at each other over the top of Huckins' bald head. The standoff had begun.

Huckins slowly retreated to the house, muffling the devastating loss. "I dread having to tell the previous owner in Clifden, Ireland." Any goodbyes to his stallion and his dreams he kept to himself.

Carrie couldn't help but note how rich and poor are all alike in the face of grief and loss. A heartbreaking sadness proved a common denominator in those whose pain and suffering she had witnessed over the years.

6

It must be the water, everyone said of the longevity of Mrs. Eugenia Finnegan and the radiant blush of her daughter, Roxanna Heloise Duprés. And it truly might have been, or indeed it had been at one time, when Silver Bow Creek arced undisturbed from its headwaters on the East Ridge of the Continental Divide through the center of Summit Valley. The view from the mountains looked like a beautiful silver Indian bow, thereby earning the creek its name that would one day resonate around the world. The pure crystalline water from snowcaps on the mountains assured a fresh and plentiful renewal of streams on the west side of Big Butte in the Deer Lodge Valley. And that is why trapper Jonathan Duprés intended to stay a long time in Big Butte.

Duprés claimed his favorite seat on a chopping block next to his three-room log cabin, and whittled a small figure from cedar wood, absently marveling again about his good fortune in marrying the red-haired daughter of Eugenia Finnegan. No man within fifty miles had been so successful in winning her hand, and many if not most, had tried. Duprés chuckled to himself, scattering the wood shavings to form a carpet that would keep down the mud and dust in the dooryard. Since Roxanna cared for her mother, he had managed to get a two-fer, two for one, when he married "Roxie," as he loved to call her, and he was quite content with the situation.

Fur-bearing animals populated the floodplain region in unbelievable numbers; even Canadian trapping was scarcely more desirable. Here the winters were hardly no worse, though not much better than his experience living a long time in Canada. Not being one to migrate as readily as the miners whose constant ebb and flow often gave him a headache, he had married and settled comfortably within sight of the knob that gave the mining town of Big Butte its name in Montana Territory.

As he whittled, he thought back a few days when Jackson Colter had raced to their cabin. The clatter of hooves on loose stones had brought Duprés and his mother-in-law, Eugenia, out to the porch.

"Mr. Colter, good day, good day. You are perhaps in a great hurry," Duprés had said.

Jackson had drawn in the reins of his hard-breathing mount. "I have to see Mrs. Tarynton about a horse. I hope I can find her at the ranch. You haven't seen her pass by have you?"

"Yestidday. She left yestidday along with Mr. Tarynton and the cowhands. They went to the Elkhorns to drive a herd of cattle home for the winter. Ye say it's about a horse?"

"Poison plants, snake bite, ticks, I don't know. Something made him sick—the import that Mr. Huckins brought in a short time ago. Sounds bad for the horse. Huckins said 'Go fetch that healer, the Mountain Woman.' I am his nearest neighbor. He is depending on me, so I cannot turn back empty-handed." Jackson's freckled face flushed with sweat as he dismounted and took a long drink from his canteen. "I feel like Paul Revere sounding the alarm."

"Ye best go back and catch Mrs. Carrie on her way up Bison Creek canyon," Eugenia said from the doorway. Duprés nodded in agreement. It seemed like the only recourse right now and anyway, Eugenia was usually right.

"I passed the Hart & Hare and the Killarny gettin' here," Jackson said. "Sure n'all, I'd 'a liked to be inside liftin' a cool one instead of ridin' in this hot sun." He had swung into his saddle and galloped back down the rough dirt road in hopes of catching up with Carrie Tarynton.

By autumn of 1875, the silver rush in Big Butte had done what gold discoveries had failed to do—attracted a thousand folks or so who bought up claims, established stamp mills for both gold and silver, and embarked upon creating their own world of saloons, stores and boarding houses, generally in that order. Affluent investors who formed well-heeled mining companies contributed to the demand for building materials, which were obligingly supplied by Samson Brothers Brick Works and Northern Rockies Sawmill. As if overnight, quaint, miniature but haphazard towns of Dublin Gulch, Finntown and Corktown formed in tight ethnic circles around their immigrants, each recognizable by their pubs.

The first gold strike, the Missoula Lode on Silver Bow Creek ten years earlier, had attracted a population half that of Big Butte now, and those had filtered away when placer gold became scarce. Many did not make fortunes, notably the Germans on Upper German Gulch, and the Chinese who reworked many of the abandoned claims on Lower German Gulch, as well as the mine dumps at Centerville. An estimated five to ten million dollars worth of relatively "easy" placer gold that reportedly left Big Butte hillsides had attracted the fraternal twins, Jackson and Patrick Colter, from Sterling.

"Jackson is a fine young man to go after Carrie like that," Eugenia said after Jackson rode away. "*Maythe Spiorad a bheith ar 'I fe'in agus an capall.* May the Spirit come upon her and the sick horse."

Among the many adjustments to married life, and there were many given that Duprés was considerably older than Roxie, was a linguistic challenge—his French—her Gaelic. Fortunately, they were united in holy matrimony by an English-speaking Irish priest, and they conducted most of their discourse in passable English, that is until it came to spontaneous healing prayers and other peculiarities that Duprés encountered, most recently about the quarry.

"Aye, and what did ye say, aye?" asked Eugenia, cupping her hand behind her sixty-five year old ear.

"The *delf*, Madame," Duprés answered heartily.

"The dell?"

"*Oui, oui,* Mum, the *delf*. 'Tis all the same, the quarry."

"Daft, it is, I daresay," Eugenia said. "So we live in the dell near the *delf*. It gives me such a turn, Roxanna will need to remind me from time to time."

"Of course, Mum, we shall walk about the quarry every day when the weather is better. Surely it was once rich with marble like those in France. Too bad it has been abandoned so. The French *delf* for quarry has a very nice ring to it, don't ye agree?"

As a young wife enamored with her husband and her good Irish luck in marrying so charming a trapper, she lost no opportunity to laud him, his accomplishments, and his distant European origin, though he was Canadian.

Roxanna looked for an answer from Duprés, who left thinking that was enough language and culture, and he would one day explain the quarry stone was granite, not marble, and that he was unfamiliar with Pyrenees marble, rich or otherwise. He shook his straight, dark shoulder-length hair knowing he would be hard pressed to translate the word *delf* into Gaelic, though he was sure they would ask him in time.

Duprés' mind wandered back to the 1860s when he originally scouted the Deer Lodge Valley, and beaver still claimed most of the streams. Extensive beaver dams formed palatial quarters for the industrious, much sought after animals whose luck was soon to run out with the rapacious demand for beaver hats in Paris and London. He was not unaware of the profitability at that time, but he had been committed to return to Idaho with a tribe of Nez Perce after their annual buffalo hunt east of the Rocky Mountains. Their homeland, in truth a reservation, was on the Clearwater River.

Duprés served as interpreter on these Native forays amid white trappers and farmers, and found the association mutually beneficial. Years had passed when he tired of the constant travel, and he knew exactly where to settle down. Finding Roxanna Finnegan of similar mind, his dreams had come true.

––––––––––––

A few days later Eugenia Finnegan made her way along the weaving paths and intermittent boardwalks on Park Street amid the congestion of delivery wagons, mule team freighters, an occasional stagecoach or buggy, and the interminable barking of dogs. The new nickname of "Silver City" added to the uncertainty of an exact name for the town after its recent demise as a gold camp. The town's revival, based on the "rainbow belt," a half-mile-wide outcropping of quartz laced with silver and black manganese, prompted citizens to describe it rather freely based on circumstances or geography. "Big Butte" had an endearing if not enduring quality for its location under the conical butte located above town, the terms "town" or "city" being loosely applied since it was a scattered encampment of hastily devised structures. Hand-sawed boards and materials used ten years earlier to build homes in the gold camp of Silver Bow had been ripped out and hauled eight miles back for reconstruction at the current site of Big Butte.

Eugenia glanced from time to time at new signs in the windows signaling businesses never dreamed of in the Territories—a Norwegian bakery with the aroma of fresh baked breads drifting through the screen door, a weaver's shop where the proprietor worked at the spinning wheel near the window, and a candle-maker's shop where scents of hot tallow, lavender, herbs and cinnamon escaped under its awning. Eugenia was accustomed to visiting H. S. Parker's Mercantile and Apothecary Shop when Roxanna had other errands. Indeed a trip to town would be incomplete without consulting the elderly proprietor, mostly about her own needs, but generally about the doings of others, it being that kind of shop; a clearing house for all public and private affairs of the gentry, housewives, and miners in Big Butte, though no one would explicitly say so and ruin such a good thing.

At last she turned into a rambling, frontier-style frame building that appeared to be an extension of the boardwalk and the hillside behind it. The wooden floor creaked under Eugenia's sure progression to the rear of the building that flared both east and west. The Apothecary Shop, an alcove, received a bit of light through a dirty window, supplemented by a kerosene lantern hung from an overhead beam.

The aging proprietor, Mr. H. S. Parker, though not as old as Eugenia, followed her, leaving his son Sherman, who had acquired his father's middle name, to tend the Mercantile's front counter.

After the usual pleasantries and, yes, Mr. and Mrs. Duprés were quite well, thank ye, Eugenia asked, "Did anyone come in for medicine for a horse?"

"Uh, hum, I do believe so," began Mr. Parker, rubbing his clean-shaven chin. His long mutton-chop sideburns, showing odd yellow patches over gray, more than made up for lack of a beard, which unfortunately would have been the same calico colors.

"A miner with freckles?" Eugenia pursued hopefully.

"I don't know about the freckles, Mrs. Finnegan. The miners' faces are generally pretty smudged."

"What did he purchase, if I may ask? Of course I wouldn't want to discuss anything personal, but ye know, for a horse—." Eugenia well knew a basic code of ethics even in the West, and especially in the apothecary, but it was worth asking considering this had to do with an animal.

"Some tinctures, I believe, and salves. Nothing exotic or of interest, ma'am, if you know what I mean. Why, Eugenia," he said familiarly, "are you up to something?"

"No, no," Eugenia laughed. She could not help glancing at the darkened top shelf lined with dusty blue bottles in the locked medicine cabinet, some unlabeled, that contained the 'exotic' preparations Mr. Parker referred to. Among the popular well-diluted sedatives of questionable native or Mexican derivation for women's troubles and headaches, were the spirits from fifty to seventy proof that Eugenia was particularly fond of.

"Not at all, I assure ye, but tell me, did he say if it was for an Irish horse?"

"Come to think of it, he did. Some fancy stallion that reared over backwards or some such thing and became badly bruised and beat up."

12

Eugenia couldn't wait to tell Roxanna that the horse lived. However, the news would not be confirmed for several weeks until Carrie Tarynton returned with her husband, Michael McHenry Tarynton, and the cattle herd from the Elkhorns' summer grazing range.

———————

Roxanna brought three chairs outside so she, her mother, and Carrie Tarynton could sit on the shady side of the cabin. Pans banged in the kitchen as Eugenia emptied three containers and brought them outside, along with a basket of dried beans to shell. Carrie was talking about the stallion.

"I found King barely alive, Eugenia. You would never have believed he would live if you had seen him when he was down with a seizure. I stayed by his side all day and night so Tex wouldn't 'put him out of his misery,' as he said. We slept on the ground, Love and I. That is what I call him. I covered him with saddle blankets that heated his body and over time he began to relax and breathe normally."

The other two women listened raptly, the beans forgotten in their aprons. Carrie's brown hair hung straight to her shoulders and curled on the ends, defying married women's custom of pinning it up in a bun, which would not fit under her husband's old cowboy hat. Her face was thin, worn beyond her years from relentless sun and winds of the high altitude.

"At daybreak I got him on his feet and pushed and pulled him out of the pen and out of harm's way. I had to or Tex would have shot him. Then my gelding took over, whinnying and nuzzling, telling Love there were great adventures to come. That way my horse and I led the Connemara across Summit Valley from Huckins' place. Love was so weak and unsteady it took us all day to go as far as Jackson and Patrick Colter's cabin. I put him in the corral with their Molly mule for company. I have a feeling this will work, but it will be a long recovery, and I don't know how his mind will be. Jackson and Patrick were surprised but they seem to have accepted him. So did the mule."

The three women cheered with a huge sense of relief that the stallion lived, and that Royal Magic O'Shannon was now paired with a commoner, the miner's mule. Eugenia confessed she had gone to the apothecary to inquire innocently about the horse. They burst into laughter—poor Mr. Parker was readily cajoled by his women customers.

"But I'm scared, Eugenia," Carrie confided. "I – I uh, in a vision, I saw Love with a pack of wolves. I don't know what that means. Surely a pack wouldn't come through the valley near Big Butte, nor around our busy ranch."

Roxanna cut in. "Maybe the gentlemen of money at the Clifden auction! Maybe that was in his past."

Carrie glanced at her gratefully for reframing the image. She could depend upon the younger woman to enliven any situation, and at times, even show some insight. "Yes, it could be past or future as these visions are wont to be. The uncertainty haunts me, though. Mac grows weary over my forever entertaining such ideas."

Shadows deepened on the side of the cabin as the women sat in silence. A hot wind whisked over the quarry and blew wood chips in small eddies at their feet. At last Carrie spoke.

"In another disturbing vision, I recently saw myself with a child. Was that child mine or someone else's? Might it have been my Christina when she was small so long ago? Or a promise for the future? Ah, my dear friends, I can't imagine bearing a child at mid-life. I find these dreams or visions very disturbing."

Carrie pressed her face into her hands. Christina had died in a flu epidemic at age two. Ten years after the birth of her only child, Carrie was now thirty-five years old and childless.

Eugenia shoved another pan full of beans towards Carrie and Roxanna. They sat together shelling them, their years of friendship silently absorbing the pain and absolving Carrie of her sense of loss and guilt.

"Don't tell anyone," Carrie whispered fearfully, "especially not my Mac. He would worry so, and he would be terribly upset by any gossip about us."

2

The human frame is, as everyone knows, constantly liable to be out of order; it would be strange, indeed, if a beautiful and complex instrument like the human body were not occasionally out of tune.   Prudence B. Saur, M.D.

Hot dry winds of early fall scorched sparse hill grass on the slopes surrounding Big Butte. The chatter of red-wing blackbirds moved to lower elevations as swamps dried up along Blacktail Creek. Even coyotes slunk back into the timber to escape the stifling heat at the 7,000- foot altitude under mostly cloudless skies. Only the industry of mineral seekers brought life to Summit Valley in the months before a predicted merciless winter would slam the mountaintops. The heat and intensity led to squalls and brawls and misfortunes of all kinds. Widow Whitmore scalded her foot when she tripped over a cat and spilled her teakettle. Sheriff Ford broke up a fist fight but had nowhere to send the bloodied fighters for treatment. Two cases of rattlesnake bites, a dog and a mule drover, more or less represented the state of medicine in the town. The dog recovered and the drover did not. Casualties below ground multiplied due to greater risks, primitive conditions, and often lack of precautions in the flush of silver mining's nascent days.

At last, after reports of numerous perilous experiences, the self-appointed civic leaders of Big Butte decided physicians were needed in town, and in Walkerville, Centerville, Dublin

Town, and all the rest of the habitations on the north slope of the mountain. These luminaries therefore placed an advertisement in Deer Lodge's *The New North-West* paper that circulated in the East, and stimulated massive investment of Eastern capital into mining operations extending south from Silver Bow to Bannack, east to Virginia City and Hot Spring, and north to Last Chance Gulch in Helena. Their notice included an appealing blurb about prospects, not in minerals but an opportunity to practice medicine in this unique locale of Montana Territory.

A physician, Dr. George Beal, had come earlier from Virginia City, but finding riches in trading rather than doctoring or mining he became a merchant, leaving prospective patients to other practitioners such as midwives, grandmothers, Chinese apothecaries, a Shoshoni herbalist, and the indefinable Mountain Woman. These healers served Big Butte, Silver Bow, and the German Gulch area, much of which was owned by the respected though itinerant Dr. Beal. German Gulch was the site of placer mining and home to many families with children, including the Chinese, all susceptible to ravages of croup, whooping cough, pneumonia, sprains and broken bones, and a myriad of other maladies. The progressive town of Deer Lodge had attracted three resident physicians, an enviable number of professionals to serve the medical needs of the city and sparsely populated cow camps such as that of Conrad Kohrs.

The advertisement proved as welcome to Dr. Beal as to all the citizens of Big Butte. "Doc" had dignified the town by platting the streets and building the Centennial Hotel, famous for its restaurant and his hospitality, in anticipation of the town's growth and acculturation. The addition of proper physicians would be an important step in that direction. When subsequent stagecoaches brought two new doctors, rumors spread like wildfire, with some mirth, that Mrs. Tarynton would be out of a job.

"She's only called upon when no one else is available," gossips said. "Folks will be in better hands with modern medicine."

The rumors inevitably and purposefully reached Carrie's ears in no time. She tossed her head, her hair flying from beneath Mac's old hat, her chin high and light brown eyes undaunted when someone said as much at Parker's store one day.

"There is definitely need for more than two physicians with so many miners and their families here now," she said. "You may find me on the mountain any time."

With a sly and knowing smile, she looked into the eyes of women in colorful bonnets clustered around her, to men chewing steadily on tobacco next to the spittoon, and at last to Mr. Parker himself. The chatter quieted. The onlookers shuffled uneasily. They sensed strange powers in this woman that were at once disconcerting and fascinating, but no one dared discount her to her face.

Mr. Parker spotted Eugenia threading her way through the crowded mercantile towards the alcove housing the drugstore. He trotted after her to fill her standing prescription for Parker's Aches and Joint Remedy for her arthritis, her joints being 'so strung up' she might need a little extra of the spirits, she said.

After Carrie left the general store, the buzzing resumed.

"Yerra, she kin be the Horse Doctor Lady from now on." That brought a laugh.

"I say Mountain Woman can treat the Indians from now on. They're the only ones unnerstan' what 'tis she does."

"I think it's witches she's mixed up with, that's what I think."

"Did you see them eyes? I sure 'n all wouldn't want to meet her in the dark."

"Specially 'round all those Irish with their faeries and stuff. It's a bad combination, witches and faeries."

"Well, we don' have to deal in magic, not with real doctors here. I think we be safer in good hands now. Ye never know aboot the Spirits. I say give a wide distance between them and ye, that's what I always sez to the missus."

"There's that dapple horse I heard was crazy as a bed bug and now's about as good as new—what do ye think about that?

It cain't be what that Molly mule done for him that brought him around."

"We should match him up against a good horse, an Arabian or one of the Serbian horses. Them's a good breed, better than the Irish horses when it comes to working. We'd see if he's good as new. I'd stake some money on the Serb, you betcha!"

The crowd laughed and dwindled away when a sixteen-mule, covered freighter towing two tandem wagons pulled up amid shouts for hands to unload crates for the stores on Park Street, Big Butte's main thoroughfare.

The new physicians reserved apartments above what would become their offices on Park Street until suitable homes were constructed on Excelsior Street heights, that is, if the doctors decided to stay in the Territory. A young man, Isaac Gallagher, M.D., claimed he'd had a thriving practice in St. Louis where he delivered babies, splintered broken appendages after horse accidents, removed infected appendices, and did his best to save clients from the ravages of colds, influenza, scarlet fever, small pox, and other devastating diseases. But the urge to go west succeeded in uprooting him for a new adventure. He reestablished himself with confidence, hardly fazed that a mountain woman, her Irish friend, and a medicine woman had preceded him in treating much of the prospective clientele.

"The women are likely social workers, quite common in the East where women are accepted in nursing. And I am familiar with the Osage, Missouria and Quapaws' quaint practices and ceremonies to accommodate the spirits—in lieu of better medicine," he said. "We may expect to encounter the use of sacred pouches, potions, and eagle feathers, as well as the sweat lodge here in the West."

"I believe I miscalculated this uninhabitable mining town with its primitive medical practices," complained Miss Adelaide

Owens, M.D. "It was entirely misrepresented in the advertisement. It's just a few buildings scattered under a perpetual cloud of wood smoke. The Irish more accurately describe this country as the 'boonies.' As far as I can see, the population is made up of males with a bent for self-destruction that surely could have been well-served by an additional general practitioner."

Miss Owens had come directly from Philadelphia's singular women's hospital, the Garden of the Holy Cross, where her short but distinguished career in obstetrics and gynecology had caught the attention of several staff physicians. To her credit, she had survived the purging—the elimination of female medical students, by gentlemen of the Old Doctors club who evidently felt threatened by the women's intellect and talent. "Saintly," some patients said of Adelaide Owens, whose misfortune it was to acquire the coveted M.D., yet failed to gain the prestige of her counterparts for the same reason she was denied a position on the hospital staff—her gender and the attitudes of her superiors, all men.

As a transplant in the mining town of Big Butte, she went shopping in H.S. Parker's Mercantile and Apothecary, meager as it was, and made a mental note that at least she would have access to a pharmacy. She smirked at Parker's custom preparation for aches and pains alongside Cooper's Vital Restorative for *"cure of loss of memory, lassitude, nocturnal emissions—and many other diseases that lead to insanity and death."* With dimming prospects for support of her profession, or recognition as "Dr." Owens, she scanned the women's section of dry goods to replace her present wardrobe. Fruit Loom cotton yardage sold for twenty-five cents a yard, the best gingham fifteen cents a yard, and bleached cotton eight cents. Not of a mind to sew for herself, she sifted through undergarments, bone corsets, drawers, chemises and hosiery. Men fared better with an abundant selection of canvas and denim overalls, ribbed woolen socks, felt hats, and California buck gloves, the gloves on sale for a dollar fifty.

"I hope they have mail order catalogs," she muttered. Her mood brightened when she found a Broadway seamstress who measured her generous figure for all-season outfits. The shop displayed clothing of superior quality. Puff-sleeved blouses and long skirts would be cool in summer yet modestly cover wrists and ankles. Formal gowns designed by the seamstress were of surprisingly rich fabrics of silk with velvet trim in the latest fashions. For winter, the seamstress layered clothing with soft lamb's wool to provide warmth yet a sense of style. None would bear the hospital monogram, GHC encircled in red and pierced by a thin gold cross, that doomed her present wardrobe.

Adelaide trudged home to her new apartment under an armload of packages containing accessories, ruche and lace collars, prim hats and a wool shawl. Everything is uphill or downhill, she panted, dodging stout canes portly men and women used as walking sticks. At the same time, she assessed the pool of potential patients in passing, including a gray-haired Irish woman with bright blue eyes whom she had seen browsing in every drawer of women's delicates in the Mercantile.

Jonathan Duprés, erstwhile interpreter, waited in Big Butte for a summons to assist in negotiations among the Nez Perce reservation tribe, the non-reservation Nez Perce, and the United States military. Both factions of the tribe were under pressure from the government to abide by the Treaty of 1863. The "Steal Treaty" as the Natives called it, signed at Lapwai, Idaho Territory, reduced the size of the first reservation to one-fifth of that allocated by the original Treaty of 1855, leaving the best grazing land and the Nez Perce homeland to settlers and gold rushers. The lost tribal land occupied the rich valleys and plateaus between the Grande Ronde River and the west side of the Snake River as far south as Wallowa Lake in Oregon, a long cherished region that had now been appropriated and occupied by force.

The loss so infuriated Old Chief Joseph that on his deathbed in 1871, he had told his son Joseph, "My son…you are the chief… Always remember that your father never sold his country."

Jonathan bent over a length of white pine with his Bowie knife, his rather sharp nose defining a long thin face with prominent cheekbones above a short, thick beard. He whittled fast and flung woodchips around the stump where he sat outside his cabin.

"You promised me you would stop traveling, Jonathan," Roxanna reminded him.

"The *Nimíi puu*, "the real people" as they call themselves, are dear to my heart. I lived as one with them one winter when they came to the Headwaters of the Missouri for their buffalo hunt." In fact, the tribe included offspring from his loins by several of the women he no longer cared to identify since his Christian wedding to Roxanna.

Roxanna could only stare at him in mute desperation, signaling fear that he would likely drop off the edge of the earth, that was surely more flat than round, if his Indian friends called him away from her. Nervous fingers twisted wisps of red hair straying from under her starched bonnet. She chewed the corner of her lip until it bled.

Duprés swallowed hard, brushed the wood shavings from his stout thighs, and dodged meeting her eyes. At last, with a peck on her cold cheek, he murmured, "I best pull up some of my traps in case I am summoned," and made his escape.

Roxanna's knees let her down on the stump recently warmed by her husband's rawhide pants. Her husband had made it clear that the Nez Perce were his people, and from recent news there was no doubt of the urgency for negotiations. She understood it was his linguistic talent that gave him stature with not only the Nez Perce, but also with other tribes in the Northwest.

"I will return to my lovely Irish maid," he had vowed, holding her chin in his rough fingertips. "I will not forsake my Irish wife and family."

Jonathan had described huge gatherings that included the Shoshoni, Bannocks, Nez Perce, and other tribes, all vitally impacted by invasion of their grazing and hunting grounds west of the Snake River. He was needed to translate the Shahaptian of the Shoshoni and Nez Perce into English, French, or trader shorthand called Chinook Jargon, and the responses in reverse order, with all parties involved in lengthy negotiations. The cumbersome and not always successful process did not reassure Roxanna that her husband's trip would be short. She only knew it would be a matter of time before he must pack to be away for several months. Anxiety overshadowed the Duprés cabin until Roxanna's nerves became taut as a fiddle string, so when Eugenia came home from town and said she had overheard threats to steal the dapple gray, Roxanna let out a long, piercing cry.

"Ye think they might steal him on a bet?"

"They might scheme to race him against an Arab or a mustang or some other bloomin' horse," Eugenia fumed, forgetting exactly what they had said.

Roxanna's voice rose in her usual hysteria. "No! Not Carrie's stallion. Not the Connemara! What are we going to do, Mum?"

Eugenia related her eavesdropping in the store. "I was about to leave the Apothecary where I picked up my remedy, the one I like so much, seventy proof, aye, when I heard the men talking and I think half of them were soused, mid-day, too, 'tis a shame. They bragged over each other saying awful things about Carrie being a witch. I was so frightened I kept to the aisles, hiding among drawers of women's unmentionables so the men wouldn't notice me."

"And what exactly did ye hear, Mum?" pressed Roxanna, impatient with the length of the story.

But Eugenia continued at her own pace. "A new woman was there listening, too. I never saw her before, but she couldn't help hearing about the Horse Doctor Lady being a witch, and the blokes cursing the Irish and faeries like they know what they're talking about, only they were talking through their bloody hats."

"But what about the horse; ye must tell me about the horse so I can tell Jonathan."

"Roxanna, my dear, I am telling ye. I fear mightily for Carrie and the horse. There you have it, aye. It is my knowing; I can feel it." She sat back in her rocker, her hands cupped in her lap, her lips a thin firm line.

Eugenia did not need to emphasize in order for her daughter to understand. Their collective experience was that Eugenia's hunches were indeed perceptive. If Roxanna were a gambler she would bet on her mum's sixth sense a thousand times over. Ye could have the gift, too, Eugenia always told Roxanna, but her daughter's usual anxiety over fearful images interfered with a proper reading of her intuition.

"Now," Eugenia said, slapping her palm on her knee, "We must inform Jackson and Patrick or Carrie about the scheme to steal the horse." A method for doing that did not immediately present itself. Jonathan Duprés was no help, since he was tending his trapline in case he would have to leave shortly for Idaho.

"If only my husband stayed home as he promised!" Roxanna persisted. No one else lived near the quarry who might make the considerable trip either to the Colters' far across town or up the mountain to Mac and Carrie's ranch. Eugenia breathed deeply with a sense of dread, remembering the wolves Carrie had envisioned around the stallion.

The empty blocks of the city on the breast of the Continental Divide quickly filled with eager entrepreneurs. From a buckshot approach to building with scavenged materials, residents now had an eye for more aesthetic and permanent structures. A fire at aging Widow Whitmore's old cabin not only ran her out of town, but the conflagration threatened the red light district and nearby Chinese laundries. As a result, Guildsmen from central Europe set to work quarrying the heights of the Divide in earnest. The yield was surprisingly handsome from gigantic, rose-colored granite blocks already split along fracture lines and stacked by nature in three-story columns. Speckled and striated gray blocks lay jumbled near the summit, and available for the taking at what became known as Pipestone Pass.

Granite quarries dotted the mountains as far north as Elk Park. Swaths of timber removed to reach the granite were bought by mining companies for their operations. For all its depths of gold and silver and accompanying zinc and lead, the surface resources—the granite and timber that built Big Butte, often went unacknowledged.

Above Park Street, the town of Centerville contoured itself around the ungainly northern slopes in an attempt to adapt to a rigid grid of streets below. Here the Cornish and Irish built tidy frame homes close to the mines. A popular pub, the Hart & Hare, kept its door open twenty-four hours a day. There Jackson and Patrick's after-work respite turned into a rare argument.

"This mining stinks." Patrick twirled his glass of warm beer until the froth flew off on Jackson's shirt. He stood at the bar, his dark features moody, eyes shadowed beneath his dusty fedora. Behind him miners jostled and hooted back and forth to comrades, the relief typical of men when they emerged unscathed from underground.

The twins were employed by the Silver Dollar Mining Company, whose massive headframe bespoke of silver millions, a prospect to be determined as the miners drilled deeper, shoring up the shafts and drafts with timbers as they progressed. Fatefully perhaps, the Colter brothers had sold their placer claims in Big Butte to speculators once the surface gold ran out. Hardrock silver mining required substantial investments which they and most placer miners could not afford. Six years ago Patrick and Jackson had also sold their placer claims in Hot Spring District in Madison County for the same reason. All they owned now was their cabin at the mouth of Bison Creek, two horses and a

Molly mule. They had no time for Carrie Tarynton's temporarily boarded stallion when they came home late.

The saloon girls in pink and green satin gowns avoided the two patrons who looked tense and angry. Jackson tried to bite his tongue, but words rushed out. "Why are you complainin'? You wanted this job, same as me."

"Now I don't. I hate the underground. This isn't what I'm cut out for, you ought to know that, or are you so fixed on marrying that little woman you need to make a day's pay? Then what will I do?" Patrick glared at Jackson's flushed face, needling him in a soft spot.

Breaking up the twin set was the crux of the problem, Jackson quickly determined, as much or more so than the mining. Patrick was the outgoing, assertive, mature fraternal twin; a handsome figure with his square jaw and straight teeth. Women gravitated to him. Gentlemen who might ignore run-of-the mill miners generally treated him with respect. Jackson, however, with roundish features and freckles was often overlooked in the stream of grimy workers coming and going from the mines. He had always taken second place to Patrick. Jackson felt a little flattered now and touched that Patrick claimed a right to him. He wondered how to bridge the present gap.

"I didn't say I was gettin' married, did I? Wouldn't you be the first I'd tell, Patrick? You're dreamin' all this up."

"Something has to change. I just don't want to work in the mines any longer. I'm going back to Boston for good." Patrick's voice was flat and cold, one he seldom if ever directed at his brother. The decision had the ring of finality.

Jackson choked on a gulp of beer, further staining his shirt. He tried futilely to wipe it away with his sleeve. "Damn it. Let's not end like this after all these years. I don't like this, Patrick. You can't pull out just like that."

"You're wrong—I can go my way, and you don't have to be a part of it anymore." Patrick stood up ready to storm out.

"Patrick, please, don't leave me. This isn't right. The folks wouldn't like it if you moved home and I didn't. "

"They need to realize sometime that twins aren't one person. That they—we—can separate, for god's sake. It's about time." Patrick's gumboots clunked on the wooden floor and echoed in Jackson's ears long after his twin left the pub.

They took King to the Tarynton ranch the next day.

"Carrie isn't here." Julianna Brom, the ranch cook, wiped her hands on her apron and reached for two cups, "but you can put the horse in the corral and come in for coffee."

Ash stains from campfires decorated the chipped, oversize gray enamel coffee pot. Coffee was a ritual with the Taryntons, black enough to float a horseshoe, everyone said, but you could come in and talk any time of day or night. Coffee was always on.

"The stud looks pretty good," Patrick offered. "I think he is coming around. He led behind my horse just fine."

"I had to bring Molly along or she'd tear up the corral and bray loud enough to attract the constable," Jackson said. "She didn't want to give up her charge." Julianna's low comfortable chuckle reminded Jackson of his mother's.

"I can hear Molly with that foghorn right now talking to her mate in the corral. Do you want to leave her? Heaven knows, Carrie owes you."

"Oh, Carrie's done right by us and the stud all along. Molly has to get on sometime. It might as well be now. Same as me. I'm thinking of going back to Boston. I might want to try sailing for awhile." Patrick talked more easily with Julianna, a tired but tough ranch woman who never quit working, than with Jackson.

Jackson listened intently to hear what his brother had in mind. "I'm looking for something other than day labor where I can get ahead," Patrick added. It was not clear if he had a plan or had decided to take a chance that "something" would turn up.

Later, when they rode past the Duprés cabin near the quarry the two women ran out of the house, overjoyed at seeing them.

"The horse, how is the horse?" Roxanna queried, trying to catch her breath. "We have been waiting to see you, to ask about Carrie's horse."

"Fine, fine. You seem to have worried all for naught. He is safely back at Mrs. Tarynton's." Molly let out another ear shattering protest. "Although I may have to get another horse to take his place with Molly," Jackson laughed.

Eugenia was too quiet, her eyes wide and fearful. The twins waited on their mounts for the women to say more. The silence became uncomfortable so Eugenia finally admitted, "We were afraid of the wolves. That the wolves might get him."

"That won't happen at Tarynton's busy place, ma'am," Patrick said, shaking his head at the silly notion. "Their dogs bark all the time. You can rest easy now. Speak with Mrs. Tarynton when she goes by."

"No, I mean, the men at the store—" Eugenia stammered, "the men who want to bet on him." Her words were lost on Patrick who was impatient to ride on. Jackson had no choice but to follow—this time. Their mutual dependence would change when Patrick left for the East on the next stage bound for Fort Benton on the Upper Missouri River.

The stallion's lonesome cries greeted the Taryntons far down Deer Lodge Valley long before they crested the hills leading to the ranch, the pioneer homestead settled by the senior Michael McHenry Tarynton. Mac, Jr., had muscled it into a sizeable cow operation, not rivaling the vast Conrad Kohrs' spread, but an impressive holding under the *TN* brand.

"Love is home!" Carrie galloped her horse ahead and dismounted on the move to see him. The Connemara thrust his head at an odd angle over the top pole of the corral, revealing the battle scars on his neck and shoulders, but his large, soft eyes framed by black lashes eagerly awaited her. That was all Carrie cared about right now. She stroked the length of his neck as far as she could reach, then crawled into the corral, cooing intimate messages that only he and she could understand, her hands expertly exploring every muscle and joint of his long but compact body, still too thin from his ordeal.

Mac rode up unobserved by the two reuniting after the lengthy caretaking arrangement on Bison Creek. He unsaddled after a long day scouting winter forage for his herd, and went into the house. Carrie came in later from the corral, poured herself a cup of coffee and wearily sat down. Mac scowled and bent over his cup at the table without a word. Carrie soon noticed the unusual tension.

"Mac, are you upset with me about Love?" She knew she had read his thoughts when he looked morosely at her.

"What is it about that horse? Is it going to be you with the stud and me having coffee alone?"

Carrie leapt to his side, almost toppling both of them. Mac stood and she rushed into his arms, hiding a mischievous grin he didn't see as he crushed her in his long, powerful arms. Carrie's head came nearly even with Mac's since she was so tall. He pressed his face against her hair.

"I thought I was your love," he muttered, nudging her cheek much like Love did.

"You are my one and only. You know that, Mac."

Wrapped in each other's embrace, memories cascaded through her mind—their marriage, their loss of two-year-old daughter Christina, the ranch work that sapped energy from their love making. A good many years had passed them by, or had they lived them to the hilt?

"Sometimes with your healing obligations I wonder if I have a wife at all. If you start healing sick horses I'll be a lonely man."

"Mac, are you pining about something that hasn't happened? You're out with cows dawn to dusk. You won't even miss me."

He allowed a snort. She laughed. He held her, rocking on his boot heels, giving in to powerful currents that always passed between them, sustaining their marriage through blizzards, paralyzing heat in the high, thin atmosphere, loss of livestock, and problems with the cowhands often related to alcohol. These they not only survived but together proved them surmountable. At last, tears mingling, Mac raised his head and sighed. Bone tired, he released Carrie, scanning her face to be sure how she felt.

"You are my only love, Carrie," he said, tender as he had proven to be at times over the years, sincerity reflected in his dark brown eyes.

Carrie stroked the boyish, red-brown curls that framed his face and matched the short beard of the same color, noting he needed a trim, a skill she had developed since Mac preferred both be cut fairly short. She smoothed her hands over his chest much as she had done with Love's, stroking over his heart and feeling its strong steady beat, the long heaves of his chest always reassuring, his breath the source of life, their lives. Carrie's hands sensed the energy centers she had learned from an intuitive healer when she was young. "You have the gift," the woman had said. The gift had given direction to her life ever since, and right now she knew her one love, Michael McHenry Tarynton responded to her.

That night Mac murmured into her ear, "I'm crazy about you, Carrie. I'll be crazy same as the stud if you'll keep me."

"Oh, Mac, you're jealous," Carrie chided, again suppressing a smile.

3

*My son... you are the chief. Always remember that your father
never sold his country.* Old Chief Joseph

An early autumn wind teased around the corners and
cracks of the Duprés cabin hinting of chilliness to
come. Jonathan Duprés laid out a medium-sized, tanned buffalo
hide on the cabin floor, and packed his fur boots, leggings and
hat. He tucked a small amount of cash into a deerskin pouch,
tightened its rawhide drawstring, and hid it deep inside his belongings. Jerky, salt pork, dried berries and hardtack went in a
small saddlebag that would hang off the pommel opposite his
rifle scabbard for balance. His absorption in preparing for the
trip to the Nez Perce reservation in Idaho prevented him from
observing that Roxanna chewed her knuckles, fist in her mouth,
to keep from crying out. Eugenia's rocking chair creaked steadily
as always. The teakettle spurted steam in loud hisses.

Last, he rolled and bound the buffalo hide, fur side out, with
leather thongs. Duprés' past diligence in accumulating handmade hide and fur clothing, as well as storage receptacles, meant
he could travel with comparative ease, especially since he would
not be taking his traps. A fellow trapper had agreed to watch his
trapline, which ranged up and down the Deer Lodge valley, and
pull them up before ice set in on the streams.

The day broke overcast, mildly threatening, a sliver of sun
scouting lower in the sky after the fall equinox. A willow basket

31

of ungainly size and shape remained to be tied onto the unresisting horse. Eugenia Finnegan and her daughter had cooked all day yesterday to ensure that Roxanna's husband would not go hungry, at least in the short term. They rose before dawn to bundle soda bread, jam, sliced cold cuts, hard cheeses, applesauce cake, and a spicy steamed rum pudding that Duprés could not resist, though he figured the aroma would attract hungry bears. All were tucked into the basket with small brown bags of cocoa, coffee and English black tea, one of Duprés many departures from French-Canadian cuisine. A pouch of medicinal herbs Eugenia had meticulously prepared was already rolled in the buffalo hide. Finally, he stuck a bone-handled hunting knife into a sheath on his belt.

"Ye make my life like royalty," he addressed the women. "Without ye two I would be nothing, not worth my salt, *n'est pas?*" He glanced around the cabin to be sure everything was taken care of, insofar as he could, before he departed for Idaho. Wood overflowed the battered woodbox near the hearth, and bales of furs were stacked in the corners to be disposed of when the women needed money. Beaver had been extraordinarily plentiful and easy to trap; their tabletop-size pelts now glistened in the glow of the fire. Long, thin mink pelts hung loose to protect the rich furs from being damaged. Muskrat hides of less valuable or luxurious fur were stacked beneath a wad of dried rabbit hides and feet, the musky odors indoors familiar in the women's lives with a trapper.

"Will ye be away long?" Roxanna repeatedly inquired.

"I do not expect to be, *ma cherie.*" The Nez Perce emissary had requested his services to interpret negotiations between tribal splinter groups and the military. "I do hope they are all amenable to solving their difficulties. I fear such a mess—but enough of the fears. Ye and Madame will be safe and warm." He tipped his hat at Eugenia who remained stoically rocking in a trance state, listening—not to Duprés, but to inner voices, with an expression of disbelief.

Roxanna followed her husband outside where he took her in his arms. "I love you always, Roxie, my lovely Irish maid." His attempts to console her over the past twenty-four hours came to naught, so he swung up on his horse and reached down, one last time, for her hand.

"Next time, if there is a next time, you can come with me," he blurted, a rash thought that he immediately regretted. "*Mon Dieu*, what did I promise? Marriage makes one say and do improbable things, my love. Truth is, we'll have to wait and see." He patted the willow basket tied precariously behind his saddle and rode due west toward the Bitterroot Mountains to a trail that would take him over Lolo Pass to meet with the Nez Perce in Idaho Territory.

The brief pang of leaving, accompanied as it was by irritation with Roxanna, was soon replaced by the exhilaration of open country and free time ahead that Duprés had not enjoyed since his vows, extracted by the Irish priest and under God, that he would love and protect his wife forever, amen. He commenced to bite off the end of a long slim *cigarillo*, a crimped tangy-smelling cigarette wrapped in brown paper that added immeasurably to his contentment. Over the next few days, he followed the Clark Fork River toward the town of Hell Gate. He stopped to camp where he had previously spent a season with the Nez Perce when they traveled east of the mountains to hunt near the Headwaters of the Missouri.

Once called Diggers, the Nez Perce had been among the relatively non-nomadic tribes that dwelled near the Columbia River, where they dug roots and fished for their sustenance. A diverse group of Northwestern tribes had acquired horses about 150 years before many of them, including the Nez Perce, had become buffalo hunters. Their subsequent need for annual trips to the hunting grounds provoked conflict with Northern Plains Indians such as the Blackfeet, who already claimed the privilege.

The Council of 1855 in Lapwai, Idaho Territory, had therefore reached an agreement between the aggressive Northern
Plains tribes and more peaceful western tribes. The agreement
partitioned the buffalo hunting grounds, giving those north of
the Missouri to the Plains or Dakota Indians that included the
Blackfeet and Sioux, and those south of the Missouri to the Nez
Perce. This enduring peace treaty that assured a relatively safe
passage for either tribe over age-old trails once claimed by both
sides was negotiated by former Idaho Governor Isaac Stevens,
superintendent of Indian Affairs at the time. The Governor
and later agents were well-known to the fur traders, including
Jonathan Duprés, who had benefited from the Governor's even-
handed ability to reduce conflicts twenty years ago. Today, Duprés proceeded west with confidence until he reached the foothills of the Bitterroot Mountains.

"Ye best turn back," settlers warned him along the route.
"Hostilities with the Indians have broken out. Whites have been
killed."

"Guard yer life and yer horse," others said.

"Cows and horses were stolen in bright sunlight from nearby
neighbors," a rancher bitterly informed him. "We aim to shoot to
kill from now on, ye bet. Everybody's on edge."

"I can't understand it," a trader mourned. "We had peaceful
relations with the Indians, same as my grandparents since Lewis
and Clark come through. Tribes hunted buffalo, and in exchange
we fished for salmon in their territory. It was working out about
right until gold was discovered in Idaho. When miners scattered
over Indian land and settlers paraded through on the Oregon
Trail conflict was inevitable."

Duprés took a short break at a small farm teetering in a clearing on the edge of the mountainside, where a settler invited him
for dinner with his family. The blue-black hue of the Bitterroots
came from heavy timber that draped the massive north-south
range from one end to the other. In 1864, the range became a

partition between Idaho and Montana Territories at the urging of Sidney Edgerton, whose untiring efforts earned him title of first Governor of Montana Territory, though he high-tailed it back to Washington D.C. so often that a semi-permanent acting governor, Col. Thomas Meagher, took his place in Helena, Montana.

"Somebody better tell me what the government wants if I'm going to be of assistance in reaching an agreement," Duprés said. "I understand the tribe is divided over how to respond."

"It's the reservation and the non-reservation factions. The military waded in without thinking of the consequences. Half the Nez Perce refused to leave their homeland in the Wallowa region of Oregon and move to the reservation. Now we have to live with violence that is yet to come."

"It's like leading a horse to water—you can't make him drink," Duprés nodded.

In the early days of competition between the Canadian Hudson Bay Company and American Fur Traders, the first white men into the Northwest encountered what was considered Shoshoni territory ranging from Canada to Mexico along the Continental Divide. This vast land was occupied by Shoshonis, Paiutes, Bannocks and Utes, all speaking similar dialects but separated by different cultures. Duprés' experience trading with the tribes in the early years taught him their languages. In the midst of this were the Nez Perce, who originally claimed the Wallowa Valley on the west side of the Snake River as their homeland. Efforts to force them onto the shrinking reservation at Kamiah met with firm resistance. Duprés knew from his past association with the tribe that roots of their rebellion were timeless.

"I hadn't believed the seriousness of Indian troubles when I moved my family West. We now recognize the danger when it comes to tempers and prejudices on both sides."

The settler's tone was foreboding, and Duprés left with a heavy heart for Fort Missoula near the town of Hell Gate.

A gradual climb over richly wooded foothills that protected lush meadows below from battering by storms brought him to Lolo Pass. Over the Pass, an ancient trail of heart-stopping switchbacks and inclines stirred his imagination—the passage of Natives with families, tipis, herds of several thousand horses, and supplies over this trail for countless years. This practical, generational use had imprinted their pathways on the ridges and crests of the Lolo Mountains high above the Lochsa River, a trail that Meriwether Lewis and William Clark followed on their journey to and from the Columbia River.

On the west side of the pass, Nez Perce guides waited to accompany Duprés on the hundred-mile-ride to the headquarters of their reservation. They continuously scouted the trails in an effort to detect government incursions in the mountains. While the guides led him along the ridges, they related their side of the stories to Duprés regarding whites intruding on their land. At last they descended at Weippe, an encampment situated in a meadow of camas. The Natives depended upon the starch of the camas root to sustain them through the winter, but settlers who remained on the reservation to farm had allowed their pigs to dig up the roots and destroy the crop the previous year.

"My people angry. Warriors tear up fences," one scout said. "White farmers call for soldiers this year. My people kept out of meadow and left to starve. Now women and children cry. They have no food."

"And what does young Chief Joseph do about that?" Duprés asked.

"He try keep his people on homeland and make peace with white people. Other chiefs want war."

There may never be a time when Roxanna could safely accompany me if all out war is in the offing, Duprés breathed, thankful she was not with him on this trip.

From Weippe, he reached the Nez Perce village of Kamiah, headquarters of the Treaty Nez Perce, located within the revised reservation boundaries at the junction of the Clearwater and Lochsa rivers. The Treaty of 1863 diminished the previous reservation to less than one-fifth of that provided under the original treaty. Lost were substantial acres of grazing lands formerly occupied by Nez Perce tribes. Now the Non-Treaty Nez Perce, those led by Chief Joseph, refused to give up their homeland in the hospitable Wallowa Valley to move to the cramped valley around Kamiah. This refusal pitted the Nez Perce against white settlers and gold rushers who preempted their land, and emigrants who demanded safe passage to the fertile Yakima Valley. In addition, the conflicts unsettled the Cayuses and Paiutes, neighboring tribes. Duprés quickly assessed that efforts by Indian agents and missionaries had proven increasingly futile in coping with rising confrontations.

Nights became frigid as autumn deepened into November. Testy winds along the Clearwater River stripped cottonwoods and willows of their bright yellow and orange leaves. The water, so clear it defined every color and contour of its stones, harbored a fringe of ice after colder nights. Duprés visited the native village of Kooskia located in bottomland along the river. Both encampments, Kooskia and Kamiah, were protected from harsh winds that raked the plateaus high above the valley. The gentler climate west of the Rockies had coaxed plentiful forage along the river, and its inlets befriended thousands of horses owned by the tribes. Duprés was aware that Idaho Territory offered everything except buffalo, principal food source for the families for the winter. Their annual fall hunts were a longstanding tradition, usually unhindered by numerous tribes on the Montana Territory side of the mountains.

Continuing on his way, Duprés trailed the scouts beyond White Bird Canyon to the Wallowa Mountains in northeast Oregon, homeland of Chief Joseph and Nez Perce Non-Treaty tribe. He soon confirmed that uniting irreconcilable parts of the shattered tribe after they were ordered onto the reservation in

Idaho appeared to be in vain. Young Chief Joseph had indeed agreed to move to the reservation, but to Yellow Wolf, also a chief, any capitulation to demands by the United States to relinquish their freedom and land was unthinkable. Yellow Wolf's followers remained at large, feisty, radical and unrelenting.

Winter occasionally inched its way across the mountain ranges of Montana Territory, but more often it swept in with blasts of Arctic ice and snow that drove even the hardiest rancher to rethink his occupation. The winter of 1876 offered no pretenses from the heights of Big Butte in Deer Lodge County to the usually more temperate Gallatin County, known as "Valley of the Flowers" by the Natives. Mac Tarynton grew up expecting the worst, and the winter of 1875-76 filled the bill.

He had bought stock from Nelson Story when Story drove longhorns from the Mexican border to Montana Territory ten years ago. Story had envisioned herds of cattle that could withstand hoofing it to market, as well as endure heat, cold and starvation conditions such as the winter descending upon Montana. Story's original stock of Texas longhorns had been tested on the three-thousand-mile drive with Teddy Blue and other seasoned (some say foolhardy) cowboys. The longhorns' three-to-four-foot spread of horns set off the cattle's distinctive, bony frames mounted on short sturdy legs. Story had foreseen a market for beef in the gold rush towns of the Territory, as well as in the East, and his wild-eyed cattle rapidly propagated to stock his spread in the Gallatin Valley. He sold livestock as far away as Norris on the Madison River in the Tobacco Root Mountains. Kent Berrigan, who lived on South Willow Creek, was not a cattleman, but he leased his prime half-section of grazing land to his neighbors. A cattle industry now flourished where cows and calves occupied vast reaches of former buffalo country which became Montana Territory. The names of stockmen were known far and wide.

Mac had taken advantage of the opportunity to produce herds adaptable to the higher elevations of the Continental Divide. Over the years, Mac's mixed-breed stock bearing his *TN* brand became a sizeable herd that wintered well on dried grass close to the ranch. Saddle and pack stock were also turned out to fend for themselves except for a few required back at the house. The reduction in ranch work associated with cattle grazing near the ranch permitted Carrie Tarynton to spend more time with her patients despite Mac's frequent complaints about not having a wife.

Cold winter months brought on colds, pneumonia, and influenza, especially among the elderly, families and children, when every available medical practitioner was called upon to treat them. Accidental exposure became an everyday hazard. Alcoholic intake was incalculable in any season—miner's lunch buckets brimming with take-home beer were handily refilled when off-duty miners lined up in the saloons. Incidents of depression, often a companion to drinking, were more obvious during winter months, and beset men and women alike. Increased incidents of suicide and occasional homicides occurred during the short days and long, frigid nights.

Carrie bundled up and asked Duggan, the ranch handyman, to bring around her team and buckboard so she could drive down the mountain to Finnegan's. Carrie would enlist Eugenia's help to check on her patients. At the cabin, she found Roxanna, seldom one to be a placid soul, still railing against her husband leaving her for the Natives.

"Ye see how easily he upsets our tranquility in answer to the Native call?"

Carrie ignored the grousing and tried to console her. "But did you not tell me he might take you with him if he goes again?"

"T'would be sad if there is a next time, as he suggested," Roxanna sniffed.

Eugenia hugged her midsection. "My stomach takes a leap when I hear these outlandish ideas. My sixth sense says no good will come of Jonathan's invitation. No good would come of a white woman on an Indian trail."

Her words were lost in Roxanna's tirade—her husband's lack of appreciation for his wife, who would do anything to be with him. Eugenia's old rocker answered with its creaks coming faster as she listened with horror to Carrie's forthcoming proposal.

"Of course you need to ride more than you have been doing since your marriage, Roxanna. A woman must always be independent in that respect. I shall be glad to help you if that is your decision."

"Will ye, Carrie? I should be grateful! I shall be so happy to show my husband I am up to it. I will surprise him when he returns!" Evidence of her recent malaise was readily dispelled. Now Carrie had to figure out how to follow up her impulsive offer. *What is it about Roxanna that makes one want to take care of her, for heaven sake?* Carrie's mused, though she did not know that Duprés had felt the same.

"Come to my place tomorrow and we shall see what we shall see, hmm," Carrie said, her mind already on another mission for the day. She turned to Eugenia. "There seems to be an epidemic of chicken pox racing from Walkerville to Big Butte. Would you be willing to come with me today?"

Eugenia bolted out of the rocker, indicating she was more than ready to get away from Roxanna and her endless complaints. She slipped into her thick woolen coat with its dozens of patches and replaced the piece of yardage tied over her hair with a fluffy homespun shawl. Her feet were already in tall warm boots because the cabin floors were chilly. Carrie drove the team to Parker's Mercantile and Apothecary.

"Eugenia, if you pick up calamine lotion, I'll shop the bins for oatmeal," Carrie said. "I suspect Dr. Gallagher will be treating most of these patients, but many families cannot afford to see him. I do know that with patience, chicken pox eruptions go away of their own accord. We might also consider the Chinese Herbal and Natural Medicine Shop for homeopathic remedies."

In Parker's apothecary alcove, Eugenia selected a bottle of pink, sickening-smelling lotion, "though some people like it," she said. She also chose spirits from unlabeled blue bottles high on the apothecary cabinet shelf—an extra large bottle that she assured Mr. Parker was not for herself, but for Carrie's patients. Carrie was not unaware of the subterfuge. Both women stepped far around a large earthen jar punctured with holes that housed leeches used for purging toxins from patients. Other means of purging were blood-letting by slicing tissue with a knife, or administering purgatives that induced vomiting.

The women walked down the street and turned on a dirt path leading to a neighborhood housing Big Butte's poorest families a few blocks from Park Street. The transient nature of the population during the silver boom limited even the pitiful subsistence allowances offered by Deer Lodge County seat miles away. Big Butte residents were widely hailed for their generosity, but efforts by public and private sectors often failed to alleviate the suffering of the unfortunate.

Ducking their heads, Carrie and Eugenia entered a dilapidated tin-covered shack huddled behind several boarded up buildings. Narrow beds filled two sides of a single room and a makeshift stove occupied a third. The rest of the family's possessions were stacked inside or outside a rattling barn door they had salvaged for their home.

"When the young 'uns broke out, I think to myself, they must 'ave been telling lies." The mother, a thin, pale young woman, motioned towards two children about four and six sitting silently on one bed. "T'would be the devil's due to make them sick if they was lying. Then I got it—see my arms and neck—and 'tis up and down my back, and I ain't lied one bit, even to their father who youse see hasn't got in the wood for breakfast. 'Tis the devil's due we live here, no matter right or wrong."

Her voice registered the flat, hopeless feeling of many miners' wives. Encountering despair was not unusual in Carrie's experience with Big Butte's residents. She poked up the fire and brought in rough boards for firewood. Eugenia talked about natural childhood illnesses that the children were likely to have, though she did not dispute the woman's beliefs.

"It be natural as the sun shinin' and the grass growin' that young 'uns get sick," Eugenia soothed while she poured a generous amount of calamine lotion into a chipped saucer. An upturned half of a whiskey barrel served as a table. "Put this on the spots to help stop the itching. It's not the spots that cause the lasting damage to the skin, 'tis the itching that causes the scars. And ye 'ave beautiful babes. Here, let me help." She fussed and clucked so that Carrie had little to do except mix up a bit of oatmeal and water in a cracked cup to supplement the lotion.

"Leave this paste on the spots as long as you can," Carrie encouraged. "It's not pretty but your back will feel better if you try it." The mother warily accepted assistance while the wide-eyed children remained silent. Carrie mixed up additional oatmeal for breakfast, since it appeared the children had not eaten. Before leaving, Carrie placed her hand on each member's forehead, checking for fever, and essentially taking a moment to breathe healing energy into the beings in her care. It was not Carrie's penchant to be a social worker, but sometimes she did report needy families to the authorities. However, welfare cases went largely untended. This family had a father, and Carrie determined that it might be counterproductive to intervene.

Further downhill Carrie stopped to see Mrs. Theresa Sawyer whom she had known for many years. Theresa lived with her husband and numerous cats in a tiny but neat house above a long set of steps leading uphill from the street to the front door. While Eugenia puffed and pulled her way up by use of the railing, Carrie's long stride took the steps two at a time. Mrs. Sawyer opened the door before they could knock.

The room was one of sunshine and lace interspersed with shy feline faces peering from behind modest furnishings. "The lace makes me homesick for me home in the Isles," Eugenia said. Irish lace with its intricate floral patterns graced the tablecloth, curtains, pillowcases, and napkins, as well as Mrs. Sawyer's cuffs and collar. "Oh dear, I am most overcome by the beauty of it."

Mrs. Sawyer beamed at Eugenia and embraced Carrie. The teakettle was already hot, and she served scones on faded, gold-edged plates in the parlour. Their social chat led Mrs. Sawyer to ask Carrie about the new physicians in town.

"Ought I make an appointment with the women's doctor, Miss Owens? Or should I try to see Dr. Gallagher? I am quite uncertain of their expertise, or whether I want to bother with further medical regimens. As you know, Mrs. Tarynton, I am doing quite well."

"By all means, do what you feel is best, Mrs. Sawyer. The physicians' arrival is timely and important to the health of the community. You may find satisfaction from knowing edema is a persistent problem for many women, and those with tumors affecting the lymph suffer more than most. Perhaps Dr. Gallagher would be helpful."

Mrs. Sawyer's hand explored the lump under her left armpit, and she lifted her long skirt to reveal a grossly swollen calf that caused her foot and ankle to be oversized for any but a man's shoe. The lump had waxed and waned over the six or seven years Carrie had known her, but did not appear to increase from its original size. Many women had reported the phenomenon regarding lumps in their breasts to Carrie, most too modest to tell their doctor, if a doctor were in their vicinity. Treatment varied, with most growths disappearing of their own accord. The human body was a marvel, and most of all a mystery, Carrie concluded from all she had seen.

"I carry on, Mrs. Tarynton, tatting much of the lace you see and caring for my kitties. I admit the steps out front are daunting, but my husband, bless his soul, has created a small ramp off the back that leads directly to higher ground."

Nothing more need be said, Carrie thought, as the women sat with only the ding of china cups against saucers breaking the silence. She noticed Eugenia's concentrated stare that indicated her third eye was turned inward, reading any intuitive voices that might pertain to Mrs. Sawyer. Carrie applauded the older woman's insight that often led to remedies they found more effective than the long established methods of purging, which struck Carrie as being dangerous to the health of the patient.

The dissonant chime of a clock brought their awareness back into the room. Carrie moved around the crowded furniture to begin her energy work with Mrs. Sawyer, who believed mightily in spiritual healing, while others saw it as quackery, or worse, witchcraft.

Mrs. Sawyer's Bible rested on a small table beside her chair, open to Jesus' healing, St. Matthew, Chapter 8.

"Lord, my servant is lying sick in the house, paralyzed, and is grievously afflicted."

Jesus said, "I will come and cure him."

"Lord, I am not worthy that thou shouldst come under my roof; but only say the word, and my servant will be healed."

Then Jesus said, "Go thy way; as thou has believed, so be it done to thee." And the servant was healed in that hour.

Carrie's sensitive hands felt the tangible, extended energy field of this faithful woman, an aura similar to those that formed a golden radiance about the saints depicted in icons of many churches. Carrie attuned her breath to Mrs. Sawyer's breathing, a quiet even pace engendering perfect trust, and placed her hands above the woman's head. Carrie's eyes flew open from her brief meditation when she felt Mrs. Sawyer's energy more powerful than her own, the two forces converging into what Carrie experienced as a hiss like that of the teakettle.

After a few moments, Carrie's hands traced the outline of Mrs. Sawyer's body and hovered above the left leg. With a last brush to rid unseen energy residue, Carrie moved quietly away. Mrs. Sawyer and Eugenia remained deep in their private prayers, the vibrations in the room wrapping them all in a single altered state outside of time and space— perhaps one where illness and suffering did not exist. Carrie signaled Eugenia to come along. Upon leaving, Carrie felt she had received more healing than any she might have given.

They next visited several men and women who suffered chronic depression in the winter, some due to alcohol, others to unemployment, and one woman so homesick she felt near death. They perched on uncomfortable furniture and drank tepid coffee from home to home, listening to often heart-breaking stories of loss and grief, of intractable ailments and other seemingly insurmountable personal and financial difficulties. In fact, Carrie's Spirit work had more to do with "dis-ease," uneasiness of the soul, than with typical medical symptoms and maladies which she felt were often ailments of the soul in disguise. This was well understood by the Great Physician, Saint Luke, according to Mrs. Sawyer, who enlightened Carrie about the work of the Holy Spirit. Jesus' laying on of hands was a teaching, she said, a model for healing at a time when uneducated folks depended upon witchcraft and alchemists, and nobility relied upon court physicians with their nostrums and purges.

The spiritual malaise Carrie encountered in many residents could be attributed to inadequate living conditions and alcohol in this far-flung mining camp isolated by the rugged, snow-capped Rocky Mountains. She also questioned the effect of dust and smoke from the mines on the health of residents, as well as the effect of the highly mineralized, gritty red or yellow tailings piled in their immediate surroundings.

But underneath, when Carrie sat and listened to her patients, she heard the yearnings—yearnings for a better life elsewhere, or for the security of extended family they had left behind. Her Eastern European patients often yearned for the intimacy of small, timeless villages, synagogues, and churches with their ancient traditions. The few Chinese she spoke with missed the love and comfort of families they left behind, those they supported by their grueling, unsafe labor in the camps of the Territories. The weather, too, worked its hardships. Extreme heat in late summer and frigid 40-60 degree below zero temperatures, driven by furious winds over the Continental Divide in winter, taxed even the strongest, most resolute residents of Big Butte.

The women completed their rounds by mid-afternoon. Eugenia's energy flagged since Mrs. Sawyer's tea and scones served as lunch some time ago. The melancholy of these last visits clung like ugly leeches, sapping her remaining strength. She sat down on a granite outcropping and tipped a bottle of spirits from her inside pocket. She offered the libations to Carrie, who politely declined, though she experienced a swift wave of intolerance toward Eugenia's drinking. Carrie noticed she had been irritated twice in one day by her two closest women friends—Roxanna's erratic moods and Eugenia's not always subtle reliance on the spirits. Beyond the obvious annoyances, Carrie realized the image she'd had of herself with a child lurked at the edge of her consciousness at odd times, perhaps prompting her impatience, but she dashed the thought and practically dragged Eugenia up the hill to the buckboard that would take them home.

4

God is our refuge indeed, our strength and our defence; in a
time of strife and trouble our very present help is He.   Psalm 15.2

Daylight shortened at the approach of the winter solstice until it was still dark at eight o'clock every morning. Eugenia and Roxanna continued to occupy the cabin near the quarry by themselves while Jonathan was away with the Nez Perce. Eugenia sat in her rocker and said ten Hail Mary's for Jonathan, ten for dear Carrie, and ten for herself and Roxanna. By then Roxanna sleepily appeared in her flannel nightgown, fur-lined slippers her husband had made, and slips of rags that formed long curls in her hair. Eugenia read passages of Scripture aloud, usually pertaining to miraculous healing that they found inspiring, as well as Psalms of praise, often rapturously reciting verses she knew in Gaelic.

'Se Dia a's tearmumm duinn gu beachd,
Ar spionnadh e's ar treis;
An aimsir carraid ags teinn,
Ar cabhair e ro-dheas.

God is our refuge indeed, our strength and our defence;
in a time of strife and trouble our very present help is He.

47

Roxanna found her refuge in her mother and her husband, Jonathan. She had been born late in the lives of Eugenia and Nial Finnegan, the advent of a first child more precious in their long childless marriage. Roxanna looked back fondly on her early years filled with lullabies, faerie tales both gruesome and terrifying, and always the exquisite Irish handmade lace that trimmed her dresses. What a contrast, she laughed, with her present costume.

The family lived in Acadia, a fishing port north of Boston, where Nial Finnegan became a skillful sailor and fisherman. But the landscape and hardships were scarcely less daunting than those of old Ireland, and he yearned to go West. One day he flourished tickets on the new Union Pacific Railroad, stunning Eugenia and Roxanna. The train sped at fifteen miles per hour to the cries and flag waving of a jubilant population along the way. The celebration aboard was no less enthusiastic. Engineers tooted ear-splitting greetings at crossings, and huge black steam engines heaved from pressure that left a trail of dirty clouds of smoke and steam.

Their rail trip ending in Kansas City was much too short for young Roxanna. The family boarded a wagon train, ponderously cutting north on the Overland Trail toward the gold fields in Montana Territory. Nial Finnegan soon proved to have been a much better fisherman and sailor than prospector, a truth revealed too late for return to the East, and he died of pneumonia before he provided security for the family. His daughter, then like a fickle Rose of Sharon, did not take transplanting well and developed a pattern of hysteria that remained with her into adulthood. She and her mother worked hard for a living like most families at the time, but they withdrew from social life as the "knowing," the mystical, became their reality after multiple traumas of their lives. Their lot became easier years later when Roxanna married Jonathan Duprés and settled, along with her mother, in the cabin in the dell.

After breakfast and more than the usual cups of coffee halved with cream, Roxanna announced that she would ride the stallion out to the pasture. Eugenia's spine stiffened when Roxanna went on. "Mum, I assure ye, these past months have been heavenly, just Love and me, playing our games to make him strong again. Truly, he is a dream and so kind with his soft nose nuzzling my pockets seeking treats. I spoil him with apples and carrots more than I should."

Carrie had given Roxanna the opportunity to improve her riding skills and also to rehabilitate the stallion to a semblance of his condition prior to his illness. Roxanna seized the chance to prepare for an eventual horse-packing trip into the wilderness that her husband had promised. Days flew by with Roxanna engrossed in making friends with Love within the confines of the Tarynton ranch corral, then leading him outside the corral at a walk, trot, and slow canter. Every day showed an increase in agility; the muscles of his chest developed in form and strength, and his hindquarters began to contour with the characteristic roundness of the Connemara. However, his ears failed to appear as alert as before, and his head cocked to the side in an odd manner, giving him a quizzical look. Most significantly, his vitality as a stud had not returned to active levels normal for a stallion in his prime, but his naturally good disposition redeemed him for other missing qualities and he remained friendly. Love greeted Roxanna as eagerly as she greeted him; his great dark eyes framed by long lashes were soft and gentle.

"I don't know if his mind has recovered, but I've yet to see any damage," Carrie said when she oversaw the training. "I'm a little jealous that he has taken up with you so readily."

She and Roxanna had ridden for days along foothills below the ranch and on the mountain above Big Butte, their laughter ringing on the wind. Roxanna's confidence grew along with Love's readiness for further explorations. For the last two weeks, Roxanna rode alone in the pastures, ambling among junipers up one gully and down the next. Love had flexed his slack muscles on the steep climbs and exercised his balance on the downhills. Today, she saddled him for a trip down the valley among the cattle and ranch horses before a coming snowstorm hemmed them in. She fastened a floppy wool hat Jonathan had made for her and left the ranch at a youthful, carefree clip.

Twelve miles to the southwest, tendrils of steam floated in the darkening sky above Gregson Hot Springs. The giant springs once surrounded by tipis were called "medicine waters" by the Nez Perces, Shoshonis and Flatheads. The area was now devoid of Native presence since cattlemen usurped a nearby pure, cold-water stream and grazed their herds on abundant grasses around the springs. The striking blue Pintler Mountains sheltered the fertile valley to the west and north. The Connemara moved out eagerly as if he owned the land, the day, and the promise of a new life. Roxanna imagined Jonathan's surprise when he came home and saw her riding the stallion. She planned to braid the horse's mane and tail, polish his hooves, and lure Duprés to the ranch for a demonstration. Oh, she would twirl the stallion and canter in short bursts across the largest corral to demonstrate her riding skill to her husband.

"He will soon be home, and *Sea, beidh sé a bheith amhlaidh ionadh*, aye, he will be so surprised." With these distractions engaging her attention, she and Love put miles behind them until Roxanna stopped to pull a bite to eat from her coat pocket. Munching at ease in the saddle, she surveyed the herd and beyond.

Cows and bulls were scattered for quite a distance up and down Deer Lodge Valley, knots of them in clusters of sagebrush, some cows still nursing oversize calves from last spring, others lying down in groups as if they all decided to take a nap at once. To the side in the protection of a few willows and a rise in the ground, forty or so ranch horses held their own counsel, a few others mingled with cows searching for stray blades of dried grass. The horses in the open with the cattle were alerted first. Heads high, eyes wide and nostrils distended, their ears stood straight up, listening, readying for flight, their instinctual response to predators. The stallion sensed something and his body tensed. Roxanna dropped her biscuit and gathered the reins. A quick glance did not reveal any threats, no moose wandering through the herd, or coyotes flashing their fat tails as they hunted rabbits. A mountain lion was unlikely in mid-day in the flat, open land. Roxanna relaxed her concern for Mac's livestock, her mind wandering to fantasies of her husband's return any day now, each time resolving a new and exciting welcome for him.

Within the next few moments the horses bolted and cows bawled, those lying down scrambling to their feet, dimly aware of a threat, but uncertain where it came from, all erupting frantically to an unknown provocation. Love belatedly whirled, but not before Roxanna saw a spotted horse bearing down on the herds, its rider light and low over its neck.

"Sweet Mary, Mother of God, Jesus," Roxanna screamed to the wind and grasped a fistful of mane along with the reins and saddle horn.

The Connemara plowed through the herd of cattle to reach the safety of other horses, but those horses plunged away and dispersed, whinnying their fear. In the chaos, cows circled, their bellows echoing Roxanna's screams. Again the horses were first to sense the ground itself move, as if the earth had come alive. Fearsome eyes above bared teeth shone among the sagebrush. Figures leapt in front of and behind the animals, their piercing cries penetrating the marrow of Roxanna's bones. She clung for her life to the wad of mane in her hands. With a sideways glance she recognized frightfully painted men in wolf hides who stood, arms flailing, cutting a portion of the herd from the rest.

The Connemara now stampeded with the horses toward the valley floor, fleeing the unknown 'pack.' Roxanna took a cue from the rider on the spotted horse and leaned low over Love's neck. Enveloped in his long streaming mane she murmured, "God in

Heaven, he's spooked to death with what little mind he has left."
She mentally crossed herself a hundred times over. Certain of
impending death for both herself and the stallion, she breathed
final prayers for her husband and mother.

"Jonathan will feel such remorse for leaving me."

The horses peeled away, further separating the livestock
from the thieves. Desperate, the lone rider became more daring,
moving at an incredible pace as if sagebrush and badger holes did
not exist. Roxanna glanced past her shoulder and shrieked—the
painted apparition was right behind her on the equally painted
steed, a blanket of white spots bright against its blood-red hide
sending chills down her spine.

"Run, run from the dastardly thieves," she whispered in
Love's ear. "Live. Live for Carrie. Ye must—I daren't lose ye!"

Just then the stallion hauled up in a tight circle and reversed
his course, throwing Roxanna forward. Pitching straight ahead,
at the last second her long skirt caught on the pommel. Dazed
and wobbling, she righted her balance. Now turned back, she
and Love soon passed the puzzled warrior face to face. He veered
off on the raid with other Natives on foot and horseback.

"Hallelujah!" Roxanna was taken by a strange euphoria, an
exultation, a joyous awakening! A babble of Irish merged with
the staccato beat of Love's hooves, sounding as possessed as the
horse she was riding—before she almost fainted and hung helplessly over his neck.

The Connemara galloped home as fast as he could go, carrying his nearly senseless rider to the only place he knew, the safety
of the home ranch. Driven by bloodlines of the wild ponies of
the Connemara highlands of Counties Galway and Mayo that
ran in his veins, his basic instinct led him to survive. His stride
gained power, swallowing the barren ground of the foothills,
leaving behind the impending doom his instinct had sensed.

The dapple streaked into the barnyard, his abrupt arrival
raising alarm at the ranch. With horror, the hands lounging in

the bunkhouse bailed out at the sight of the limp rider on the sweat-stained stallion. Cursing in fear of a misdeed for failing to protect a novice rider, the men lifted Roxanna from the saddle and carried her into the house. Carrie was out on her rounds. Mac, roused from a nap on the settee, barely heard Roxanna's feeble story before he yanked his rifle from its pegs on the wall and stormed out, barking orders while he saddled his horse. The men caught their mounts, none sure how he felt about Roxanna's ride. No one questioned his determination to retrieve his livestock, but they figured there'd be hell to pay.

All hands rode out except Duggan who drove Roxanna home in the buckboard.

"Thank ye, Duggan, and thank ye, Lord. Ye brought this willful, headstrong woman home in one piece." Eugenia murmured while she put her daughter to bed.

After resting and supper, Roxanna told her story between sharp intakes of breath. "I let Love go, Mum. He ran like the wind with the spotted horse gaining on us every step. Then he circled back—I almost flew off with the about-face—but I hung on and we passed the Indian eye to eye, we did!

"He wanted that horse bad—or me—," she shuddered and paused as the fears she had suppressed crashed over her. "Then the whoops of the wolf-men faded away and they took a bunch of Mac's horses and cows. He was so angry. And Carrie, dear Carrie, she wasn't home, but I brought Love back aright."

Eugenia wrung a lace handkerchief between sweaty palms, her open, wrinkled face an expression of one who had met her worst fears—and they came to naught.

I feel a great weight has been lifted from my shoulders, as long as Roxanna and Carrie's stallion survived the attack. "Surely the vision of wolves Carrie had seen when she first rescued Love has come to pass."

Not long after, Carrie saw a light in Eugenia's cabin and stopped by on her way home. Stunned by Roxanna's story, she murmured, "I shouldn't have let you go—"

"Sha, 's nothing, Carrie. The joy, the ride of my life! And the wolves, just like the vision ye saw! It's true—it came true!"

Carrie moved her hands in an odd way, as if sifting and weighing something between her palms, her presence removed from the women in the room. The Finnegans waited. At last Carrie looked up. "Love took care of you, he said. He doesn't know what happened in the valley, only that he is still shaken from the frightful experience. He is afraid of predators that rise out of the earth, and of poison plants that make him sick in this strange land far from his birthplace on the island."

"He knew to go home. That's good enough for me," Roxanna declared. The women's nervous laughter sounded like chimes out of tune in a capricious breeze, teasing about mysterious seen, unforeseen, and unbidden turns in life.

———————

Pursuit of the horse and cattle thieves by Mac and the *TN* crew was short, fast and reckless. The predicted snowstorm whipped sideways over the Pintlers, creating a pageant of hunched, moving forms on the valley floor. The rancher caught sight of the Indians after a couple hours of hard riding. Mac guessed they were Sioux, the notorious horse thieves riding Palouses stolen from the Nez Perce. The warriors were encumbered by the stolen herd, and a number of them had been on foot, their horses hidden in the willows. By the time the raiders had gathered their horses and the livestock, Roxanna and the dapple had been well on their way to rousing the ranch crew who easily tracked the separated part of the herd in the new fallen snow. It appeared the thieves would attempt to drive the bunch across the Clark Fork River before dark, but Mac and his men spurred their mounts to push ahead of them and prevent the crossing.

"Shoot the bastards," Mac ordered, though it was hard to draw a bead on galloping riders, many in wolf hides disguised by snow. Some wranglers circled the sides of the herd, while Mac and Pete forced their way toward the rear, chiseling remnants of the herd away from the thieves. Soon the valley rang with shots coming from both sides, echoes muffled by the storm. A Native hit the ground in front of the ranchers. An arrow blew up the heart of a wrangler's horse that went down without a sound. The wrangler, Antonio, bailed off and ducked down, but the Native ran and dodged in the opposite direction.

Antonio loosened the cinch to pull his saddle and blanket from the dead horse. He removed the bridle, avoiding blood gushing from the horse's nostrils as its eyes stared sightlessly at him. Antonio threw his saddle on his shoulder and walked out of range until the battle was over and the crew could rope another horse for him. Near him one Native lay dead, a Sioux. The gaping mouth and shining eyes behind the wolf hide looked very alive.

Other *TN* wranglers had ridden ahead, shooting and yelling. Dozens of cows broke from the herd and fell behind with separated horses that sought security among Tarynton horses. Under intense pressure, the warriors quit the raid to escape across the river with what livestock they had, still firing randomly behind them.

"Mac is hit!"

"Hell no...."

"Hell yes."

Pete witnessed the bullet's impact hit Mac's thigh. Mac's horse dodged, jolting Mac sideways but he stayed in the saddle.

"Give me a hand," Pete yelled and grasped the reins of Mac's horse. Sidling next to him, he steadied his wounded boss until two wranglers pulled up their wheezing mounts. Together the men bound the wound, while Mac remained in the saddle swearing he'd ride to hell and back to "get even for what they done." Another wrangler guardedly backtracked to pick up Antonio. The crew found two ranch horses had been wounded, but they would recover with treatment, leaving only one killed. Gradually night closed in. Silence hung huge over Deer Lodge Valley once the rifle shots ceased. Only the anxious mooing of cows for their calves accompanied worried wranglers, who hauled their boss home as best they could.

A few hours later the horses were back in their pasture and cattle close to the ranch with the exception of a few stolen horses and one dead. Mac lay on the long, wooden kitchen table when Carrie came in from an emergency with one of her patients. Julianna, the ranch cook, had torn strips of a sheet to bind the deep wound on Mac's upper left thigh. She had cut away his pant leg on that side. Blood soaked through as fast as she applied more bandages. Two wranglers stood by, hats in hand, their Adam's apples tightly rising and falling with their boss's cursing and cries of pain.

"My Mac shot? What are you saying?" Carrie stumbled to Mac's side, the usual glow in her face drained of color. "NO, NO!" She hovered over him to see his face, touch his brow, his hand, make it all go away, make it not have happened. His lips were clenched and only a flutter of his eyelids responded. At sight of a thin stream of bright red blood pooling on the table beneath Mac, Carrie's legs weakened, collapsing under her. Falling, she slipped from the frantic grasp of the wranglers who saw her going down. Julianna threw all her weight on Mac's chest to keep him flat on the table.

"You can't move, sir. She will be all right. I'll fetch the salts."

Mac heaved back, pain wracking his body, contorting his face into a grimace as the young men carried his wife to the horsehair settee and laid her down, her long legs propped over the armrest. Julianna passed the bandages to Pete and nodded that he take over. She whipped towels through cold water from the pitcher for compresses to revive both Mr. and Mrs. Tarynton.

Antonio had immediately ridden to town to summon Dr. Isaac Gallagher. The doctor arrived about midnight to find Mac still lying on the kitchen table for fear movement would reopen the wound. Mac fell intermittently in and out of consciousness until Dr. Gallagher administered morphine. He gave Carrie a dose of laudanum, also an opiate sedative, for her agitation, and ordered that she be put to bed. For the next several hours, the crew held all the kerosene lamps Julianna could find in the house to provide light for Mac's surgery.

"This will require a good many stitches," Dr. Gallagher determined. The thigh was pulpy, ragged and swollen from a deep hole, but it was clean. Julianna had doused it with lye soap and cold water that spread all over the table and floor. Knowingly or not, she had sanitized a good part of the kitchen.

"There's a good chance of saving his leg," Dr. Gallagher continued. "How the leg will be is the question." He set a smooth mahogany box of surgical instruments on a side table. The red velvet interior displayed knives, probes, needles, and sutures. A compact bone saw lay nearby. Selecting a slim, hooked probe, he fished for the bullet that had hit bone and angled off, ripping more flesh. Beginning inside, "Doc" sutured severed muscle and sinew, then worked his way out to close the ugly wound. Fortunately, the femur, artery and sciatic nerve remained intact.

The Tarynton ranch owner was not a big man in terms of a large body for he was tall and slim with the wide shoulders and broad chest of a Westerner, but he was heavily muscled, with strong hands, forearms, and long sturdy feet beneath steel-like calves. It took a bunch of hired hands to move him to the spare bedroom. Carrie recovered to hold a lonely vigil at Mac's bedside.

Dr. Gallagher slept on the horsehair settee, his legs dangling over the arm under the goose down coverlet Julianna had thrown over him. He awakened to smell some of the blackest coffee he had ever seen, but the taste called for a second cup. He was therefore fully awake when Duggan brought his horse and buggy around to the front door. Doc lowered his head into one of the infamous blizzards of the winter of 1876 and drove back to town.

As winter days wore on into weeks, recovery from shock and depression for Carrie Tarynton was more prolonged and complicated than that of her husband. She blamed herself for training Roxanna to ride the stallion, knowing of Roxanna's hysteria. Her sixth sense had failed her, leaving her unaware of what turned into a tragedy—Mac nearly losing his life and his leg. Right or wrong, she sensed Mac blamed her. The lack of foresight led to her questioning her intuition and visions, even her relationship with Mac. Would he blame her forever for his wound? She could not forgive herself for being away from his side that night, and coming home to find him almost mortally wounded. But what was she to do with her healing gifts—if she retained any? This exaggerated self-condemnation appeared perfectly warranted in her state of mind—a state she refused to divulge to Mac or her friends. Already thin, Carrie's inability to hold down food soon became an emergency.

To Mac her moods became even more worrisome. "I will be all right. The herd has been collected. You needn't fret."

Yet Carrie was unable to make her rounds. Her patients' requests to see her went unheeded; the need for her personal touch and counsel, an alternative to that offered by doctors on Park Street, went unanswered. Days, then weeks slipped past. Christmas and the New Year came and went without more than a lit candle at the Taryntons. Carrie prowled the house at night, hearing voices shrilly whispering on the wind, her usual clear mind cluttered with dire images, sapping her powers of healing for either Mac or herself.

Mac's early rage at the Sioux now fueled a persistent, low key anger that continued long after the raid, diverting him from Carrie's troubles. The wranglers moved stock onto sheltered ranges with more feed during the blizzards. Julianna had gone home for the holidays, and on Jackson's recommendation, Mac hired Nettie from the Norwegian bakery. Jackson wooed Nettie every minute he could spare from shifts at the mines until Mac hired him as a night watchman on the herd. The household ran smoothly with young people providing a ray of sunshine. But the Tarynton tranquility was gone.

A melancholy overcame Carrie, merging with sad and restless energies she frequently encountered with her patients. Failing to confront her own, the household no longer reflected love and peace between the Taryntons. Carrie knew it and her depression worsened. Mac knew it and he became angrier. He hobbled on a crutch since the thick thigh muscles required time to mend. The doctor had warned him against exercising that leg, another frustration adding to his inner turmoil. Incarceration, as he saw it, upped his irritation and the feeling of being helpless shortened his already short temper. Carrie overheard his conversation with Dr. Gallagher.

"What is it that is so disturbing?" Dr. Gallagher inquired one day on his regular visit to check Mac's wound. "There seem to be more problems here than this wound, which is doing very well by the way, though I can imagine it is difficult for you to curtail your work."

"Doc, the frustration keeps my gut churning. I can hardly eat or sleep sometimes. Sure, I'm anxious to get back to work, but I'm more concerned about my wife. It isn't like her to be moody and upset for so long—since that damn Indian raid, I think."

"Did she say anything about that?"

"She says she's lost her ability to heal others or herself. You know, the healing she does. It's as though she is lost. She cries and refuses to let me comfort her. That hurts me the most." Mac scowled, his look imploring the physician to help Carrie.

"How old is she? Thirty-five? Too young for the change, or maybe not, since women differ. Well, I am sorry to hear this. I understand she is a remarkable woman who has helped a good many people. Perhaps the Spirit comes and goes. I find that myself sometimes. She may have suffered a prolong shock brought on by your injury. It would be treatable if she were amenable to my care."

That not being the case, he treated Mac for dyspepsia, leaving preparations of *Nux Vomica* and *Lachesis* for settling the stomach and improving the appetite, doses to be taken three times a day, along with a recommendation for easily digested foods such as venison, wild birds, and beef tea, as well as baked apples or fresh fruit. Nettie had despaired of suiting his appetite with her lovely baked breads and desserts. She was pleased to follow the doctor's advice for meal preparation. In fact, the beef broth was already simmering on the stove.

Eugenia and Roxanna came a few times and enjoyed Nettie's lace oatmeal cookies, but Carrie was too distraught to talk openly as she had before.

"I should have stood by Mac during the surgery. Instead, I welcomed the oblivion of the drug Dr. Gallagher gave me when—when Mac was in such pain—I thought he was dying." Carrie dared not tell Roxanna she regretted having allowed her to ride the Connemara, and that she blamed herself for Mac getting shot. And she dared not admit her failure to foresee the consequences.

"Sometimes I need laudanum to calm my hysteria that is hard on my loved ones," Roxanna said, trying to smooth Carrie's guilt.

But Carrie's mood failed to lift, and finally she would not see her friends at all. Nor could she look at the Connemara. She also refused to discuss her personal difficulties when Dr. Gallagher visited Mac. When she heard that the doctors' medical practices on Park Street in town were thriving, she muffled her cries. Miss Adelaide Owens became an ogre in Carrie's feverish mind, an identifiable threat amid her otherwise unexplainable trauma. She only knew that she was shaken to the core with a perceived sense of her shortcomings and uncertainty about her healing, about her love for anyone, even for the stallion she called Love.

A grim outlook beset her fine features and made them hard, un-caring, a stranger to her husband and household.

The couple now sat at opposite ends of the long kitchen table.

"It's that damn horse, isn't it?" Mac flared at Carrie one morning. "Nothing has been right since he came here. Roxanna shouldn't have been riding him."

In Idaho Territory, Jonathan Duprés sat up long nights with his friends, the Nez Perce. He heard their stories and sculpted their arguments in preparation for days of negotiations with the government. Interpreting for the Nez Perce meant doing the same for the United States military, though Duprés was not on the U.S. payroll. Scouts of both contingents went back and forth attempting to work out a satisfactory agreement between the un-settled, hostile Nez Perce and Agent John Monteith, who spoke for General Oliver O. Howard, a Civil War hero tapped to sub-due Native populations in the West. Duprés exercised his utmost skill in interpretation and diplomacy to no avail. He conceded the issues must be settled in Washington or on the battlefield, since Non-Treaty Nez Perce grievances failed to be addressed.

With a growing sense of dire outcomes for his beloved tribe, Duprés realized his services were not immediately relevant to the outcome, and he turned his attention toward home and re-uniting with Roxanna. He had ridden hundreds of miles to con-sult with the tribe's factions, and spent months involved in their negotiations, so it was far into winter when a Chinook melted enough snow on the passes to permit his return to Montana Territory. In gratitude for his services, the Nez Perce gave him a fine horse, dried fish for the trip, and beaded jewelry for his wife. Three scouts accompanied him as far as Lolo Pass, where he could make his way through the Bitterroot Valley back to Big Butte.

As he approached the Deer Lodge valley his mouth watered for the fatty mutton stew that Eugenia was wont to make on cold winter days. And he thought of—uh, the dalliance he'd had with his former "wife" in the tribe—the scent of dried fish on her breath and bear grease on her hair, the times they coupled when drums distracted the attention of the tribe, heated moments in a buffalo robe when she slipped away from her husband. He dashed the thoughts from his mind and swore to keep the secret from Roxanna. Pure Roxanna, she was too good for that.

Two days later he arrived at the Duprés cabin where he first heard the news of Roxanna's narrow escape on the Connemara.

"She has taken ill and lies in her room," Eugenia said, cementing the one-two punch.

"*Quoi? Quoi?* What are ye telling me, Madame?" It was Duprés turn for hysteria, his voice rising. "*Non, non* such thing, *n'est pas?*"

He peeked into the darkened room to find his wife asleep, her fair skin pale against her red hair. The "in sickness and in health" words of the wedding ceremony churned in his mind.

Eugenia came up behind him. "She was fine—until the after effects."

"By all the saints, whatever are ye talking about? Ye are frightening me—," Duprés shouted, a string of French expressing his consternation. "I need an interpreter for you, woman. What Indians? My Roxie riding the stallion for her life?" He stormed about upsetting furniture in the cramped room. "What happened here while I was away?"

"She didn't want ye to go and leave her. She nearly lost her life for love of ye. Now how do you interpret that?"

"She's lying in bed like a corpse. Is that a woman's love?"

"She wants to go with ye next time," Eugenia said simply.

The "for better or worse" part of his vows sunk in and numbed his mind. He wanted only to eat supper and bed his wife.

"Indians came on spotted horses to steal Tarynton's horses and cows. Roxanna rode to the ranch and told Mr. Tarynton. Carrie thinks they were Sioux. They had stolen horses from a

Nez Perce hunting party about the time ye married Roxanna. Remember?"

Duprés could not remember or comprehend any of what Eugenia tried to tell him. He only heard "she wants to go with you next time," and "married." Unable to comprehend the story or sort out his vows, he left his bound, buffalo hide pack on the floor, grabbed his fur hat and went out. Snow came down thick and heavy on his bent shoulders while he made his way to a Finntown saloon. He drank with complete strangers until his promise to his wife, and the injunctions of marriage became a dim memory.

———————

Three days after his initial visit home from his trip to Idaho, Jonathan Duprés again showed up at the cabin, this time disheveled, foul-smelling and contrite. Eugenia cautiously let him in, now like a creature of the back alleys she often saw on her rounds with Carrie. His buffalo robe pack had been cleared from the room. Duprés wondered if he would be thrown out with it. Roxanna slowly opened the bedroom door and gazed at him. It was not the homecoming he had envisioned on his return, his dreams of her warm body enveloping him for overdue marital bliss. Stung by her pale face and long stringy hair, he traced a fuzzy memory that she had wanted to go with him. Had she tried to follow? He knew it was time for a reckoning. He braced himself for their first fight.

"I wouldn't want to criticize my son-in-law," Eugenia said, chucking a hunk of firewood into the stove and slamming the lid, "but the Canuck looks like a common bowsy."

She rattled pots and pans while she made coffee and put on a large pot of water for his bath. Undercover of her mother's outburst, Roxanna spoke to her husband while she helped him slip off the filthy wool coat that smelled of stale fish and bear grease. Duprés' hands shook and his lips trembled.

"It looks like a long night ahead with the tremors," Eugenia observed, not bothering to be discreet. She put supper on the table and proceeded to offer lengthy prayers thanking God for Duprés safe return and Roxanna's recovery from near death with the Indians. Amen.

The sobering thought of the two women stripping him down for a bath in the galvanized wash tub made Duprés figure he'd better get through the meal without creating a reckoning—a man doesn't stand a chance fighting two women in his underwear, or worse, stark naked.

Roxanna recited her story to him over coffee. Duprés waggled his head, pursed his lips, and closed his red-lined eyes, admitting the story was beyond belief. Not Roxie on the stud. Not Roxie face-to-face with an Indian. Not Roxie run down by thieves. Even the delirium he had been through in the past few nights created more conceivable images than that of Roxie's wild ride.

5

The neuralgias, nervousness, fidgets and hysteria which afflict some women at this period are such as to make life miserable.   Prudence B. Saur, M.D.

When Mac blamed the Connemara for the plagues that visited the house of Tarynton, Carrie knew that she must shake herself from despair and do something. "It's that damn horse, isn't it?" Mac had said. "Nothing has been right since he came here. Roxanna shouldn't have been riding him."

Stunned by Mac's tone of voice with her, with his accusation that Love was, bizarrely, the source of their problems, and she to blame for allowing Roxanna to ride him, Carrie put on her coat and went out into the storm. Her footsteps automatically turned towards Silver Bow Creek, a good distance from the ranch, but downhill on a trail she trod in the early years when Natalya, a Shoshoni medicine woman, taught her herbal medicine and traditional healing. Carrie chose to walk to the Shoshoni camp, horses now escalating her general nervousness and anxiety. Tears froze on her cheeks, only to be warmed by more tears and frozen again into painful crystals. She curled her fingers inside her pockets to keep them warm, her legs, weak and cold, moved automatically.

Mac was the kingpin of her life, her very existence. Though marriages were common at seventeen and eighteen years of age, they had not married until later; she had been twenty and he twenty-five. They felt it was a mature decision, one they both cherished.

Carrie had been a shy child and a reserved young woman, often unsure of herself and frightened by visions that appeared in her mind and sometimes came true. The currents that surged through her slim body and pulsed in her palms alarmed her even more. At age two or three she found some people drawn to her while others shunned her eyes. "You have a strange child," she overheard friends whispering to her mother. Some said "that child is possessed by spirits." Others felt sure "she looks into one's soul." At these times Carrie hid under the table so no one could see her eyes. As she grew older she ran among the coulees behind their home in Nebraska, exhausting her long legs and tangled emotions.

The dark, anxious feelings began when her father announced that the family would move to Montana Territory to homestead. Carrie began suffering moments when the shock and fear of being uprooted were followed by more intense images fleeting through her mind. She told no one. For lack of an alternate on the long, lonely Overland Trail, Carrie learned to visualize herself in the safe place under the old family table. Not knowing what to do with the "crazy" ideas, as her father called them, she contained her near madness by walking the entire distance from Nebraska to Fort Laramie, Wyoming. There the family took the Bozeman Trail over rugged, blue mountains and across the forks of three rivers until they reached the vicinity of Big Butte, a site chosen by her father because there were few conflicts with the Natives. In addition, the grassland of Deer Lodge Valley where buffalo herds had previously grazed, was lush and plentiful.

The biting, fresh air strengthened Carrie over the years. She felt accompanied by a sense of almost tangible spiritual guides cavorting among the peaks of the Rocky Mountains, sometimes teasing her for her uncertainty, until the hazy visions she had experienced in childhood became an astounding progression of 'knowing' that later informed her life and led her to spiritual healing. Yet Carrie now felt she could not heal herself, nor Mac or their marriage.

Her head bent beneath the wide fringes of a plaid wool shawl, her eyes seeing one boot placed resolutely ahead of the other as she neared Natalya's home. Her usual intuition offered her no comfort: no images filled her mind, no guides prompted her to do this or that, no yearnings led her one way or the other. She vaguely wondered who would find her if she collapsed and became a frozen lump in the snow.

But Natalya would know she was coming. Carrie knew her mentor would read it in leaves and stones and bones. Mountain Woman is coming, only she wouldn't know when. The leaves and stones and bones did not tell of time. Days and weeks and years melded together for the Shoshoni who had all the time and no time, they were one and the same. Natalya lived with her husband in a tipi south of Big Butte among seasonal Native residents from Idaho, who camped close to town for fear of hostile settlers in the valleys.

Today, enveloped in a sense of despair, Carrie stumbled down a path between ice-crusted arms of aspens. "I must see you, Spirit Woman. I feel my life draining away." Carrie's voice trembled from the cold.

Natalya pulled back the flap covering the door, and Carrie slipped inside. The flap closed like a womb around them, shutting out elements of a disturbing world, yet the spacious tipi opened to the heavens through a smoke hole above a fire pit in the center. Carrie sat on the floor in her old place, eyes downcast, hands in her lap. Natalya's husband snoozed on buffalo hide rugs at the edge of the room. Great willow baskets stuffed with dried bounty of the natural world spread over the limited floor space. Bundles of sage scented the air, stalks of stinging nettle filled one basket, and a bouquet of herbs nested in another. Little altars of smooth stones were heaped among the baskets. Above hung eagle feathers and plumage of wild turkeys and geese. Clusters of willow sticks for weaving, tidy rolls of sinews for lacing, and stacks of tanned deer hides all spread odors that mingled with the sage.

Gradually Carrie released sobs in her coat sleeve, the sobs rounding into cries she did not try to hide. Natalya wiped out a cup and boiled water for tea of chamomile and valerian root to calm her guest, Mountain Woman. Carrie's stories flowed one upon the other, leaving out nothing. She poured out her soul to this woman who sensed the very fabric of the earth and heavens. Outside, the women's spirit guides made their presence known by lifting the flap at the door, whispering in the aspens, and chiming little tunes in dry yucca pods, their messages portending a happy resolution. As usual, no time was specified; it could come soon—or after a long while.

The hot tea lent a penetrating balm to a fragmented mind. Carrie soon toppled over on the buffalo hide and fell into a deep sleep, perhaps like Natalya's husband. On an epic journey into unconsciousness she encountered a figure who asked, "What are you seeking, Carrie?" She opened her eyes wide to see the wizened face of Natalya before her.

"Did you ask me what I want?" Carrie asked.

No words came.

Natalya could wait. Embodied in nature, she had waited since the first hour of the rising sun for this moment. Carrie blinked, round eyes opening and closing. She swallowed hard.

"Ask me something easy, my friend Spirit Woman," Carrie pleaded, her voice high and thin. Tears threatened to again overwhelm the visit.

"You must ask yourself," Natalya encouraged.

Braced by the soothing voice, Carrie noticed an assortment of small stones from the altars lay in a paisley pattern within a frame of larger stones and bone shards on the earth in front of her.

"I see a lost part of myself," she said instantly, placing her forefinger within the pattern where two lines curled but did not touch.

Natalya said nothing. The guides shushed. Only the electric pulse of the collective energies seemed to stir. Natalya bowed her head in recognition of the powers.

Carrie's breath came quick and sharp. "I feel my breathing," she said in wonder. "I thought I was dying, but I am not." She glanced questioningly at her mentor's bowed head. Natalya's thick, gray-white hair fell to her round figure covered in bulky winter clothing of threadbare green and red wool blankets—trademark of the Hudson Bay Company, likely traded for beaver or tanned deer hides long ago. Natalya tucked her feet under a wide skirt where she sat on the buffalo hide on the floor. Carrie drew strength from the beneficent presence, but she wanted to see Natalya's face, to take refuge in the fathomless dark eyes.

Her husband rose on stiff legs and moved haltingly across the fire from Carrie.

Bunching the stones in her hands, Carrie stammered, "I –I – want to be whole."

The elder shook his long pipe and took his time tamping and lighting it. Eventually the faint smell of tobacco mingled with the wood smoke, sage, and overheated body odors.

"You are whole," Natalya said, nodding in Carrie's direction. "What do you need to believe in yourself?"

Carrie suddenly felt the impulse to tear herself away from responsibilities that come with being whole, to avoid admitting the illness of her mind was a creation of her imagination. Lost in the deceptions of judgments and guilt that robbed her of self-confidence, Carrie tried to defend her distancing from Mac, from her friends and patients, and for alienating herself from healing entities that had slowly become a part of her. Distraught, she wailed, the sounds akin to those of a stricken animal in a distant hollow.

Natalya's hand firmly grasped Carrie's forearm. Carrie crumpled next to the older woman, the flashbacks pirouetting in fantastical colors of jade and burgundy, taunting her to believe in herself or go mad, the tension daring to rip the room apart, yet strangely, the old man smoked his pipe as if nothing were unusual, his eyes squinting at a farther realm.

"Oh, dear God, is nothing real?" Carrie groaned at last. "I see myself falling down Mrs. Sawyer's long stairway. She is at the top of the stairs reading to me from Scriptures about Jesus' healing, but I cannot understand her words. I am reaching for the words to heal her, to heal myself, but they escape my fingertips. I am at a loss, help me please—"

Natalya would understand, Carrie sensed, relinquishing the psychic battle with light and shadow, good and evil. The Shoshoni woman had been christened Natalya and had suffered missionaries' Christian teachings that often conflicted with her Native beliefs.

"I was once torn. These days I feel whole. You will find a way to believe in yourself."

But Carrie did not find a way at Natalya's. She would have to come to terms with her disbelief, her uncertainties, on her own. She gathered her wits for the long walk home, thanking both the old woman and her husband. When she trudged back uphill, she noticed her footsteps were lighter, though her mind was not necessarily at ease.

A horseman followed her when she crested the hill towards the ranch house. She turned to see Jackson trotting his Molly mule towards the ranch. He greeted her merrily.

"I'm bringing Molly to keep company with King," he said, "I hope Mac will agree to it."

"King would be so happy!" Carrie answered. He would be whole, she realized, startled at the thought.

Another start came when Jackson said, "Yes, I know first-hand what it is to feel like half a person. Patrick is my twin brother. He moved back to Boston some time ago."

And he has not felt whole since, Carrie filled in for herself. Or maybe he is finding his other part with Nettie. Astounded at the possibility that wholeness could be achieved by others at the ranch in the midst of her daily life, Carrie smiled.

"What a blessing you have found Nettie. She is a darling girl. And I know she loves you, Jackson."

Jackson dismounted to walk with Carrie. He glanced sideways to be sure this good humor was genuine—Mrs. Tarynton had been sad and distant for such a long time.

"Thank you for being with me right now," Carrie said warmly, tucking her hand under his elbow.

———————

Each spring the Tarynton range stock almost doubled when the cows dropped their calves in the dried grass of open grazing land. Likewise, as silver mines proliferated, the population of Big Butte redoubled almost overnight, and so did orders for beef, making the *TN* brand known throughout the Territory. To Mac, the market appeared inexhaustible. He had the foresight to hire enough men, in addition to Jackson Colter, to manage the herd. Ranching went on though Mac remained sidelined from heavy labor or hard riding on doctor's orders. The extensive damage deep in the tissue of his thigh left him in constant pain. He called his slight limp "getting old."

Jackson's responsibility was to keep water holes and spring-fed tanks open and free of ice for the livestock. On the mountain near the ranch, the natural, year-round springs managed to flow without freezing up, but southwest on Silver Bow Creek he had to chop holes in the ice every day if the creek froze over. With the size of the herd, it could be an all day job, only to repeat it if temperatures dropped below zero. When March and April thaws began, Jackson's miner's eye noted bright mineral colors of the streambeds against glistening rims of ice.

He began riding the Connemara on these trips, telling Mac that he wanted to exercise the horse. He did not want to admit how much he cared for the once battered creature that had spent months of his early recovery at the Colter brothers' place. King's formerly thin frame had filled out; a shining coat covered many of the scars. Royalty showed in the refined features of his somewhat wide, short head. His ears had become alert, and his overly friendly disposition captured Jackson's heart. Yet no one knew precisely if the stallion's mind was normal, or ventured to guess whether he would pass on defects to his offspring.

In the saloons, the story of the Connemara outrunning the spotted Indian pony earned the horse a lofty reputation. One night in Killarney Pub, Jackson overheard Duprés embellishing the story while Duprés drank pints with the miners, a bit of socializing the Frenchman enjoyed more frequently these days, sanctioned by his marriage to "that Irish woman who chased the Indians." Duprés did not deny any of the wild speculations that Roxie saved the Tarynton stock single-handedly, hence he also stood taller as a result of the episode.

Wagering occupied many a night when blizzards whipped the mile high atmosphere into a frenzy. The pub proprietor signaled his helpers to keep the wood stoves blazing, or "the blokes will freeze to death on the bar stools."

The blokes in question proposed racing the Irish stallion against any four-legged that could run. And for another poke of gold, they bet on Duprés' wife riding against any woman in town, or in all of Deer Lodge County. At the first opportunity Jackson informed Mac of both the mineral buildup in the streambeds and the plots made in jest or in earnest about the stallion.

"I've heard rumors of that nonsense. Wal, they won't be racing Carrie's stud." Mac cussed the Irish, Cornish, Finns and Serbians for spending too much time in the dives.

"Don't they have families to take care of? It's the Irish with their wagers that makes a man ashamed to be a McHenry," he fumed to Carrie, Jackson, and anyone who would listen. "Don't they have enough to do in the mines?"

Mac put a night guard on the Connemara stallion. "I'll get

the cowhands to take turns for awhile in case those liquor-fueled gamblers connive to race the horse or some fool thing."

Winter eventually wore itself out and the horse problem was solved, at least for the Taryntons, when Jackson Ulysses Colter married Nettie Francine Holmes in a ceremony with a justice of the peace at the Tarynton ranch in late May.

"You were out in 25 to 40 degrees below zero with the wind blowing like hell caring for my stock," Mac said. "That makes you part of the family."

"You're my only family in the Territory. You know my twin brother, Patrick, is in Boston escapin' from the mines."

The reception was held at the Continental Hotel in Big Butte, and the couple lived in the Colter cabin on Bison Creek, chaperoned by the healthily blaring Molly mule and her favorite charge, the royal stallion. Word reached Patrick Worthington Colter a month or so after the wedding; his congratulations came back by mail months after that. By that time Nettie was with child.

Carrie had given King to the happy couple for a wedding gift. This magnanimity was endorsed with Mac's blessing. As these things go, the Connemara was soon sought by horse breeders who wanted to improve the endurance of their stock, and perhaps did not know the history of the stallion. Jackson knew the stud fees would amount to considerable income if the horse proved to be a good producer.

Whether or not Mac was glad to see him go, he did not say.

Jonathan Duprés seldom ventured up the mountain. A fur trapper by heart, he scouted the lower basin and followed the creeks, but at daybreak he rode up to catch Mac at the ranch house. He tapped at the kitchen door and came in to find the rancher lingering over coffee. Mac was clean shaven, his rust-colored hair clipped fairly close with slight curls on the ends. Duprés' disheveled long greasy locks wandered into his thick beard, matching the condition of his slouchy coat and trousers. He removed his hat and shuffled to a chair opposite Mac.

"The water's lookin' bad some places." He spoke with care, always intimidated by Mac's authority and now perpetually stern demeanor. The remark caught Mac's full attention.

"I had been trappin' up Silver Bow where it swings by Blacktail crik, then yonder down past the old diggin's at Rocker, but the trappin' ain't good close in anymore. I had to set a line far down the valley."

Mac leaned back in his chair knowing he was in for a long, rambling story—one that was important to a rancher.

"The beaver are scarce and the muskrats all but pulled out. There's hardly a mink within five miles. It ain't like it used to be." Duprés described the abundance he had seen in the early '60s. "Trappers made good in this country since I was a lad. We caught tons 'a beaver an' mink an' rats. The fur companies hauled out boatloads of baled furs, you bet. The traders run furs down the Upper Missoura and made fortunes long afore gold was discovered." His gaze drifted, as if seeing the hustling business in furs and hides that once broke the isolation of the West from the rest of the country.

"Yestiddy, I saw *TN* horses back off from the stream without taking a swallow—like it stunk."

Mac jolted his chair upright.

"Maybe it was sulphur from Gregson Hot Springs."

"I don't trap in warm streams. I went north down the valley. The horses may be right about the smell, Mr. Tarynton. Those criks show a yellow, scummy slime along the edges. I'm finding dead muskrats and fish here and there. I wouldn't want it myself." Not knowing what to do with his hands without whittling, Duprés spun his hat around on his thumbs.

"Poisoning the creeks—that could be mercury the miners use in sluicing," Mac said.

"The crik bottom is green and red where claims up and down the valley turned up minerals. It's bad stuff."

"Jackson mentioned seeing color up next to the ice."

"Now the Chinese are reworking the old tailings."

"And that means exposing more ore to rains and runoff. They probably add more mercury for amalgamation of the little gold that's left."

"*Oui*, sir, everybody uses mercury, even placer miners left workin' the criks. The ore that's turned up oxidizes, they tell me, and leaves the colors ye see in the streams. Even the quarry by my cabin has putrid water seepin' in."

"You best be careful of acid in the water. You can't always see toxic minerals. As you say, you only know they're there when you see dead animals and fish. I'll have to look into the sources of the minerals in the streams. It sounds like it's getting to be a problem I can't ignore."

Mac was on his feet, plans obviously rolling over in his mind. "I should put you and Mrs. Duprés on the payroll for looking after my stock," he grinned.

Preparations for the annual cattle drive to the Elkhorns began later than usual this year, increasing the vitality at the ranch as if it were coming out of hibernation with renewed vigor. Lights in the two-story frame house went on earlier and blazed into the night when Julianna resumed cooking after Nettie left the ranch, a role that Mac titled "Chief Cook and Nursemaid." Julianna had been the only one with stomach enough to change his bandages between doctor visits five months ago.

Farriers and skilled wranglers shod horses, others mended tack or repaired and outfitted the chuckwagon. The barn, framed like the house in rough-cut lumber, rose to a high ceiling over a center aisle with low, wide wings that covered these activities during frosty mornings and periods of slushy rain.

"Big Butte is gettin' too crowded to trail cows across town to Bison Creek," advised Antonio, Mac's foreman. "We'll need to move 'em below the town."

"Yeah, I 'spect those old cows and steers won't take kindly to headframes in their way, nor the Alice's open pit. We might drift the herd down a southeast route, bypassing Ian Huckins' place on Blacktail Creek, then turn them north towards Bison Creek," Mac said. Towering steel structures over mine shafts, known by miners' wives as gallows frames, clutched the hillsides of Butcher, Town, and Dublin gulches. Homes scattered from the foothills onto the flats.

"Antonio, you and Pete ride with me to check for foreseeable problems. The cattle will be wild in the spring air, and ornery enough to fight a buzz saw to protect their calves. The whole bunch could spook at anything or nothing."

The scouting trip revealed what Antonio had suspected, that the Tarynton ranch was pretty well hemmed in on the east side.

"With the town spreading there'll soon be no way to cross the valley, not with two to three thousand head stampeding through the kitchens of these folks," Mac growled. "I'll be forced off the ranch if I can't get my stock to the Elkhorns for summer grazing. We need to save feed in the valley on the west side here for winter months."

On the return trip, they pulled up their horses at the old quarry near the Duprés cabin. Ten years ago its stone had served for foundations, retaining walls, and a few small buildings for the short-lived Silver Bow gold camp. Later, builders envisioned more permanent structures of granite blocks from the Continental Divide. Left in the quarry beneath tumbleweeds and dried fireweed were pools of rainwater discolored by leeching minerals.

"This is the rusty scum that Jackson and Jonathan Duprés warned me about," Mac said. "A geologist told me there's arsenic, sulphur, iron, copper, and a mix including cadmiums. He says it lets you know if the concentrations are toxic—it stinks and has a sulphur or metallic taste."

He grimaced. "My father wouldn't have homesteaded here if

the water hadn't been perfectly good. That tells you the mining operations have changed Big Butte."

Mac paused for reflection, tamping down indignation. "We weren't the first to find it in prime condition. First it was buffalo country, then came the Indians and after that the fur traders. Like Duprés says, these waters used to be full of every kind of creature.

"Then small outfits like my father's came with a few horses and cows. The first big spread was Johnny Grant's. He built up his herd by trading one fat cow for two tired, thin cows from settlers passing through. That way Grant came by fine breeds of English shorthorns and Herefords. Conrad Kohrs bought out Johnny Grant about ten years ago when I first started ranching. He built a fine house for his wife, Augusta. I been there a time or two for supper.

"Wal, Kohrs started with longhorns from Nelson Story like we did. Now he has tens of thousands of good, mixed stock. My herd is puny in comparison. He runs 50,000 head on ten million acres, a lot of it in Sun River Valley west of Great Falls. He grazes his herd plumb into Canada, the Dakotas and Wyoming, and ships out 10,000 head a year to Chicago. The market's there for beef, but the demand here from folks working in the silver mines suits me."

Mac crossed his good leg over his saddle horn and rolled a smoke. He offered the drawstring bag of Bull Durham to Pete and Antonio and launched into another one of his stories.

"When my family first came here grass was belly deep on a tall horse. My dad and I trailed 200 head of longhorns that Dad bought from Story while they were still on Bozeman Trail in Wyoming. We had two Mexican drovers and my cousin Tad, fifteen or sixteen years old, to bring those cows in ahead of Story.

"Somewhere this side of the Yellowstone, we ran over a patch of ground bees that swarmed up with a terrible revenge. The cows high-tailed it out of there, bawling in every direction.

To please my father, Tad rode into that cloud of bees that were buzzing like the devil, and tried to gather up the cows. In no time his horse reared and bucked with bees in its ears and stinging its belly, and threw Tad off right there in the midst of the stampede. We couldn't see nothing for the dust and bees flying sky high, but we forced our horses in and around expecting the worst. All of a sudden, Tad comes walking out of the herd, hat in hand as good as you please—like parting the waters, Carrie says." He chuckled, savoring the story and the storytelling. "It was enough to make a man religious."

The men laughed but made no move to ride on while Mac was in a talking mood. From the height where they sat on horses above the quarry, they viewed a dozen or so headframes uptown, each mine representing finger-like tunnels probing the earth's veins for riches.

"We're all just creatures on this earth," Mac philosophized between drags on his handmade smoke, his arm gesturing toward the ant-like activity around the mines that had rapidly altered Summit Valley's landscape. "There's the source of raw ore that is leeching minerals into our pristine streams. I don't know when or where it's going to end."

His horse shook flies off its head, jangling the copper bit with its long metal shanks. Mac swung his leg back to the stirrup and touched the horse's sides with his heavy steel spurs, setting the rowels singing. Lost upon Mac was the connection between mining and a rancher's dependence upon metal products that was almost as necessary as the need for grass, air and water. The blunt fact was that he only foresaw the Tarynton style of ranching threatened near Big Butte.

6

The greatest physicians are good water, sunlight, and exercise. As a tonic, exercise is better than medicine. Prudence B. Saur, M.D.

After scouting a new route to drive a herd of cattle east past Big Butte, Mac grumbled about the inconvenience and the dismal outlook for ranchers if mining continued at its present rate.

"They dealt their final card by spoiling the water," Mac told Carrie one morning. The 'stinking' water had worked on his mind for a couple of days. "We need to take a position before it's too late. I'm going to send Antonio to Deer Lodge to ask if Kohrs and other ranchers feel the pinch over there."

He stared out the window with a long, faraway look, seeing the country as he imagined his father saw it when streams ran with pure snowmelt through wide open valleys. "I don't know if silver will amount to anything or not. These discoveries have gone bust before. I hear talk they'll next want to mine copper, manganese, and zinc. We may have to organize to get any clout. Not that it could stop mining in its tracks, but what can a man do? Go to the capital in Helena and raise hell? Maybe get on the Territorial Advisory Commission?"

The matter rode for several weeks with little concern expressed by neighboring small ranchers or by Kohrs vast spread, none of which had been significantly affected by mining in the Pintler Mountains. Mac was resigned to taking his concerns to

Virginia City or Helena. Less eager to storm the capital, he chose to assess the water situation in Madison County. They had experience with long-term, residual waste in streams from mining in Alder Gulch, Sterling in Hot Spring District, and Silver Star's Green Campbell, as well as dozens of other operations in the county.

The stagecoach offered Mac a one-day trip to Virginia City, an alternative to enduring several days on horseback over rough terrain. The wound in his thigh ached beneath the ugly scar and generated considerable pain when he overtaxed that leg.

His first impression of Virginia City was that it surpassed Big Butte in its maturity. Nice stone buildings anchored the east end of Wallace, the town's industrious main street, where a gleaming brick courthouse towered above streams of ox and mule teams pulling freight wagons. Above and below Wallace a number of two-story Victorian homes gave the town a respectable face. Women in remarkably current fashions, wide feathered hats and bustles, hurried past an arrastra consisting of ore-grinding discs turned by a mule.

"But a mining town is a mining town in my opinion," he muttered. The distinctive yellow tailings had greeted him on the outskirts. "I doubt they'll be sympathetic to ranchers."

Uncertain who to see, Mac stated his business at the sheriff's office, where a tough-looking deputy sent him to a temporary Madison County Commissioners office. A group of formally attired gentlemen stood chatting in the doorway, their session finished by noon. He recognized a dignitary from Butte, Francis Millhouse, owner of the Daylight Silver Lode. Millhouse offered his hand.

"I'm Mac Tarynton from Big Butte. I need to see somebody about toxic water that's affecting my livestock. I haven't been able to raise anyone's interest in Deer Lodge Valley."

Alerted by the combative tone, Millhouse tipped his hat towards a tall gentleman in a top coat and Homburg, introducing him as Kent Berrigan. "You need to talk to the ranchers among us."

"I'm not much of a rancher," drawled Berrigan, chuckling. "To these miners, if you run one cow you're a rancher."

Mac relaxed a bit. "You gentlemen leaving for dinner?"

"About to. We had a special meeting regarding the need for more court justices, better roads, mail offices, and more of just about everything. It's likely the same in your county with towns like Big Butte growing so fast. They'll take you on the board just because you walked in the door." Mac and Kent laughed along with the departing Commissioners.

"I'll show you around, then we'll go eat," Kent said. "Looks like you could use a good meal," indicating Mac's gaunt frame.

The two men, Western cattleman and Southerner, were half a head taller than most, well dressed, and carried themselves with a surety that turned heads of tired miners and the few women who stepped wide of ruts and broken walkways. Chinese in long tunics hurried among teamsters and mule skinners. Freighters' shouts and the grinding of wagon wheels bounced off the narrow slopes along Daylight Creek. Mac hunched his shoulders against the reverberations of the closed-in space, choking from dust and cigar smoke that made a further onslaught on his senses.

"I've seen enough of the city," Mac said by the time they toured the end of Wallace.

Cautious of Mac's souring mood, Kent invited him to a point overlooking Alder Gulch, where William Fairweather discovered gold in 1863. Mountains once heavily timbered with pine rose on both sides of the deeply eroded creek known for its alder thickets with their glistening, sculpted leaves. Only a few pines and alders had survived the spate of claims that had uprooted and turned over every living thing, tree, stone, and soil from Virginia City to Summit, a mining town five miles up the creek on the crest of the Gravelly Mountains.

"The ravage of God's green earth," Mac said, his voice low and bitter. "All for what?"

Kent nodded. "I had similar feelings about tearing up the earth when I mined in Hot Spring District ten years ago. The stagecoach came through my place before you hit the Bozeman Trail at Norris."

"I wonder what Millhouse is doing at your county meeting. Likely nosing around, trying to influence you folks according to mining interests."

"There's not much to see. The counties are hamstrung about doing anything that costs money without a Territorial or state tax base. Gold mining has all but run out in Madison County. Pockets of silver mining continue as long as reduction facilities exist to separate it from other minerals. Population has dropped in ten years from a high of 10,000 or so in the early days to a few thousand. The final blow came when the state capital was relocated from Virginia City to Helena."

Mac's perpetual scowl grew deeper. Realizing that mining was not what the rancher came to Virginia City to discuss, Kent steered him back uptown past sagging frame businesses with boarded up windows to the Varina Inn, a congenial location for dinner and conversation. The Inn had been a holdout for Confederate miners who provided much of the workforce of Montana Territory following the war—an occupation in terms of numbers only, not in political or economic power. Higher positions of authority were held by those appointed by the government that held the purse strings.

"Southern Democrats often won at the polls and in rabble-rousing causes, but we lost even our favored name, Varina, for the town," Kent drawled. "Yet the Varina Inn, named after General Jefferson Davis' wife, remains a durable presence. Virginia City was named after Thomas Jefferson's wife, the Northerners having won that dispute, too."

Kent chose a table and waved Mac to a reasonably comfortable chair. "I had better explain about my so-called ranching. My half-section is on South Willow Creek north of here. It is good grassland that I lease for grazing and haying. I'm so involved in county affairs I find it hard to stay home anymore." He leaned back, not appearing to be displeased about that.

"I prospected years ago when I was more ambitious, so my mining days are behind me." Kent laughed easily, his grey eyes lighting up fine features, emanating a gentleman's good life and upbringing.

Mac was struck by his cultured manner. In an attempt to appear accommodating, he allowed "mining has its place, but there's places it shouldn't be. You're talking about the influence of investors and politics. That's what we may be up against in Big Butte."

"I'm interested in hearing what brought you here."

Mac had picked at the Inn's excellent prime rib roast, mashed potatoes and brown gravy while Kent was talking, aware that the market for beef was steadily growing in Madison County.

"Cattle ranching," he said, pointing his fork towards the roast. "We are getting pushed out of Big Butte. At first I thought the miners would be gone when placer gold ran out, but I was wrong. Those black-lined quartz rocks we see everywhere turned out to be rich in silver. I'm sure you are aware that hardrock mines haul up the bowels of the earth and drop the innards over the sides. The gold and silver miners haven't been at it much more 'n ten years, but the tailings and runoff are beginning to mess up the streams."

Kent nodded. "I saw that in my mining days on Norwegian Creek. The effects are apparent now, a decade later."

"My stock got into stinkin' water, probably sulphur, arsenic and lead. I'm worried. I can't raise beef on foul water. It sure as hell wasn't that way when my father pioneered the spread I have today." Mac soon lost his appetite altogether, a signal to Kent of the depths of distress the rancher was experiencing.

"The issue of water contamination in and around mining camps has not been seriously addressed as far as I know," Kent said. "Ranching and mining are both relatively new fledglings in the Territories. At this point no one knows or notices the limits when they intersect."

"But cattle ranching is the largest industry in the Territory, followed by fur trapping and trade with the Indians. A trapper told me that twenty-foot beaver dams have been torn out so that streams can be diverted for mining. What's left is water so nasty even the muskrats left. This affects all of us one way or another. It's only going to get worse." Mac searched for words to describe the predicted upward curve of what he was seeing.

"Does the Territorial Advisory Commission propose regulations or legislation to govern these operations, or do they let them mushroom out of control? Damned if it isn't a frightening prospect." His wary, uncertain look told Kent that Mac sensed the situation had already developed past an individual's power to intervene.

"How are the other ranchers feeling about the water issue?"

"You may be surprised, but I haven't found anyone who is interested enough to get off their backside and confront the big bosses. The problem is my ranch is located closer than others to the silver mining in Big Butte. Mines are propagating faster and deeper, hauling up tons and tons of ore that the smelters process, creating dirty smoke and acid drainage. I tell you, Mr. Berrigan, it is a one-two punch for our *TN* ranch."

"I can understand your situation," Kent replied. "We saw streams run red, yellow and green in Hot Spring District, and that was only what was visible after placer and hardrock mining."

"Other ranchers are too busy and too short-sighted to raise a voice about it. It may be fear of making it an issue, but I don't think cattlemen of Deer Lodge Valley see the effects that are happening. They will, come shipping time, and their cattle are sick or underweight. And like I said, I'm unfortunately a lot closer to Big Butte than the others."

The subject was not uplifting to either man. Kent shifted the conversation, and explained what the Territorial Commission does and the current issues before it.

"Who is on it at present and why are they there?" Mac asked.

"Generally, representatives of banks, mining companies, and other monied interests sit on the Commission. They have the wealth and motivation to protect their businesses. Most citizens around Big Butte are barely surviving. They often lack education to act on their own behalf, much less in a leadership position. That's likely what you're seeing in Deer Lodge County. The Commission makes recommendations to legislators, but legislation often stalls, usually over finances. The District Courts are spread too thin to be helpful, and circuit courts are understaffed. Until we get statehood we don't have a prayer of resolving issues across the Territory."

By the time they left the Varina Inn, Mac felt that statehood was a piper's dream, but he had a connection with Berrigan. They shared many of the same views. He was pleased therefore when Kent invited him to stop at his home on the way back to Big Butte so they could further discuss what might be done.

The Virginia City to Big Butte road bisected the Berrigan holdings. Mac got off the stagecoach to meet Kent at a line of massive cottonwood trees bending under the weight of heavy boughs, outlining the course of South Willow Creek. To Kent, Mac's wide shoulders, slim cowboy hips and awkward walk left him looking uncomfortable without a horse. When they walked along the creek Kent mentioned Mac's limp.

"Souvenir of the Sioux," Mac said, rubbing the indentation where good muscle used to be. "Say, this is a nice spread you have here."

"It suits me, though I don't have much time for it anymore. The land is leased, the neighbors supply eggs, butter, milk and beef. Elk come right down to the pasture. You'd think with all that I would have time to paint the house, but it's been ten years and it hasn't happened yet."

"You must have horses." Mac was still under the impression that Mr. Berrigan came from a family with higher aspirations than driving a herd of cussed longhorn mixed-breed cows and bucking stock.

"One old timer and a companion for him. What are you raising?"

"A bunch of longhorns, a string of ornery mustangs, and we just gave away a Connemara stud for a wedding present," Mac replied, his mood rising to the occasion.

"An Irish horse?"

"My wife dragged in a broken down import that had been poisoned by eating weeds or something he shouldn't have. He recovered, but it's not clear how much it affected his mind."

"Come meet Ben, my thoroughbred."

They circled past a sturdy home distinguished by its Queen Ann style of decorated eaves. From beyond a few outbuildings an exceedingly large Percheron-thoroughbred bay lumbered over to Kent. Flecks of gray hair speckled his heavy coat and muzzle. A wide neck and barrel suggested his fourteen-to-fifteen years of age.

"He'd make a good workhorse in deep snow on my ranch," Mac chuckled.

"He's done his share and gone to California and back with a wagon train. I ride him now and then. He can go the distance when he needs to." Berrigan's other horse was a cinnamon-red unbroke mustang with a crooked blaze and the wispy hairs of a broomtail.

The rush of South Willow Creek on its steep, short course from the Tobacco Root Mountains towards the Jefferson River formed a backdrop to their conversation.

"Spring runoff is heavy this year after that severe winter," Kent said.

Mac stood on the creek bank and marveled. "This is the clearest, purtiest water I've ever seen. Untouched. You're a lucky man."

"Relatively untouched. It escaped much of the placer mining that occured on Norwegian Gulch to the south and recent placer discoveries at Pony on North Willow Creek just beyond us."

The two men pursued the topic of water over supper and coffee at the house. It was clear to Kent that Mac had a grasp of the potential size and threat of water contamination from Big Butte mines, and more importantly, that it weighed upon him.

"I don't want to discourage you, but support would be hard to come by. Money is on the side of big mining companies. They generally buy out regulatory commissions by packing them with their men. Mining is particularly notorious for flaunting the few regulations that exist, much less enforcement. The West also lacks effective means of recourse in the judicial courts, in my opinion. Frankly, I don't see that the cattlemen have much power unless they organize and load local and Territorial commissions with their people."

In Kent's experience, the battle for water fell to the rich; consequently, so did the respect—or rather lack of it—in the treatment of water. He was no stranger to the controversy. He recalled that the ditch from North Meadow Creek to Norwegian Gulch was financed by Midas Mining Company, then appropriated by separate claims and landholders when Midas dissolved. Kent's neighbors, the Sayles and Williams, desperately needed water for their homesteads after the once plentiful flow of creeks in the area was siphoned off into smaller and smaller units until many people had little or none.

"I understand it's the same in Helena, where mine operators obtain ditches and diversions at a cost to other enterprises. I doubt we can expect much help from our Legislature in the capital."

The men mulled the problem while they ate biscuits, gravy and salt pork, then sat back.

"Would you run for the Territorial Commission to represent this section of southwest Montana?" Mac spoke his mind, parsing his words.

Kent paused. He had previously served as Justice of the Peace—though he had no background in law, but he could read and write intelligently which evidently met the meager criteria. A few former Confederates had run successfully for the Territorial Legislature, but one refused to take a loyalty oath required prior to serving. The Legislature later abandoned the practice. Kent had served for years on the local County Commission, where his low key approach to conferences and negotiations earned him respect. "Charm," someone flattered him, "can go a long way."

"Let me think about it," Kent said when he walked Mac back to the road to catch the evening stagecoach into Big Butte.

By spring of 1876, notices for upcoming elections went out in the few newspapers of Montana Territory, papers which maintained a nationwide distribution extolling investment opportunities in the West to entrepreneurs in the East, and drawing massive Eastern capital to the region. The *Montana Post*, published since 1864, had ceased publication and also the *Bozeman Avant Courier* which had picked up the slack. Elsewhere, news included completion of the new Madison County courthouse in Virginia City, a long needed facility to house offices spread in temporarily rented spaces since the days of gold discovery in Alder Gulch.

The *New North-West* newspaper of Deer Lodge that Mac had given Kent squeezed news of Indian conflicts, acquisition of mines and local lore between prominent advertisements for Dr. Liebig's *"restorative for lost manhood, a result of youthful imprudent years."* The popular German tonic competed with Sir Anthony Cooper's Vital Restorative claiming *"cure of loss of memory, lassitude, nocturnal emissions,"* as well as *"loss of vital fluids passing unobserved in urine, and many other diseases that lead to insanity and death."*

Not only unimpressed but annoyed by the extravagant claims, Kent sifted through the paper and found notices of open elected and appointed positions in the governing bodies of the Territory and local communities. A single position stood open on the Territorial Commission, where the issues were familiar yet daunting—the need for better roads, bridges, and law and order were highest priorities. The Commission would study the issues and bring recommendations to the next session of the Legislature. In addition, it had some clout on lower level bodies such as county commissioners.

At present, the Territorial Legislature had pending administrative actions pertaining to spending powers of the Territory, clarification of criminal codes, and jurisdiction of the courts. Two hefty problems, refinancing debts and subsidizing railroads, remained leftovers from previous sessions.

"You would think the Territorial Legislature would bend over backwards to bring in the railroads," Kent muttered, but no one heard. He sat alone in his home on South Willow Creek near Norris, where a spur of the proposed Utah Northern Railroad or Union Pacific would have been welcomed by cattlemen and miners alike. News reports of the Legislature's failure to do so surprised him. Elsewhere, cattlemen like Conrad Kohrs had to drive their herds from Montana's Sun River to Cheyenne, Wyoming, or to Iowa for shipping by rail to processing centers in Chicago. Mac Tarynton's herds were smaller, but he still needed to hoof beef to market. Kent made a mental note to talk with Wilber Fisk Sanders, Territorial representative in the Legislature, whom he knew in Virginia City.

Kent folded the papers and removed his spectacles. The current Commission composed of five members representing vast areas of the Territory had been largely obscure since few of their positions on issues were reported in the newspapers. It was therefore difficult to know exactly what they did, he concluded, but he had indicated to Mac Tarynton that he would consider running for the open position. His aversion to controversy and politics notwithstanding, it was time to step forth or forever wonder if he could have made a difference.

Kent had come to love the wild open land of the Rocky Mountain West where it was often said, "you could see for a hundred miles on a blue sky day." No longer did he yearn for the steamy hot Georgia climate or shady days under dense sycamores, or even miss the Georgia pines. That was one kind of beauty; Montana had another—soft violet blues of distant mountains, steely crisp skies that showcased mauvy-red sunsets, and startling yellow-greens of willows in spring that yielded a tangy, fresh-born scent. Here he had a stream all his own on one side of the half-section along South Willow Creek, an exclusive and safe playground for "brookies," native brook trout, since Kent was not a fisherman.

Beneath the benign brow of 10,600-foot Mount Hollowtop, rivulets of melted snow formed multiple creeks that graced the east side of the Tobacco Root Mountains. In sheltered draws and shady nooks lay secret gardens of glacier lilies and pockets of tiny blue violets, but the real gold, Kent thought, was the cold, delicious spring water that he had piped into his house.

Again amazed at the contentment he felt in his home, all of it derived of his own ambitions and none from an inheritance, Kent reflected on his former aimlessness and indecisiveness when he had emigrated to the West with an unknown destination. He had fled the ravages of the Civil War and avoided the homecoming of his older brother, Rand, who had sided with the Unionists. Rand returned to Georgia, solely inheriting the family estate, an eighty-acre tobacco farm that Kent had never expected to leave. The estate would have more than adequately supported two families, his and Rand's, had they come to an agreement, yet that possibility faded when the war split their loyalties.

I was more a blind follower than a leader, Kent realized. What now? Accept a leadership position in the Territory? The notion of accepting responsibility on a scale he had avoided since his days in the Confederate Army was unsettling. He knew from experience that finding consensus among opposing parties was a thankless job.

Yet, Mac had a point about organizing to address the water issue. Kent respected the rancher for assessing the pulse of both Deer Lodge and Madison counties to determine the situation and ask for help. His forthright approach would raise hackles, though neither he nor anyone else could confront the problem alone. That meant reaching out to parties with similar or vested interests. Kent again found himself aligned primarily with those who would protect the land and its assets, even if the legitimate pressures of an expanding population and various industries meant they could not always preserve it in its pristine condition.

After Jackson and Nettie Colters' wedding the Tarynton household regained a measure of tranquility. And following Mac's trip to Virginia City, his earlier angst seemed to have subsided. The possibility of gaining alliances for the mutual benefit of ranchers in preserving water quality downstream from Big Butte mines had relieved his mind. Carrie had heard a steady tirade of his fears and sense of responsibility for months, and therefore welcomed a respite when he threw himself into late spring chores.

Life softened around the edges at the ranch house. Carrie tousled Mac's curly brown hair in the old playful manner. He chose to ignore it, but she knew he was pleased that she had returned to her normal, pleasant self. She resumed her rounds with former patients such as Mrs. Sawyer who had become a friend, but did not accept new referrals.

Mac and Carrie's April birthdays had passed uneventfully, though Mac remarked, "we're no spring calves." He turned forty-one and Carrie became thirty-six; their lovemaking had marked a celebration of sorts after a dispirited, celibate winter due to Mac's wound, Carrie's malaise, and doctor's orders.

Carrie breathed in the moments of peace, wanting to settle in for a long deserved rest rather than tip toe around the edges of Mac's temperament as she had done all winter. The checked power, the tension and grit made Mac the man she loved, the rough loving Westerner who gave her a sense of security when she wanted to hide under a table from visions that often tortured her mind—Michael McHenry Tarynton, the man who was also hard to live with at times.

But instead of tranquility, dreams came again, filtering snatches of the other world, conversations of spirit guides, and messages from One known as *Yahweh*, God of the Hebrews. Carrie had become familiar with "the unnamable" God from Mrs. Sawyer's reading of the Old Testament. Usually, a sense of suspension in the spirit world felt inviting, as natural as her own heart beat, but lately the vivid images frightened her. Punctuated by the "screeeee" of ravens outside, Carrie would startle from a dream-like state, always finding solid ground in Mac Tarynton, son of pioneer stock.

Then one day Eugenia and Roxanna came to the ranch for tea and biscuits with Carrie. In the course of her excited conversation, Roxanna mentioned the vision Carrie had spoken of some time ago, a vision so indefinite and disturbing that she had cried.

"Remember, Carrie, when you saw yourself with a child?"

Carrie's alarmed look alerted Roxanna that she overstepped.

"We were shelling dry beans at the cabin. I wonder why you had a vision of a child."

"What child?" Mac demanded from the back room, where he was cleaning his guns. His tall dark form filled the kitchen doorway.

"There is no child," Carrie said, her jaw firm, squarely facing Mac. "It was a passing image."

"What are you withholding from me—all of you? These superstitious babblings have got to stop."

"I've never withheld anything from you, Mac. Never." Carrie dully viewed her real-life dream to restore calm in her marriage capitulating under his withering gaze.

"Faeries and voices and visions! Women are worse than the drunken miners in the saloons," he stormed on his way out, then halted and yelled back at Carrie, "You tell me first if there's going to be a child, you hear?"

The door slammed behind him, drowning Roxanna's wails. His voice and footsteps echoed and reechoed like cracks of thunder gone haywire long after he left. Carrie's face paled. She slumped, bracing herself on the table, her fragile hope for reconciliation with Mac stricken.

"I know how you feel," Roxanna whimpered, fists in her mouth. "My husband often hurts my feelings, bless his soul." Roxanna's gush of tears dampened and spoiled the starched apron she threw over her head.

Eugenia remained planted in her chair, her lips whispering "Jesus, Mary, Joseph, Lord and Holy Ghost." Moments past before she said, "Carrie, my daughter, my friend, this may be hard to believe in light of what is happen'n before my eyes, but my soul tells me there is to be a good outcome. What, pray tell am I not understanding?"

Carrie's stoic acceptance of Mac's charge rooted her friends in their chairs. The laughter, the shared pain of their daily lives, their common purpose as healers among a handful of women on a remote windswept mountain all vanished in an instant. Only sobs rent the hollowness of the formerly vibrant kitchen.

Eugenia finally turned to Carrie. "'Tis the feelings, love. He can't bear his feelings for ye—"

"But what about my feelings—? What are his feelings? Tell me, Eugenia," Carrie caught her breath and gasped, attempting to counter resentment, yet an angry flush betrayed the hurt.

"'I love ye, Carrie, heart of my heart and soul of my soul—'"

"Then tell me, Eugenia, for god's sake, what is it about Mac's feelings for me?"

"I am telling ye—'heart of my heart—' he says."

"You know something, I am sure," Carrie pressed, without fully hearing Eugenia, or failing to understand that she spoke words Mac was unable to express. She sensed only rising anxiety not only in Roxanna, but in herself.

Eugenia's mouth opened and closed, opened and closed again without uttering a single word. The women waited, held captive in the wake of Mac's fury. The teakettle sputtered water into the firebox. At last in a flat, trance-like tone, Eugenia spoke. "'If I could cut a great piece of the perfect heavens with all the rainbows, the golden rays of the sun, and infinite stars and give it to ye, Carrie, it would not be enough—.'" Her voice trailed off and tears pooled on her wrinkled cheeks.

"That's how Mac loves ye. And the Lord, too," she whispered through dry lips.

A faint scent of lavender and sage from the basket of dried herbs and flowers on the table, and perhaps myrrh from another sphere, enveloped the three women of Big Butte; a softness crept into the room among the shattered pieces of their previous contentment. The women sat in a rarefied glow, touched by love revealed, their collective intuitions and wisdom acknowledged within the greater harmony of the universe. It was much later when Eugenia rose from her chair, and she and Roxanna went on their way.

7

It is said, 'a little knowledge is a dangerous thing.' I contend that no knowledge is a greater calamity.   Prudence B. Saur, M.D.

The dapple gray foal came at a busy time of calving and hardly caused a ripple in affairs at the ranch. One morning the miniature replica of the Connemara lay beneath her mother, a black ranch mare the cowhands had trapped from the wilds. Wisps of dark mane and furry tail matched the mare's coloring. Swirls of black over light hair on the foal would fade to dappled gray as the filly grew older. She struggled to her feet, bracing long straight legs in front, and toppled over. She tried hoisting her petite, rounded rear end with hind legs, an ungainly move that set her on her tiny nose in the rough dirt corral. The mare nuzzled her to try again. The newborn must suckle, and the foal was only too eager, after she figured out the physics of balance and trajectory.

"I guess the stud had more in him than I expected," Mac admitted. He told Carrie it was her foal to keep. That was the end of it—no flap about a half-breed Connemara filly. Carrie guessed his giving her the foal was a loving gesture, although it did not feel like it at the time. Neither she nor Mac had bridged his outburst about Carrie's vision of a child. Both bristled over the smallest encounters, and the whole house felt like a tinderbox.

However, the foal with its beautiful, well-shaped head and trim, strong legs had her own way of becoming a delightful handful. She played coy around her mother until her curiosity prompted her to snort and dance and venture forth when anyone came near the corral. She was soon a favorite of the staid wranglers and ranch hands.

Carrie determined from the start to avoid falling hard for the offspring of the errant parent, Love. Mac's accusation that the Connemara had been the source of their problems remained a raw spot with Carrie. Therefore, the foal had a mother, and that was that. She would leave it be. But an inkling persisted, is this the "child" that came to me in a vision? As quickly, she dispelled the notion. The mystery of the vision haunted her but seemed no closer to resolution. The constant worrying and second-guessing became exhausting. Carrie knew she must again visit her mentor, the medicine woman.

Natalya puttered outside her tipi removing last winter's dried stalks and leaves from crowding dog-toothed violets bordering a small spring, her large feet slipped into the thinnest of soft deerskin moccasins.

"What is it with Mac?" Carrie asked, following Natalya around a small patch of wild onions, and the domestic herbs she had planted behind the small community of tipis.

"I am at a loss to explain his behavior. He never used to be this way." Carrie gathered brave shoots of mustard and chickweed in her apron while Natalya raked back aspen leaves with her hand to find tiny fresh dandelions. With their spring harvest, they moved inside around the fire pit. Natalya's husband was not present in his usual place on a buffalo robe.

Today Carrie's impatience with Natalya's slow tea-making ceremony left her restless and irritable. Made from a rich, sodden mixture of nettle leaves and steeped in boiling water, the tea smelled and tasted like wet hay.

At last Carrie burst with pent up anxieties. "I don't want to believe Mac no longer loves me. My life would end if he didn't.

Eugenia claims that he loves me dearly. Is he short with me because he's now forty-one and 'old,' as he says? Is he ill? Is it the pain from his wound?"

Natalya sipped her tea without haste.

"He is angry or tender or indifferent—I don't know what to expect from him, but it is wearing on me."

Natalya appeared as unhurried and hard of hearing as her husband had been, Carrie thought, and pushed small stones around in front of herself. For long moments the stones, too, held their implacable silence. Carrie dashed the last of her tea in the fire.

"I fear he regrets our failure to have another child—my failure to have another child—and he is afraid to tell me. He harbors such fury at times." Carrie impulsively reached for a small pile of bone shards. Her strong, capable hands swooshed a jumble over the stones. "There, that is how I feel, my friend, Medicine Woman. It must be my fault—I do not please him anymore."

The old woman did not address the troubles directly. Carrie became increasingly frustrated. It was too hot inside by the fire on such a nice day. She moved to go as if daring Natalya to object, when a kind voice welled from a place deep within the Native woman.

"Your husband will be wise one day."

"How do you know, Natalya? I am not finding wisdom in his words or actions. I cannot be sure."

"He will grow old." The old woman spoke evenly, the slits of her eyes revealing a glance toward the doorway beyond the fire. Carrie wondered if Natalya's husband would appear, no different from any other time she had been here.

"We are both growing old and, and losing each other," Carrie murmured.

"He will grow old and sit by the fire."

Carrie waited for what seemed a long time. The pronouncements made no sense. The elder man did not appear.

"I already know that." Carrie shifted again, only half attuned to her mentor, her lips pouting.

Eventually Natalya finished her tea and poured herself another cup. "He will grow old and sit by the fire and keep his mouth shut," she said, her merry eyes dancing behind hooded lids.

––––––––

I am young yet at thirty-six, Carrie told herself as she trudged back uphill to the ranch. Natalya is truly an elder and her husband much older. I'm not sure if he still has his hearing. Oh, to have Natalya's maturity and wisdom and wit, but I am so impatient. Grow up, she chastised herself—even if Mac does not, she added with a grim sense of satisfaction.

Putting Natalya's mostly nonverbal teachings into practice was not easy. Shortly after the dapple gray foal was born, Carrie began a regimen of disciplining herself. She tried sitting in a chair like Eugenia every day, one hand cupped in the other, feet flat on the floor. She began with two minutes at a time, stretching it to five minutes over the next few days. Soon she avoided sitting in the chair altogether.

Eugenia's habit of meditating did not come easily to Carrie, nor the connection with her natural style of healing. Her gift of intuitive powers, the link between the ethereal and earth, had gone missing in her scramble to find herself and her lost art. Unheard were the Spirits who sang mystical songs and whispered secrets at the edges of everyday human life—the Spirits who had given her intuitive powers to nurture others, and indeed, had given her a sense of self as a woman and a wife.

Carrie copied Natalya's veiled eyes, tuning to the world beyond the world. "I have forsaken her long years of teachings," she murmured. Merging with the flow of the often intractable universe depended upon patience, and Carrie again despaired of opening to the secrets of the guardians.

"It will have to come of its own accord, as it always has. I cannot make it happen."

Suddenly the future loomed long, lonely and empty. How do I live like this and not lose my mind as well as my gifts? Why do I think I can heal others when I fail to heal myself? But the daily demands of the ranch proved overwhelming and disrupted Carrie from further contemplation. Inevitably, she substituted the washboard that hung on the back porch for introspection.

Julianna's services were unneeded since Mac had been away a few days, so Carrie did the washing. She heated water in pans on the cookstove and carried it to galvanized washtubs on a sturdy bench in the yard. She gathered lace curtains from all over the two-story house and threw them in the hot water. Gently rubbing the soft, filmy material up and down, up and down, circulating it between her palms with a bit of lye soap, and scrubbing it with her knuckles bump, bump over the ribs of the board somehow generated a sense of well-being. Washing away soot and dust meant the curtains emerged white, fresh, and new again. She soused them in rinse water next to the washtub and hung them on the clothesline to dry. Driven by inner forces she pulled sheets from all the beds for a good soaking before the water cooled, added more lye soap and a little bluing, then stirred the bulk with a long stick. With the sheets on the line, she went in search of more laundry—Mac's riding pants, trousers, flannel shirts, longjohns and socks. As she flew through their bedroom, she yanked open drawers of the wardrobe, a free-standing closet with drawers beneath, and dumped underwear on the floor. Her camisoles, stockings, petticoats, nighties, all went into a burgeoning pile, then her cotton and gingham dresses. Left were a few wool dresses and her riding habit—those would be hand-washed later.

"Antonio," she called out the back door towards the bunkhouse. "Please heat more water." This was going to be an all day job and she expected Mac home that night. Carrie twisted her hair in a knot high on her head, securing it with combs to keep it in place over the steaming tubs. Her knuckles became raw and swollen from the washboard's textured tin ribs that increased agitation of the laundry, but her mind cleared, restoring a sense of purpose. Antonio chopped and hauled sticks of wood for the cookstove, a huge black, eight-lidded affair with a water reservoir attached to one end. *Monarch Amalgamated LDT*, an elegant raised script, decorated the firebox and oven doors, a craftsman's art that taught many small children in the country their first letters and words.

The foreman carried heavily laden baskets of wet laundry to the clothesline on the west side of the house that received the strongest breeze. Mac would have left basket carrying to her, Carrie noted, washing being women's work, but ranch chores were slack and Antonio thankfully had time. The lace curtains dried within minutes in the mile-high atmosphere around Big Butte, the unique landscape that lent a comforting sense of stability when she was upset. Sheets, pillow cases and delicates were hardly up before they were dry and back on the beds or in the drawers. Only Mac's heavy clothing hung on the line when he rode in for supper.

Carrie freshened her hair and set a small table for two by the window. She had made beef stew, cornbread and applesauce early that morning. Antonio brought in a bucket of cold water from the spring, set an armload of kindling beside the stove for breakfast, and slipped out, pulling the door behind him when Mac came in.

As usual, Mac wearily hung his hat on a peg and poured a pitcher of water into the blue enamel pan on the washstand. He sloshed cold, bracing water over his face, ears and neck then smoothed back curls on his damp brow.

"Duprés took me to see more stinkin' water down the valley today. There's evidence of effects of the mining beyond this side of the mountain."

When he straightened to towel dry his face, Carrie stepped beside him, tall, clear-eyed and direct, holding his gaze. He startled when she moved in front of him and placed a hand on each of his shoulders.

Steeling herself, Carrie said, "Mac, I want you back."

The towel loosened from his grip and dropped to the floor. His hands slowly lifted. Hesitating, he took a half-step toward her, his lips forming 'yes,' his throat catching the word unuttered.

A world of hurt peeled away from Carrie; a dizzying array of distractions fell aside as she stood firm. She read Mac's boyish heart and knew this was what he most desired—his struggle with emotion written all over his face. His hands rose to enfold her close to his heaving chest. The swelling part of his yearning dashed his last defenses and confirmed her belief that she'd had to make the first move. And that this was the right one.

"Carrie—," he mumbled in her hair. "Carrie—I uh, I am so sorry—there is no way I can make up—undo what I said." She yielded, soft and warm, as if there had never been anyone or anything, not even hurtful words, between the two of them. Carrie's initiative spoke for both of them; nothing had come or would ever come between them. Mac's long embrace welcomed her back, closing the rupture, erasing their differences, and healing the hurts.

When they reheated the stew, cornbread and coffee around midnight and ate supper at the little table, Carrie said, "I won't be spending so much time with the Finnegans."

Mac bit his lip, acutely aware of his outburst and insults of her friends. "Carrie—"

"Roxanna went with her husband to the Nez Perce in Idaho. Eugenia will care for the people I look after. You will find me staying home, Mac." Her eyes remained candid and lacked resentment, and most of all, expressed her resolve.

"It seems like a sacrifice," Mac said carefully, "one I wouldn't have asked of you. We might have to do different someday, but right now I think it would hurt you, Carrie, to give up your people. I suppose I can share you." His eyes twinkled the way they used to.

The Continental Divide thrusts skyward in one startling peak after another, creating an endless range from Canada to the Mexican Territory border. Beneath a portion of the mountains crossing Montana Territory lay the 75-mile-long Boulder Batholith, extending between Big Butte and Helena, as well as underlying much of the Deer Lodge valley to the Missouri river. Volcanic origins millennia ago had been altered beyond recognition by glacial action across the Northwest, leaving mountain lakes in hollows of the Rocky Mountains. Deceptively blue in dense atmospheric conditions, the distant range fades to hazy violet in the clarity of mid-day sun.

In the heights above Big Butte, nature had stacked columns of granite blocks that rode the backs of overlapping strata of basaltic rock, layers of fused sandstone and quartz. In places cavernous limestone cliffs had eroded over time to form craggy cliffs rimming the foothills. Among the mountains' many resources, besides its peaks sheltering folks in Summit Valley, were the nearby stands of timber, quarries, and quantities of minerals that at one time or another catapulted miners and investors to fame and fortune.

Kent Berrigan had visited the gold camp of Silver Bow in its early placer days, sniffing out prospects like many other miners. William Farlin had placer-mined for gold during Silver Bow's heyday in the early 1860s, before following a star to other boomtowns, taking with him samples of ore from his claim. The ore proved to be so rich in minerals that he later hastened back to what became Big Butte with a population of fifty dwelling in scattered buildings on the hillsides.

He held his cards close knowing that at midnight January 1, 1875, all unrepresented claims would be forfeited under a new

Federal law. On that date, Farlin claimed the Travona silver mine and other lodes under the blatant act that essentially legalized takeovers. Kent had heard that others, among them Andrew Jackson Davis, Marcus Daly, and William Clark, had also seized the opportunity the law provided to aggressively acquire a string of mines with good potential. For a sliver of time silver, not gold, was king, and so were the visionaries who flocked to Big Butte and bought out two-thirds of the independent silver mines, including the Alice, the Neversweat, and the Lexington.

A year and a half later, Kent found the silver-mining town of Big Butte that had taken the placer gold camp's place was an eye-opener. Uptown blocks of streets assumed formal definitions around hotels, boarding houses, stores and saloons, shaping a lively commercial center bookended by headframes and smelter stacks. The Continental Hotel, a two-story frame building with a restaurant became a center for business, socializing, and politicking.

Francis Millhouse, the burly Big Butte gentleman Kent had met earlier in Virginia City met the stagecoach when it arrived.

"Mr. Berrigan, welcome to the forum. We publicized this event as an opportunity to meet the candidates for the Territorial Commission. We should have a considerable turnout. Weather is good. Folks are looking for a little entertainment," a slight Millhouse intended as a joke that did not go unnoticed.

"I am already nervous," Kent admitted, sensing the gathering could escalate to a showdown between rival constituents. Millhouse directed him to a rough-hewn dais that served as a platform for the candidates outside the Continental Hotel.

To Kent Berrigan, the bald-faced, usually underhanded "claim jumping" was reminiscent of buy-outs of miners and small mining companies in the mid-1860s in Hot Spring, his home district in Madison County. The leap into hardrock mining occurred after placer gold deposits were exhausted. It attracted eager investors, who heard glorified reports of the vast wealth to be reaped. Experts in Hot Spring District had predicted that gold-bearing veins went deep, a premise that cost the investors when veins proved to be superficial. The frenzied exploitation had left mountain streams and creeks lined with tailings, and piles of gravel similar to those in Alder Gulch outside Virginia City. Kent noticed similar mine dumps outside Big Butte's mines, the distinctive yellow of oxidizing ore filtering into streets, backyards of workers' homes, and every waterway.

"Are you representing the cattleman, Mac Tarynton, whom I met in Virginia City?" Millhouse might be a coordinator for the forum, but he was a canny politician at the same time.

"Mr. Tarynton is from a family that settled in the Territory back in the day of trappers and traders. He posed a rational reaction to water issues affecting his ranching. I hope to represent a good many individuals, not just the rancher. As far as I know he is an upstanding citizen with an interest in the future of Big Butte and Deer Lodge County."

Millhouse left to greet other candidates. Kent bought coffee in the hotel and chatted about mining with men who hung around waiting for the speeches to begin.

A haze of dust and smoke hung over the town from processes used to release minerals embedded in granite, igneous basalt, and quartz from the mines. Steam-powered mills used 10 to-20 piston-like feet called stamps to crush ore that then required heating in smelters to separate the minerals. Silver was usually bound with other less desirable minerals such as zinc, copper and manganese at the time of their volcanic origins. Given this complexity, samples had to be assayed to determine the value of a claim. The processes involved in hardrock mining depended upon significant capital. In addition to the investment in heavy machinery, it had to be transported by mule trains from the nearest railroad in Corrine, Utah, or from the inland port of Fort Benton on the Upper Missouri.

"It is apparent that the expansion of silver mining impacts multiple problems that will confront the Territorial Commission and eventually the Montana Territorial Legislature," Kent mentioned to several of the other candidates. Heads nodded, though it was unclear where they stood on the issues.

It was stream contamination and unregulated development of numerous mining operations that had stirred Kent to action. Goaded by Mac's solid reasoning, his own experience and his conscience, Kent had decided to run for the lone seat that was open on the Territorial Commission. It represented much of Southwest Montana, the vast reaches of mountains, valleys and rivers that Kent had come to love and wanted to preserve, including the Big Butte area.

However, Kent was relatively unknown in Big Butte or Deer Lodge County despite his tenure as a Madison County Commissioner. Evidently few Commission reports were deemed newsworthy in their papers. Outcries for better roads garnered ongoing publicity, yet there were few articles about water quality. Kent read this lack of interest as an ominous sign for both ranchers and mine owners. He resolved to avoid campaigning on either side of the roads issue. To date, citizens' demands of the Territorial government to end toll roads and cease awarding contracts to incompetent road builders proved futile. Previous attempts to improve hazardous, bone-jarring roads had resulted in little success, given the challenging granite walls and rugged sedimentary and limestone cliffs of the Rocky Mountains. Instead of inserting himself in current intractable problems, Kent knew he had to present himself as one who would work toward restoring balance on the Commission between corporate and ranching interests.

At the appointed time, Kent stepped on the dais with seven other gentlemen dressed formally in top hats and coats with tails. Starched and ruffled white shirts marked the vested outside interests as opposed to the more conservative and less expensive tucks and blousy style of Westerners. A half-dozen dignitaries vying for appointments on other boards or to governing offices followed. Francis Millhouse introduced the speakers in turn, asking for quiet and consideration for those who would "deal with important subjects that have come to the attention of the citizens of the Territory. The gentlemen you see before you have come forward to serve the public in some capacity."

Several candidates from Helena's Last Chance Gulch spoke in favor of representing business interests. Others spoke of the need for additional public servants, money to address welfare needs of families, improve the justice system ("we're not far removed from the Vigilantes," one warned), and establish a movement for statehood.

This last topic was roundly cheered by citizens in the street. Colorado, with its wealth of silver and gold, currently pushed for statehood, trailing Nevada, whose spectacular mineral booms had led to early statehood in 1864. Statehood united Montana residents pleading for better roads, bridges, schools, and improved courts. Many investors shrewdly resisted, foreseeing that statehood would bring regulations and taxes where presently few of either existed.

In turn, Mr. Millhouse announced, "Kent Berrigan of Hot Spring District is a former Justice of the Peace and longtime Commissioner in Madison County. He has served on numerous boards and panels, demonstrating his experience in both mining and business. Please welcome our next candidate for the Territorial Commission."

Kent had studied the makeup of the crowd packed in the intersection of Park and Montana streets. He guessed the miners in hard, round jerry hats or battered fedoras and baggy coats and trousers outnumbered ranchers and settlers eight or nine to one, despite a good showing of landholders from the Deer Lodge and Boulder river valleys. The Tarynton ranch had prodded these farmers, small ranchers, and horse operations to look after their interests and their future. Mac had formed his own delegation that stood on the street to Kent's left.

In a diplomatic effort, Kent praised the vigorous nature of Big Butte, "much respected for its citizens of diverse cultures and for its industries essential for the nation." Hoots and applause sporadically erupted across the crowd when Kent paused. He nodded slightly in the direction of the *TN* bunch, and outlined emerging areas of dispute that would benefit by early and dedicated attention "to resolve in the best interests of all parties."

"One of the critical issues brought to my attention," he said, "is that of preserving the clean, clear water of our streams, surely a priority we can all agree upon." With this approach, he laid out the need for members on the Territorial Commission who would represent the people's concerns for the next two years.

At that moment Kent looked up to see a woman moving confidently through the crowd of mostly men. A wide green hat trimmed in cream satin, and the mass of rusty-gold hair trailing from beneath the brim, did not disguise the person he knew so well. Nine years—he had often counted days and months since her abrupt departure—dissolved in an instant. The woman so full of life who had once fulfilled his life now stood almost within a whisper of the dais: Miss Marion Patton, his former common-law wife.

His train of thought interrupted, Kent attempted to conclude his remarks. "I, uh, I am pleased to have your attention today, and umm, I believe I can objectively represent the citizens of this community if I have your vote in the election."

Fortunately, the next speaker was on the way to the podium after the brief applause. Kent absent-mindedly returned to his seat, struggling to adjust his cravat as if it were cutting off his breath. His mind and soul rocked, not by politics unfurling in historic proportions before him, but by the improbable presence of Miss Patton, who had obviously traveled some distance to see him.

In 1866, he had pursued her from Montana to California and from the East Coast back to Montana Territory the next year. Marion, the wood sprite, the astute businesswoman, the enigma who loved and finally left him. She stood quietly on the outer right side of the crowd, ignoring curious glances from the men, while maintaining her attention on Kent, a disconcerting experience that shook his determined efforts to sit still on the dais with a facsimile of dignity. His heart took extraordinary leaps with fantasies as rapidly following. She is no doubt making a thorough assessment of the mining and political situation in Big Butte, Kent assumed, from his long and intimate time with her, though regrettably, it had been not long enough.

The shock that had sent his heart racing and mind into a tailspin worked itself out during the last painful hour of speeches. He felt his breathing even out, and the program agenda he held ceased to shake. Finally the candidates shook hands and filed offstage behind Mr. Millhouse. Kent immediately exited to greet an eager, smiling Marion who moved smoothly towards him in long strides as if she had never been away.

He took her gloved hand and bowed deeply, rising slowly, savoring the touch and prolonging the moment. Swallowing hard, he choked back the aching question, "Why did you leave me?" that would have been hard to explain to his supporters–or detractors in the crowd. He also refrained from offering open arms, though he wanted to blindly enfold her, to hold her close once again, to confirm that her appearance here meant she cared for him.

"Marion, I'm delighted," he managed to say, his drawl rich and full as straight bourbon. A daring merriment in her eyes may have meant equal pleasure in seeing him—or something unreadable. It was enough that the warm presence of the woman who had brought joy to his life, and ultimately despair, had come to see him. Pages of the past flashed intimate moments through his mind, one of a private swimming hole on Norwegian Creek, her body lying in the chilly depths next to his, another of their travel up the Missouri by steamboat, the cabin enveloping their first union. Memory of the squatter's shack they lived in prompted a wave of regret that he had not yet built a home worthy of such a woman, though they had shared their passion beneath a patchwork "crazy" quilt, which seemed about as crazy as he felt right now.

Checking his impulses, Kent found a middle ground. He needed to gravitate to the Tarynton crew who were waiting to take him to dinner at the ranch. "Please come meet an extraordinary rancher."

With Marion's hand tucked into his elbow, he led her across the noisy, congested street. The crowd dispersed, forming groups of three or four in animated conversation that may or may not have related to the candidates' speeches.

"I read about your running for the Commission in the newspapers," Marion said. "I maintain several subscriptions since our close affiliation—er—to keep abreast of the news in your area. I have been aware of your civic participation over the years. This time I could not resist coming to hear you speak in Big Butte. Travel is much easier and faster than it was when—when—we met," she faltered, finally betraying a reservoir of feelings she had carefully concealed. Kent sensed this was more than a casual reconnection on her part, that she had kept abreast of life and news in Montana Territory because of an attachment to him, or to Montana, or both. Most dear to him was that she had made the effort to see him, though what her intentions were he couldn't begin to guess. He prayed they might be similar to a flurry of his own that he dared not dwell on.

"Miss—is it Miss or Mrs. now?" Kent asked, approaching Mac's crew, who stared at them with amused interest, mouths half agape and cigarettes dangling from wry grins, signaling that a woman of her style and bearing was rarely seen in Big Butte.

"Miss Marion Patton," Marion said forthrightly, extending her gloved hand to the lean Westerner whose towering presence and self-assurance marked him as the ranch owner.

"Mac Tarynton," Kent said. "He persuaded me to run for office. And Antonio, Pete and Jackson." The other hands drifted away to bring the horses and a buggy around. "Miss Patton is widely traveled and we crossed paths when she visited Montana Territory a good many years ago." The men tipped their hats good naturedly. Only Mac knew that Kent lived alone on his land in South Willow Creek and had not spoken of a woman. He was clearly puzzled now.

"My wife invited you all to come to dinner," he offered. "We can ride out in the buggy and have time to talk about the campaign." His boot heels thudded on the gravelly street as he gave orders. "Antonio, go on ahead and tell Julianna we'll be there in an hour." He would discreetly take care of letting Carrie know to set an extra plate.

For the benefit of his host, Kent related the story of the first time he met Miss Patton ten years ago, a non-committal bit of conversation to ease his own tension if not his host's. They had shared a stagecoach out of Virginia City. "We boarded with two German miners who spoke little English. I understood enough German to know they had visited H.S. Gilbert's brewery in Virginia City and praised its *Kolsch* ale." He did not say he was so jealous of their eyeing Marion that he wanted to push them out the door over a cliff.

Kent and Marion's mature figures fit tightly in the buggy seat across from Mac, who used the extra space on his side to extend his left leg. "Buggies have not broadened much over the years," Kent noted, and they joined in the laughter. Pete drove west out of town past a curiously colorful quarry.

"That quarry holds evidence of the problem. It used to be a source of rock for building foundations because it was close and easy to get. That stale water you see is runoff from the mines," Mac indicated pools with his thumb. "The hills and gulches above were dug up first for gold, now for silver. This quarry and mining tailings all over town represent disturbed rocks and soil that leach minerals into the water. In concentrations, the acid is toxic as hell to livestock."

"My family moved to Coloma, California, during the '49ers gold rush," Miss Patton said, further introducing herself to Mac. "The difficulties are not new to me, nor the dangers. It is well you are confronting the problems early."

"This could mean survival for the ranch, Miss Patton, if the Commission sees things our way. That's where Mr. Berrigan might be in a position to help us. Wal, here we are."

The Tarynton's rustic ranch house and outbuildings were framed by a half-dozen pole corrals meandering among the pines and slopes of the mountain.

"This is a real treat to come up here," Kent said. "You have created an impressive spread back here in the timber."

"You can credit my wife for the flowers and garden."

Miss Patton mentioned the Sayles, a family she had known ten years earlier near the town of Sterling in Hot Spring District. "Samuel and Genevieve produced good crops and gardens in the short growing season of this northern climate. I understand it can be quite harsh. I have become accustomed to the deserts of New Mexico for most of the last decade."

Her brief smile at Kent threw him for a loop—he had assumed she had returned to California when she left him, never dreaming she would venture anywhere else, much less the arid Southwest. He started to inquire when she added, "Look at the views here," and Mac intervened.

"You see the snow-covered Pintlers off to the west and south. Of course you came in over the Continental Divide. We're a mile high and a dollar short, they say," Mac grinned.

Carrie came out to greet the visitors, extending her hand to Miss Patton with a warm welcome, and exchanged glances with Mac, indicating she was unsure of the relationship. Mac did not have a chance to tell her the little he knew.

"Come inside. Julianna has outdone herself for us today. Thank you, Julianna. This is Miss Patton. And where are you from?" Carrie asked, intrigued by this poised woman five or six years younger than herself.

"I have lived in Santa Fe for many years—since I knew Kent in this region some time ago. I manage our family-owned telegraph company there." Miss Patton's unaffected manner and fresh, tanned face with a few freckles made her immediately likeable.

Mac sat at the end of the long table with Carrie to his right and Miss Patton next to Kent on the left. A huge basket of dried flowers with sage, lavender and spruce decorated the other end of the table.

"And how were the candidates?" Carrie inquired. "Does it appear the Commission has a chance of becoming more balanced—in our favor?"

"Most of the speakers were supportive of the coalition of investors. I'm worried," Mac said. "We are clearly outnumbered. Kent appealed to their public conscience about the water. I don't know how that will go."

"My guess is that most citizens are hard pressed to provide for their families," Miss Patton said. "That was my experience growing up in California at the height of the gold rush. Civic responsibility is beyond their immediate needs. Single men move on after the boom and leave the problems to others. Yet mining communities continue with a life of their own. It is the same everywhere."

Mac gazed intently at this remarkable woman, nodding when her view was compatible with his own tendencies. Carrie observed his fascination with Miss Patton while he waited for her to continue. Without her bonnet, her hair fell from a bun in fashionable curls around her face.

Kent intervened, hoping Marion would not discourage the Taryntons' efforts to literally save their ranch, their way of life. Or that she would appear too forward. "Water adjudication is a long and torturous process that has already begun in parts of southwestern Montana, particularly in districts around the Territorial capital of Helena. However, water cleanup is a relatively new and untried concept. True, I do not know what will become of the controversy."

His soft drawl lent a cultured charm to the occasion, as did his stiff new clothing, though he had hung his coat and top hat on a peg by the door. Carrie's glance lingered on a watery silk vest that flattered his wide chest. She caught herself and said, "It is our privilege to have both of you here today. I'm wondering how you know each other."

"We met in Virginia City on separate business, and traveled together to Sterling. I—I lived with Kent for a time as his wife— in name only," Marion said, lifting a thin chain with two gold rings from her bodice. "I returned to my family in California, and we have not seen each other since. He was surprised to see me today." The same daring merriment returned to her features. "I read about the campaign in the newspapers and came uninvited. It has been quite a shock to Kent, I'm sure."

Her candid remarks visibly put the Taryntons' at ease, though Kent raised his brows at the forthright admission. "I didn't expect any of this earlier this morning," he conceded, knowing it was better they knew the truth. "I am pleased she made this visit." His words sounded both too casual and too formal even to his ears. The sentiment he felt was entirely lacking, evidence of his discomfort.

Both couples finished their meals, engrossed in their own worlds of relationships, knowing how difficult they could be. Struck by Miss Patton's statements suggesting that their trust and intimacy had apparently ended, no one at the table dared pursue the subject. Current tender, if not raw emotions swam beneath the surface for Mac and Carrie. Kent betrayed little other than his obvious astonishment that Miss Marion would turn up unannounced and alone in Big Butte. Julianna's tapioca pudding with raspberries, canned from last season's harvest, barely garnered a comment.

"Come, I will show you my garden," Carrie said to Marion, "though we are too high to raise many ordinary garden vegetables. We have friends down by the quarry who supply much of our fresh produce during the summer. The raspberries did come from our bushes."

After the men had their smoke on the front porch, their conversation addressed ranching and mining, realizing how the two would fundamentally fail to coexist. Words trailed off as the enormity of the issues became clear. Before long Pete brought the buggy to transport the visitors back to Big Butte.

The respectable formality between Kent Berrigan and Miss Marion Patton lasted until after supper when both found their rooms at the Continental Hotel and occupied only one. Marion left early the next morning for Santa Fe.

8

We come from no country. We were always here.

Yellow Wolf, Nez Perce Chief

The townspeople had not been surprised when Roxanna Finnegan rode out of Big Butte with her husband, the interpreter, to assist the Nez Perce in Idaho Territory.

"She kin ride, that one," said some.

"Will she ride the Connemara?" others asked over a pint.

"Sha'na, she out ran the Indians on the Irish horse and saved the Taryntons' herd."

"How did the Canuck trapper git so lucky to marry Roxanna Finnegan? Where were all the good Irish boys at the time?"

Oblivious to the chatter, Roxanna prepared for the extended journey. She traded her bonnet with wide silk ties for a floppy wool hat Duprés felted for her from sheep's wool, rolled her belongings in a buffalo hide as her husband had done, and bid her mother goodbye for the first time in her thirty-one years.

Jonathan Duprés' ambition to settle down having gone awry due to his mission to meet with the Nez Perce, he left behind Big Butte and his beloved Silver Bow Creek, headwaters of the Clark Fork River. He would follow the gently winding river to Hell Gate and over Lolo Pass into Idaho. The tribe was near the brink of war with the United States over their land, their birthplace known as far back as the Nez Perce' creation story.

Hostilities had worsened. Duprés had been summoned to interpret among the many factions. He was therefore riding the tribe's old buffalo hunt trail that spanned the border of Idaho and Montana Territories, and against his better judgment, he was taking his young wife along.

After the tender moment when he had invited her, and in unguarded times when he had boasted of her riding, *Que fait il?* what could he do? He could do no less. Roxanna expressed no surprise that she rode with her husband, both bundled in and among furs in the crisp spring air, her husband hoping in a superstitious Irish way that went against his gall, that she would not be a burden, or worse yet, bad luck.

For the first three days Roxanna sang Irish songs and questioned Jonathan interminably about the Indians, and what they would do if they were attacked. Beginning to regret having brought her with him, Duprés muttered under his breath, I can't get away from the wretched woman long enough to fart. He grumbled and shifted in his saddle so often that Roxanna inquired of his health.

"I'm accustomed to riding alone, my sweet. My bones are weary." He grimaced, and turned his back on her.

Roxanna continued to sing, head held high, ignoring his increasingly sour mood.

Does she never tire? Fifteen years younger, she kin ride all day and be no worse for wear, Duprés groused to himself. But at night when they rolled into one of the buffalo hides, he forgot about the Nez Perce 'wife' they would inevitably see, and he did not complain.

The riders left the Bitterroot Valley and ascended the mountains to Lolo Pass above the Lochsa River, where they chanced upon a military encampment awaiting orders to advance if war was declared against the Nez Perce. When intercepted, Duprés rightly claimed he was a trapper on his way to translate for the tribe. The presence of his wife was more difficult to explain. They stayed near the encampment for several days, where he gathered information that might be important for the tribe, and taught the troops a few words of Nez Perce language in the interest of furthering positive relations.

What he heard was unsettling and potentially dangerous for their passage into Native land over the next 200 miles along the Lochsa and Clearwater rivers. Two settlers had accused young Nez Perce of stealing their horses. In the altercation, a Native had been killed. The settlers later found their horses had not been stolen, but tribal retaliation for the death threatened to spill over. The settlers claimed land in Wallowa Valley in Oregon at any price, and who was to stop them? Duprés moved on, wary of the intentions of both sides.

Duprés had friendly relations with old Chief Joseph for many years when Duprés was a young fur trader in the Bitterroots. Joseph was one of the first eager converts to Christianity by Presbyterian missionaries when white men came West with their "good medicine," reading and writing. Wishing to emulate this powerful medicine in their tribes, the leaders embraced the teachings with all its contradictions and judgments as early as the 1830s and 1840s. The willing faithful learned to speak and write passable English, skills that later proved invaluable in negotiating treaties with agents, territorial governors, and the Great White Father in Washington, even as their faith unraveled under cruel punishments by the missionaries and lack of accountability by the United States Government.

Now the government had to decide whether to hinder spreading white settlements in Idaho and Oregon, or force the tribe to less suitable life on the reservation. The Treaty of 1863 sliced Nez Perce lands to a fifth of earlier agreements. Only the Treaty Nez Perce accepted this new treaty. Young Chief Joseph refused to accept the ruling based on a deathbed promise to his father, the elder Joseph, that he would protect their homeland; therefore, he and his followers became the Non-Treaty tribe.

Duprés was acutely aware of the significant opportunity he had to bring opposing factions together. To fail would invite

an undesirable outcome, if not war. Nez Perce guides met Duprés and Roxanna on the ridge trail and led them from the Lolo
Mountains down to the Nez Perce camp on camas meadows at
Weippe, high above the Clearwater River. They were warmly
received and given provisions and current news of difficulties
ahead that they might face. In turn, Duprés advised them of the
location of the military encampment, the number of men there,
and their mission.

The descent into Kamiah, headquarters of the Treaty Nez
Perce, soon initiated Roxanna in the perils of Idaho's steep ravines. She clung tightly to her horse on switchbacks curling a
mile down from the plateau to the confluence where tributaries
of the Clearwater merged. From their high vantage point, two
prominent mounds of grass-covered basalt near the rambling
Indian village appeared entirely out of place on the meadows
far below.

"The mounds are the heart and liver of Monster that Coyote
destroyed and cut up to create all the tribes of Indians," Duprés
said. "That is their story from ancient times. Coyote saved the
best to make the *Nimíi puu* and gave them this beautiful valley."

"I learn a great deal on my travels with ye," Roxanna whispered, in awe of the creation story and sight of the mounds.

The village of Kamiah presented an odd mix of nomadic life
squeezed into a semi-permanent settlement, a striking portrayal
of the transition to white man's ways. Tipis made of hides followed the contours of the river's edge like a spiky white garland,
and centuries-old trails formed roads among small frame houses
hidden in pines. Ragged garden plots and small pastures fenced
with sticks copied the whites' means of marking possession,
whereas formerly all had belonged to all.

Duprés, the long awaited interpreter, and his red-headed
wife accepted gifts of handmade horsehair bridles with exquisite
beaded tassels for the couple's horses. Roxanna sat quietly aside
while the men talked in the strange Shahaptian language, her
eyes wide and alert.

"I can't help remembering the Sioux warrior chasing me," she whispered to Duprés when she had a chance. Adding to her discomfort, she noticed the dark eyes of one of the women peeking at her from behind tipi flaps from time to time.

Duprés left her to her fears and waded into discussions with agents of Indian Affairs, British and Canadian traders, as well as settlers and white missionaries present when representatives of the tribes gathered. The process often took days to assemble. Translation was also lengthy. Many Nez Perce spoke English learned in schools established by Henry Spalding, a former missionary. Each sentence in English had to be translated into French for the traders, Shahaptian for the Nez Perce and Shoshonis and WallaWalla for the Cayuse and Bannocks. At the end of multiple translations of a single sentence, a chief made a statement in a loud announcement to the gathering. A response was translated in reverse order, one sentence at a time.

It soon became clear that Northwestern tribes, including Umatillas of Washington, found the immense migration along the Oregon Trail an unacceptable encroachment across tribal lands. The tribes had become surrounded, their lives throttled by settlers, gold rushers, and United States military sent to quell uprisings. Clashes led to violence perpetrated by all sides, often ending in thefts, murders and scalping. Indian and U.S. military courts of justice often found their counterparts guilty of murder, generally hanging those accused but not always guilty. In addition, the Bannocks with a modest population of 2,000 or so, had already been moved to Fort Hall reservation in Idaho, where they chafed under unequal or insufficient distribution of goods by the government.

"The agents do not agree with their own leaders. Who do we believe?" one chief asked, referring to the military, the Office of Indian Affairs, and the Governor of Idaho Territory.

A fiercely painted warrior beat upon the ground and said, "What does the ground say? Can we divide the Great Mother?"

A Bannock chief complained, "Our families are starving. The Great White Father did not send enough food for the winter as he promised."

Dozens of voices rose in agreement. "The promises were broken. The Treaty is broken. The Indian no longer believes in white man's medicine."

The Natives sat on the ground, many in buckskins, others in white man's trousers and hats from trading posts. Discussion lasted far into the night. Many representatives spoke eloquently, desiring only peace on their lands.

"I hear ye. And ye hear each other," Duprés said at last. "I cannot fulfill the promises. I can only tell ye what I know from the white man's side. Ye must make your needs clear to your chiefs and to the government of the United States."

Hours later Native representatives reassembled with their tribes, their chiefs debating in long speeches in their own languages. Night deepened under a lacy swath of silvery stars. The women remained apart from the debates, many wearing elk tooth necklaces over clothing also purchased at trading stores. Several women started a small fire with *Artemesia* bark tinder, the sharp smell of sage smoke soon biting Roxanna's nose. Early hours of morning found the encampment still awake and active, though communications were subdued. The women formed a circle, gesturing for Roxanna to join. A low keening emerged from the depths of their throats. Almost imperceptible at first, it gained volume and strength as the fire burned down. Sounds rough to her ears, multiplied, dipped and swelled with benefit of only a rawhide drum and rattle.

Roxanna did not remember falling asleep in the circle when Duprés awakened her at first light to continue on to Wallowa Valley. "We ride today to 'country of the winding waters' between the Grande Ronde and Snake rivers, to Chief Joseph's homeland."

They left Kamiah where the Clearwater ambled with the innocence of pure, sparkling snowmelt of the Bitterroots from the Lochsa feeding into its channel. Willows draped over river-banks, shadowing hollows for fish that for centuries sustained tribes year-round in the deep valley. Alders, cottonwoods, and chokecherry bushes hugged the valleys where wild currant bloomed prolifically in the underbrush.

Duprés and Roxanna followed the seventy-five-mile long Clearwater, distances being seductive in the repetitive landscape of chiseled ravines, where wild burros frequented almost perpendicular slopes. Along Lapwai Creek, the riders came upon an oasis revealing the village of Lapwai in a sheltered valley known by the Nez Perce as "place of the butterflies."

"Ah, fine food and a good bed," breathed Duprés at the sight of the Mission. Here reservation Indians established houses and rather extensive gardens including small crops of potatoes and corn.

"But see, buildings have been burned." Roxanna pointed to several chimneys standing amid blackened timbers. "And fences torn down."

"It looks peaceful enough now. We'll soon hear the stories."

In years past, angry bands of Natives had overrun Lapwai Mission in an attempt to drive out Presbyterian and Catholic missionaries who fought with each other and failed to uphold their promises to the Natives. But authorities at the Mission assured Duprés they maintained peace, and that a boarding school served the church and government's goal to convert the Indians to a non-nomadic way of life.

"More of the tribe speaks English than I expected," Duprés said of the thirty years of on and off missionary education offered in what became Idaho Territory. He thumbed through an eight-page primer in Shahaptian, a beginner's text in translating a heretofore oral language into written form by the long-time missionary, Henry Spaulding. The primer, titled *Numipuain Shapahitamanash Timash*, had been printed by the Clear Water Mission Press in 1839.

"I dunno how they done it. The Nez Perce didn't have an alphabet to begin with. They had no way to write or spell."

The startling contrasts they encountered, the so-called uncivilized Natives whose culture was now embodied in written form, and the serenity of Lapwai Valley with its starkly burned remnants, caught Roxanna's breath.

"I am aware, my husband, of a great sadness settling over this land. The farther we go it feels like the depths of currents from which one cannot escape. Strangely, I do not fear for myself or ye as much as for these lovely people." She added "I have spoken," as Eugenia did when she made intuitive pronouncements.

"Am I knowing like my mother, do you think?"

"I do not know, my sweet, but these lovely people find ye a lovely white woman."

Roxanna almost choked on the unexpected response. "Ye mean that, do ye?"

"Aye," Duprés said in the way of the Irish. "I mean it."

Roxanna's voice broke. "I want to shout, but more likely I'll cry," she whispered. "I will listen to my knowing. I will not doubt myself as I have done—I feel layers of doubt peeling away as I speak." She glowed, relishing a newly kindled serenity and basking in the recognition of her intuition that she had discovered on the trail of the Nez Perce.

9

Treatment should be one of prevention rather than cure.

Prudence B. Saur, M.D.

Mac couldn't remember having so many distractions before a spring cattle drive. He and Antonio had plotted a new route around Big Butte, and he had dealt with runoff from the mines seeping into water for his livestock as much as he could at this point. Now he was hard-pressed to get his men and outfit lined out to leave with the herd for the Elkhorns. But he and Carrie had had dinner guests, and Mac stood on the front porch of the *TN* ranch house, his eyes following the dust down the road. Pete drove Kent Berrigan and Miss Marion Patton back to town, their laughter drifting over the barren hillsides below the cone-shaped knob called Big Butte.

Dinner at the Tarynton ranch with a prospective Territorial Commissioner and his former common-law wife had been a novelty not soon dismissed by Mac or Carrie. Still caught up in the visit Mac paced between kitchen and living room, spattering coffee on the linseed-polished wood floor. "She didn't come here to listen to his speech."

"They obviously care for each other. I wonder how long she will stay in Big Butte." Carrie tried to be noncommittal, to avoid making too much of the visit. She had noticed Mac hanging on Miss Patton's every word, his manners rising to the occasion of dining with a refined couple. She had also seen Mac recoil when

Miss Patton said she had left Mr. Berrigan. She wondered if he feared she would leave him.

"A woman like her, wal, it could be a day or it could be a week, but she's got bigger fish to fry somewhere else. Santa Fe did she say?"

Carrie motioned for him to sit next to her at the kitchen table. They'd had too many misunderstandings this past year— over the stallion, her vision of a child, and Filly's place at the ranch. Carrie was not going with him on the upcoming cattle drive, and she did not want him to leave in this mood. Her hand gripped his tanned, heavily muscled arm, bare below rolled up sleeves of a cotton shirt. Mac could chase her fears and loneliness in an embrace with these arms, or he could throw a calf by the fire for branding; his strength was her center, a pillar against which she measured her own, indeed meted out strength to friends and patients. Mac's scowling face bore years of weathered lines, peeling sunburned skin exposed childhood boyish freckles. A short, raggedly trimmed beard betrayed he had taken scissors to it himself.

Carrie sought his often sleepless eyes, and held his with the power of her own, both conveying messages back and forth from years of intimacy. Carrie remained calm, even maternal, reflecting the way she felt but did not want to reveal to her husband. The totality of her life experience in healing taught her to hold the uncertain self of Mac Tarynton, the man she loved; to hold his fragile sense of who he was at moments like this, until he could again get a grip on how to be his own man. She felt her chest expand with compassion, with the need to meet him where he was and hold that moment, to be the shoulder his wavering soul chose to find. She would be there for a day, a week, for uncounted years, unlike Miss Marion Patton. It would be no chore as long as she had Mac.

When the stockmen finally moved cattle to the Elkhorns by a circuitous route south, then north around the growing settlement of Big Butte, their collective unhappy opinion was that the miners had already won. Below the slopes and foothills in Summit Valley, small frame homes hunkered among chicken yards in dirt and rock debris of earlier gold diggings that pockmarked both sides of Silver Bow Creek. Beyond the town, free homestead allotments of one hundred sixty acres eroded cattle trails from mountains to valleys, an accomplishment encouraged by the Federal government's Homestead Act. Like a giant bull snake swallowing a chicken egg whole, emigration was beginning to devour the open range and life of the ranchers.

Mac had not expressly forbidden Carrie from going on the cattle drive as usual. The couple had discussed the matter prior to the men leaving, but he had already lined up a cook recommended by the Kohrs' ranch. He suggested he best get on with the job and see her when he got back. Mac and all the ranch hands except Duggan would be away for several weeks. Torn by the break in their tradition of driving the cattle together, Carrie had avoided being home when the herd left the ranch. However, the change meant she could settle into a time of peace and quiet that generally did not exist around her husband—not with Mac's restless energy, short Irish temper, and the burdens of responsibility.

Instead, the gentleness of Kent Berrigan lingered with Carrie long after their dinner at the ranch. In his presence, the household atmosphere had absorbed an inner peace that was evident in the man; time slowed after the casual connection to the world outside Big Butte, and prompted even Mac to dally over coffee. Mr. Berrigan had appeared calm except for the sudden, disconcerting appearance of the woman who had lived with him as his wife years ago, yet his solid, unruffled maturity and innate good manners had set those around the table at ease, and he had shifted the conversation to a less personal subject.

However, Carrie agreed with Mac that Miss Patton's visit was certainly not to hear Kent's speech—it seemed strange their lives ran parallel to each other's, while their attachment apparently lingered, perhaps thrived and obviously strained to reunite, though it failed to do so until she returned.

Carrie's fantasies and conjectures also ran parallel to the spoken and unspoken romantic tale that had unfolded in front of Mac and herself, one that inspired Carrie, who now remained alone in the unusually quiet ranch house. Miss Patton's unconventional daring to speak openly of their common-law marriage was generally unheard of. Her travels across the continent and the fact she managed her father's telegraph company in Santa Fe marked Miss Patton as an extraordinary woman.

But it was the Southern gentleman who distracted Carrie from the deadening routines of washing dishes, mopping the kitchen floor, and peeling potatoes for supper. Privately she smiled at the ease with which Kent seemed to live: old wealth, refined manners and a relaxed assurance. How different it would be to live in that culture compared to the rigors of life in the West with Mac, the cattleman. Why Miss Patton would ever leave him, Carrie could not imagine.

In the empty spaces of the following days, a return to reality contributed to Carrie's sluggish feeling of discontent. In his insecurity, Mac had insinuated that she might leave him. The house soon became haunted with his presence, rather than the haven she had anticipated. Yet Carrie had to admit Kent Berrigan stayed in her mind, and teased her frayed emotions—the way his grey eyes had searched Miss Marion's as if reading pages of lost years, filling in the blanks with long-held fantasies of his own, writing a different outcome. She sensed that his low voice, wrapping words in a long drawl, came from a deep place born of suffering. His courtly demeanor crept into her consciousness at odd times, beckoning a respite from the current turmoil in her own relationship.

"Life would be much easier with a gentle soul," Carrie sighed, "but I would never leave Mac. I don't know why he doesn't seem to trust me."

Carrie intended to practice patience in all things as Natalya had taught her, but within a day or two her pulse pounded in her temples. Patience, acceptance, the long view, were not to be. Determined to avoid the medicine woman at all costs, Carrie fled to her room with an opposite plan.

She pulled her good gray dress with the broad white collar from the back of the wardrobe. The wool felt exquisite to the touch, yielding a warm, pleasant elegance to a style that flattered Carrie's spare frame. Tucks under her firm bodice were caught at the waist with a silver belt. The dress hung freely in soft folds to her ankles. Since she intended to take the buggy, she selected a pair of high-top leather shoes with a medium heel. Women's fashions must be designed by men to try women's wits, she groaned, bending over to thread the fine, round shoelaces through tiny eyelets on either side. Nor did she approve when women cinched themselves into tight corsets. As caregivers, she and Eugenia encouraged their patients to forego large bustles and heavy gowns that strained their posture. Carrie imagined how high-fashion crinolines would look like over her thin frame, or for that matter, how that would go over on the Tarynton ranch.

Ready to go, she dashed to the back door to call Duggan. With growing excitement, she tried on her widest brimmed hat which now appeared too plain for the occasion. She rummaged through her sewing basket for suitable decorations. "Color. I need color." She unfurled a roll of wide pink satin ribbon and tied a bow around the crown of the bonnet with the ribbon falling halfway down her back. On the way out the door she stuck a sprig of lavender in the crown for a jaunty air.

"Ye look mighty fine, Miz Tarynton," Duggan said, giving her a hand up to the buggy seat.

"We will take the back road to Walkerville and into Big Butte." Carrie meant to avoid passing Eugenia's in case she might want to join her. She knew that Eugenia had been too much in her cups, her favorite Irish coffee "tonics," since Roxanna had gone with her husband. It was not always pleasant to be with her, but Carrie promised herself she would bring her along next time, an evasiveness uncharacteristic of her, but today she had to go out alone.

"I am going shopping if you will be so kind as to transport me from place to place," Carrie said to Duggan. "We may be gone for quite awhile. You will have free time to visit your friends and get a bite to eat along the way."

The driver's old face crinkled into an almost toothless grin and his watery blue eyes danced with joy. "It'd be me pleasure, ma'am, only too happy to oblige. 'Tis a fine day to be about, aye." His small but tough body bent to reach the reins.

At Parker's Mercantile and Apothecary, Duggan tied the horse to a rail and bounded off to the nearest pub, clearly de-lighted with a day away from the bunkhouse, a lonely place now that the men were gone. Carrie glided into Parker's, her soft soles barely exerting a squeak from the worn wood floor.

"Mrs. Tarynton, how fine to see you!" Sherman Parker greet-ed her at the front counter as his father, H.S. Parker, looked twice at the sight of the stunning woman with sparkling eyes and a demur smile. Carrie usually came to town in Mac's old riding hat and her brown split skirt over scruffy riding boots. Other men in the store gave her appreciative glances that brought a blush to Carrie's weathered cheeks. She welcomed the attention with an uncertain smile.

"'Tis a wedding today or a christening, Mrs. Tarynton?" Mr. Parker asked, as usual angling for news that would be passed on to other customers.

"Only a day for shopping, Mr. Parker," she assured him, be-fore rumors ran rampant about escapades that would inevitably reach Mac's ears. Carrie had planned it as a day for finding a lost part of herself, to follow yearnings she had expressed to Natalya. The lively, self-confident Miss Marion Patton had succeeded in jolting her into soul-searching, Carrie mused. Her fingers ran over rolls of cotton, gingham and muslin yard goods suitable for summer skirts and blouses, and traced the rose patterns in old lace. Strangely, today the bolt of tightly woven white cotton for aprons appealed to her.

"White cotton will take the bluing," she said to the shop clerk. While the material was being measured and cut, Carrie hastened to the alcove to assess whether Mr. Parker's standard stock of herbal medicines and drugs had expanded to accommodate prescriptions by Big Butte's new physicians. This is a backdoor way to see what kind of medicine they're practicing, Carrie admitted, though I ought to be more up front about it.

To Mr. Parker she said, "There may be recent medical treatments I am not aware of that would benefit my patients. If I knew, I would refer my people to Dr. Gallagher or Dr. Owens."

The pharmacy carried bottles labeled with traditional antidotes, supplements, tonics, and tinctures: *Pulsatilla* to treat suppression of the menses, difficulty breathing or stomach problems; *Aconite* for fever; *Nux Vomica* as a laxative and treatment for ulcers. Commonly used minerals included *Mercurius* for soreness in the mouth, dysentery, and many other purposes; *Sulphur* as a remedy for ailments of the bowels and stomach, and *Chamomillia* for colds, fever and croup. Carrie noted the usual presence of foxglove, a stimulant for dropsy, and quinine for fevers and malaria. All these fit into cabinets that rose on two sides of the alcove, where a tall ladder led to the upper reaches beneath ornate tin plates on the ten-foot ceiling. Glass doors on the upper cabinets shielded the contents from view, but Carrie knew, as did Eugenia, that alcohol-based preparations were safely stored there behind lock and key. Protected as well were opiate derivatives, such as the laudanum Dr. Gallagher had given her, and homeopathic substances made of deadly nightshade plants.

Accessible on open shelves were dried herbs and minerals in dusty blue bottles of uniform size, all hand-labeled in a quaint italic script. Many of the labels had browned and curled, others were stained from being handled. The equally marred and dented tin countertop of one cabinet was worn from the pounding, grinding and chopping in the process of formulating prescriptions. At one end of the counter pestles and mortars ranged in sizes from very small to fist-sized stones. Carrie's practiced eye quickly ran over the inventory on the shelves, avoiding a nearby earthenware crock punctured with air holes for leeches.

From *Angelica* and *Arnica* to Zinc, most of the labels were familiar to her. It was not typically within her scope of practice to recommend medicines, but on occasion, she discussed certain options with her patients.

"I see you have stocked additional supplies for Dr. Gallagher and Dr. Owens," Carrie observed to the trained and obliging pharmacist. An open, polished mahogany box displayed surgical tools, including a short bone saw. Carrie shuddered, vividly recalling Mac's exposed flesh, her fear he would lose his leg from the gunshot wound, and her collapse.

"In accordance with demand," she dimly heard Mr. Parker say beyond the overpowering images inspired by the bone saw. Hauling her attention back to the present, she focused on inventorying the pharmacy.

Natalya and Carrie occasionally ordered specific items such as ginseng. Other customers often requested botanicals for unusual remedies native to their country of origin. These special orders came from larger cities and required weeks or months in advance to arrive in the remote town of Big Butte. Less essential, but on hand by popular demand were trademark Holloway's Pills and Ointment, and Pipestone Springs mineral waters that *"stand unrivaled in their curative powers,"* according to the label, though they had no known connection to the local Pipestone geothermal feature.

Today Carrie asked Mr. Parker for preparations of St. John's wort and valerian root to alleviate dark moods that frequently swept over her these days—a melancholy she had uncomfortably fought to displace with recurring images of Kent Berrigan, she chastised herself. She also bought essences of oil of wintergreen and helichrysum for the still aching wound in Mac's thigh. Her reputation as a healer precluded the need to mention for whom she chose the medications, nor did Mr. Parker prevail upon her to do so.

Back on the street, face to the bright sun, Carrie breathed in fresh air and enjoyed a sense of well-being that had escaped her for a long time. Duggan hopped back on the buggy seat in anticipation of their next stop. "I must go to the Chinese apothecary," Carrie told him.

Duggan failed to pick up the reins.

"To the Chinese shops on Mercury Street," Carrie affirmed her request. He well knew the way, having passed through the congested streets of the Chinese section on many occasions, but he paled and fidgeted.

"Mr. Mac—," he stalled.

Carrie knew Mac had berated him for driving her on their previous episode.

"I dunno, Miz Tarynton. Ye don't want to go near them dens with the smoke 'n sticks 'n all. Mr. Mac, he wouldn't like it a'tall."

Carrie didn't know how much was superstition and how much fear of his boss, but Duggan clearly struggled to avoid complying this time. "Go," she ordered. "You can stay in the buggy."

Giving up, he picked up the reins and clucked loudly to the horse. Once underway, he brazenly dodged pedestrians and teams of horses headed uptown on Big Butte's nearly vertical streets. As they neared the Chinese stores, Carrie's attention shifted from Duggan to the twisted handkerchief in her hands. She remembered why she was going there—to ask for help— help for her marriage, a thought her mind hardly entertained; only her practice of healing gave her strength to carry on.

A flood of images of Kent Berrigan and Marion Patton's "marriage" prodded her—especially the way he obviously opened his heart to her again, or more likely, never closed it over the long years they had been apart. His grey eyes had softened, his wide firm mouth hinting an indulging smile at this woman who exposed the most intimate passages of their lives to people she had just met. She managed him, and probably most men and women around her with her outspoken manner, including me, Carrie conceded.

She recalled the long *TN* ranch dining table had seemed crowded with the commanding presence of the individuals who were seated for dinner that day. Mac's intensity had contrasted with Kent's reserved manner, though Kent could not contain his pride in the petite woman with the pert, oval face whose striking dress instantly made Big Butte look like the common camp set among cow paths some claimed it to be.

Miss Marion, so much more a woman in a man's world of industry; Kent's voice, rich and low, both born of cultures Carrie barely knew. She only knew that his soft palm had lingered a moment in hers when he expressed his profound pleasure in meeting her.

It is the way he excites me—Carrie bit her lips before the thoughts became words spilling over into Duggan's ears. Oh, I could never, ever let Mac know I even thought these terrible things. Oh, it is much too painful. It would end our marriage. And I would never, ever tell Eugenia and Roxanna—they talk too much. Breathing hard, Carrie put the stream of fantasies and fears aside as if she had once again hidden beneath a table and they no longer existed.

Duggan had his hands full driving the horse that startled and flared his nostrils at the unaccustomed smell of cooking oil, and spooked at steam billowing from several laundries. Carrie took a moment to survey the few blocks that had risen from the hillsides as fast or faster than the rest of Big Butte. She had passed through Mercury and Galena streets many times, but today she found the community vibrant and thriving with triple the number of residents as before the silver boom. She recognized a few Chinese families from German Gulch who evidently moved here. Up the street, families occupied rooms above narrow shops that fronted Mercury Street. Down the street, small homes each displayed a red scroll over the doorway, a symbol of protection, Carrie had learned from conversations with Chinese healers, yet it all felt unfamiliar, as if she had stepped into a foreign land.

Duggan's jitters are getting to me, or I'm a case of nerves, she muttered. What do I really know about the Chinese, and what assumptions am I, like Duggan, making that are an injustice to them and to me? They belong to Companies designating the Province they came from in China. The People of the Tang, I've heard, often consider themselves superior, likely inviting disrespect in Big Butte—that and their willingness to rework mine dumps, discarded ore that continued to yield rich minerals.

To Carrie, the street looked like a mural painted with handwritten, artful characters of Chinese signs and arrangements of produce and goods in the markets, a portrait of individuals of all ages. Bright orange candied ginger next to white coconut candy looked delicious. Children darted around corners calling one another. Mothers hurried to prepare their wares, offering good buys with the English they had absorbed. Grandfathers with white braided queues walked with stick canes or sat on small stools among outdoor markets. Portly men seemed to be in charge of small dining nooks, noodle parlors, and trading shops. An absence of young men suggested they were employed elsewhere during the day. Carrie found the shop she was looking for, and asked Duggan to halt the buggy long enough for her to step out. He then pulled a considerable distance down the street to wait.

She approached the Natural Herb Shop with a sense of humility amid the proprietors' bows and warm greetings that felt almost reverent in nature. To Carrie they were the healers, having inherited thousands of years of Chinese medical knowledge and practices, the art and artifacts of which were displayed around her in plain packages bearing circular black and white symbols. Healing is in their everyday practices and diet, in their upbringing, in their consciousness, the *yin* and *yang* that balances Mind and Body, the *Qi* life energy of which we are given only so much, and the discipline of *Qigong*. I can feel it, she breathed, and sensed the beliefs and practices were life-affirming and inviting.

"I am so glad I came," she managed to say to the first English speaking shopkeeper she met, offering her hand which was taken between two gentle palms. The women's energy mixed, magnifying one another.

"You are Horse Doctor."

The statement was matter of fact. The woman's plain elderly face softened and sharp brown eyes crinkled. "We know you. You save the horse!"

Carrie chuckled, feeling more comfortable.

"And you help women and children."

"Now I need help." Carrie's inner world crashed into this receptive reality. I did come for help. I feel welcome. I wonder that my feet led my head and heart here, but I shouldn't impose upon this elderly woman burdened with cares herself. No, I shouldn't stay—what if I expose my inner self, a white woman crying with the Chinese? Oh, my—I might fall asleep like I did at Natalya's— Duggan would be so frightened. But I am here, leaning toward staying—the wave of push-pulls left Carrie's head making dizzying leaps into and out of facing the present.

"May I help you?" ventured the woman with a wide smile that showed several teeth missing behind incisors on both sides. "Why did you come?"

"Please, ma'am, please help me with medicines for my husband, no, for myself—for a broken heart," she ended, astounded at the words she had uttered. Carrie blinked at her own request. Who has a broken heart? Words were flying through her mind as if she did not own her brain. My heart opened—but to the wrong person—Kent Berrigan of the gentle smile and soothing voice. Frantically, her awareness shifted back to the quiet woman who stood as if suspended in time in front of her, a woman she sensed that she had always known. Carrie's footsteps had led her here for healing, even overcoming Duggan's pleas.

"I - I need help—"

Understanding at once, the woman said, "I am Li An. Come." She reached for Carrie's slack hand. "You not find healing in herbs and medicines."

She led Carrie back through the store, where long strands of mossy, ocean-scented seaweed hanging from the ceiling brushed Carrie's tall figure. Bins held grotesquely shaped, preserved sea creatures, bits of dried turtles and snakes. Crates of sliced, dried mushrooms looked dark and uninviting, though Carrie knew the shitake were effective for treating many ailments.

They passed a small dim room containing Asian apothecary preparations. At a glance, it was similar to Parker's in that the bottles were colored, these dark brown, to prevent deterioration of the contents. The pestles, mortars, and small glassware were all familiar, also the ginseng that Mr. Parker had to obtain from San Francisco or New York, but the Chinese probably imported it directly from China. Woven floor mats served to direct the steps of the women to a low door leading into a courtyard. The overflow of the store's goods was stacked outside under a lean-to. A small garden plot started plants unknown to Carrie. Boxes of porcelain pottery and dishes were interspersed with gum boots, work shoes, and slip-on sandals.

Li An seated Carrie, now moving like a sleepwalker, on a low outcropping of boulders, secluded behind a high fence. She left briefly, returning with four other women who placed themselves on rocks or small folding stools in a circle around Carrie.

Eyes cast downward, they sat in their plain, loose-fitting dresses, dusty calloused feet exposed in sandals woven of reeds. Without introductions or preamble the women's breathing soon became as one, and Carrie's vision cleared to see herself among them, a scene not unlike that in Idaho where Roxanna sat with the Nez Perce women. A rooster crowed in a back alley and hens cackled, flapping their wings to avoid his pursuit. Carrie relaxed with a grateful sense of being where she should be, permitting tears to settle like dew on her cheeks.

Li An took Carrie's hand as well as that of the woman next to her. That woman did likewise until Carrie felt a current circling their joined hands. Minutes passed, Carrie did not know how long, while the energy evolved into a vertical mass of whirling pastel colors that obscured their view of each other and the sky. Each woman was caught in the *Qi* and chose to remain there in a deeply resonant state. Carrie rocked with the movement, caught in a sense of timelessness, aware she had let herself be drawn into a betrayal of Mac in her thoughts, but she did not feel she must hide under a table as she had as a child. Sounds subsided as only the earthy smell of the courtyard anchored her to her former life.

Woman to woman, they know, Carrie realized at once—their power and energy born of suffering for families, husbands and children felt overwhelming. She envisioned desperate Chinese families driven to brave the perilous Pacific Ocean, then cross the prairies and mountains, exposed to elements and dangers where many suffered sickness and loss. Images occurred to her of women in childbirth, some with complications or death of the newborn. In Big Butte many became widows of miners who had perished in mine accidents. Nearly overcome with the intensity of the revelations, Carrie opened to the grief and wailing of women around the world— their loss of mates, children, or security through hunger and war, many having nowhere to turn. Perhaps relying only on other women in their lives—mothers, daughters, grandmothers, or women they did not know, such as these she had sought today.

A pervasive sense of peace settled upon the obscure courtyard, a postage stamp of earth on the slope of a mountain pockmarked from a frenzied search for silver that lured ambitious and often unscrupulous individuals from afar. And here are the Chinese, so separate in language and custom, yet a part of the very fabric of our lives, a part of me, Carrie noted, one of many passing thoughts that coursed her mind.

With a deep sigh, she again found solid ground beneath her feet, feet she imagined bare with dusty toes peeking from under her dress like those of the other women. An awareness settled upon her like gentle rain, the recognition that not a woman among them did not also have a broken heart.

And I came here crying inside over the tenderness I had witnessed of a man to a woman. Woe is me for betraying Mac and chasing someone else's dreams. Worst of all, I could not heal myself, or did not want to release my attraction to Kent and Marion's story, failing to honor my own. Their energy knocked me out of my self-indulgences, thank goodness, saved me from inviting bitter wrongs into my life, Carrie acknowledged, feeling hidden pools of despair and sense of isolation draining from deep within.

Their gifts! These women from China teach me to heal. And to find the power of the unbroken circle right here in Big Butte!

Carrie walked lightly back to the buggy, not daring to question the healing, not wanting to impose doubts, desiring only to take with her the release from dark forces she had experienced.

10

Contentment is the finest medicine in the world; it not only frequently prevents disease, but, if disease is present, it assists in curing it. Prudence B. Saur, M.D.

The experience with the energy healers was so profound that Carrie stayed home for the next week to work in her garden, meditating on the rich traditions and wisdom of the Chinese women. Barefoot, or in open sandals, she dug in the dirt, kneeling to plant rows and rows of hardy vegetables that would grow on the mountain. The wizened handyman came around regularly to check on her.

"Are ye all right, Missus?" he asked a number of times a day. Carrie laughed heartily for the first time in months. When she had come out of the Chinese Apothecary shop she had found Duggan stone sober and blanched beneath his whiskers, eyes round and terrified, fearing she had been devoured by the jaws of the occult. She knew if ever an Irishman needed a stiff drink it was then. On the way home he said Mac had told him to "take care of Carrie."

"'Tis a right honor, ma'am, and I be pleased, but ye scared the bejesus out of me. I fear the wrath of the devil if somethin' bad happens to ye."

"Thank you for your concern. I am very well," she replied then and again today when he hovered nearby. She suspected he was lonely with the crew away on the cattle drive. By week's end when she prevailed upon him to drive her into town, apprehension curtailed Duggan's usual banter, a sign of his uncertainty about what this willful woman would do while her husband was away.

This time Carrie went to town in her everyday riding skirt topped by a blousy gingham shirtwaist and Mac's floppy old hat. She first visited Mrs. Sawyer while Duggan leaned back on the buggy seat for a short nap. She took the stairs two steps at a time, almost laughing with the feeling of being more alive than she could remember.

"Have ye fallin' in love?" Theresa teased her for the bloom on her cheeks.

"Yes, with my husband again!"

Mrs. Sawyer had no idea what she referred to.

"I know women have their ups and downs with the monthly troubles, and I've found that healers have their ups and downs, too," Carrie admitted. "Isn't there something in Scriptures about doubt?"

"Doubt, certainly! The Bible would be a slim volume without admonitions about doubt." She read passages about Thomas and Saul, and added, "I've had my own doubts about ignoring the swelling in my legs. I went to see Dr. Gallagher about the tumors. He checked me thoroughly, and suggested I might need surgery. Removal of the tumors may or may not cure the edema, he said, and since I have had them this long, he is fairly sure they will not worsen. What do you think, Mrs. Tarynton?"

"You were wise to see him. Modern medicine is often lacking in the Territories. He brings both knowledge and experience to Big Butte. I shall be ever grateful he was able to save Mac's leg. I would like to meet Miss Owens, too. Perhaps I will stop by there today."

Carrie took Mrs. Sawyer's two hands, inviting their mutual good will and energies to merge and swell until Carrie saw the violet and blue colors she carried from the circle of Chinese women. Smiling, she left knowing that both she and Theresa had entered a mystical realm, perhaps the larger universe of women yearning for peace and healing for all.

Uptown, a rough frame building housed Big Butte's doctor offices and the upstairs residence of Adelaide Owens. Her clinic occupied the right half of the downstairs while Dr. Gallaher's was on the left. Carrie glanced back to see Duggan hurrying into a pub up the street before she entered Miss Owen's lobby, where a string of small bells jingled when she opened the door. Straight-backed chairs lined the front hallway, and subdued wallpaper with small pink flowers decorated the walls above traditional varnished wainscoting.

Miss Owens stepped out of her office when she heard the bells. She was known as "Miss" instead of "Dr.," indicating her marital status in contrast to the recognition given to Dr. Gallagher, a male physician. She squinted to view the exceptionally tall, spare women with a plain but striking appearance standing comfortably before her. Miss Owens, presented a substantial figure with a wide, unsmiling face. Thick hair pulled severely back in a knot at her neck showed some gray, though Carrie guessed they were close in age. The doctor did not invite Carrie into her office.

"You are the mountain woman, I assume."

"Mrs. Tarynton to most," Carrie said. "I am pleased to make your acquaintance. You have been an asset to the community. We are fortunate to have you and Dr. Gallagher. He treated my husband day and night for a week when Mac was wounded last winter."

Miss Owens frowned and folded her arms across her breasts. There seemed little to be said after Carrie spoke. Adelaide turned to leave, a signal to the unscheduled visitor, or perhaps her answer to Carrie's forthright initiation of conversation as if they were equals. Carrie redoubled her efforts.

"If you would care to come to the ranch for dinner tomorrow or the next day, I would like to hear of recent discoveries and practices in medicine, especially those concerning infections. I encounter many ailments specific to women, which would benefit from professional treatment from a woman doctor. I am sure we both also encounter home situations needing improvement in sanitation by furthering the education of women." Carrie's round brown eyes softened, a contrast to her mannish riding habit, and Mac's old hat, both smudged with garden dirt.

"My practice is quite overloaded at present," Miss Owens said, declining the invitation, but she abruptly turned back towards Carrie. "I don't suppose you are familiar with the recently proven germ theory of diseases that any practicing physician would know."

"I understand some illnesses are contagious and that contaminated water can carry disease."

"Big Butte will be subject to epidemics of cholera, typhus, and typhoid fever in time, despite the fact drinking water is piped in. Of course I would not expect you to know about the causes or treatment of amoebic dysentery."

"I do know that belladonna may be administered for bloody flux, but preferred treatment is mercury, especially if fever is present. The diet should be flour porridge well boiled, rice water, arrowroot, or sago."

"Where did you say you received your training?"

"From women," Carrie said. "Where did you get yours?"

"I completed studies in obstetrics and gynecology, and served a residency at the prestigious Garden of the Holy Cross Medical School in Philadelphia."

"Your training came from men—who have never given birth even once since the beginning of time. God chose women to be in charge of their own procreation. It has been unduly appropriated by men." Carrie did not see how a woman physician in obstetrics would or could argue with her basic premise.

"Why, you blasphemous, heretical witch," Miss Owens fairly screeched, shaking her finger in shame at Carrie.

"You say so, not my patients," Carrie said evenly, without so much as backing up a step.

"Shaman, pagan. I don't know—I never—"

Carrie breathed deeply for both of them. I'll have another patient on my hands if this escalates, she thought, noticing purple splotches creeping above Miss Owen's neckline. The doctor glared at her before ducking into her office.

"Pleased to have met you," Carrie called after her, smiling though she did not feel that good about her own temper.

Quickly back on the street, Carrie calculated pluses and minuses of the visit, determining that for a first unannounced contact it could not have been worse. She looked for her driver. He was not in sight, but she had glimpsed where he had headed. Poking her head in the pub door, Carrie heard Duggan in full-throated brogue regaling his companions with an Irish faerie story. Carrie lingered near a light post and waited for him to come out, or for someone she could send in to get him. The gist of the tale entertained her as well as the rapt audience.

"The pub it was in County Cork by the edge of a great field that belonged to the faeries, ye know, and it was said if'n ye crossed the field, ye would be swept up in the most awfullist storm and whirled about and finished off in no time. And all the men they go round the field and go to the pub and drink to the faeries, the good and the bad. But one night, the blackest of nights and the foulest of weather, Jerry O'Houghlihan was late and he wanted to git to the pub in the worst way, and he says to himself, 'Jerry, 'tis only a scare that ye be taken by the faeries in the field, and because I be so late gittin' to the pub, it be best if'n I cross the field.' And he did. Only he could not find his way across to the pub. The light of the pub shone in the dark and he would go to it, but it would move. He ran as fast as he could in that direction, but the light, it moved again. And this went on most of the night, and Jerry O'Houghlihan became tired and afeered. He decided to make a last run fer it, his legs going as fast as they could toward the light."

Duggan paused for breath and a nip, dangling the story before his rapt listeners. The pub was known for Sean O'Farrells, one ounce of whiskey in a pint of beer, a combination that contributed to a teller's volubility.

"Wal, Jerry, he did run, and he was caught up jist as they said he would be, and he was whirled around at a turrible pace with the field falling below his feet and the wind crying bad things into his ears, and he fell to the ground in a heap." Duggan's voice trailed off. "And that is where they found Jerry O'Houghlihan in the morning. Daid in the field."

The believers in the pub savored the grisly end and the non-believers guffawed. They all lifted their pints. After an appropriate interval, Carrie motioned to Duggan, who was quite drunk on the brew and his stature as a storyteller. Carrie paced his loopy walk up the street, wondering if she should let him drive. She hoped he wouldn't fall off the driver's seat under the buggy—the horse would run away and the large, iron-rimmed wheels would run over him. The gruesome consequences reminded her of the adventure of Jerry O'Houghlihan. Smiling, she absently pondered what she would she tell Mac!

"Duggan, I know you have had enough of Big Butte, but I want to drop by a Serbian meeting hall that members have told me about. This seems like a good opportunity to visit it."

Caught between his promise to Mac and his obligation to the Missus, Duggan's manner became one of insubordination—he refused the request, and he was drunk enough to think it would work.

"I dunno, Mrs. Tarynton, they'se awful strange and ye might not want to go there."

As if the stories and the superstitions of the Irish were not strange, Carrie murmured, taking the reins of the restless horse while Duggan hauled himself into the back seat. Mac had notions from his Irish lineage that were not that different from those of Duggan, Eugenia and Roxanna—confounding, to say the least, humorous at times, and endearing if one was in the mood. Checking her impulses, she turned to Duggan.

"What do you know about the Serbians? Please tell me," she urged, unwilling to abandon her day in town on account of Mac's or Duggan's certain disapproval.

"They speak Greek in the holy communion. That's how diff'ernt. Who knows what it is they're sayin." He shuddered, though the missionaries' Latin masses were surely up there with the unintelligible.

"You must encounter Serbs and other Slavics when you mingle uptown. Some of them must speak a little English."

"If'n they sit on the barstool next to me, they talk to their kind and me with mine. They is serious people and work hard in the mines. I don't say nothing bad about 'em. They don't have no troubles with nobody."

"I am acquainted with several Serbian families with children whom I have treated for coughs, fevers, scrapes and minor burns. I would like to better understand them," Carrie assured him.

The buggy drew near a frame building used as a church. "Thank you, Duggan. This is a Christian church, so you need not worry. I will be out soon." She tried not to laugh at her driver, who looked as if he was doomed for the rest of his natural life.

"Holy Trinity, Archangel Saint Michael, and all the saints, what will this woman do next?" Duggan muttered, crossing himself. "If an idle mind is the devil's workshop, she be in deep trouble, aye." His lips moved in prayer. "And me, too."

Carrie pulled a scarf over her head and followed two parishioners into the hall. The Slavic community was relatively small compared to the Chinese and Irish, but the congregation aspired to build a church with a traditional onion dome in Big Butte. Gold-gilded icons brightened the interior of the present hall. Statuary was notably absent from the church, though a Greek cross was displayed on a wide altar. Apparently preparations for the evening service were underway. The women draped a floor-length white linen hemmed with heritage lace over the altar. The psalm books were written in the curious letters of the Cyrillic alphabet, and the services conducted in Greek, as Duggan had said.

In the absence of pews, Carrie stood for a few minutes of mediation in the somber surroundings. She was no stranger to the Catholic Church, held in a similar primitive meeting hall, and attended by many of the people she treated. In both churches, women wore hats or headscarves. Carrie slipped out feeling as though she had expanded her world, not in the sense of the cross-country travels of Mr. and former Mrs. Berrigan, but by circulating among the diverse assembly of immigrants in Big Butte, Montana Territory.

"How many more days 'til your husband comes home?" Duggan pleaded. Carrie's light hearted laughter carried above the rattle and jangle of the horse and buggy.

When Carrie and Duggan wheeled past the corrals at the Tarynton ranch, the foal voiced her plaintive, come-see-me whinny. Carrie had hardly given a thought to the first foal of the sire, Love—Royal Magic O'Shannon, or King, as they now referred to the stallion. Except for occasional intuitive communication, she had closed the door on their painful separation when she had given the stud to Jackson and Nettie Colter for a wedding gift. Now his offspring, the lovely little filly astounded Carrie with her beauty, her head held high on an elegant, arched neck, her tiny ears as alert as they could be. Large curious eyes surrounded by black lashes begged Carrie to come to the fence. The foal had the distinct wide head of the Connemara, but the bushy black mane and tail of her mother, a solid black mare that had come in from the wilds to join the wrangler's bunch. Early mottled baby fuzz was giving way to Love's gray dapples.

She is intelligent and seems to be sound, Carrie noted, knowing full well that Love's mind had been deranged when he suffered poisoning or an unknown ailment, possibly contracted during his importation from Ireland. Yet he had sired a foal that appeared to be perfectly normal, possibly exceptional. If his progeny turn out like this one, that will mean a great deal in terms of stud fees for the Colters.

"I am happy for you, my little filly, and more than happy for your sire," Carrie said. The filly playfully dodged back to her mother's protection then ventured forth again, her timid steps drawn by curiosity.

"The boys have been giving you treats, you little beggar," Carrie whispered, wishing she had a nibble to give her. Carrie took advantage of the contact to run her hands over the long neck and the gentle curve of the withers, caressing her fine legs and tummy. Antonio must be working with the babe for it to be so gentle, the babe that has no name.

For the next few days, Carrie pondered names when she spent time in the corral getting acquainted with the smart little female whose soft dark eyes captivated her. "I don't remember what Mac said to do with the foal," Carrie mused, "but I find it comforting to be with her. Now I am afraid to bring up the subject with him."

Mac came off the cattle drive ruddy and well, having gained a few pounds from the cook's culinary skills with a Dutch oven over a campfire. Tired horses had been let in the lower pasture by the crew that was equally ready to be home, back to their bunks and Julianna's beef pot pie with cornbread.

"Last night on the trail we had an all-out feast. Harvey stirred up a double chocolate cake with pie cherry filling and baked that thing right over the coals." Mac smacked his lips as if he could taste it all over again.

"And he boiled up a pan of brown sugar with a little water till it started to caramel, then poured in the dregs from the coffee pot. It was the best caramel-coffee cake I ever had."

"So you 'spect me to make double chocolate cake with coffee topping, do you?" Julianna said over her shoulder as she scraped the pans after supper. Julianna could be counted on to go the extra mile for the family when she had time away from her own brood.

"Sure, anytime! I saw him make it. We were having a little drink around the fire." He glanced at Carrie. "The men deserved it. We were kept busy. Those longhorns can hike and not always in the right direction. Besides, those critters don't much like the domestic stock and try to run them out of the herd."

He and Carrie sat at the end of the long kitchen table; her hand resting on his arm reflected her concerns about their re-union after the cattle drive. He had left an unsettled situation between them following the visit by Kent Berrigan and Marion Patton. Not knowing his current mindset, she feared what might continue to be a troubled relationship. Maybe I'm too guarded and a bit defensive, she conceded, privately treasuring the two weeks of being 'single' for the first time in years—I found that I could amuse myself.

After Julianna finished washing the dishes and went home for the night, Mac kissed Carrie's nose and said, "I missed you, Carrie."

"I missed you, too. More than you know." Her long brown hair, loosened from its pins, fell over her shoulders when she leaned her head against him.

"You'll go with me after this. It isn't good when we're apart."

He had not had time to hear of her adventures, Carrie thought with some satisfaction. Instead of moving to his favorite chair, Mac hung out at the table. "I was afraid you might leave me," he confided in a low voice.

"Mac, you feared I might?" Carrie asked, alarmed. "You were worried while you trailed the stock? Worried about that?" She reached for his hand and found her own was trembling, shifting her mood from the pleasant interlude exploring her interests to that of her very real, underlying fears for their marriage.

"Yeah, a cattle drive gives a fella a lot of lonely days and nights to think about things. I thought about that woman leaving her husband, even though they weren't exactly married."

Carrie started, chin up and eyes wide. Kent and Marion's visit had indeed created a rift between them, and Mac had carried the residue with him for the past two weeks. Surely the guests' story needled Mac, as it brought up uncomfortable feelings for me, Carrie thought, but it's not like Mac to distrust me. Heavens! That never crossed my mind. Floored, she could only reply, "Oh, that was them, their lives years ago. It has nothing to do with us, Mac."

Mac continued as if he hadn't heard her, not recognizing how incredulous the notion of separating was to his wife. "I knew he'd been broken up when I saw them together in town. Berrigan looked like a sick calf compared to how steady he was when I met him at his place on that trip to Virginia City. He seemed settled then, at peace."

He paused with a long exhale. "Men and women just can't walk out on each other. It isn't right."

"Mac, who left you in your life that you would fear being abandoned? I don't understand this feeling of yours. Did I do something?"

"It's not you, Carrie. 'Tis myself. I –I am sorry I talked mean to you that day your friends were here—about there being a child, that I yelled like I didn't care about you," he whispered, half turning toward her. His tortured face bore regrets much deeper than the current misunderstandings, lines drawn from furrowed brow to wide pale lips. Carrie moved to see his eyes, bloodshot and sad.

"Mac, you haven't been sleeping. Who left you in your life that would bother you so much?" she insisted, her voice low, urgent. "There must be something in the past that would make you feel this way."

He shook his head wearily, unable to answer to that question. Carrie slid onto his lap and wrapped him in her arms.

After that evening, Carrie found Mac hung around the ranch house, winterizing drafty cracks with chinking on the outside and bits of rags stuffed between door and window frames inside. His voice became gentle with Carrie as if he rediscovered her, as if he had been shaken to depths even he did not realize, only knowing he needed her now as never before. He bought her a stylish coat he had seen in the window of the weaver's shop downtown.

A subdued atmosphere hung over the usual activities on the ranch while summer transitioned into fall. If days were peaceful, turmoil often claimed the nights. Mac rarely slept a full night, and once he fell into an exhausted slumber, he had worse nightmares than before.

"I guess it's my turn," he said one night, referring to Carrie's bout of depression and bad dreams the past winter.

"What is it that haunts you, Mac?" Carrie asked, lighting a candle so they could talk in bed.

"Mostly I'm falling and screaming—then I wake up." Mac lay with his hands behind his head, staring at the ceiling. "Do you ever get any sleep with me, Carrie?"

She blew out the candle, not wanting to reply.

At breakfast Julianna asked if they were sick. "You are both looking poorly sometimes. I'm wondering if it's something in the air. Let me know if I can do anything."

Jonathan and Roxanna Duprés ferried their horses across the formidable Snake River at its convergence with the equally swollen, rambunctious Clearwater. The Snake formed on the Continental Divide some distance south in Yellowstone Park, and twisted its way north before angling west and south. Its perseverance through eons of time had cut a veritable Hells Canyon into enduring basaltic rock below the trading port of Lewiston, former campsite of explorers Meriwether Lewis and William Clark. Weathering and erosion by the river had worn mile-deep valleys with narrow, sheltered banks habitable to humans and their livestock.

Above sharp incisions in the earth's surface, grassy plateaus lay exposed to sun and wind that proved merciless at times, even with the usually benign temperatures between the Cascades and Rockies. Pacific storms dropped precipitation on the west side of the Cascades, but bestowed a warm climate and shorter winters to the east. Blooms came early to the abundant serviceberry and yellow currant bushes. Indian paintbrush in its flaming orange and red finery appeared in semi-shady nooks by streams later in summer, along with crimson wild geranium that natives used to treat stomach ulcers, all bits of information that Roxanna absorbed on her maiden journey into Indian country. Topping the slope on Camas Prairie north of the Snake River in central Idaho, Duprés and Roxanna found vast numbers of horses grazing the plateau above the rivers, apparently without herdsmen for none were in sight. Some horses were branded, most were not.

"The spotted ponies are *Palouses*, named after the Palouse River." Duprés waved, indicating the Appaloosas, distinguished in the herd of Indian ponies by their height and soft white or brown blankets with spots over their hindquarters.

"Oh, my husband," Roxanna grasped her throat. "Sioux rode horses like these when they tried to steal Mac's herd, and the warrior almost caught me."

Duprés ignored Roxanna's fear couched in a boast to avoid a recurrence of her hysterics.

"The *Nimíi puu* know horse breeding. 'Tis like yer Connemara. They select the best to get one like that."

"Why do they need thousands of horses?"

"For their buffalo hunts on the Missoura."

"Surely there aren't so many hunters—or warriors?" Roxanna's anxiety rose unbidden from the memory of her recent escape from the horse thief.

"Maybe a thousand Nez Perce on this side of the Snake and fewer Bannocks. This was all Shoshoni country at one time, and the tribes were river people called Salmon Eaters. Later they traded goods for horses from Crows on the other side 'a the mountains. The tribes became separate after they started using horses, and spread out north and south."

"Look! Two young boys ride like the wind over the prairie!" Roxanna clapped a hand over her mouth, again re-experiencing her own mad flight from men in wolf hides.

Miniature dust storms swirled from the hooves of the spotted horses, the boys bent low over the horses' necks, their bare legs clamped securely over the bare backs of the steeds. Involved in a race or a high-spirited run on the limitless plateau, the boys apparently did not see the two white riders.

Roxanna shuddered. "Rivers and tribes—I don't know where I am or why I'm here. I am afraid, my husband. I should not have come among the Indians."

Duprés pulled in his horse to see his white-faced wife hanging back as if to turn around. "*Oui*, my sweet, we are deep into Indian country. The Bannocks who live here kin ride and shoot. They about wiped out the Shoshoni and Nez Perce until those tribes traded for guns, too."

"Oh, don't tell me such stories! I am afraid enough already. How can I possibly proceed?"

"'Tis true. Traders and missionaries brought guns and traded for these good Indian horses. Now ever'body has guns and goes to war."

"Are there bears?"

Jonathan laughed. "Of course, my dear, there are bears and wolves and cougars, too. The Nez Perce hunt the great white grizzly. But 'tis the settlers and gold seekers who are the nasty varmints, according to our friends, the Nez Perce."

With her fears expressed and her husband joking—or was he? Roxanna sighed and urged her horse forward. Having found no recourse but to continue, Roxanna followed her trapper husband, the interpreter, into southeastern Oregon rather than turn back toward home.

Gradually she expressed delight in the passage. Wildflowers bloomed earlier in spring, shooting stars and yellow bells double the size of those in the Rockies. They came upon a meadow of cornflower-blue wild camas that promised life-sustaining roots in late summer, a principal food source of the Nez Perce. The camas, the startling blue Idaho skies, and the impenetrable blue of Wallowa Lake melded in prismatic spring light into one endless tapestry.

"Truly, the land is an inheritance the Natives sorely need," Roxanna said of her wide-eyed tour. Wallowa Lake occupied a gentle valley of meandering foothills clothed in rich grass to summits that bent over onto plateaus. Here Chief Joseph and his band had lived in relative peace until conflicts began with white men.

In Wallowa, Duprés again heard of the horse-stealing episode in which horses had not, in fact, been stolen, yet two natives had been killed in retaliation for the supposed theft. Duprés had heard both sides of the story, evidence of the grave misunderstandings between settlers, who wanted to create small farms, and Natives who required open land for their partially nomadic lifestyle. Duprés met with principals from both groups, those of Agent John Monteith of Indian Affairs, and those of General Oliver O. T. Howard. Their positions were generally supportive of Nez Perce claims. Duprés was pleased with the conciliatory tone until he met with a party of settlers who refused to back off.

"It's them or us." One burly settler wielded his shovel like a weapon. "You can tell 'em we're stayin'," an oath generally carried out in the formation of citizen militias.

Under pressure from distant Washington D.C., Monteith set a deadline of April 1st for the Non-Treaty tribe to to remove themselves to the Lapwai reservation. Unfortunately, spring presented almost insurmountable obstacles for travel with herds, families, their tipis and belongings, and certainly provided far too little time for the extended tribe to make arrangements.

"The Canyon of the Snake is running too high to cross," the chiefs said. "Our families and horses will be lost."

This logic was met with stern enforcement on orders from Washington. If they had not moved by the deadline, the cavalry would force them across the river and onto the reservation. In desperation, chiefs ordered young men to round up stock dispersed over thousands of acres of deep ravines and river bottoms where they had foraged for the winter. Days slid away faster than the roundup could be completed. Hundreds of horses and cows of the hastily gathered herd were lost to settlers, who considered it payback for Indians grazing on land they now claimed. Clearly, collision was in the offing. Young Chief Joseph gathered his people. Duprés could do no more— he had to get his wife safely out of harm's way.

"What if we get trapped here?" she asked.

"Why, we would live like the Indians."

"Ugh, roots and chokecherries crushed with the seeds in them? I'm not squeamish, but I couldn't butcher a deer like the squaws do."

"Or eat a raw liver?" Duprés could not resist teasing her. But Roxanna remained unnaturally quiet over the next few miles of endless plateaus.

"Ye saw the beautiful camas. We would make flour from the roots and ye could make bread, *n'est pas*? And pick serviceberries and buffalo berries. Ye could make kouse from cowish plant roots."

"I –I –don't know how."

"Remember, my sweet, ye married a trapper. Ye want to eat, we gather food. Ye want a warm blanket, ye trade furs at the post, ye see how life goes on." His voice softened as if tutoring the young.

"I see how the land nourished the people. I feel the nice climate. 'Tis truly the best land." Roxanna fingered an Indian hemp bag Duprés had bought for her, its tightly woven pattern a simple diagonal with plant-dyed red and blue fibers. It held a few small treasures the women had given her, and a hand-woven cornhusk wallet filled with precious pine nuts the tribe had gathered on their annual trip to the Yellowstone. Prairie hens and sage grouse scurried out of the riders' path, waterfowl shrieked and chattered in every body of water, and elk in their tan and brown seasonal coats grazed nearby.

"The *Nimíi puu* did indeed live from the land," she admitted.

Over the two hundred mile reverse trip from Wallowa to well within Montana Territory, Duprés carried and relayed messages between the Nez Perce and emissaries of the U.S. military, as well as between settlers and Indians. However, President Ulysses S. Grant in Washington, steadfastly refused to redress Nez Perce grievances concerning settlers' claims to Nez Perce land. Chief Joseph had promised his dying father years before that he would protect and preserve their homeland in the Wallowa Valley in Oregon Territory, but the spring military offensive forced him to forsake his vow and move to the reservation on the Clearwater. Other chiefs in his tribe refused. Before leaving, Duprés had admitted to all parties he could do nothing to alter the opposing forces within the Nez Perces, or between the Non-Treaty tribe and the United States government. Subsequently, Joseph's tribe found they must flee ahead of the military to safety across the mountains.

"*Ma cherie,*" the trapper said one night after their Nez Perce escort turned back at Lolo Pass in the Bitterroots, "ye be good ambassador to the tribe. My friends, the *Nimíi puu*, accept white woman in their circle. I am proud to take ye." Jonathan's long, agile fingers found Roxanna's in the dark and gave them a squeeze.

'What? Proud of me?' Roxanna returned the squeeze and asked," What did ye say?"

"I be proud of ye, my sweet!" he chuckled.

"Did I hear ye aright?" Roxanna asked, now fully awake. "Ye be 'proud' of me?" She rolled over in the buffalo robe and caressed his grizzled beard and stringy hair.

The burdens of long days of riding and cold nights of camping appeared to be lighter for Roxanna if not for her husband, who worried about impending battles that did not bode well for their friends.

"I feel rewarded ten thousand times over for coming," Roxanna marveled, expressing joy in her husband's acknowledgement of her. "'Tis rare, 'tis rare, indeed in my life," she added, repeating the praise, exercising a new feeling of confidence in herself that Duprés could not fail to notice. "'Tis like standing on firm ground for the first time."

Eventually, her thoughts turned to her mother, whom she had left behind months ago to follow her husband into the wilds. "Mum will be worried, but her 'knowing,' her foresight will keep her informed that I am safe," Roxanna assured herself over the miles.

Duprés and Roxanna cut off from the Bitterroot Valley towards the Clark Fork, then traveled northeast until they came through Deer Lodge Valley on their way to Big Butte. Their fare, dried salmon strips from the Columbia River and plentiful camas root hardtack, at first seemed fit for kings, but days into the return trip Roxanna would have given an arm and a leg for double chocolate cake if she had known of Mac's feast.

11

The important object of my work is to show that this universal suffering is not the result of excessive mental development, but a lack of physical culture, a want of balance between excitement and rest. Prudence B. Saur, M.D.

On the outskirts of Big Butte, early spring grass, once tender and green, was beaten into a well-trodden path to the highest point above the quarry. Eugenia padded up in her slippers to gaze longingly toward the west hoping to glimpse specks of two riders moving across the still barren foothills. Her watery, red-rimmed eyes squinted to see if her daughter and son-in-law were coming until a flurry of sleet drove her back to the cabin. Each time, disappointment echoed in the lines of strain on her face, the slump of her shoulders, and the rapid depletion of a well-fortified tonic that she acquired regularly from Parker's Apothecary.

"Even Carrie has forsaken me in my time of need," Eugenia complained, as months wore on and the loneliness deepened like night around her. She pulled her rocking chair close to the fire so she would not have to get up to heat the coffee. Dishes with dried food particles formed a mound in and around the dishpan; an unmade bed poured its duvet coverlet onto the floor, along with a heap of dirty dresses and stockings. Even the chamber pot was unattended, now reeking and full to the lopsided lid.

The stench of the pot and rotting food hit Roxanna when she burst into the cabin, the interior dark behind closed curtains in broad daylight. In the dimness, she saw her mother asleep with her mouth open, her gray head leaning back on the rocker. Roxanna stumbled in, babbling, feeling her mother's pulse, her temperature. Startled, Eugenia righted herself and twice rubbed her eyes to determine if she were awake or dreaming that Roxanna had come home.

"Mum, we have safely arrived home at last! Are ye surprised? Or did ye know the very day?" Roxanna edged past the furniture left awry in the small room. "Mum, tell me, be ye well?" Leaning over Eugenia, Roxanna gasped at the alcohol fumes on her mother's breath. "Mum?"

Roxanna fell to her knees beside the rocker, shaking Eugenia's hands to dispel effects of the tonics. "Mum! Are you awake? See, Jonathan is here. Please say something. Ye give me such a fright." Roxanna tried to maintain the calm she had learned on the Nez Perce trail.

Eugenia struggled to her feet, sending the rocker careening to the side. Her lips moved automatically in Hail Marys while Roxanna and her husband glanced at each other, saying without words that their months away had been easier for them among the Indians than it had been at home for Eugenia.

"Start the fire to make fresh coffee, Jonathan, please." Roxanna opened the door to let in a stiff blast of fresh air, and fetched her mother's shoes to replace the worn slippers.

"I did not know ye be coming today," Eugenia said. "I have lost my knowing."

"Mum, it cannot be—surely ye've had a bad spell, but ye have your gifts—ye will find them again. I shall tell Carrie."

"I didn't see Carrie," Eugenia said. "Some people came to the ranch to visit, and I have not seen her since."

"Oh, I have a lot of catching up to do," Roxanna moaned, and began washing dishes and putting the cabin in order. I am so happy to be home, but what I have to relate will come later. Surely she will not believe her ears when I tell the tale!

Aloud she said, "Jonathan, there is no room for our buffalo hides and packs inside. Please hang them over the fence." Outside she muttered to him, "Mother is in no condition to hear about Indians today. It is her tonic."

"Her tonic?"

"Spirits, 50–70 proof, I think. Mr. Parker must be mixing it stronger for her. No wonder she feels as though she has lost her foresight. I wonder how long this has been going on."

"Ye talk to Mr. Parker, not me," Jonathan said in a split second of grim assessment. "Yer old woman would beat me to death with a broom if she found out I talked with Parker."

A few days later, Carrie hastened over to see Eugenia. Two saddle horses grazing beyond the quarry meant that Roxanna and her husband were back. Roxanna threw open the cabin door and ran to greet Carrie.

"Lord Almighty, I am so happy to see ye. Ye see I am all of one piece, even after the wilds and the Indians! But mother had a more difficult time. Ye must come in."

Carrie stepped inside to find Eugenia stirring a cook pot on the stove, the teakettle whistling so loudly she was unaware of a visitor. Eugenia's dress was clean and starched, her feet shod in flat-heeled walking shoes. A neat bun topped by a lacy cap restored her matronly looks and dignity.

"Oh, come, come, we shall have tea!" Eugenia rose to the occasion in her best form.

"I am so sorry I have not been more attentive while Roxanna was away. It is my fault entirely. Please forgive me." Carrie noticed at once the deep hollows under Eugenia's eyes and the pallor of her skin. Seeing that her own exploits had led to neglect of her friend, Carrie's lips twitched with regret.

"Never mind, my family has come home, thanks be to God," Eugenia said. "Now I am making Jonathan's favorite tapioca pudding with nutmeg and cinnamon. Sit down please, Carrie.

The biscuits are in the oven." The industry obviously helped Eugenia overcome her melancholy. Roxanna motioned Carrie aside and informed her that Eugenia felt she could no longer go about healing.

"She says she sees and hears only dreams with terribly violent scenes that awaken her in a sweat. Garbled sounds like cries in the wind over the quarry disturb her waking moments. I do not know what to do or say, Carrie. She is frightened. Can you help her?"

Eugenia's best china cups rattled in their saucers when she poured comfrey tea with trembling hands and passed thick cream. She served ginger biscuits hot from the oven, and sat down at the table.

"Tell Roxanna about the people who visited," she said wearily. "It has all been too much for me. I have missed ye, Carrie. I'm afraid me fears took hold of me."

"Dear Eugenia, how could this come about? Your fears sound awfully similar to my own when I doubt my feelings. I have felt lost lately, too, but I am terribly sorry I did not first come to you. This was not a good time for me to become distant from you—or from myself," Carrie apologized, "but I do know that much turbulence is afoot, and you may be intuiting more than you realize."

"What is it?" Roxanna asked. "How can it be turbulent here when we are so safe? Our homeland is not threatened like that of the Nez Perce. We had to get out to save our lives. Jonathan did not say so, but I knew it, truly. A great battle is coming with much weeping—surely our problems are minor in comparison."

"Minor in comparison perhaps, but serious nevertheless. Difficulties remain about the acid in streams that we depend upon for the livestock. Mac is worried. And I worry about him. Sometimes he is quite irrational."

The three women smiled and nodded in agreement that men can be unreasonable, but Eugenia unexpectedly added, "And distrustful?"

"Strangely, at times it seems he does not trust me, though we have had complete trust in each other in the past." Carrie said no more, never hinting even to her friends of the trial brought on by Kent Berrigan and Marion Patton that left her and Mac floundering, nearly spinning their marriage out of control.

───────────

The chairs in Dr. Isaac Gallagher's lobby usually filled shortly after his office opened at 8 a.m. For that reason, Mrs. Baumbier, wife of the Montana Territorial Bank president, insisted upon an appointment at 7 a.m., before "the hordes arrive and everyone knows everyone else's business." Doctor Gallagher humored her, and opened his office early once a month for her regular checkup.

She arrived five minutes early for her appointment, puffing from the short walk. "I do believe I inhale too much smut from wood fires and dust from the mines, my good doctor," she declared, trying to catch her breath. Her husband routinely parked the buggy a discreet distance from the doctor's office to further protect his wife's privacy.

"Come in and be seated," Dr. Gallagher insisted, offering her his chair, its classical tapestry upholstery secured by shiny brass tacks over horsehair stuffing.

Dr. Gallagher knew Mrs. Baumbier's self-diagnoses were generally accurate to a fault, omitting only that she was seriously overweight, an oversight that contributed to her current ailments. However, he had never thoroughly examined her, by her choice through a series of maneuvers and postponements, therefore, his treatments were rather more palliative than allopathic in nature. Granted, Mrs. Baumbier's healthcare may have been compromised, but certainly his purse was not. Her husband paid in full immediately after services were rendered.

"What is it today, Mrs. Baumbier?" Dr. Gallagher seated himself on a high wooden stool where he felt more authoritative around this outspoken woman, whose body was encased inside a black, full-skirted silk gown that had managed to have more tucks and pleats than a dress shop. Mrs. Baumbier attempted to remove her wool shawl without displacing a wide-brimmed straw hat framed in creamy-hued feathers.

Dr. Gallagher leapt from his stool to assist her with the shawl, enabling her to fan herself.

"I suffer terribly, Doctor. Even my husband agrees. He is now sleeping in the spare bedroom at the end of the hall." Her voice trailed away.

"The symptoms, please, Mrs. Baumbier."

"Yes, the symptoms. Mostly my stomach with the most awful cramping that keeps me awake and thrashing about all night." She flourished a bottle of Hostetter's Stomach Bitters from Mr. Parker's, an over-the-counter remedy claiming to treat heartburn, nausea, stomach, intestinal and bilous symptoms.

"I find the bitters very disappointing. No wonder my husband has moved out of the bed chamber."

Dr. Gallagher sidestepped potential collusion or debate about the quack medicine. "If you don't mind, Mrs. Baumbier, may I inquire whether you are wearing those dreadful corsets so many fashionable women insist upon wearing?"

"Stays only, my good doctor. Thank you for inquiring. The stays keep me in place so the dress will go on as it should. Goodness, no. I gave up corsets when I had my first child, a good idea, wouldn't you say?"

"A very good, life-saving idea which many women would benefit from emulating. Now if I could examine you, we may determine your general state of—"

"Of course, of course. Can you take the blood pressure over my sleeve? It is a chore to roll it up or remove it." Mrs. Baumbier readily extended her arm fully clothed in puff sleeves that ended in tight cuffs around her wrists. She just as cooperatively opened her mouth and stuck out her tongue for the depressor, though the thing tasted like "a dry stick of firewood," she always said.

Dr. Gallagher gently pushed back her thick gray hair to check her ears, though he had to dodge the hat brim that remained balanced atop her head.

"If I may," he said, delicately lifting her skirt about six inches to check her ankles. She wore men's brown leather oxfords, and her flesh had swollen over the tops of the shoes despite the restraint of thick cotton stockings.

"Quite sensible shoes," he said quickly before she could launch into an explanation. The reason she wore low-heeled shoes was evident; the woman's ankles, and he suspected, her legs were grossly swollen and no doubt painful. "I wonder if you sit too much, Mrs. Baumbier, with the fluids settling in your legs and feet?"

"I suppose I do. It is inevitable. The house consists of two floors, and we live primarily on the ground floor due to my delicate condition. The hills of Big Butte forbid one from any kind of decent walking out of doors. I do believe my life has taken on a sedentary nature, especially since we acquired two young German girls for household help. They need the work, you know, and I dearly love to help them learn English."

"You have a positive outlook, Madam, all the better for your health. I should like to further examine you regarding the stomach problems."

She hesitated, fiddling with her hat that had tipped askew. Dr. Gallagher waited. He had allowed a full hour for this patient.

"And what would that be, Doctor? I am afraid I cannot disrobe here in the office, and anyway, the preparation you gave me last month was extremely helpful. I would like a refill." Mrs. Baumbier squirmed and clamped her mouth shut.

Dr. Gallagher was not inexperienced in the practice of medicine with women. He scribbled a prescription while Mrs. Baumbier slowly rose and replaced her shawl. He kept the diagnosis of flatulent colic to himself but ordered preparations of *Pulsatilla, Nux Vomica, Colocynth* and *Sulphur* with appropriate intervals of oral administration noted. In addition, he handed her a list of easily digested foods recommended by a women's physician he had met in Philadelphia, Mrs. Prudence Saur, M.D.

"Mutton, venison, hare, sweet bread, young pigeons, partridge, pheasants, grouse, beef, tea, mutton broth, milk, turbot, haddock, flounders, sole, fresh fish generally, roasted oysters, stale bread, rice, tapioca, sago, arrowroot, asparagus, French beans, cauliflower, baked apples, oranges, grapes, strawberries, peaches, toast water, black tea, sherry, claret."

He failed to note the list included ocean fish and shellfish, and that Montana Territory was as remote from the ocean as an inland island. To his patient, Dr. Gallagher said, "I advise you to see Miss Owens for a complete physical as soon as possible. Routine examinations are highly desirable for a woman of your age. In the meantime, elevate your legs several times a day and limit salt intake. And I would see about the cooking, if I were you. The German girls may be overly dependent upon cabbages, onions and sausages that would provoke your condition."

The gentlewoman hastened out with the prescription, the list tucked carefully in her bodice. Dr. Gallagher peeped out the window to see her climb into the buggy. Mr. Baumbier eased the bulky dress in a somewhat orderly fashion in beside her.

Across the hall from Dr. Gallagher, Miss Adelaide Owens opened her office promptly at 8:30 every morning, a blessed relief from early rounds, which she and Dr. Gallagher would have been required to make if Big Butte had a hospital. Many of the "hordes" Mrs. Baumbier referred to were Miss Owen's patients, a wide ethnic range of miners' wives, often wearing long stained aprons, and accompanied by their gingham-outfitted older daughters. The Chinese generally doctored their own people. Occasionally, a few of the dismal collection of women from the brothels came for treatment. Lacking an assistant, Miss Owens admitted all patients herself, and allowed only short appointments so everyone could see her that day. She treated many child-bearing women who were grateful that a physician was available in the mining town. Miss Owens, M.D. winced when they invariably referred to her as a midwife.

Nettie Colter was pleased to come in regularly since she did not have relatives in the West to turn to during her 'confinement,' a misleading term in her case since she remained highly active. Miss Owens was equally pleased for a different reason. Mr. Jackson Colter, Nettie's husband, was one of the few who paid for each visit with cash.

"Chickens, what am I to do with another chicken?" she asked Isaac Gallagher one day. "They pay me with a chicken, dead or alive, or a sack of potatoes—once a box of warm, freshly made tortillas that looked delicious, but my office smelled like a market for three days."

"Times will no doubt improve and working people will have better lives and wages," Dr. Gallagher often consoled her. They were both aware that wealthy clients of the upper north side preferred a male physician with a medical degree to the questionable care of a woman with the same medical credentials. For some it was a common belief that women were of lesser intelligence, and that those women who undertook "excessive mental development" were surely devoid of other human qualities. Even ladies in the red light district usually preferred treatment in his office, and distanced themselves from the woman who practiced "mid-wifery." At times, Miss Owens drilled Dr. Gallagher about his beliefs when she caught him mid-sentence unconsciously falling into similar patterns of thinking.

On the other hand, Miss Owens found her popularity with the working class about on par with that of Mrs. Tarynton, the mountain woman, as far as she could tell. Adelaide's patients included women of all ages and backgrounds, as well as men who could not pay the higher fees of a general practitioner. She also made frequent home visits as midwife at any time of day or night, thereby closing her office for a day or two. These visits often prompted more of her complaints to Dr. Gallagher since he was the closest person to whom Adelaide could turn.

"I ran into that Irish woman, Mrs. Finnegan, three times today when we crossed paths caring for patients. I don't know what she does, but they like her. She used to be midwife to half the children in Big Butte."

"She and Mrs. Tarynton apparently have established practices, an enviable accomplishment, I would say," Dr. Gallagher admitted.

"Mrs. Finnegan seems to have good luck counseling, teaching basic health care and sanitation in her homely way. I will say the families and their homes have improved since she's been out and about."

"Then I cannot see the matter with it. Many of these women come from different ethnic cultures and often have only a minimal education."

Still, Adelaide felt slighted, as though the services she provided were no better than those of the Mountain Woman and the itinerant woman near the quarry. *Why, oh why, do I study and work in the shadow of men like Gallagher who believe a hysterical womb makes women insane?*

Aloud she noted, "There is something to be said for common sense in medicine, and it is lacking when women with serious complaints continue to tightly lace their corsets until their waists are twenty inches, give or take a few inches. It is a crime and many lose their babies meeting this abominable expectation of fashion."

"Adelaide, my dear, if you can change their minds, then please do so. In my experience, I have found women tend to disregard physicians' admonitions. They are often unwilling to deviate from the latest fashions." Dr. Gallagher laid down his spectacles and took up a microscope to examine a specimen he had recently scraped from a newsboy's throat.

Gallagher's remark "Adelaide, my dear," struck her finely tuned sensitivities as evidence of his patronizing. Stomping back across the hall, she remarked over her shoulder, "I wonder that I remain here in this desolate, uncouth community, where I am subjected to going about with untrained women who deal in superstition and witchcraft?"

Out of sorts, even reduced to a few tears almost unknown to the hardened professional, Adelaide stared out the window over the green and white checkered half-curtains that provided privacy from the street, rethinking her unfortunate decision to practice medicine in the West—why did I think attitudes would be any different in the Territories than they were in Philadelphia? Men are men, and they act out of a misbegotten sense of entitlement. Women can be even more biting with their condensation born of ignorance.

Chewing her lip in frustration, she locked up and left early for her apartment upstairs. The small dog that was her only real companion needed walking, but Adelaide begged off.

"It's too hard to walk up and down these hills and I'm too tired," she told Poochie, excuses that Poochie did not accept. He ran back and forth to the door until Adelaide put on her coat and went out.

Seasonal hot winds and bracing cold signaled the arrival of autumn days. Mac Tarynton grumbled about the "do-little" Territorial Commission that barely met over the summer, let alone made any worthy decisions regarding stream contamination from the mines in Big Butte. The election had come and gone with Kent Berrigan from Madison County winning the seat, which in the end went uncontested.

"Damned if I don't have to start over to get anybody to listen to ranchers' problems this year. I'll soon have cows back from the Elkhorns that we'll have to keep off creeks closest to the mines. Meanwhile headframes are sprouting like mushrooms. Besides the Alice, Travona, and Lexington, there are a bunch of others. The mine owners aren't considering the effects on the rest of us. Mining dumps are growing every which way, and I don't see an end to it."

The tailings, piles of undesirable ore, were indeed next to every claim and had been since the early days of placer mining when prospectors shoveled aside debris from their gold pans and sluice boxes. In addition, the overburden of soil and rocks removed to explore veins beneath the surface likewise formed discarded heaps next to the mines. Hardrock miners, who drilled straight into hillsides or tunneled far beneath the surface, also deposited tailings over the edge adjacent to the mines, unless it was used to build roads or level inconveniently located gulches. Weather and erosion oxidized the ore, oozing red and yellow run-off along streets, back alleys, and railways built to transport ore between the mines, stamp mills and smelters.

Since workers' homes crowded near the mines and ethnic villages sprang up block after block above, below, and next to every thriving industry, in this case, the open pit Alice, residents near and far shared the escaping dust and water laden with toxic minerals. Rain and snowmelt later flushed cascades of soil and mineral-laden silt from "the hill," as Big Butte's seemingly inexhaustible north slope was called, into Silver Bow Creek and down into Deer Lodge Valley. Effects of the leeching steadily progressed to lower flats and creeks, eventually flowing toward the Clark Fork River.

Mac's disgust and restlessness with the stalemate carried over in the household. Julianna had been let go for a few months during slack time. Gardens were harvested and preserves tucked away. Carrie cooked dinner for Mac, and she would cook for the crew on the cattle drive this fall when they brought stock home from the Elkhorns. Mac made preparations with pent-up energy and bottled resentments of which Carrie took the brunt—the visit of five months ago stayed with Mac as well as with his wife.

"That woman, Miss Marion Patton, she spoke her mind like the women campaigning for women's vote. I wouldn't put it past her to stump for the vote. Sounds like she runs the family company telegraph office in Santa Fe." Mac jabbed his fork in the air for emphasis.

To Mac, Miss Patton appeared comfortable in her own right, an emancipated female, few of whom he had ever encountered and, on the surface, he would not have liked. She could stand up to her man, he speculated privately, forgetting that Carrie occasionally did the same to him. The disturbing residue of the fateful coming together of the two couples was that Marion had 'left her husband' to whom she admitted being only nominally joined. The words "I left" repeated themselves insidiously in his mind day after day at unexpected times, triggered by the most benign events or comments.

"That woman could talk business with men, but she left her husband. It gets so a man can't depend upon a damn thing anymore." He shoved aside his plate, his dinner barely touched.

"Mac, if you are suspecting I am not trustworthy, I assure you that is not true." Carrie let the words fall as if she was throwing out the dishwater, an announcement he could take or leave. "Furthermore, if you think I am failing in my duty to bear all things, you can tell me about it." He had not mentioned whether Duggan had told him about her adventures in town.

"I'm not sure what I started, getting Berrigan to run for the Commission. It seems his coming here stirred up more than it solved, and their meetings haven't amounted to a hill of beans."

"He needs a chance to change things on the Commission. And if you are imagining I would be like Miss Patton and leave you, Mac, I tell you honestly that notion never entered my mind. You are taking their visit too seriously."

Mac didn't admit the charge, nor did he deny it.

"I found the couple interesting, even charming, which may further annoy you, but their lives have nothing to do with ours." Carrie's direct gaze met his until he changed the subject.

"I need a word with Kent about the crik water smelling like sulphur and running muddy as hell. See if he has any interest in standing up for the cowmen, or the guts to do it. Nobody pays a man to complain about the mines. More than one's been run out of here already for complaining. Despite the risk of alienating myself and other ranchers, I need to put in my two-bits worth ahead of the Territorial Commissioner's meeting, or I'll stew about it on the whole cattle drive. They are meeting in town, and I don't see anyone else coming forward to do it."

The Commissioners met for briefings in a number of different locations in the Territory. Newly elected Kent Berrigan would be seated among the officials when they visited Big Butte. Accordingly, Mac sent word to the County Commissioners in Virginia City and Deer Lodge urging them to attend the meeting. Support would be crucial in calling attention to the issue of water quality that would affect citizens in the wider Big Butte area, ranchers in particular.

Mac and two of his crew gathered with the crowd to meet the stagecoach from Virginia City near a building established for the new Masonic Lodge. Streets filled with dog-tired miners coming off shifts, townspeople in suits and snappy fedoras, and newsboys with the hyperactivity of a field of grasshoppers. Women inched around freight stacked on the sidewalks of what looked like a makeshift plaza. One-horse buggies and two-horse hacks jostled among larger carriages, weaving past incoming freight wagons pulled by teams of mules. Merchants, shopkeepers, and Big Butte's two physicians joined the crowd, fine hats defining their presence.

Mac had cleaned up for the day, slicked with a fresh shave, starched pinstripe shirt tucked into new pants, and a Stetson in place of his worn riding hat. Antonio dressed smartly in Southwest style, a string tie over a black shirt. The apparel set off his moustache and shoulder length-straight black hair. Pete came in his best dusty bunkhouse attire, not too concerned about wrinkles and down-at-the-heels boots.

Finally, a team dripping with sweat and heads reared high, angled the Concord coach toward the walkway to unload the passengers squeezed inside. Other Commissioners would come separately. The gentlemen disembarked, straightened their coats and gathered their small bags from the leather-covered rear compartment. Mac and Antonio quickly strode over to speak with Kent before dignitaries swept him inside for a meeting that would or would not have significant consequences for the rancher.

As Mac approached, a rifle blast at close range slammed into Kent's chest, toppling him instantly. The blast hung in the air, echoing off the distant East Ridge, followed by silence. Moments passed, stillness prevailed. No one seemed capable of moving. Mac's arms flailed the air in an attempt to fly to Berrigan's side, but his body felt leaden. His boots stuttered on the walk, an unsteady dance on a left leg that had suffered its own bullet. A curse caught on his breath at the same time he lurched, his hands reaching and grasping to catch Kent and failed. Kent's frame rose precipitously in the air, twisted, and spun in slow motion in a grotesque pose before it collapsed, the momentum rolling both men off the boardwalk into the street. For the longest time Mac sensed himself airborne—heaving forward, his Stetson spiraling across dusty footprints that now scattered like little animals in every direction, his instinctual need to run and hide countered by an effort to throw himself over Kent.

Landing hard on the rough gravel, Mac lay beside the prone figure. He saw Kent's face contorted in shock, a bizarre contrast with his formal wear. A gush of air escaped Kent's lungs. Mac felt the newly elected Commissioner's body go slack next to him— the man who had visited the *TN* ranch so recently lay in repose, his features softening from the grimace into a more recognizable natural look.

Lifting himself on one elbow, Mac became aware of bedlam surrounding the assassination, while he sheltered Kent Berrigan as best he could.

"Pete, get Doc," barked Mac as his wranglers hovered over him.

The excitable stagecoach team bolted and rammed a team of mules next to it, causing the Concord coach to collide with a heavy freight wagon. A piercing scrape of their iron-rimmed wheels rent the thin air of Summit Valley like the rifle shot. A sustained grinding of the wheels further inflamed the animals. Drivers hauled on their reins, their "hold 'em in" warnings to others averting a stampede. Painted women on the outskirts of the crowd screamed and ducked into the nearest buildings, their flamboyant clothing markedly noticeable next to the plain garb of fleeing miners' wives and store clerks. Men in the street flung themselves behind freighters, many with firearms in hand. The ranchers' saddle horses reared, whinnied and plunged away with riders cursing and shouting at each other.

Mac waited—an eerie tension enveloped the scene, slowed time—held him motionless, waiting for more shots that did not come. He pulled himself upright. Bright blood smeared his pinstripe shirt.

"Antonio, find the thug."

Mac dragged Kent by the armpits from under the chaos of wagons and teams to the side of the Lodge, and jammed his wadded up shirt into the gushing hole in Kent's chest, already knowing it was too late.

Dr. Isaac Gallagher and the coroner took charge of the assassinated figure on Park Street. Sheriff Ford arrived awhile later. Mac's face was ashen, the front of his body covered in dark, drying blood. His hands trembled when he reached for the coat Pete handed him from his saddle pack.

"Let's get out of here," Pete hissed, prodding his boss's back. "It ain't safe."

"I have to—"

"The sheriff can find you, sir. Maybe somebody been shootin' at you and missed."

"God, who knows? Yeah, that could have been me. Carrie would be scared to death." Mac forced his unwilling feet to move out of range around the corner. Pete covered him, disregarding how much Mac complained. With the big to-do downtown no one noticed that they left.

The trip back to the ranch was markedly opposite of that just hours ago when Mac was doubtful about Berrigan, now deceased—angry about his purpose and the futility of the issues they faced together. The hot imprint of the Commissioner's bloody body on his own remained with him, while he replayed the shooting in garbled utterances that Pete partially heard above the clip of horses' hooves on the rocky road.

"A fine man now gone. One I admired." Mac unloosened his neck scarf and wiped his brow and hands.

"We shared the same hope to save the damn land. Berrigan was a man confident in his own right, one who loved and lost." Privately he acknowledged, yeah, that could be me, too. I feared he would attract my wife.

"But I pushed him into public service. Oh hell, Pete, it's too late for regrets. Too late to relive the brief time I knew the man. I sure hate to have to tell Carrie."

That evening, Mac and Carrie waited up for Antonio's tap on the kitchen door, their conversation punctuated by long silences after Mac broke the news, each separated in swirling rehashes of their recent images, thoughts, and feelings associated with the man Kent Berrigan, few of which they were ready to share with the other.

Mac's stare hung over their long kitchen table, unaware of Carrie's basket of dried sage, stems of wild geraniums, and sprigs of lavender. He saw himself lying on the table semi-conscious after being shot during the Indian raid. The drama replayed in his mind, not for the first time, but it recreated the sensations in his stunned state of mind.

Carrie set two cups of coffee on the table, distracting him. He shook his head as if awakening, took out his handkerchief and blew. The scene before him became one of the visit—the lively Miss Marion seated next to Kent Berrigan, their conversation with the Taryntons' parallel to a private exchange beneath their spoken words, portrayed intimately in smiles and flushes and startling admissions between them.

"I feel terrible for him, but also for Miss Patton," Carrie whispered, apparently reluctant to intrude on Mac's obvious shock, yet needing to say something. "Mac, you did what you could. I'm so sorry."

Antonio showed up late that night, stooped and exhausted, his Colt revolver swung low in a holster.

"Come in, come in," Mac yelled. "What the hell is going on? Did you find anything? You all right, man?"

"*Si, bien, gracias*, everybody talkin', nobody knows nothin'. I asked everbody. Went to every saloon. Nothin'. Somebody knows but they ain't tellin.'" His voice rasped, disappointed and strained from his covert inquiries. Carrie took this news stoically, as she had taken the news that Kent Berrigan had been shot and killed.

"Thugs! Hired thugs of the investors, that new coalition taking over. They want to keep power in their hands. My guess is they wanted to rig the Commission, and if they can't do that, they kill the opposition—early, before complaints reach the Legislature—not that the Legislature represents us either." Mac whirled to face Carrie. "Power. It's about power to run out small outfits like us."

Any opinions Antonio had he kept to himself, and he quietly slipped out to the bunkhouse where Pete was already snoring.

12

Our God is our strength...be still and know that I am God.

Headlines the next day in a special edition of the *Butte Miner*, a new Big Butte paper, read *COMMISSIONER SHOT IN BIG BUTTE*, subtitled *Kent Berrigan Represented Ranchers on Water Issues*. Stories related the short stint of Kent Berrigan of Hot Spring District on the Territorial Commission, noting he had spoken for ranchers and *"all those who have an interest in maintaining clean water."* Speculation on motivation of the unknown assassin ranged from protecting mining interests to that of a supposed political rivalry between Berrigan and other rising stars, including Wilbur Fisk Sanders, an attorney who held a seat in the Territorial Legislature.

"Berrigan, former Justice of the Peace of Madison County, and a man of considerable charm and talent, may have presented a threat to less comfortably situated yet more ambitious men with political aims," the article said.

Little was reported regarding Sheriff Ford's investigation to date. Eye witnesses professed to hear a close up, deafening crack of a rifle, and see Mr. Berrigan's body fall before the ensuing chaos. All onlookers present when the stagecoach arrived had desperately tried to escape the scene, their flight evidently masking the getaway of the assassin. None were able to identify the shooter. His whereabouts remained a mystery.

A short notice stated that interment would take place immediately on the Berrigan property at South Willow Creek near the Jefferson River in Madison County. Graveside services would be conducted after next of kin were notified, allowing travel time for their arrival.

The New North-West brought the news to Santa Fe two and a half weeks after the assassination. Fortunately, the Taryntons' first thought had been to telegraph Miss Patton, sadly notifying her of the shocking event, and that a memorial service would occur when family and friends arrived. Mac and Carrie offered their sincerest sympathy. Miss Patton immediately replied that she would make all haste to come for the service.

Life at the ranch went on automatically, the ranch owners preoccupied and biding their time, the prospect of a memorial service for Kent Berrigan a weight upon their already burdened marriage.

Several weeks later, Marion returned to Sterling, where she had lived with Kent years ago. Pale and stricken, her sparkling personality altered beyond recognition, she came to the memorial dressed somberly for mourning but short of masquerading in widow's weeds. A bronze silk gown and a hat tied under her chin with a matching wide ribbon set off her rusty-gold frizzy hair. Mac and Carrie met her at Kent's place where Kent's older brother, Randolph Berrigan, arrived after a hasty train trip from his home in Georgia to Salt Lake City, then on to Sterling by stagecoach.

"You must be Kent's brother," Carrie guessed. "You have strikingly similar family features." He extended his hand, introducing himself as Rand, and nodded politely at each of the ranch crew. He was nearly gray, with deep creases in his face. He walked with a halt.

"Due to the war," he said when others noticed his limp. He was well-dressed but not fashionably so, and seemed out of place, uncertain among individuals who knew his brother well from long association. "Mother would have dearly loved to be present. She has taken the news extremely hard. Unfortunately, her health does not permit her to attempt such an arduous journey."

"I'm sure this is a very difficult time for her. We're so sorry for your loss," Carrie said.

At the memorial service Mac shuffled uncomfortably, intensely aware of his intimate contact with the dying body, the victim's blood pouring over Mac's good shirt. He reached for Carrie's willing hand. Jackson Colter and Nettie, showing she was with child, drove up shortly before Jackson's twin brother, Patrick, who had unexpectedly returned from the East. Trying to hide his delight, Jackson edged toward Patrick during the brief graveside ceremony on the foothills near South Willow Creek. The Tobacco Root Mountains loomed over the small gathering at high noon, their rarified climate circulating the peaks, sending wisps of clouds cavorting along the timberline, and altogether diminishing human significance on the open range below.

At Marion's request, Samuel Sayles, Kent's neighbor and a good friend of both her and Kent, offered graveside readings and prayers.

"He stepped forth in service for the greater good and a higher purpose. Mr. Berrigan was exemplary in this respect. Indeed, he served as a citizen, County Commissioner, and justice of the peace when duty called over the years."

How Rand, a Unionist, interpreted this was anyone's guess. Many in the gathering knew that his brother, Kent, had fought in the War of Rebellion as a secessionist, and that he had mourned the downfall of his beloved homeland in the South. Rand could not fail to recognize that his brother was accorded the highest of honors by those who knew and loved him.

Miss Patton nodded, not only honoring his achievements, which were high on Marion's priority as a pace-setting businesswoman, but primarily her personal loss.

Mac realized the crushing blow of Berrigan's death, not only to Rand and Marion, but to the need to address challenges ahead—had he lived, Kent Berrigan may have altered the course of events. Mac had clung to the hope they could save the originally pristine waters of Silver Bow Creek and its tributaries as far as the Clark Fork River. Together, their insights, Berrigan's as a former miner and Mac's as a rancher, had recognized early warnings. Would there be others who would take a stand? The service weighed heavily on Mac beyond the immediate grief so clearly etched upon the faces of those present.

Rand accepted the flag of the United States that had stood in the Justice of the Peace office where Kent had officiated, but declined to display it at the service, stating "I don't know how Kent felt since the war. I do know that many veterans are still fighting it in their minds, myself included."

The barely audible words of the Lord's Prayer took on a life of their own, hitching on air currents, whispering among dried bunch grass, and seeking solitary nooks behind sagebrush and boulders. The cluster of neighbors, the folks from Sterling, the Big Butte rancher, his wife, wranglers Antonio and Pete, and next of kin represented by Randolph Berrigan and Miss Marion Patton, lingered after the service as if none could break away from their connection with Kent Berrigan, the tall gentleman each had known in their own way.

In the quiet interlude on the hill, views in every direction evoked a sense of endless seasons with Montana's astounding changes sweeping over the gravesite—pungent spring buds spicing the air, autumn turning aspens a golden hue, and the natural and inevitable time of rest prevailing in winter. Water falling over rocks on South Willow Creek reminded one of the eons it took to carve the valleys and rivers and benches below, a statement of sorts about the eternal.

Jackson Colter took Nettie home after the Kent Berrigan memorial service, but not before he had a chance to talk to Patrick who created a sensation in his Eastern attire.

"Patrick, you've sold out on me," Jackson complained, slapping his twin on the back. "Look at them duds, man! Clerking in a law office must be rewarding!"

Patrick tossed off the compliment, accustomed as he was to appraising stares of men and admiring glances of women. His sleek black hair was cut square at the neck and his sideburns were trimmed to accent a thin, black moustache. Hatless, Patrick showed off his first new set of clothes in years, a fine cotton shirt with blousy sleeves and cuffs wide enough to show some class, or lack of. Tethered by slim suspenders, his trousers rode high at the waist under his formal dress coat.

"Hey, brother, I've grown to like a desk job and the pay isn't bad." He displayed clean fingernails and palms without callouses.

"Things must have worked out for you. I'm glad," Jackson said. "For me, too. Come stay with us when you get back from checking out our old mining claims and cabin. I'd like to see Norwegian Creek and Sterling myself, but I'm a family man, you know."

Patrick stayed to mingle with neighbors from Hot Spring District, where he and Jackson had mined for five or six years. The Williams had a big family now. Callahans had owned the boarding house in Sterling. Their two children, Angel and Finn, were almost grown up. He didn't know the Sayles very well nor the tall, dark woman with them introduced as Miss Danielle Hartman. They all heartily embraced Miss Marion, a favorite when she lived with Kent near Sterling. But later her privacy was respected when she walked through the Berrigan home alone.

Marion ran her fingers over the cherrywood dining table and lid of a mahogany box labeled *Brogan Premium Cigars, Woodland Hills, Georgia,* the Brogan for Kent's father who had abandoned his young sons. Strange, the loyalties that held Rand and Kent despite their differences over the war. A hand-hewn bookcase of prized classics did not escape her glance. I did not share the academic world with him, only the natural, she mused, remembering their secret swimming hole in Norwegian Creek. Nor did I share this house or the modest four-poster bed.

At sight of the bed, visible through the bedroom door next to a bureau strewn with masculine toiletries, her knees nearly buckled. She clung to the back of a dining chair, half slumped over the brightly cross-stitched seat.

"Our first night in nine years—our only night since I left him—I held him and oh, he held me. If only—if only—" She sensed again his warm breath on her cheek when they shared a room in the Continental Hotel in Big Butte. She could hear him asking, "Marion, are you sure?" His soft, knowing grey eyes had searched hers for any hesitation, any uncertainty; a wrinkled brow registered his concern. She had sensed him waiting all these years, wondering what was in her heart, what she felt when she left him, what she felt now they were together again. No words had risen from her throat.

"My god, he can't be gone. He was so well, so alive and handsome, his face lined by Montana wind and sun. I could not or did not tell him why I came back, or how I felt—I failed to answer, and now it's too late. Too late to tell him that nothing about my leaving had to do with him, only myself, my restless ambitions for I knew not what."

Marion belatedly murmured the words. "He's mine—was mine. If only, if only it had not been our last night—"

His eyes had sought the chain with two gold rings she wore tucked between her breasts, one ring of gold from his *Marion* mine, the other a symbolic wedding ring. His slight smile told her worlds—he remembered their common-law marriage—he had forgiven her leaving—he wanted her now—he was hers. For once Marion's bold gaze had dropped under long moist lashes. A convulsive sob bent her slight shoulders when Kent lifted her to the hotel's plain iron bed. Mammoth goose down pillows over a white scalloped coverlet welcomed their embrace in an otherwise austere room. An oval mirror, hung crookedly on water-stained wallpaper, witnessed the reunion.

Today she straightened, her fingertips unable to leave the cherrywood tabletop, reluctant to give up the only way she could touch him now. The sweetness of it, she thought, our reunion, our one and only night in the hotel—truly the glory of our love. We always knew it. Both of us. It was there despite all the others, for me, at least. A deeper, mature love that night, no less passionate—maybe more so—yes indeed, more so—at least I could give him that. Marion now smiled into another world of her memory, perhaps into a world Kent now inhabited.

At the memorial service she felt numb, grief erasing their years apart, filling her heart with the poignancy of the time they spent together, realizing that Kent Berrigan held a prominent place in her affections the past nine years, even though she lived in Santa Fe and he in Sterling, Montana Territory. Her aspirations and urge to take risks in business had taken her away. Managing Barnstone Telegraph Company in the Southwest now felt like a lesser conquest than that of Kent Berrigan's devotion, which she had given up to carve a future of her own. And her passionate affair with the *mestizo*, Ramos, had burned itself out, not to be replaced by a single, lasting relationship, though she was barely thirty years of age.

Standing next to Carrie, she had been dry-eyed and stony, distant from her and the others, cherishing private thoughts, wrangling with others, knowing only that a senseless tragedy had robbed them all, as well as Kent. Kent's final courageous stand as a controversial commissioner confirmed Marion's belief in the man she had known, followed to Montana Territory, and eventually left—her belief that he would rise to his convictions. She saw him achieving that which would have been most meaningful to him in life—honor.

She had sensed that Mac Tarynton felt somewhat the same, his frame stooped, his hat hanging loosely in his hands in front of him.

Antonio had stood watch on high alert even here, as if an attack on his boss might spring from the earth at any moment.

How far the reaches of conspiracy? Where next? From whom? And most of all, why? Antonio's eyes had darted after every able-bodied man who had gathered from what was once the gold camp of Sterling in Hot Spring District. Not least did his eyes follow the figure of Danielle Hartman, a striking, reserved woman who had accompanied the Sayles family to the memorial celebration. Widowed by the war, someone said. However, he and Pete had left soon after the service to ward off any repercussions in Big Butte or at the ranch. Though considerable time had passed since the shooting, anger and fear in town had not subsided in the aftermath.

A knock at Kent Berrigan's door brought Marion back to the present. The Callahan children she had known at the Sterling boarding house came to see Miss Marion. Angel, a lovely shy young woman at sixteen, asked, "Would ye be wanting yer trunk back, ma'am? I took good care of it."

At this touchstone to her previous life with Kent, the trunk marking her abrupt departure when she forfeited most of her personal belongings, Marion's strangled emotions burst forth in tears. Angel stood by dabbing her own eyes and sniffling. Her long blond hair, plaited into a charming braid, exposed her pale Irish cheeks.

"Goodness no, child. It is yours to keep and may you be happy," Marion answered, greatly moved. Kent loved the children, and called them his godchildren, though they were Southern Baptist, he an errant Catholic. "It was just right that he gave it to you, Angel." She supposed her green silk gown, acquired with such excitement in New York City, had likewise been charitably given away.

Genevieve Sayles, Kent's former neighbor, invited Marion and the other guests to come to their place for coffee and sandwiches. Rand urged Mac to stay with him at Kent's place and keep him company while the women visited. Mac agreed, weary from the recent devastating events.

At the Sayles log cabin, Genevieve served sweet tea halved with thick cream from their Jersey cows. After they had eaten, her husband, Samuel, read somber Scriptures that promised a brighter road ahead for those who suffered. Candles burned down while the women gathered in the parlour. Unpretentious with each other in the tranquil home, they talked far into the night. Genevieve's sister, Danielle, mystery woman at the graveside ceremony removed herself from outward mourning.

Marion suspected she had shared confidences with Kent, perhaps allowed herself notions of taking Marion's place in his favor, but apparently they had not become close. Marion wondered why they had not, then recalled Kent's words their last night together, "You were, you are, my only love." Miss Hartman had evidently recognized his deep though futile devotion. Her austere demeanor seemed to indicate she accepted her life as single since her husband had been killed or missing in the war over fifteen years ago.

"Pardon me, Miss Patton, but would you be willing to share with us what came between you and Mr. Berrigan?" Carrie asked the unspoken question suggested by the women's stares and raised eyebrows.

"I was young and impulsive," Marion answered. "It was mostly on impulse that I dared to live with him." A long silence followed while Marion gathered her fragile feelings and tucked them into a less charged place in her heart. "I –I left him abruptly—when we were so happy. I felt dreadful afterwards about what I had done to Kent, and to myself. I do not understand it, except that it was not in my nature to stay."

Her voice choked, faltered. "He was badly torn by the war. You would never believe it from seeing him as he was at your home, Mrs. Tarynton, but when we lived together he suffered terribly from nightmares and endless regret and guilt. I am pleased to hear that he may have come to terms with the war trauma and family upsets that haunted him."

She looked helplessly at each of the women, her small oval

face with round hazel eyes unbearably sad. "Now he rests in peace. It is my loss—I love him still."

"I understand." Carrie broke a long silence. "My husband is something of a tortured soul as well. It is all very hard—"

"But you have the strength of a mountain," Marion interrupted, then paused to sort out the churning events of past years, separate them from her current perspective. "I never married though I loved several other men from time to time, or thought I did. Regrettably, I am not so faithful as you."

Carrie wrapped her arm around Marion's slim shoulders, the woman she had envied now a subdued, smaller presence than when they first met.

"It was a privilege for Mac and I to have known him even so briefly. Surely he was an extraordinary man and loved by so many here in Hot Spring District. I offer my deepest sympathy to you and to his family."

Randolph Berrigan walked downhill with Mac after the memorial service to a weathered, unpainted house with a look of solidarity with the land, a house in keeping with the nature of Montana itself, except for minimal Queen Anne embellishments on eves and gables.

"Kent's place evidently represents how he came to be after all these years on the frontier," Rand mused. "Refined, but earthy and strong."

He followed Mac inside, still shaken with uncertainty about visiting his brother's home. Kent had fled the South for the gold fields of Montana Territory after the war, along with a historic exodus of other displaced individuals. Rand had searched for him the next spring, hoping to fulfill their mother's longing to see her younger son. However, the rift between the brothers, one a Unionist and the other a Secessionist, had precluded mending their split loyalties at that time. Now Rand had a feeling of intruding because Kent had refused to take him to his squatter's shack during his earlier unannounced visit. This home was far from a temporary shack. Unpretentious yet imposing and masculine, it had a look of prosperity—but for Rand it still felt like crossing a personal boundary, though they had healed much of the breach in their family over the years.

"I regret that I have missed a great deal of his life since we lived on opposite sides of the country."

"I was here for lunch with your brother in better times. We worked up the idea of him running for the Territorial Commission, so I feel responsible in a way. I'm sure sorry and wish to hell it was diff'ernt. He was a fine man and good to me," Mac said.

Rand nodded and stood in the doorway, shaking his head in disbelief that his younger brother, Kent, was dead. "I feared mightily that something might happen to him in the war, or during his prospecting days in the Territory. Mother worried endlessly about his safety. Newspapers reported hostilities with the Indians, which have now become full-scale Indian wars. The Territory seems raw and lawless with those incursions when an elected official is shot down while appearing with other dignitaries in Big Butte."

"This isn't the time or place to vent my anger." Mac gritted his teeth, attempting to avoid stirring the pot already overflowing with rumors, innuendos, blaming and threats. He also did not reveal that he might have been the target instead of Kent.

"It could have been revenge by a bluecoat—Kent had said the aftermath of the war remains in the Territory—I'm sorry as hell for how it split our family, but I can't go back down that road. I have a family to think of. Perhaps the assassination occurred for some other reason—I don't know what the investigation will find, if anything."

Rand stepped outside to break the tension. His gaze swept the far horizon over bench land that dipped down to the Jefferson River, then swung to view the mountains behind the house. Observing the wide open acres cut by creeks and the abrupt rise of timbered blue mountains lightened his mood.

"These are astounding views. I can see why Kent loved it here. It does seem peaceful, a balm to one's mind—especially after the war. It was quite a coincidence, or natural inclination of tobacco growers, that both of us dug in the dirt to right ourselves, he on his claims and me in the fields."

Mac prowled around the house, brought in firewood, and sank into a rocker by the hearth. "I have to say your brother has an uncanny way of separating women from their husbands, if my wife sleeping at the neighbors and me here is any indication." Mac's lack of tact betrayed earlier fears that Carrie might leave him. "I wonder what happened between the two of them, Kent and Miss Patton."

"Kent never disclosed much of his personal life other than that he never found another woman to take her place. This is the first time I have met Miss Patton, but I find her to be a remarkable woman, confident and successful, though I am not familiar with her business. No doubt, she is attractive."

"Oh, she is confident and outspoken all right. I understand she established a telegraph service to Santa Fe. I just wonder what influence she has on my wife. I don't mean to slight Miss Patton—or him after his death. I appreciate the stand he took attempting to help us in mining communities across the Territories. I don't believe anyone has done that before."

Rand opened cupboard doors and poked futilely around the pantry for a bottle of Southern Comfort or other spirits only to find several polished, hardwood cigar boxes with gold gilt trim.

"Help yourself." Rand offered a box to Mac. "We grow the tobacco on our estate in Woodland Hills, Georgia. Kent taste-tested for us—not under duress," he chuckled.

The *Brogan Premium Cigars* contained fat rolls of yellow-brown leaves inside a lighter yellow-ochre layer, each with a red and gold band around the middle denoting source, year, and numbers relating to Rand's experimental crops.

"The 'Brogan' is for our father, bless him. He disappeared from our lives when we were young. He was a sturdy Irishman with ambitions of high adventure. Not so for us. We both wanted to stay on our estate, but the war came along to define our destinies, mine tied to father's side in the North, and Kent's with mother's in the South. The estrangement was more painful than I can say, although over time much of it has worn away."

"He seemed at ease with his conscience when he visited my ranch," Mac interjected, "if that is any comfort to you."

"I am glad to hear it. Thank you. Mother and my wife will be relieved to know he found peace here on this property. Elena would have been pleased to come, but we have three children, the youngest a son, four years old."

Night settled over the Tobacco Roots and long shadows stretched out the back door as the moon rose in the east. A great horned owl lifted from the topmost dead branch of a cottonwood on his nightly excursions. Mule deer emerged from the undergrowth of dogwood and yellow willows. Purple spears of dotted gay feathers bloomed where other vegetation had begun to die back. A breeze chilled by Mount Hollowtop hinted of deepening seasons toward year's end.

The men walked out to feed Kent's horse, Ben, a seventeen-hand Percheron-thoroughbred that eagerly came to the fence.

"He's getting pretty old, I think," Mac said. "I wonder what will become of him."

"I found only an informal letter in a desk drawer indicating disposal of property in case something happened to him. It was signed, giving everything to the neighbors, the Samuel Sayles family, who have been *"my dear friends, family, solace and inspiration, and looked kindly after me, thanks be to God."* I have not yet told them," Rand said. "He designated his books for the 'godchildren,' Angel and Finn Callahan. Elena had sent Kent's childhood collection for their education."

Rand's voice wavered. The last will, his last words, revealed volumes about Kent's life in the West—evidently a life with warm, supportive folks from the North, as well as Confederate émigrés, who met the rigors of pioneering face to face.

A profound sense of aloneness overcame Rand; the brother he had tried to father had rebelled against him and fought his native country, ultimately leaving the family just as their father had.

"Mother had kept Kent close to her," he murmured, but he had to break away.

Wind whipping down the mountain brought neighs of wild horses in the foothills, reminding him of riding thoroughbreds with Kent over the red soil of Georgia's Uplands. Savoring the reflections, he smiled at their adventures catching small bass with Gracie, the cook, hovering over "her" two lads. They had worked the tobacco fields under the tutelage of Ephram, their foreman, and the half-dozen men and women they owned, producing the cigars which bore the family name.

That night Mac insisted upon throwing his bedroll on the floor. Rand took Kent's bedroom. Out here in open country breathing in the sweet scent of dried prairie grass, Rand realized that Kent, like their father, was an adventurer after all.

At last he sighed, regretting their lives had been so distant. *Our loss, but I am beginning to understand why he chose to live here.*

Carrie drove Miss Patton back to the Berrigan home at first light to have coffee, buckwheat pancakes and chokecherry syrup with Mac and Rand before they went their separate ways. Rand would accompany Marion on the stagecoach line to Salt Lake City, where she would board a train for the Southwest and Rand for the Southeast.

For weeks following the assassination, riotors convened sporadically in Big Butte to throw rocks at an opposing crowd, breaking windows and hitching rails. Many bore the stench of sweat-drenched miners just off work, others included settlers with ill-concealed shotguns who lingered on the fringes of the crowd. Whether they were for or against the Commission or stood for an undisclosed coalition or company was impossible to determine in the dark. More evident was newly aroused strife between rivals of the War Between the States. Occasional taunts of "Yank" were countered by "traitor," clashes verifying that the war was still alive in the West eleven years after the surrender. Sheriff Ford swore in a few miners to wear a badge and beef up security, but made no arrests.

Antonio and Pete rode back into town from South Willow Creek in time to witness the unrest, both bearing arms but remaining out of the riots. They saw trapper Jonathan Duprés heave rocks at the miners while he had a chance, shouting in a stream of French and English something about "even the rats are better'n you scum." Constables monitored the conflicts but stood on the outskirts of the flurry. If there were thugs in company hire or assassins among the crowd, no one pointed a finger. The air remained tense and ominous over the growing mining town that many now considered "Butte City," a place that showed little sign of becoming citified.

13

A universal culture is now demanded. The mental, affectional, (sic) moral, aesthetical, and spiritual departments of our being re-quire no less development and fullness of expression in us, if we would do our noblest work. Prudence B. Saur, M.D.

Following the memorial service gathering, Patrick Colter met up with the Callahans, his longtime friends who ran a boarding house in the early days of Sterling. The Callahans had provided the closest family for Kent Berrigan and the Col-ters with their lively children and pets, at one time bestowing on Mr. Berrigan a pup he called Shag.

Patrick wondered if many of the 'old timers' like himself were left in Hot Spring District, or if more recent comers even knew Kent. Still in his formal dress clothes, Patrick asked Har-land Callahan if he could ride back to Sterling with his family and spend the night at the boarding house.

"Sure 'n all, the boarding house is mostly torn down now. Ten years it's been since the gold rush and Sterling is gradually fading away. We were some of the last to leave. Aye, ye come stay with us at our small store in Norris."

The junction town near the single hot spring was on the Bozeman Trail that led to Virginia City. To the east the Trail fol-lows the winding Madison River towards the headwaters of the Missouri.

"Norris is the stage stop now, and there is a school," Harland said. He had gained weight that seemed to shorten his stature and slow him down, partly the years, too, but his Boston accent was as familiar to Patrick as his own.

"I just returned from a year in Boston." Patrick's experience came out in bits and pieces, the Callahans chiming in with questions about how it was in the East.

"Aw, are you folks getting homesick? I guess I came back to the West for the same reason. I miss this place. I'd like to stay and look around tomorrow, maybe see some of the people I used to know. You say the mining's gone bust? I guess my brother and I were here in its heyday."

The wagon lumbered slowly behind an old team, allowing Patrick time to reminisce with the Callahans. Most surprising was that their children, Angel and Finn, had grown up. Angel had finished school and was looking for a suitable position. She wanted to work for someone other than her parents since she had helped in their Sterling boarding house as a child. Finn, now fourteen, was studying to enter an academy, possibly in Boston. He was a quiet lad with large, watchful eyes, whereas Angel's nature was outgoing and talkative, though she appeared shy around Patrick.

"You played pranks on us at the Sterling school," he reminded Angel, who still had a mischievous look.

"Mr. Berrigan helped me with my studies and let me read his books," Finn said. "I would like to be an accountant like him, but I am not so clever with arithmetic," as solemn a tribute to the fallen, his 'godfather' and mentor, as any given at the memorial service.

Patrick patted the lad on the back and encouraged him. "It's all right, Finn. You and I, we have to figure out what we are clever about and what we want to do."

"When are ye going to know?" Finn's round eyes remained serious in a boyish face that reminded Patrick of his brother,

Jackson. Finn was so lanky that Patrick hardly recognized him as the five-year-old in knickers who had wanted to attend the Sterling school where Patrick taught one year.

"Hmm, I worked in a law office in Boston, and the work interests me. I came back to Montana to stay, so I had better decide."

Harland drove the team down the Sterling road to show Patrick what remained of the once thriving gold town. Patrick recognized the mills and several dilapidated false-fronted buildings.

"Say, that was the old Golddigger Saloon. I remember that, and over there was the Dixie Saloon where Southerners held out. Jackson and I lived on Norwegian Creek near the Confederates. We had claims there and occasionally worked for Mr. Berrigan. I'd say he helped me more than any man in the Territory by providing me with the classics and starting me, as well as Finn, on a path to higher education."

Finn absorbed this talk, likely impressed that he and his former mentor were influenced by the same man for the same reason, and that they both had higher aspirations than mining.

"I remember when our neighbor, Jake Hanson, was killed on Norwegian Creek. Did they ever find out who shot him?" Patrick asked.

"Never did," Harland said. "There wasn't much justice in Hot Spring District then, and there ain't much more now."

The pall of the two murders stifled the conversation, the men mulling the incidents. Would Berrigan ever have sensed he might be gunned down like Jake for no identifiable reason? Certainly each were killed by an individual who escaped to possibly stalk and kill again.

"He hadn't lived his life in fear that I know of. Ye could see he lived in plain sight and served on the County Commission and as Justice of the Peace and over here for quite a few years. Some said he was the voice of reason. I knew that when I first met the man. I says to him, 'whyn't ye run for higher office' many a time before he did it. I feel like we put him up to it and look what's come of it." Harland broke off, the pain of loss evident.

Patrick guessed the old businessman had needed to get the confession off his shoulders. Shifting the subject, he said, "Say, what did you think of Miss Marion Patton showing up? I wonder if she had planned to return and take up a life here."

"She's always been independent," Mrs. Callahan cut in. "I think a lot of her. We used to have good times together. I knew her fairly well, but not so well that I wasn't surprised when she left Mr. Berrigan. That poor man was terribly stricken. I hear they met in Big Butte recently. Perhaps they made up before he died."

The loss settled again over the group. They quietly trouped into Callahan's small quarters behind their store in Norris to find their way into beds for the night.

The next day, his good clothes packed, Patrick dressed in a suitable riding outfit and borrowed a horse to visit the old claims he and Jackson had worked before they had given up and sold out. Land had become cheap when claims were soon worked out. Midas Mining Company of New York had folded shortly after startup. Years later only the Revenue and Galina mines continued sporadic operations.

Back on a horse after a year in Boston, Patrick struck out across country, relishing the discovery that miles and miles of range grass on the benches remained open, though much of the best farmland had been claimed under the Homestead Act of 1862. He and Jackson had come West in 1865 before settlers sliced the land into fenced parcels. Today, he rode straight north for Norwegian Creek, a substantial stream bounding from the steep incline of the Tobacco Root Mountains, cutting a gulch lined with dark junipers, and lower down, clusters of cottonwoods. At first he could not detect the exact location of his old home, a makeshift cabin perched on the edge of a gully, until he realized it had been converted to a cow barn behind a settler's new log home. A flourishing apple orchard served as a windbreak around the house and barnyard.

"All these changes make me feel old. Old and alone." Patrick couldn't remember feeling lonely out here before, but then his twin Jackson had always been with him. They had been a constant in each other's lives. Their former diggings were now filled in some places and left as pits in others. Piles of tailings sprouted mullein, hounds tooth, and thistles everywhere. He soon felt he had seen enough and hastened back to Norris to catch the stagecoach for Big Butte.

———————

Patrick's nostalgic excursion stayed with him long after the stagecoach left behind old Hollowtop peak on its lonely vigil, and Madison County's purple ranges rolled into the distance. Reflections coursed through his mind engaging his deep attachment to Montana Territory, his need to stay, to become a part of it. Eventually he dozed, the crunching of iron-clad wheels of the Concord coach over stones a jarring percussion concert until the team arrived in Big Butte, where a dense haze and intermittent clangs of the mines claimed his senses.

"I want to stay in Montana Territory," Patrick later told Jackson. Their coffee cups were still on the table and a kerosene lamp burned low. Nettie had gone to bed and the twins talked long into the night. "But I've seen too much violence close to home with Jake and now Berrigan shot and killed. They both meant a lot to me. Maybe it takes more man than I am to stick it out and make a living here."

"I want you to stay," Jackson interrupted. "That is, if you prefer the West and want to remain here."

"With folks gone from Sterling and corporate mining companies taking over Big Butte, it's not the same. It isn't like a fella can do what he wants anymore, not that I know what I want,"

Patrick continued, hashing over the shock of Berrigan's death and changes that had occurred in the past year.

"We need you, Nettie and I," Jackson pleaded, the same boyish look on his freckled face that Patrick knew as well as own face, better even, since mirrors were few. They had always been dependent upon each other until a year ago when Patrick had abruptly gone back home.

"I'm sorry I left the way I did—having a blowout to make myself go. That was cheap of me, Jackson. I've felt bad about it."

Jackson nodded, "I've felt bad we parted that way, too."

Patrick scrunched his tall frame down in the chair and hiked his feet up on another one, exhaling long and loud as if letting a lot go. "I discovered what I'd left here after I got back to Boston. I hadn't missed the city when you and I came out for the gold rush. My only connection was with the folks, of course, and they're getting on. By the way, they're coming when the grandchild arrives."

"Naw, you don't say? I can hardly believe it!"

"Sure thing. And more than that, they sold some of their land, so they're giving you and Nettie your inheritance early. They gave me mine before I came back here."

Unable to speak, Jackson propped his chin on his hand, elbow on the table, eyes misty.

"I thought you'd be pleased to know," his twin finished the thoughts for his brother. "There is rail a good part of the way, which makes the trip easier. Yep, they're coming to see you, Nettie and the baby. But tomorrow you better show me that stud horse Mrs. Tarynton raised from the dead and brought here." They clasped hands with that special twin look, a seal that all was right with the world.

The next day King raised his head high over the fence to check out the visitors. The stallion that whinnied and trotted over to the two men proud as could be was filthy dirty, his silky dapple gray well disguised beneath dirt and manure that he'd rolled in. His tail fared little better having picked up mud, spears of dried weeds and hound's tongue burrs.

Patrick laughed. "Is this the famous start of your horse breeding operation?" He crawled through the pole rails as King nuzzled his pockets and sniffed his ears, knocking off Patrick's hat.

"He knows you well. They never forget—neither the good nor the bad. You were pretty good to that horse," Jackson said.

Patrick ran his hand over scars from injuries the stallion had sustained from throwing himself when he was loco, an undetermined condition from toxic weeds, or an illness contracted in shipping to Big Butte from Ireland. Patrick felt for the huge welts that had covered the stallion's body, and found only blemishes. The Connemara took off with a snort for the other side of the corral to investigate a noise and loped back, a reunion that welled up in the twins' throats almost as much as the one between themselves.

"You can't beat that for a comeback," Patrick said at last. "He looks good. How is his mind?"

"Seems to be normal. You'll hear tales about him saving Roxanna Duprés from the Indians, though I don't know how much to believe. The fact that a woman can ride him shows his good nature, and she isn't a world class rider. He seems to have good sense. I rode him so often the Taryntons gave him to Nettie and me for a wedding present.

"But here's the thing. He's sired one foal that we know of, and I need a higher corral fence or he'll be off siring them for free. There's a lot of demand for his services, and I'm not comfortable taking him to folks' places where he could get hurt or stolen."

"How was the foal? Is its mind all right?"

"She's a beauty, same dapple gray but with a black mane and tail like the mare, a wild one that came to the ranch. She seems to be exceptional in body and mind. In fact, she's a better looker than this one in terms of longer, slimmer legs."

"You've got it in your blood," Patrick teased. "You'll be betting on this horse same as the blokes uptown before you know it!"

"About that corral—"

"Sure, I'll help you. We can cut some posts and rails, and make this one quite a bit larger."

"We better do it while you're in a good mood and before you get a job."

"Say the word. In the meantime, I'll clean up this stud. He's no show horse today and wouldn't be worth a cent to you."

Patrick edged away with a sense of loss. Jackson had found his way in life without him.

The twins rode north up Bison Creek early the next morning, Patrick riding King and Jackson on his saddle horse. Axes, chains, and a short crosscut saw jangled in a pack on Patrick's old horse. A settler on the flats would be along with a team and wagon to haul their poles home if they cut an equal amount for his use.

Scandinavian woodcutters often provided vast quantities of firewood for steam-driven stamp mills, smelters, and engines, and harvested much of the easily accessible timber for commercial buildings, boardwalks, homes and corrals. Patrick and Jackson had to ride further up the creek, and climb the eastern slope of the Continental Divide to find a good stand of timber, where they snaked poles down to the road with their horses and the chains. By mid-morning they had worked up a sweat, even on the shady side of the mountain. Taking a break, they sat on an outcropping with a view south across the valley to Blacktail Creek that ran into Summit Flats, flats that were once lush and green and now had the churned look of giant badger holes. Not a tree, shrub, or pasture remained along the creek after a dozen years of mining. Few birds other than scavengers drifted aloft in the dark haze rimmed by the mountains.

The men, prospectors in the high-rolling days of Hot Spring District, sat in silence until Patrick stretched his shoulders. "This is work. I'm not used to it." He grinned as though it was good to be working anyway, and a good day to be in high timber.

"You look good, Patrick, even if you're as dirty as that Connemara was yesterday. Say, that's Huckin's place, the grand new house, at the end of the valley. I wonder if his money comes from Dublin. We don't have that kind of wealth here yet, though some folks have mighty big ambitions."

"How about the companies associated with the mines?" Patrick asked, shifting to face Jackson. "I've been thinking about the murder. They have to be connected, wouldn't you guess?"

"I've been thinkin' about it, too. Everyone has. There's been no clues that I know of. It's damn strange nobody knows. That shot had to come from someone hidden up close in one of the wagons, then hauled out in all the ruckus."

"Why? There has to be a motive in a case like this. Someone protecting their interests." Patrick realized he was thinking like those in the Boston law office. The notion of analyzing a case had a certain appeal to him. "You remember the Bosworth & Son law offices? The old man is shifting workloads to his son, Lucas. I served as a law clerk in their offices and took notes in a few court cases."

"I'm not one to speculate, and I for sure don't have any answers." Jackson hesitated. "I don't like where you're going with this. There's more than enough rumors circulatin' already. Berrigan set himself up on the side of the ranchers—and against the miners. If you're lookin' to get involved, Patrick, you can read the tea leaves—or talk to Mac Tarynton. He could tell you more'n me." Jackson grabbed an axe handle and got back to work.

With the settler's help they hauled the sturdy posts and rails home, stacking them alongside the old corral just as the weather turned bad with rain showers, lightning and ground-rattling thunder. Jackson agreed to let the rain soak the ground to make posthole digging a little easier.

"I'll use the time to ride to Taryntons' ranch. I'm considering running for the position on the Commission that Berrigan held," Patrick announced before he left.

"NO, Patrick. No. It's too dangerous," Jackson cautioned.

"I'll be discreet, I assure you," Patrick promised. "I'd like to get a foot in the door in law, maybe politics—I learned fast in the law office. What I've found is that I don't want to be a day laborer. Don't get me wrong, Jackson. I love to work hard, but I've seen another way."

"Don't tell Nettie and worry her." Jackson turned pale. "I'll keep a lid on it. She's close to having the baby. Be careful, Patrick. You can't mess around with things like this."

Patrick smelled the coffee and freshly baked bread before he knocked on the ranch door. Carrie invited him in for coffee that was black as the inside of a coal stove, and set out a plate of hot raisin scones.

"Between you and Nettie, I might not need to find myself a good wife after all," Patrick joked. "I've gained weight since I've been back from Boston, even though Jackson works me like a dog building a new corral."

"The crew is fixing fence here, too. Mac is always expanding the ranch, this time with new corrals. You'll find them down on the west side in a grove of junipers where the wind isn't as bad as it is up here."

Well fortified, Patrick rode down to the site and pitched in to help. He had met Duggan in the pubs when he and Jackson were miners here, and recognized Antonio and Pete from the memorial service, but the others were new to him.

"I'd like to talk with you if you have time later, Mr. Tarynton. Jackson suggested it might be a good idea," Patrick mumbled, uncomfortable making a request of the ranch boss.

"Oh yeah?" Mac said, looking up from driving a nail. "What's on your mind? If you're looking for work, it's slack time here until we bring the herd in this fall."

"About the vacancy on the Commission—I'm wondering if—"

"Not me, if that's what you're getting at. Carrie and the crew wouldn't let me run for it if the world was coming to an end," Mac interrupted.

"No, not you. Me," Patrick pursued, becoming more unsure of himself. "I'm wondering if it might be a suitable position for me."

Mac set down his hammer and stared at him. "We better have that little talk. Hey men, take a break. Antonio, come on over. This is Patrick, Jackson's brother. Antonio is my foreman."

Mac led the way to a wagon where a pair of matched Belgians dozed in their harnesses. Mac hefted himself up on the wagon bed, his long legs dangling, and pulled out a sack of Bull Durham and cigarette papers. Alert to Mac's immediate tension, Antonio and Patrick seated themselves on stumps close by.

"I know this is audacious of me to speak up, Mr. Tarynton, but Jackson and I were neighbors of Kent Berrigan for many years on Norwegian Creek. We've both been hit pretty hard by his death. I'm interested in justice—whether it is about the murder or water or other issues. I'm trying to find a way into public service since I've come back to Big Butte." Patrick's disclosure ended uncertainly, leaving a prolonged silence. Mac was either a good listener or busy rolling his smoke. Same with Antonio. Patrick had declined the tobacco.

"Wal, it's a helluva thing, the ambush," Mac finally said. "Nobody feels safe anymore. It's a good thing we're away from the house. I don't want my wife hearing this talk." He scratched a match a few times on his boot heel and tossed it for another one.

"I am being hasty, I know, and I am not well informed about the dispute over the toxic water, but I had exposure to the law the past year with a reputable firm in Boston. I found I have an interest in cases and possibly an aptitude for the work. Do you think Berrigan was shot for the position he took, posing a threat to the mining activity?"

Mac snorted and hooked his thumb towards his foreman. "You tell him what you heard, Antonio. Then he'll not be likely to walk into anything dumb and blind—like I did."

Antonio was a soft-spoken yet hardened wrangler of middle age with a clipped moustache and deep dark eyes. More than a head shorter than Mac, he still carried a restrained authority that made a man listen up.

"I better get Pete over here, too." Mac yelled over to the crew. "The trapper, Duprès, said the water in the streams was so bad the muskrats left. We saw colors collect in the moss—copper, iron, lead and so forth that build up where water is slow. It's bad for stock, but I dunno that Berrigan was shot for speaking up for protection of pristine steams. Tell what you heard in the saloons, Antonio."

"There's a lot of talk, some sayin' it was a personal grudge, some sayin' Berrigan and the cattle industry could take down the coalition of investors and stop the mining."

"No doubt the cattlemen have built an industry that is as big or bigger than these piddling mining companies, but I couldn't get Kohrs innerested," Mac admitted.

"I heered they meant to kill someone else and missed," Pete cut in. The wranglers inadvertently glanced at Mac.

"Why me, I don't know," Mac said, "but these guys won't let me outta their sight—no mingling out and about on my own. They're like a bunch of old women."

Patrick caught himself holding his breath. This was already far more than he dared venture, and he hadn't heard it all, maybe not the worst yet.

"Couldn't be you, Mr. Tarynton, sir," Patrick gushed, thinking how much Jackson and Nettie loved the cattleman and his wife, and how much they owed them for the job, the wedding, and the stallion. He felt crushed, sick at what they had said and not said. He knew he could get himself killed.

"Wal, it could be something none of us knows about." Mac tried to diffuse the tension.

"Didn't Berrigan get off that stagecoach with other members of the Commission, any of whom could have been a target?" Patrick asked.

"Yeah, four men came on that stage, and the others came separately. Maybe Berrigan was just unlucky, but some people fear the idea of a Southerner taking over. There's still a lot of hate carried over from the war."

Mac's subdued speculations seemed a stretch to Patrick, but plausible nevertheless.

"Years ago, I lived among Southerners including Kent Berrigan on Norwegian Creek near Sterling. It is true, a few Rebels continued the conflict and Federals baited them, calling them traitors or deserters. We never found out who shot one of my neighbors, Jake Hanson, a Southerner. We figured he was mistaken for a man who lived in the next cabin, but we never knew." Patrick sensed he was already honing his mind for case studies, an exercise that set off a shot of adrenalin.

Pete reeled off what he had overheard in the saloons. "That Commission was already loaded with coalition men. One owed gambling debts from when they met in Big Butte a year ago. One was a captain in the war said to have run Union prison camps. You kin hear the bad blood every night of the week downtown."

"What do you think, Antonio?" Mac asked, though they had plowed this ground many times before.

"Straight up, it looks like a power grab by the mines, but I ain't sure. Maybe settlers want to drive out cattle outfits, and claim grazing land for farms. Duprés says same is happenin' in Idaho." He scratched in the dirt with a stick, then glanced up at Patrick.

"It pays to be careful. We wait. See what happens."

His word sounded like law to Patrick, finding he had a healthy respect for the foreman, the wrangler Pete, and the beleaguered rancher.

"I'm not going to tell you what to do, son, but you best be on your own for now, and not make enemies by coming here until we know for sure," Mac said, echoing Antonio's warning.

Pete, guileless and irreverent, chipped in, "The killer might 'a been hired to git the Commissioner who spent his time in the brothels last year, and he got the wrong man." This broke the tension and they all laughed.

"I should spend more time in the saloons. You men round up more scuttlebutt than a newspaper gossip column," Patrick said.

————————

Of all the harrowing experiences Patrick had encountered in mining, including deep in the silver mines beneath Big Butte, none compared to the sobering revelation from Mac and his crew that a man might be easily targeted, that a citizen could be assassinated and the killer remain at large. His skin crawled at the thought.

"It could be me. I might put my neck out for public office and barge into a controversy I know nothing about. Damn, this is putting years on me."

Leaving the ranch he slumped in the saddle, a contrast to the high hopes he'd had on a spirited ride up the mountain. Still, he wanted to serve in a public or private capacity. The notion was not unreasonable; it only needed to be pursued with caution. "I've been forewarned. I have better sense now," he tried to convince himself. He took the following day off to settle his nerves and think this through. He had moved out of the cabin when his brother's wife's confinement advanced, and it felt good to have his own place, even if it was just a room above the Tavern.

That afternoon he walked from Park Street up Main to Walkerville, then beyond to the unsettled, rounded foothills where natural hill grass crunched under his boots and sage raised its pungent, nose-tickling fragrance, a scent he had sorely missed in Boston. The city served me well when I landed the job at Bosworths, he mused. It set me on a path I might be good at if I stay with it. Of course, I don't have a law degree, but I can learn, maybe more easily than Jackson. After all, we're not identical twins, so why not? The idea seemed like a betrayal but failed to thwart his ambitions.

By the time he headed back into the dusty streets downtown he felt determined to hammer out his future. He put on his coat and braved a wind that whipped hats off passersby and flapped crudely made signs along the street. After supper he stopped at the Tavern saloon to spend the evening among the jostling, raucous men, a welcome contrast to his solitary day on the foothills. I couldn't ride herd on night shift like Jackson, he thought. Not out there alone with thousands of cows, surrounded by wolves and mountain lions. I don't know how he does it. That's not for me.

He had already had two shots when a well-dressed gentleman sidled up to him at the bar. "Hector Winship here." The man extended his hand. A thick brown beard covered his mouth and flared beyond the broad cheekbones. "Could we sit at a table over there? I'd like to make your acquaintance."

Patrick noted the man's eyes beneath the Homburg were cool, intelligent, and appraising. He nodded and followed, though the gentleman had not waited for an answer. The case of nerves he'd felt that morning set off alarms—is this a set up? His palms felt sweaty, but he seated himself across a small table and leaned forward to catch Winship's low voice.

"I've seen you around. I'm staying at the Continental Hotel. Big Butte is quite the place. It is rougher than I thought, but there are decent folk like yourself." He waited, yet Patrick remained an alert listener. Hector's story unfolded. "I came on the rail from Newark to St. Louis. That port is a real circus with wagon trains outfitting for the Overland Trail. I chose a nice steam riverboat instead, the *Chippewea*, to travel up the Missouri to Fort Benton. We do a lot of business on that route. Fortunately, we caught good weather and sufficient water levels. It has been an excellent season for the steamers, I'm told. It is remarkable that the Fort provides the country's farthest inland port. Say, is that a Boston accent?"

"Yes sir, it is," Patrick answered, though he wasn't aware of having said anything to the gentleman. That meant he had been watched up close for awhile. He shuddered, sensing an undertow he wasn't sure came from Winship or his own apprehensions. He wished Winship would get down to "business."

Winship's self-indulgent gaze shifted, observing that Patrick was no fool. "We plan to hire good men who have local ties, those who know their way around the mining community. I understand you did some mining here at one time. I'm not looking for a day laborer, though."

"Who are you representing, please?" Patrick questioned Winship politely, at the same time chilled by the nondisclosures accompanying the conversation.

"A coalition of investors engaged me to further its interests in the Territories. I am not an investor myself. Rather I work for an intermediary company with small offices across the continent, all the way to the gold fields of California. In fact, our company first built its fine reputation in San Francisco. We're heavily engaged in silver mining in Nevada. Montana Territory is the next step for us. Big Butte has potential.

"Forgive my forthright approach, but I did not want to miss this opportunity to discuss the matter with you. We have openings in many of these offices due to the extraordinary growth of mining operations in the West. Do not underestimate the resources of the mining and shipping companies in this country. You could hardly do better than position yourself with a forward looking company such as ours."

Patrick balked—the man's tongue was slick as glass, but he still hadn't revealed who he worked for. "What exactly are you proposing?" Patrick's voice was thick and shaky, but his fears were lost in the loud, shuffling crowd around their table.

"Several opportunities have, uh, presented themselves," Hector Winship pursued, which felt to Patrick like a hound on the trail of a hare, or more predatory like an eagle after prey.

"One is to get an interim appointment to a seat on the Territorial Commission."

"That is a public rather than private position."

"Of course, but individuals occupying seats are employed by or affiliated with the private sector. We are willing to pay you well, you understand."

"At any rate, I understand that appointment has already been made."

"Ah, my good man, yes indeed, one has already been made, but we have another seat coming open that has not been publicly announced. You see, our companies would like to align our interests with those of a potential candidate. As I say, we treat our people well."

No sign of interest or affirmation followed Winship's announcement. He upped the ante since Patrick was not an easy conquest.

"Have another drink?" An offer Patrick waved off, having had his limit before he met Winship. "The second opportunity would be a position such as mine--mine, if the truth be known. Family affairs require my presence in the East. We are looking for a replacement, someone whose life may not be as divided as mine." He paused.

"We've found that communication with our Eastern headquarters requires considerable effort that would best be served by someone knowledgeable and free to travel. Of course, when the telegraph and railroad reach Big Butte, these tasks will be greatly simplified."

An electric tension sliced between the two men.

"That is my proposal," Winship concluded, his voice now flat and edgy. He withdrew a folding purse from his inside pocket and tucked it beneath his sleeve out of view, except for that of his prospective hire.

Patrick gulped, feeling he had aged ten years in one day, having had the devil scared out of him earlier by Mac. Tailed, targeted for hire, and propositioned—he figured he had a dollar sign on his forehead and a public enemy if he refused. He sucked in a breath and took the honest route.

"I don't know what to think, sir. This comes as quite a surprise. No doubt I could use the money. Would you mind if I got back to you in a few days, here after supper?"

Winship had already risen and the purse had disappeared inside his coat.

"Whatever you say, Mr. Colter. Certainly, the choice is yours." He was soon lost in the crowd, but easily overheard saying one did not have much of a life if he lived in a rented room above the Tavern.

Patrick's head reeled and his eyes glazed as if he had the biggest hangover he had ever experienced, and it wasn't from the two shots.

Patrick did not want to tell Mac of the shrewd proposition. It might bring more danger to the man he knew and had come to love; nor could he tell Jackson and jeopardize his family in any way. Alone that night he lay awake until early hours sorting out Winship's daring manipulation.

Before daylight, Patrick met the outgoing stagecoach with a letter to be delivered directly to the telegraph office in Virginia City. Instructions required an answer to his telegram within the next several days. Then he ducked back into a nearby cafe and drummed his fingertips on the tabletop for an hour, his eyes searching every movement outside. Wary, he checked to see if he was being followed or would be accosted by anyone connected with the nebulous coalition. He had learned to distrust coalitions by reputation and association since his early days of gold mining in Hot Spring District back in '66, where Crocker Mining Company tried to force miners off their claims. After a couple stacks of pancakes, he went back to his room and lay down on the bed, hands under his head, and stared at the water-stained ceiling.

The notion of being an intermediary interested him. The theory of having feet on the ground well-suited him because he knew the community, but his gut sense rejected any connection with what appeared to be a shifty outfit. Hector Winship is some kind of front man, Patrick told himself. Involved in the murder? I don't know. Maybe that's an unjust suspicion—one can't outright accuse a man.

He sat up and pulled hand-scrawled notes from his pocket, notes for the telegram he had sent to Bosworth & Son Law Offices in Boston. *"In Position to Further Interests of Firm in Territories. Opportunity for Legal Services. Please Respond."*

Arguments went on and off in his head about the merits of his proposal until he put on his cap, old miners boots, and a drab coat and went out, hoping he would pass unrecognized in the crowded streets. The ruse was successful when Charlotte, the woman he had been unofficially courting, did not recognize him in front of Montana Territorial Bank.

Charlotte preferred being called Shelley. She worked half-days as a file clerk in a rear office of Parker's store, and cared for her young sister in the afternoons, freeing her mother to work part-time in the store. Twenty years old to his twenty-six, she had a youthful sense of fun while seeming more mature for her years. Her five-year-old sister's first word had been "Shelley" for Charlotte. The name was as dear to the older sister as was little Neva. Neva's twisted leg left her limited in what she could do.

"I entertain her when I can," Shelley said. "We have to watch her in case she falls." All of this only made Shelley more endearing, Patrick found, and harder to see alone. Walking with her from her front door down to Parker's and back again was about the size of it, but he could bide his time. His prospects had not yet materialized that he could start making overtures.

For the next several days Patrick met the stagecoaches from Virginia City, his hopes for a telegram plummeting. Hell, I could have ridden the stallion over and telegraphed the law offices faster, he fumed, but it didn't seem like a good idea to skip town right now, and he could not force a quick decision from the Boston firm. He changed from miner's clothing in case he needed the disguise and stayed to face Hector Winship at the Tavern. Now it was a matter of how to turn him down in the manner expected of "decent folk like himself."

"I'm expecting an offer from a firm I worked for in Boston," he said truthfully. "I'll have to wait and see how that pans out." It felt good to use the old mining expression because he sure enough did not want to impress Mr. Winship.

"I'll be around if you change your mind." Winship brushed past him to join a group of men inside the front door. It occurred to Patrick when he went out that they could monitor the street from their table.

Four days of waiting seemed interminable, Patrick found, and tightened his belt to take up slack from weight loss. Walking above town in the brush, wrestling with his current problems, and waiting didn't seem much easier than hacking out his livelihood with a pick axe. Like prospecting, it was chancy making decisions without a guaranteed outcome. More enjoyable was meeting Shelley at Parker's and walking her home, a good climb up Main Street to a small frame house in Walkerville. She was fairly tall and of athletic frame with wide shoulders and strong arms that she swung in an unladylike manner. Halfway up, out of sight of most homes, she removed her bonnet to let her heavy blonde hair fly in the wind. Without blushing, she hiked her skirts half up to her knees to "cool off."

"Your legs must be strong as a logger's," Patrick laughed, trying to keep up with her hiking pace and not stare at the exposed limbs.

"Thank you, Mr. Colter. You can be so charming."

"I beg your pardon for my lack of tact, Miss Norton."

"If you lived up where I do, you would have loggers' legs too," she giggled, then chatted about her day and her family. "Miss Owens came into the Mercantile and cornered Mr. Parker about stocking leeches in the apothecary store, and asked if he encouraged such a medieval practice. And yesterday little Neva limped down the street to meet Mother, who stepped out a minute to go to the corner grocer's. A runaway horse and buggy careened down this hill, and nearly ran over both of them. Mother saved Neva but she dropped the grocery basket and a dog grabbed the bacon."

She could enliven my day just by breathing, Patrick sighed, and I'm falling for her whether it's a good idea or not. He reached out and took her unresisting hand, prompting a series of flushes and blushes.

"I haven't had many beaus," she said without looking at him, her hands nervously waggling with the admission. "I'm afraid I'll be an old maid. We depend on each other in our family."

Patrick squeezed her palm and let the matter be. "You brighten my day, Shelley. I am happy to be with you." Inside, his hopes soared. He determined to see if her family would spare her at some point, because he was sure that he couldn't.

The telegram from Bosworth & Son Law Firm, Boston, Massachusetts, USA, shook in his hands. Patrick retreated to his room to open the envelope, double-wrapped to secure it for the rough stagecoach trip from Virginia City. *"Interested. More to Follow. Son will Come Out. R. Bosworth."*

The tide may be turning, Patrick breathed in relief, until a momentary hesitation struck him. I better do some fancy footwork and find where and how the firm could become established in this town. Big Butte is crawling with spiffy, frocked attorneys associated with the larger mining companies. Maybe I was hasty and evaluated the opportunities for my own benefit. I do not want to mislead Mr. Bosworth or Lucas.

But the second-guessing passed. They will find a well-publicized murder, riots in the streets, and tensions growing every day indicate that Big Butte is open for legal business.

14

Dyspepsia…is found in every country, among all classes, and more frequently in persons of middle age. Those who are of sedentary habits…those addicted to the use of liquors, tobacco, etc., are more subject to it than others. Prudence B. Saur, M.D.

"There's no place at the kitchen table to set down a cup of coffee, let alone find a bite to eat." Mac stood, shifting one boot after the other, holding his cup while he talked with Carrie and Julianna who had every baking pan out. Flour covered Carrie's arms up to her elbows, and her hands were sticky with bread dough. She wiped back strands of hair that fell forward from a loose bun on her head, and left a trail of flour on her cheek and forehead. Julianna rustled up a couple potholders and pulled a huge tray of fat pasties from the oven.

"The pasties are for dinner," she warned, seeing Mac eye the lightly browned mounds of pastry-wrapped meat and potatoes.

"Makes a man hungry right now," he called after her when she went out for more firewood, though the kitchen registered about ninety degrees and sweat ran off his brow. The Monarch stove put out the heat, but it couldn't be beat for cooking on the stovetop or in the oven. Mac came up behind Carrie and kissed the back of her neck.

"If you are thinking I'm cooking on the cattle drive, I have news for you," Carrie said. "I can't compete with Harvey's double chocolate cake—but I am going with you."

Mac saw that she meant it and took her in his arms, dough and all. "You'll ride with me, Carrie. Harvey will do the cooking." He kissed her hair, cheeks and nose until she smiled, and Julianna noisily made her way back into the kitchen.

The crisp days of September brought dazzling gold and yellow to aspens and cottonwoods across Deer Lodge Valley to the west. Mac hired cowhands "still wet behind the ears," and drifters from Wyoming and Colorado. He set the men breaking broncs, an effort to train saddle horses for the trail, and at the same time keep the lads from sprees in town. His own crew was restless to start the drive to the Elkhorns. The excessive food preparation had gone on for weeks including canning summer garden vegetables, and making apple and berry preserves, all meant to feed a larger crew as well as supplement winter staples. Now the baking would be part of a daily routine since there was no way to keep bread, pies, cakes and cookies fresh for long.

"Let's step out a bit. I'm cooked in here." Mac poured himself another cup of coffee and filled one for Carrie. Carrie wiped her hands on her apron and flung it aside. She followed Mac out to the corral where Antonio patiently led an uncertain dapple gray filly with a halter and rope.

"She wants to follow. She just has to make up her mind," Mac noted.

Ignoring the distraction of visitors, the baby reached her nose out to Antonio and took several tentative steps. Antonio came back to her side to reassure her that they could go forward safely without a big fuss. Sure enough, within minutes the filly became a believer and followed him around the corral, dancing in small sidesteps, her tiny hooves nimble as a ballerina's, teasing the rope with little stops and starts. Learning quickly, she soon earned her freedom to run about with the other horses.

"What are you thinking of for the Connemara's foal?" Mac asked Carrie.

"What do you mean? I—I –don't have any plans."

"Wal, she is yours. She ought to be trained."

"I, uh, I wasn't sure it would be a good idea to keep her—"

"You don't want to keep this one?"

"I mean, you were so against Love being here—"

"I was angry about that stud. He took over the place with his whinnying for the Molly mule and for the crew to hop to it and fetch him grain. I was afraid he'd take over you, too—you named him Love. I wasn't too far off, was I?"

Carrie half nodded, clearly tired of his ragging about the Connemara, but Mac persisted. "That reckless ride of Roxanna's could have been a tragedy. We didn't need a stud on the place, Carrie. Not one with a deranged mind."

"We don't often see horseflesh like that on the ranch, my apologies to the cowhands' broncs. You like a good horse yourself, Mac."

"Geldings. We have geldings for work, not pleasure."

"Are we going to go through that again?" Carrie's hand flew to her heart. "Mac, you can be hard."

"Hell no. I'm tryin' to make it up to you for saying the stud caused all our problems, that's all."

Shadows ran over Carrie's face before she slipped her arm through Mac's elbow, accepting what amounted to his apology. "He turned out to be a good horse with a good mind. He'll help Jackson and Nettie get started," she said evenly.

"How did you know to give King to the Colters?"

"I asked him."

"You asked him?" Mac drawled, his words dripping disbelief of another one of his wife's illogical notions. "Wal, wal, so ask this one."

Carrie set her cup on a fence post and automatically weighed the communication in the palms of her upturned hands. "She says she wants to be with Antonio!"

Mac gave a quizzical shake of his head and something akin to a 'harrumph.' "Then I guess you better work with the filly," he said to Antonio who couldn't suppress a grin.

"Fine with me, sir. She's goin' good in the halter. She'll soon be drivin' in the long reins. She's a smart one and outdoes these other horses two to one."

"Now don't you forget, she is Carrie's horse," Mac ruffled. "You needn't get too attached. You can get her under saddle when it's time, but never mind what the filly wants. Are you going to spoil her or somethin'?"

"I can't help liking her a lot, sir. Everybody does. She'll be a good mare for you, Mrs. Tarynton."

———————

In Big Butte, H.S. Parker assigned the Mercantile to his son, Sherman, for the day, freeing himself to update the apothecary inventory depleted by an unprecedented demand, due of course, to the residency of two new doctors in town. Procuring new stock according to lists provided by Drs. Gallagher and Owens often took several months, given that most of the herbs and supplements came from San Francisco, New York, or China. The mining camp that had barely cut its baby teeth now postured to become "Butte City," an honor shortly cut to "Butte." Health care, formerly served by the Mountain Woman, Eugenia Finnegan, and the Shoshoni medicine woman, was second in the Territory only to the city of Deer Lodge, which had fortuitously acquired three physicians.

"The practice of medicine is harder to keep abreast of than women's fashions, and that's not stretching the truth," Mr. Parker complained to Sherman. "By the time East Coast trends reach the Territories the fashions are often out-dated. I wonder how they fare in distant California, but I suppose goods round the Horn in about the same length of time they are shipped overland."

The proprietor marked down outdated inventory of men's and women's wear for miners and their wives. On the side, madams purchased high fashion gowns, boas and bustles for their girls in the brothels—no small business in itself.

Mr. Parker always stocked choice selections of yardage and trim for seamstresses who sewed for the banker's wife, Mrs. Baumbier, and Dr. Gallagher's wife. Few other women could afford the finery.

In the apothecary shop, Mr. Parker forced himself to concentrate on the Latin names for supplements that needed to be replenished. Most essential in preparation for winter were those for treating pneumonia: *Aconite, Bryonia* for fever, *Pulsatilla, Phosphorus* and *Mercurius* for cough and difficulty of breathing, *Opium* for delirium, *Camphor* and *Coffea* for cold extremities, *Hyoscyamus* for cough spasms, *Arnica*, administered when there is no delirium, and finally *Veratrum*, when a patient's pulse is weak and strength is ebbing.

Involved in ascertaining the contents of existing bottles and jars and writing his orders, he failed to hear Carrie approach.

"Good day, Mr. Parker," she said, startling him. Carrie wore one of Mac's plaid flannel shirts tucked in at the waist and held in place with a wide leather belt. Her riding skirt stirred dust from the wooden floor when her long strides brought her into the alcove. "It looks as though you're making out a large order."

"The largest one I've ever had to send out. I don't know if it's because of more sickness or because we have more doctors."

"There are more people these days. Surely that accounts for the increase in your business. I came in for Eugenia. She says she has an attack of the fidgets."

"The fidgets? I dare say, she has had the fidgets before. She takes *Compound Spirits of Lavender*, one dram; *Aromatic Spirits of Ammonia*, eleven drams. A teaspoon to be taken at bedtime and repeated in the middle of the night if necessary. But, I must ask, Mrs. Tarynton," he hazarded an opinion, "do you know why she cannot sleep? Surely an active woman of her constitution would sleep soundly unless something is bothering her."

"Thank you for your concern. Eugenia would be most grateful. Confidentially, she is besieged by dire intuitions and fearful images that disrupt her dreams. Surely many wives and mothers have similar fears, but Eugenia has a sensitive foresight. I am afraid these are not idle imaginings, but the clairvoyance of one closely connected to the Indians by her daughter and son-in-law. So, you see, Mr. Parker, there is hardly a resolution within our means. Perhaps the valerian root, would you say?"

"I would prescribe the belladonna."

Carrie recognized the voice behind her as Miss Adelaide Owens.

"It sounds as though her general system may be reacting, possibly with spasms, which would keep her awake. I wonder that she does not see a physician for her maladies." The note of disapproval accompanying Miss Owen's comments immediately put Mr. Parker on guard.

"Certainly she must be attended by a physician," he hastened to say. "It would be in her best interest—"

"But the belladonna would not," Carrie curtly replied.

"May I ask, Mrs. Tarynton, if you are formally trained in prescribing medicines such as these you so freely advocate? I question whether the knowledge and practical application of drugs lies within the province of spiritual healing."

Mr. Parker saw his prosperous business as apothecary rapidly going awry if these two women maligned him as they were each other. He swore under his breath and rattled the blue, hand-labeled bottles in a futile attempt to disrupt the conversation.

"In all due respect, Miss Owens," Carrie said, "it is my belief that worry, anxiety, and sleeplessness as I was discussing with Mr. Parker are symptoms of an emotional nature, more so than physical. Therefore they respond to an empathic or spiritual approach without the necessity of administering powerful drugs, especially an inappropriate use of a nightshade such as belladonna."

Color rose in Miss Owens' neck, tingeing her flared nostrils and wide brow with splotches of red. "Be that as it may. Your friend is quite eccentric and no doubt finds solace in the tonics, according to some of her patients."

Mr. Parker's labored breathing punctuated her insults, akin to an alchemist caught between two incompatible substances. "Ladies, please," he cautioned, putting his finger to his lips.

"And your clients are permitted so little time in your office that they go away not having told their stories," Carrie hissed. "That is what I hear from your patients."

"Stories? Who has time for stories? Must I listen to stories for a dead chicken?" The heels of Miss Owens' hightop shoes slammed into the floor with a final epithet, "Horse Doctor." She whirled to flounce out of the store.

"She's out of my store, likely never to patronize it again," Mr. Parker lamented, peeved with Carrie who remained pondering this latest flap with the woman physician. "She means well. You needn't offend her. 'Tis a hard life doctoring in Big Butte. She frequently complains, and who am I but a sounding board."

"I'm sorry, Mr. Parker. That was thoughtless of me, but, please, Eugenia will be expecting the sleep aid as I promised. I have concerns, as you might, that she overdoses on tonics, but given the seriousness of her anxiety and melancholy, the aid seems appropriate this time. Indeed, I was grateful myself for Dr. Gallagher's prescription when Mac was shot."

The elder Parker mumbled and shook his head, confounded about the ways of women, while he pulled one substance after another off the shelf.

"The stories—I do not understand how listening to patients' stories helps, as you hinted, though Lord knows I do it every day with customers." Clearly puzzled, he poured and measured the prescription at the well-used cabinet where he reigned among supplements, tonics, and tinctures, as well as the mahogany boxes trimmed in brass bearing sets of surgical instruments, all answers and antidotes for discomforts, injuries and diseases. These, along with less-used crocks of leeches, represented the artifacts of modern medicine.

"Ah, telling their stories. Therein lies the healing in many cases, sir," Carrie answered quietly.

Ian Huckins' two-story house of peeled logs chinked in white grout stood out against shadowy, dark green timber that met Summit Valley at Blacktail Creek. A massive stone chimney, visible on one end of the house, indicated a huge fireplace, while ornate lanterns lined a spacious curved driveway that connected the home with a hip-roof barn to its left. White rail fences continued the curving lines well back into the woods. Several fine horses pastured in nearby fields. Missing were any of Huckins' preferred breed, the Connemara.

"Time will tell whether I try that experiment again," he said to his wife. "Importing breeding stock from Ireland proved to be a sizeable undertaking, and a costly one if the animal does not survive or adapt well to new surroundings." He recalled how his imported stallion, Royal Magic O'Shannon, the horse better known as King, had become poisoned by locoweed or a near-fatal cause that led to seizures.

Today, Huckins requested that his buggy and best pacers be brought around for a trip uptown, an hour's drive. In his dress clothes, a top hat and a formal black coat over a vest and white ruffled shirt, he had the appearance of a much younger, dapper gentleman.

"To the Continental Hotel please, Martin." He had scheduled a series of meetings in a private side room at the hotel, hoping the individuals he had invited by hand-delivered letters would be interested enough to attend. With the assassination of the Commissioner still unsolved and the motivation of the killer undetermined, he exercised prudence to maintain a low profile regarding the meetings.

The Continental, located on Park Street opposite Montana Territorial Bank, was Big Butte's premier hotel, restaurant, and gathering place. Three gentlemen representing independent investors were present when Mr. Huckins arrived. Dressed in daily business wear, they shifted uneasily when he appeared in formal attire.

"Gentlemen, Ian Huckins here. It is my pleasure to make your acquaintance." His accent was that of the West Coast Highlands of Ireland. "Misters Nottingham, Hinshaw, Foreman," he nodded in their direction as each responded. "You understand the clandestine nature of my visit since rumors are rife that mining interests may be involved in the murder of the Territorial Commissioner. One cannot be too careful with whom one speaks, aye."

Not expecting any divulgences as to whether or not they had been informed about the plot, Huckins continued. "I have established myself as a good citizen of the Territory for the past few years, and witnessed immigrants such as myself pouring into Big Butte, though most without the resources I am privileged to have. The population growth of the mining community has doubled and tripled, showing no sign of abating. It is this growth with all its attendant pressures and difficulties that brings me here today. I would like to get a sense of which way the wind blows as far as investors are concerned." He felt that was open-ended enough that he could sit back and listen—to spoken and unspoken responses.

Mr. Nottingham leaned his slim, bent frame forward and spoke first. "I've been a miner all my life in Colorado, Nevada, and Wyoming. I can say without a doubt, I believe the Big Butte granite with its mass of embedded igneous rock is rich beyond our present expectations. Investors want to rely on that kind of projection, a sound reason to do business here." He cleared his throat and left further statements to the others.

Mr. Hinshaw and Mr. Foreman appeared reluctant to take a stance with Mr. Huckins, a citizen "with resources" they did not know, but felt obliged to make some contribution. "I don't know what you are looking for exactly," Mr. Hinshaw began. "Perhaps you can be more explicit about your–um, intentions." He was sharp-eyed for such an unassuming gentleman.

"I intend to further my interests in the area," Mr. Huckins said without hesitation. "This could mean a run for mayor, accepting an appointment as a justice, or a run for a seat on the Territorial Commission. My wife wants me out of the house," he added, grinning. The men relaxed as a group when they felt there was no hidden agenda—Huckins might be a straight shooter.

"We ought to have you representing the investors," Hinshaw laughed. "There would be no time to see the missus! But you're going to come up against resistance in any one of those seats. And with the Territory being new and all, it has more than its share of problems."

"Just what are you dealing with as independent investors?" ventured Huckins.

"We have run head-on into several difficulties. Not that the recovery of minerals is out of the ordinary, but there is cutthroat competition among owners of silver mines to consolidate ownership of their companies, and I'm told, to buy out mines for their abundance of copper. Of course, the side effects on local citizens also run these operations into trouble. With vested interests, someone gets stepped on."

Huckins waited, but nothing more was forthcoming from any of the gentlemen. Mr. Foreman had not spoken. The sense that they had buttoned their lips forced him to wonder aloud, "Which means my interests as a citizen are sure to be in conflict with those of mining interests."

"At times, yes," the gentlemen agreed, "depending upon the issue and the side you take. At the very least you could become drawn into a controversy where things might get rough."

"I believe in the good people of Big Butte. There may be enough Irish, sober and willing to vote to get me elected."

The men laughed and their discussion turned to the weather, getting supplies hauled in, and finding time to travel back East to the States or south to Colorado or Nevada. They parted, assuring each other they would keep abreast of developments.

After the meeting, Mr. Huckins remained at the hotel to meet over dinner with Dr. Gallagher and Mayor Baumbier for another exploratory conversation, this one following the stuffed, filleted brown trout with fried potatoes and coleslaw. Relaxed among previous acquaintances, he disclosed a bit of his personal life.

"I came to Big Butte purely as an adventure to start a horse breeding operation in this beautiful land. The Territory with its wide valleys and plentiful water became well known across the Atlantic after the gold rush, and Summit Valley seemed relatively safe from Indian incursions. I find the snowy peaks surpass even our Twelve Bens or Maumtuks ranges of Connemara in western Ireland. Of course, what could compete with living right on the Continental Divide? My wife and I find it quite a spiritual experience. I'm wondering, if I may ask, what attracts professional people like yourselves to Big Butte, and what might stand in the way?"

"I came to practice general medicine, but I did not expect a ready cadre of practitioners of sorts." Dr. Gallagher's tired face matched his rueful remarks. "However, the West has always held a particular fascination for me. It was a matter of convincing my wife that we should take this opportunity while we're young enough to do it, but she is a concert pianist and we've yet to find concerts of any distinction in the Territories."

"You must be something of a humanitarian to practice in so remote a location," Huckins observed.

Mr. Baumbier laughed heartily, knowing that his wife would see only Dr. Gallagher. "We need a humanitarian to head up a hospital to serve Big Butte and outposts of the Territory as soon as possible. Naturally, our own Montana Territorial Bank would willingly finance such an undertaking as a hospital."

"I would agree with you, Mayor. I have seen outbreaks of pneumonia, chicken pox, diphtheria and whooping cough. We have not had any devastating epidemics since I've been here, but they could happen. For now, injuries from fist fights are at the top of common occurrences—along with mining accidents and occasional gunshot wounds."

"Surely building a hospital is a priority whether it comes from the public or private sector," Huckins pursued. "Do you get a sense of any other health-related problems that ought to be taken up by the Territorial government?"

"Interesting queries, Mr. Huckins. I wonder what you're getting at. Could it be whether we consider the toxicity of exposed minerals a public health issue?"

"You have likely noticed the heaps of tailings and the smell of residue, including the odor of sulfur. I am concerned about minerals that might accumulate in harmful concentrations in soil, water or the air. I had an expensive horse—quite a dream of mine—that nearly died. We were never able to determine whether it was from poisonous weeds, an illness related to heavily mineralized water, or to shipping."

"Yes, yes, the horse Mrs. Tarynton treated," Dr. Gallagher said. "We all heard of that incident. She was lucky. Many plants can be hazardous to stock when ingested at certain times of the year. You might ask old-timers who are familiar with this area which plants are poisonous at certain times of the year.

"As far as water quality and exposure to minerals, I am of the opinion that we need to determine these situations before people become sick, and take preventative measures. However, I am inexperienced in that type of analysis, or how a citywide problem might be remedied. I am quite unprepared to intervene, although I treat miners' for work-related exposure as best I can."

He is not sticking his neck out, Huckins concluded. Neither did I, but it's helpful to know his patients are not yet knowingly suffering from these causes.

Late that afternoon Mac Tarynton inquired at the front desk of the Continental Hotel where he could find Mr. Huckins who was expecting him. Pleased that the individuals he invited had all showed up, Ian Huckins further let down his guard and talked person to person with the cattleman.

"You and I have interests in common with your livestock and my horses," Huckins began. "But first let me say that I admire your wife for saving that stallion of mine." His voice dropped, evidence of emotion still related to his prized Connemara. "Now my object is to help preserve the land and the pristine qualities we found when you and I came here. Since I have established myself and my wife here at considerable effort and expense, I would like assurances that those qualities remain."

"Thanks for your appreciation of my wife's horse doctoring. I wonder myself how she does it." Mac's gaze shifted to the view out the window where a heavy layer of soot and smoke lay across the valley.

"About preserving the land, I couldn't agree with you more." He removed his Stetson and hung it on the back of his chair. "But I was more outspoken about keeping our water fit for the stock until the former Commissioner, an acquaintance of mine, was shot dead. What do you think it'll take to make any difference?"

"The assassination was a senseless outrage. Nobody wants to talk outright anymore, and I do not blame you. No one needs to tackle these issues alone. I am of the mind that it will take some of us working together. The mining interests are fully entrenched given their substantial financial backing. It will take a heftier justice system than presently exists in the Territory to ensure that murder is not an option, especially for those inserting themselves in land and water conflicts."

At the thought of the ramifications, Mac sagged in his chair considering the uphill political challenge Huckins suggested.

"It sounds like you might become a part of it. You're a better man than me. My men, the cowhands, are waitin' out front to escort me home. That's how uncomfortable we are these days. I'll do what I can when the time comes—unless I can see another way around these damn problems."

15

I am quite sure that there is nothing more conducive to health than the wearing out of lots of shoe leather, and leather is cheaper than physic.   Prudence B. Saur, M.D.

Sixty million years ago, the Rocky Mountains rose from dramatic shifts of the earth's surface, allowing wildly explosive volcanic pressure to free itself in geysers, hot springs and fissures. Later, ancient seas poured into valleys and plains of the northwestern parts of the country, and eventually subsided, leaving distinctive geological characteristics to the work of sun, wind and rain. Erosion sculpted granite ridges bound by sedimentary layers above limestone caves and contours, all hiding deposits of minerals long sought by man.

These mountains fostered the headwaters of the Columbia River far to the west, its origins in twenty miles of lowly Silver Bow Creek. From Big Butte, it gathered tributaries from the Pintlers and Bitterroots to create a river Lewis and Clark called Clark's River or Clark's Fork. The fork, long claimed by Indians, cut a hundred and twenty miles or more through a valley toward Hell Gate, later named Missoula. The drainage was destined to carry trademark mineral residue in perpetuity from the mines in Big Butte, Montana Territory.

Several times a week Antonio and Pete circled the *TN* ranch to check on livestock and the water, also maintaining a visible presence to forestall Indian raids. Patrick rode King out to meet Antonio on the west side of the ranch in the Deer Lodge Valley.

"I'm killing time walking and riding around waiting to hear about a new job. I have connections in the East. I hope they will finance a law office here."

"I'm killin' time with my own life," Antonio confessed, a disclosure contrary to his reserved nature and undisputed loyalty to his boss. "I keep thinkin' maybe nex' year I get on with it, but *nunca*, the year go by and here I am."

The uncertainty grabbed Patrick's attention. "I felt that way mining one year after the other. I quit for a year and went to Boston, but I'm no better off. A man's got to have a dream."

Antonio chewed off the end of a *cigarillo*, spit it aside, and offered the pack to Patrick.

"I'll try that."

They rode up close to share a light, allowing an opening for Antonio.

"My dream, I not forgot. Not over these many years." He slowly breathed out the smoke, his gaze wandering over the stock that loitered in the bottomlands, and scanned the distant Pintler range. "*Ma familia, los* Delgados, run cattle on *grande rancho* near Black Mountains in Territory of New Mexico. Cattle graze hundreds of acres on desert. Little grass, only sagueros, choizios, yuccas and black bush.

"Indians of South find work with my grandmother an' my mother and father in hacienda and gardens, and on the land with horses. *Hermosos caballos del desierto, paso finos. Sí, hemos tenido grandes caballos.* Fine horses of the desert, *sí*, we had fine horses."

He turned to his audience. Patrick sat rooted in the story, amazed how this quiet cowhand had spontaneously burst into his language, a rapture of sorts, in remembering. To Patrick, it was an entirely new concept that Antonio had a dream or came from a family of Spanish land barons in what had become the

United States. He waited for the story to unfold at its own pace. The two riders had all day.

In the lack of consciousness of time characteristic of a lone range rider, Antonio eventually continued. "Mexico spread all the way north to Utah, but war in '47 and '48 beat it back to 'bout where it is now. I be seven or eight when United States claim our land. Soldiers used *hacienda* my great-grandfather built for bunkhouse. My brothers fight, but my father too old. He sent me and my sisters away till it was over."

Heaviness settled over Patrick, distracting him from how hungry he was.

"No place left for me. I go to Nevada then come north. I find Taryntons. Good people an' treat their men right, so I stay. But I still have a dream."

He hadn't yet said what it was, but Patrick hoped that he would, that he would make the dream real by talking about it— so that he, Patrick, could do the same. He patted his stomach impatiently. Antonio read the sign and they pulled up at a stand of aspens along a creek, tied up their horses, and worked out the kinks after sitting for hours in the saddle. They rustled in saddlebags for the standard lunch put up by both Julianna and the Tavern, slabs of homemade bread filled with thick slices of roast beef. Large, flat boulders provided a place to sit.

"These *grande* cattle ranches will come to end." Antonio motioned towards Deer Lodge Valley. "I'm sorry to say for the Taryntons. Cattle ranchin' takes lots of land. Navajos and Hopis in south had big herds 'a cattle and thousands of sheep. Government took their stock and put people on reservations."

Patrick raised his eyebrows, trying to fathom the displacement of Navajos in the Southwest, news he had heard while he was teaching at the Sterling school years ago.

"You're right. It's a way of life that can't go on with settlers fencing their homesteads." He thought of the Natives' way of life about the same time Antonio did.

226

"We're takin' Indian land right where we sit. No wonder we lose stock overnight. I ride with Duprés on his trap line down here. He says Nez Perce bring several thousand horses west of these mountains for buffalo hunts. Settlers and military, they don't like Indians passing through. You see why it ain't goin' to be open much longer."

"What do you want, Antonio?" Patrick ventured to ask.

"I want my own spread. Only small. Maybe fence it and carve up the country like these damn settlers. But what's a man to do?"

They laughed and stretched. Antonio seemed to enjoy the company and offered another *cigarillo*. The sun winked in and out of the clouds and they mounted to ride on.

"Mostly, I been thinking about a woman." Patrick laughed again, this time feeling like the confessor. He couldn't get Shelley out of his mind for more than a minute, and any talk about a dream had her in it, front and center.

"*Si!* Me, too!" Antonio's mood lifted.

"That tall dark woman at the graveside ceremony?"

"She maybe give me ideas, only I ain't set on anyone in my situation."

"Well, I don't have a nickel to my name, not even a job, but I hope to change that." Patrick told him of Miss Shelley Norton, "the woman I care about. Her father was hired as an expert by the owners of the largest silver mine. In fact, the company paid his way and that of his family, and set them up in a little house in Walkerville right after the discovery of silver."

"Expert in what?" Antonio asked. "I know about silver mining in Nevada."

"Geology and minerals. His daughter claims they did not like his report, so they shorted him on his contract, and refused to pay the family's way back to Nevada. He's been a poor laborer in the mines since."

"I wonder what he report." Antonio was alert once again to the perils of dealing with mining companies.

"Eastern capitalists put up money when gold and silver discoveries were big news, and what Mr. Norton found was copper, zinc, and lead. They were not interested. They feared losing their investments and not cashing in on the silver boom."

"I be damned. We see rusty copper color in streams ever day. It ain't news to anybody who's lookin'. But I guess copper ain't worth much either."

"Not if they're investing in gold and silver." After a moment, Patrick's thoughts exploded. "The injustice makes me angry—the way they treated Mr. Norton. Copper or not, a contract is a contract, and they left him nowhere to turn. That is what I would like to change. If we could start up a law office here, one not bought and paid for by the mining companies, regular citizens like Mr. Norton would have a place to take their cases."

The discussion reinforced Patrick's resolution to pursue his newfound passion. "That reminds me, I best scoot back to meet the stagecoach in case Lucas Bosworth arrived from the Boston law firm. He may be our man if we can persuade him to stay in Big Butte."

———

Carrie's indecision regarding the beautiful, spirited offspring of the stallion she privately called Love kept her at a distance. The foal that stole men's hearts became the filly she would not allow herself to become attached to. During Love's life and death ordeal in his new country, Carrie had touched his spirit, and he hers. She frequently 'talked' with him, even though he belonged to Jackson Colter. They had developed a remarkable distant communication—Carrie never really felt they were parted—in spirit they connected in a far more intimate way.

You are a precious part of my life and I want to be a part of yours, she told him. In this way, she opened to sharing feelings between them that no one else would know or understand, their loneliness at times being the most poignant.

He has been doing well, Carrie assured herself, aware that the stallion's potential would come through those he sired—like Filly. Filly became the foal's name through common usage, and lack of another to take its place. She was not a Princess from royal lineage, nor a Missy, a Beauty, or a Queenie. She was neither black nor gray nor spotted, but a mixture of all three, forming the distinctive dapples of her sire, set off by her black mane and tail inherited from the wild mare. Names did not come readily to suit her appearance or her elfin manner of teasing, prancing and frolicing. One moment she could be forward, led by curiosity and her fascination with anything new, or a she-devil gleefully kicking at other foals. At four months old, she became the sweetest charmer around if it was to her advantage, if she sensed the men might have pockets full of apples. Filly was Filly. If she had been a woman, you'd better watch your wallet, Pete often said.

"We don't keep many mares around here, so your name will not cause a mix-up," Carrie whispered into Filly's soft, rounded ears. She fluffed the fuzzy, baby mane while the stubby tail whipped joyously back and forth.

She put a small halter on Filly and led her out of the corral through the orchard and over the tilled garden spot. Filly danced and spooked and whinnied, turning both ways to examine scary objects such as an upturned bucket, a shadowy stone, or chickens scurrying from beneath her feet. She nosed a pile of leaves to see if they were edible or just crunchy things that rattled and skittered under her hooves. Carrie delighted in the foal's excited discovery of the world outside the corral. They took a serpentine path among the outbuildings and came around to the back porch of the house where Carrie stored a pan of apples. Filly snorted and snatched a bite before becoming distracted by birds in the trees, then nibbled again at the offering.

"You are a spoiled rascal," Carrie said, but she was pleased. The halter training could not have been better. Filly came along without testing the rope.

Back at the corral Filly's companions dashed around as excited as if she had been away for days. Carrie laughed and gave her charge a gentle massage, paying special attention to energy centers that calmed Filly's excitable nature.

"I don't know much about your mother, little one," Carrie told her, wondering if the mare was responsible for Filly's high level of energy. "Surely your good temperament came from your father, Royal Magic O'Shannon."

The Continental Hotel's two-story frame building had weathered considerably in the past few years, until owners and patrons pitched in to give it a coat of white paint. On the other hand, Mr. Baumbier's Montana Territorial Bank across the street maintained the new look of locally made bricks. If the downtown made an attempt to rise from its tent city origins, the wide dirt street jammed with miners, horses, mules and wagons revealed its still rude awakening. Day and night, shouts from rowdy miners filled the dust and smoke laden air. Iron wagon wheels of freighters churned through mud and over stones, adding to the bedlam. Immigrants, often in their colorful national clothing, spoke languages representing several continents and many countries in this remote, mile-high town of Big Butte, Montana Territory, in autumn of 1876. A considerable number of the newcomers were Chinese, while a significant proportion of the female population were known as "women on the line" on Mercury Street.

Patrick steered Lucas Bosworth, Esq. into the Continental's dining room to a private table. The son of Reuben Bosworth, he represented a long line of Boston Bosworths. Lucas was a few years older than Patrick. They found that they shared common interests when Patrick worked for the firm in Boston.

"The frontier appears to be more civilized than I expected," Lucas said. They were seated at a table covered with a burgundy linen cloth and matching napkins; clean, thanks to one of several

Chinese laundries. Sterling silverware reflected light from tapers in a triple candleholder. Patrick felt the crunch to his pocketbook, but this would be his only extravagance; from here on out was the moment of truth. He desperately needed the credibility and security of being employed.

"You'll find a homegrown city, pulled up by its coattails into an increasingly prosperous if not necessarily respectable town," Patrick grinned.

The waiter, a distinctly Cornish immigrant, had taken his guest's top hat, cane and dust coat in the lobby, revealing Lucas's impeccably white, ruffled shirt, typical of attorneys who filed in and out of the Bosworth office in Boston. The sight gave Patrick a pang of jealousy, soon followed by an amusing image. What would Shelley think of me dressed like that! He chuckled aloud and told Lucas what he was thinking, prompting a companionable roar of laughter.

"You better tell me about this Miss Norton," Lucas urged after the waiter took their order for drinks.

"I had better discuss business first, or Shelley or any other woman will be out of the picture. You know, Lucas, I have fooled around a long time doing this and that, but my experience at your firm this past year made me seriously consider working within the justice system, such as it is. If your firm is interested in a western office, I am willing to be the feet on the ground in any way I can to make it a success."

For the next two hours, Lucas proved to be an excellent listener, weary as he was from overland travel. Patrick's stories revealed the limitations of lawful governance of the Territory, despite token appointments and official titles. Nor did ordinary citizens generally have recourse to justice regarding numerous cases of labor disputes, bodily injury in the mines, and conflicts over private property and land use.

"Vigilante myths and legends are not only deeply entrenched, but still alive, arousing fear of action by the self-empowered few after the murder," Patrick added.

"The Judicial system grew out of the Organic Act of 1864, signed by President Abraham Lincoln. The Act separated Montana from Idaho Territory and established boundaries, executive and legislative powers, and district and supreme courts. These courts presently depend upon only three justices who serve as both Territorial and Federal judges. Obviously, there are insufficient numbers of justices to serve this part of the country. As you know, lower courts include justices of the peace and probate courts. I might throw in miner's courts because you will hear of those soon enough!"

"I assume these are all appointed officials, with the exception of the miners."

"Yes. Federal officials, marshals, surveyors and the United States attorney are all appointed. Notably, they are all non-residents of Montana with little experience in Territorial government except for a few Republicans in another county. Our Deer Lodge County is underserved because of too few justices."

"I see where you stand. The Territory is too new and raw to have developed its judicial branch, perhaps the other branches as well."

"Some folks are talking statehood to better govern ourselves. However, most expect to make money and leave. In the meantime, there is enough lawlessness that the daylight assassination of Kent Berrigan, an elected official, has gone unsolved. How does this bare bones summary of the situation here sound to you?"

"I am listening."

"Mr. Berrigan initiated the issue of water contaminated by mining companies. We do not know if his stand was linked to his death, but cattlemen claim streams are carrying mud, silt and minerals that threaten their livelihood. I have examined local waterways and tend to agree about the discoloration. I also hear that residue from smoke spewing from the smelters, is affecting the health of livestock in Deer Lodge Valley. I don't have to tell you that the air in Big Butte isn't what we've come to expect in the Northwest."

"At the very least, these issues must come before Territorial Commissioners who should oversee and advise other arms of government," Lucas said. "Eventually the judicial system must hear the legal cases, foremost that of the assassination if they determine they have a case. However, I understand your frustration. In my experience I've found that not everyone wants to redress grievances, particularly those between vested interests and the law." He tossed up his hands, not an encouraging sign to Patrick Colter.

"I'm not aware of regulations concerning mining tailings or the effects of runoff from them. Frankly, I was as inattentive as anyone to side effects when my brother Jackson and I were placer miners."

"Well, Patrick, you have my attention about the potential for opening a law office here."

Grateful for a foot in the door, Patrick leaned forward to relate what clinched the deal for him personally, and he hoped that it would for the Bosworth firm. "A geologist I know who has a contract dispute is an expert from Nevada, brought in explicitly to find clean veins of gold and silver deposits in mines at that time. He analyzed the mines as well as strata of surrounding creeks and foothills, wherever a cut had been made. He found major copper deposits in astounding quantities. For his efforts he was fired and shorted on his contract."

"Not being a miner or metallurgist or even a particularly adept visionary, I'm not sure I understand the implications." Lucas did not react with the excitement Patrick sensed the discovery warranted.

"There is enough copper under Big Butte to light every house in the country from Boston to Los Angeles, according to Mr. Norton." Patrick spoke with a surety that likely set off lights of its own for Lucas Bosworth. "And enough copper to string that newfangled Bell telephone to Kingdom Come and back." Patrick relaxed heavily in his chair, slipping his shaking hands into his coat pockets.

"Of course, this is highly confidential," he added, wishing to protect Shelley, his inside source who, like Lucas, apparently did not recognize the immensity of the findings that would put Big Butte, Montana Territory, on the map.

"I understand," Lucas said. Patrick knew that professional ethics of the firm would prevent any untoward disclosures.

"I'd like to talk to the banker, Mr. Baumbier, and any members of the Commission who live in town. Did you say Mr. Huckins aspires to, or was appointed to, a seat? I believe we can have a productive day tomorrow and the next, and come up with something that you will be pleased with."

Three days later, Patrick met Shelley at Parker's and kept a straight face when he walked her home. She entertained him with anecdotes from the store.

"One of the brothel women comes in almost daily to buy taffy and strike up a conversation. Miss Meyer is from Germany and quite interesting, though I compromise myself by becoming friends with her. My little sister insists upon writing her alphabet upside down. I wonder if she has eyesight problems as well as a paralyzed left leg. That would be doubly crippling. Oh, a bunch of newsboys tricked Mr. Parker out of candy, saying they would give him free newspapers for life. I think he has heard it all before. He gave them broken peppermint sticks from the bottom of the display case."

"Altogether, that sounds like a day in the life of downtown Big Butte." Patrick squeezed her hand harder than he meant to. A rust-colored calico pinafore gave her a girlish look, but worn over a plain, full-sleeved blouse and long skirt, she appeared a mature young woman. He couldn't take his eyes off her shining face, especially when she told stories, and that was most of the time.

Once they reached Walkerville he motioned toward a stone retaining wall, an inviting and oft used perch for those hiking the strenuous, winding dirt road that served as Main Street. The sun warmed their faces and cast their two shadows as one to the north. Patrick's face glowed, too, not from the midday warmth but from a flame sparked by his dream. He described the new Bosworth law office that would open as soon as he rented an appropriate space. He explained that as representative of the firm, he would be responsible for coordinating affairs of the office throughout the Territory. That meant frequent trips to Virginia City, Deer Lodge, and Helena, as well as between the firm in Boston and its local clients.

"We talked about the telegraph and railroads extending over the Continental Divide in the near future. They will transform the way Big Butte does business." Patrick's voice dropped. "I want to be a part of it," he whispered, fearing saying it aloud would break the spell.

"I have never heard you talk like this. I'm not sure I know who you are or what you're talking about." Shelley shifted her position to sit facing him.

"I believe I have found a sense of purpose—what I want to do is realize my dream."

Miss Charlotte "Shelley" Norton attempted to respond, her eyes reflecting the earnestness in his face. Her fingers smoothed his knuckles that tightly clutched her hand. His dark eyes searched hers, wondering, hoping that she would care about his dream—that she cared about him.

"I want to marry you, Shelley, when I get settled in the new office," he said simply. Her startled look almost made him laugh, but he was so nervous he blurted, "I suppose I need to talk with your father first."

For once Shelley did not say a word, nor did Patrick give her a chance. He loosened the ties of her bonnet and let it fall, and took this woman in his arms at last. She soon wriggled to free herself. For long moments, Shelley sat on the stone retaining wall in Walkerville and stared at her feet. The ruffles of her petticoat flounced up beneath her skirt, exposing her ankles. A fiery flush spread up her neck and into her cheeks. "You want to marry me? Marry *me*?" She shivered and grimaced with the unlikely notion.

"Shelley dearest, are you all right? I didn't mean to frighten you. Tell me what you are thinking," Patrick urged, scared that he might have acted brashly.

"I – I never thought of myself of having much of a future, of belonging to someone else. My family, my sister, you know—"

"You are unable to leave your family? Or not sure about me?" Patrick feared the turn his overture had taken.

"Only that I'm not sure I could belong to someone else. I only belong to Neva and my family—how could I?"

"Whoa, let's think about this. You are such a strong, independent woman, carefree and happy—at least that is the way I see you, what I have come to love about you. Do you think I would want to take all that away from you?" Patrick spoke from his soul, never more earnest in his life.

She blinked unsuccessfully to hold back tears. Patrick took her rough hand in both his large palms, confronting her as gently as he could. "What does love mean to you?"

"That I have to give up something," she replied instantly.

The answer struck Patrick as one he could not argue with— he would not be convincing if he protested for or against.

"Listen to me," he pleaded, kneeling to look into her face. "I am a twin, as I have told you. I have not told you how hard it was to be my own self, independent like you, even as recently as a year and a half ago. Jackson and I were like one. I thought that was what love is. Eventually I fought to break it with every bit of strength and will power I possessed. Love like that is too binding. Does that make sense?"

"Would you break away from me?"

Patrick grasped for straws. Shelley was either having a hard time understanding what he meant, or she had little concept of what he thought married love was." Patrick realized he was sweating. "Whew, I didn't know this would be so hard.

"It is like your parents, your family, you. There is enough love to go around and get through the hard times together. That's how I love you, Shelley."

"Did you and Jackson make up?"

"Of course, better than ever. He knows he can belong to someone else and still be the best brother in the world to me. That's what I want for you and me." He wiped his brow with one hand, still clinging to her with the other.

Shelley wearily rose from the stone wall as if she had aged years, and began the steep uphill climb to her home. Patrick fell into step beside her, a deep uncertainty chilling his ardor, but he dared not leave her in this mood, this distancing he had never before experienced with Shelley. They walked past the usual places they enjoyed: the bakery, the small grocery on the corner with wrinkled apples in tubs out front, the barbershop with a revolving red and white barber sign.

"We do not have to rush this. It will be awhile before I am fully employed," Patrick managed to say, trying to lighten what appeared to be a burden on the woman at his side. "Do you think your father would talk to me about us? Would you even allow me to call on him? You seem awfully upset."

She paused for a long, somber search of his dark features, a face she had only known as boyish and grinning that now showed distress. "I want to know what you mean about love."

"Shelley, my dear, we need to talk more about this, please. And I want to see your father soon."

"And I would like to meet your brother."

This sounded to Patrick like both a challenge and a willingness to consider his proposal.

16

It is really surprising, in this present enlightened age, how much ignorance there still is—they fancy labor to be a disease, instead of being what it really is—a natural process.

Prudence B. Saur, M. D.

Nettie's housecleaning went into high gear the closer she came to term with the baby. Her industrious scrubbing meant that the two-room log cabin had been washed from top to bottom with hot water and fragrant, rose-scented lye soap. Floors shone with a double coat of linseed oil, hand-wiped over the freshly cleaned surface and allowed to dry before furnishings were replaced. Shelves laden with apple pies, fruitcakes wrapped in rum-soaked dishcloths, and layers of molasses and oatmeal cookies separated by wax paper filled Nettie's favorite cabinet, a green tole-painted pie saver. Small holes in the metal doors let in air but kept flies out.

"I haven't done this before. I have to be prepared," she told Jackson, when he cautioned her to leave tasks for the rest of them. "I don't know how long birthing will take, but just in case, I planned plenty to eat. If Miss Owens stays, we will need extra. And I expect Patrick to come right over."

No arguing with a pregnant woman, Jackson found, so he beat the dust out of the braided rug hung on the fence, laid in a supply of firewood, and cleaned the chimneys of two kerosene lamps and three lanterns. A white candle embedded with dried blue violets that Roxanna had made rested on a chipped Blue Willow saucer on the nightstand. A woven-reed laundry basket nearby would be the newborn's first bed. Nettie, Roxanna and Eugenia had stocked the basket with tiny baby garments and fresh flannel receiving blankets.

"You must fetch Carrie when it's time, please Jackson. I do so want her to be here to hold my hand."

"Don't I get to hold your hand?"

"Oh, husbands never do that, but you can hold me until then. I am kind of scared, Jackson. Aren't you?"

"Yeah, me too." He muffled his concern in her hair. "I've been a bachelor too long. Me and Patrick spent too many years minin' when other young lads married and raised families. Now it's my turn, and I'm more scared than I was lightin' gun powder my first time blasting."

"Well, I'm not really frightened." Nettie tossed her loose hair, defying anything in the world to steal her moment. "Miss Owens will be here and Carrie and maybe Eugenia. You and Patrick can stay out with the horses."

Another week passed before labor pains began in earnest. Nettie set out the washtubs and laundered the last bit of clothing she could find, throwing in the towels and dishtowels for good measure. A stiff wind dried them on the clothesline as fast as she hung things. The activity felt good, but pains continued so she walked back and forth to the corrals, finding King and Molly to be compassionate distractions when they ran to the fence each time to greet her.

The twins had built the new pole corral a good distance from the cabin because Molly's loud, hee-hawing brays were annoying. Gray hair sprinkled the mule's nose and flecked the wispy brown hair in her mane. She ambled after the Connemara in an unsteady gait, evidence of aging. King nuzzled her neck, urging her to be playful. Nettie decided to tell Jackson to ride him more often to keep him friendly and outgoing—then a wrenching pain sent fluid dribbling down the inside of her legs.

Holding in her skirt against any more of the flood, Nettie walked back to the house as Jackson rode up with Carrie. "What are you doing out here?" he demanded.

"Walking. You have to ride King more. He's bored."

"Yeah, I'll get to that," he grumped, taking Carrie's reins, freeing her to help Nettie into the cabin. "I'm sorry it took so long. I couldn't find Patrick."

Nettie continued to pace inside and out until an evening chill sent both she and Carrie inside where the fire was roaring, and they soon had to open all the windows. Miss Owens came just after dusk, wearing a prim black hat. With her usual authoritative manner, she set down her bag and hung her coat on a peg, then addressed Carrie.

"I will take over now. You are free to leave." Her voice was flat, as unapproachable as her demeanor.

"Oh, of course she will stay. She must. I invited her," Nettie insisted, alarmed at the unexpected glitch in her otherwise thorough planning. "She will hold my hand."

"And what is it you do? Deliver babies as you go about?" pursued Miss Owens. She jerked a chair from beside the table and sat down as if staking her territory.

"We have been friends for a long time," Carrie said easily. "I am here as a friend only, if you will please permit me. They were married at our ranch and her husband works for my husband."

Jackson stepped in the door in time to hear the altercation. "She'll stay."

Miss Owens received the message in no uncertain terms. Jackson poured himself a cup of coffee and escaped the birthing rooms. He cussed his way out to the corrals and cussed Patrick for not being there when he needed him. "'Tis going to be a long night, I see that already," he muttered.

A few breeders as far away as Philipsburg and Bozeman had approached Jackson about his stallion, and readily agreed to bring their mares the distance for his services. The stud fees paid Miss Owen's mid-wife fee, "but I wonder what kind of woman we've engaged. I want this to be good for Nettie," he said aloud. Only the dapple gray with the long silhouette that shone white in the dark heard his plea. He whinnied, expecting a pan of grain. Grateful for something to do, Jackson fed the horse and paced, always aware of Nettie's pacing back and forth past the low kitchen window. Illuminated by flickering lamps, she appeared as beautiful now as when he met her at the Norwegian bakery. While Molly shoved for her share of the feed, Jackson recalled he had last seen Patrick at Parker's Mercantile. They were both running errands for their employers.

"News for you, brother," Patrick had said. "Huckins took the empty seat on the Territorial Commission. Surprise, yeah? It's an appointment only until elections come around again. I wonder what he's up to."

Jackson had passed the information on to Mac. Huckins had the money to exercise some clout and no mining interests that Jackson knew of, but there was no telling his aim. He had learned as a lad in Hot Spring District to be distrustful where there was money to be made. Generally it would benefit only a few lucky miners and the rest would go to capitalists, likely located in New York or Missouri.

That was a couple weeks ago. Now he rubbed the thick coat of the stallion's broad sides, and scratched his wide forehead and belly. The hardy Connemara breed made a good transplant from the Old Country, one of Huckin's good decisions, he concluded, noting that he had managed to while away another hour. Somehow he would get through the birthing alone.

When he checked in, he found Nettie watching minutes and hours pass on the wind-up kitchen clock. Miss Owens had insisted that Nettie lie down in bed, but Nettie and Carrie opposed the order, saying she should walk as long as she wanted to in keeping with gravity. Jackson stepped outside when a truce of sorts came about between Miss Owens and Carrie.

He realized Miss Adelaide Owens would not be robbed of the opportunity to midwife as she saw fit, and she would expect a prompt cash fee for what she considered superior service. She had restrained herself in the presence of Jackson and the two women, but he heard her swear when rattling and shouting occurred outside. Jonathan Duprés pulled up in a buggy he had borrowed, and called for Mr. Colter, who sprinted from the barn. Carrie opened the door to find Eugenia and Roxanna unloading bundles. With excited squeals and hugs around armloads of gifts, Roxanna and Eugenia bestowed blessings upon Nettie and the soon to be born child.

"You came! You came! I am so glad," Nettie cried in relief. "I am so lost without Jackson. I do believe I need all of you to keep my spirits up."

"Jackson and Jonathan, you can come in for a moment—if you don't mind, Miss Owens." she added, already opening the door and calling the men.

Jackson appeared strained and tired, freckles reddish in his pale face. Nettie put one free arm around him, the other on the bulge in her belly that was now low and prominent. Someone poured coffee for those at the table, and Nettie opened gaily wrapped packages of knitted booties, a tiny crocheted hat, a stack of hand-hemmed cotton diapers, and box after box of sweets. The "ohs" and "ahs" warmed the already over heated kitchen. Nettie paced again, then announced that she was going into the bedroom.

"Please, stay inside by the stove," she urged Jackson. "Thank you all for the party and for keeping Jackson company." Under her breath she added to Carrie, "and I'm thankful they all wouldn't fit in my bedroom."

"Have you seen Patrick?" Jackson asked those left around the table, more to make conversation than really wanting to know. He wasn't here, so why bother to know his whereabouts.

When I seen him in town, he talked of traveling to Helena

and Fort Benton on business," Jonathan said. "One time he was escorting a woman."

This was more than Jackson wanted to know. They were twins, had lived like twins all their lives until the last year or so, but Patrick had not told him about a woman.

"When it's important that he be here, he's off with a woman. He is single. I guess he can be irresponsible," Jackson grumbled, wondering if this father-to-be business would go on all night, and if he would be this miserable the rest of his life.

Eugenia busied herself washing coffee cups and tidying up the kitchen. Roxanna refolded the gifts and smoothed wrapping paper and ribbons to be reused. The men extended their feet towards the stove from habit rather than necessity, and leaned back in their chairs. The long hand on the clock crept slowly around while the other neared eleven o'clock.

"We'll know by midnight." Eugenia sat down with a small piece of fancywork, her deft hands flying with the needle, while Jonathan dug his pocketknife out of its sheath and whittled a stick of wood.

The baby cried at the predicted time. Jackson nearly jumped out of his skin. The cries of his wife had numbed his ears. Now a baby? He bolted upright as they all waited in silence for Miss Owens or Carrie to come out. At last the doctor emerged, nodded at the assembled group, and smiled encouragingly.

"Mrs. Colter will talk to you soon," she said, going about her business of cleaning up and readying mother and newborn for visitors. "The baby is very healthy."

Roxanna clasped her hands and danced for joy.

Jackson smoothed the sweat from his brow over his unruly hair. "If ever there was a good birthing, this has been one," he said, even before meeting his child, which he did not yet know was a girl or boy. He shook hands with Jonathan and gave Eugenia and Roxanna pecks on their cheeks.

"I'm most grateful to the best Irish family I know," he murmured over and over again until Miss Owens allowed him inside

243

the bedroom. It had been transformed with down pillows piled everywhere and a pile of used linens stacked on the floor. Only a tall lavender-scented candle shed light, and Nettie held the baby in its glow.

"Your son," she said. "What will you name him?"

Carrie unwound her fingers from Nettie's free hand and slipped out, patting the new father on the back as she went. Jackson sat with Nettie a long time, neither saying much, feeling the quiet comfort surrounding another little soul whose tiny breaths made his eyes flutter and nose twitch.

"How about Patrick Mac Colter? We can call him Tucker."

Unable to sleep and wearying of stains on the ceiling in his room above the Tavern, Patrick rose early to make arrangements for a buggy. He planned to pick up Shelley at Parker's at noon and drive to the family's modest home in Walkerville to pick up Neva. The plans arose after a dreaded but ultimately satisfying discussion with Mr. John Norton, Shelley's father, at their home the evening before.

Charlotte Reese Norton, the Reese in honor of her father's silver strike on Nevada's Reese River, had not disclosed the nature of Mr. Colter's impending visit. Patrick hoped he would find him in a good mood. Mr. Norton had spoken at length about mining prospects in Montana Territory when they previously met.

"We are sitting right in the middle of widest mass of mineral deposits you could ever imagine," he said, becoming unusually animated, his conviction unquestionable.

"From Last Chance Gulch in Helena damn near to the Idaho border, the granite you see with quartz outcroppings is rich with veins."

"I know the quartz—" Patrick had said.

"You'll find it at the Kelly mine in Silver Star. The formation runs forty miles wide. A fella couldn't miss it with a shotgun. But silver is mixed with other minerals, and copper gets in the way. It costs money to separate it." His tone had registered his disgust with his experience in Big Butte.

Patrick had summoned his courage to face the man he hoped would be his future father-in-law. Mr. Norton, once a proud, vigorous man sought after to find lucrative silver lodes in Big Butte as he had in Nevada, was now stooped, his sad face worn but resolute.

Patrick was not well-acquainted with Winifred, Shelley's mother, who kept Neva out of the room so the girls' father could meet alone with Mr. Colter.

"Neva is so attached to Charlotte that she has been like her own child, which is helpful to my wife but it limits Charlotte's future."

The mention of 'future' prompted Patrick to outline his own prospects, not terribly solid at present, but encouraging. Evidently Mr. Norton did not need much persuasion, or he had confidence in the young man speaking so earnestly before him. Most likely, he wanted Charlotte to freely make her own decision. Patrick never knew exactly which it was, maybe all three.

"Charlotte won't leave that child, but if you can deal with these women, you go right ahead. I'm outnumbered here," Mr. Norton conceded, with resignation and a wry smile.

Patrick chose to overlook the warning in his tone. Mr. Norton was forthright, fair, and above all he wanted what was best for Shelley and Neva. As it turned out that was pretty much the same thing. If Patrick got one, he got the other.

"Damnest deal I ever heard of," Patrick mumbled to himself, half-awake the rest of the night. He was not dissatisfied with it, though he wondered what he had waded into, perhaps blind to the reality of taking on a child, and a crippled one at that. I will become a husband with a step-child and an uncle at the same time.

How am I going to explain this to Jackson? He will hoot, and ask, Have you lost your mind, brother?

A tall black pacer pranced smartly up to the Colter cabin with a buggy about two o'clock the next day. Neva proudly held the reins under Patrick's steady hand as if she had done this all her life. She could not stop smiling her five-year-old smile for a second.

A very surprised new father stepped out the door, quickly revising his prepared give-him-hell speech, Where were you?

"Patrick, I'm glad to see you." Jackson's stored up resentment vanished when his twin handed Shelley down from the buggy, then little Neva. Neva, a sprightly blonde child in a polka dot dress beneath a white pinafore, limped off to see Molly, whose head reached through the pole corral to greet her.

"Please meet Miss Charlotte Norton," Patrick said. "Shelley, this is my brother Jackson." Shelley, now completely silenced, extended a gloved hand.

Jackson grinned, figuring he would get the whole story later or ask a damn lot of questions. He ushered them inside, realizing Patrick was somewhat a stranger in what had been the twin brothers' bachelor cabin. Now Nettie sat by the fire rocking a baby basket that held a newcomer. Patrick gasped.

"Patrick, meet your nephew, Patrick Mac Colter, Tucker for short."

"I wasn't here," Patrick uttered, looking helplessly from one face to another, overwhelmed by a sense of having failed Jackson again—"I missed your wedding, too, a fact I'll never forget or forgive myself."

"Not much you could 'a done, man. It's for the women, but to tell you the truth, I would have liked another shoulder to lean on."

"Yeah, I bet. Damn. Good of you not to kick me out right now," Patrick said, forgetting he wanted to show Shelley how much, as twins, they loved each other.

"May I see the baby please, Nettie?" Shelley whispered, her instincts cautioning her to be quiet in case the baby was asleep.

Nettie was only too happy to pick up the chunky, two-day-old sleeping boy and show him off.

"Oh, he's precious," Shelley said, reaching out her arms. Patrick shifted from one boot to another and finally gave up. I figure she will see us as we really are. This is going to work out even if I did everything wrong.

For a big man, Mac Tarynton had the nightmares of a small boy, his arms thrashing about, legs pummeling the bedcovers. The movement often awakened Carrie, or he cried out until both of them were up and irritable. Sitting on the edge of the four-poster bed with his head in his hands, Mac despaired of ever escaping the dreams that haunted him. Carrie knew that the sense of being targeted by an unknown assailant heightened the scenarios lurking in his mind, but that his anguish also related to times or events that neither Mac nor she could fathom. These rampages in the night were nothing new. In the days after their marriage twelve years ago, Carrie sat and cried with him while he attempted to hide his fears, to be the husband he thought he should be—the man he thought he should be. But now he rejected her comforting, barring her from his private hell.

"I keep hoping these damn demons'll go away. Oughtn't I outgrow them at some point in my life? How but by a miracle does one find peace of mind?" Certainly, Mac had been master of his fate in the ranching business; now that was gone, too, with possible threats against his life. "I'm forty-one years old and sittin' here crying like a baby," he railed, though he held the cries inside.

Carrie knew he held in much more, consciously and unconsciously, and wondered at her inability to sense the source of his difficulties. But none of the torment escaped her; she bore it even more torturously than her husband.

"I feel helpless when I can't help you, Mac." Her face reflected an unbearable sadness when Mac refused to share part of his life with her. "If you tell me about it, maybe the two of us can come up with a way to ease the pain."

"It's not the pain. The goddamn pain is in my leg. This is all in my mind." Mac crushed a pillow between his fists.

In the early days when internal storms banished sleep, Carrie urged him to share the nightmares with her, and they curled up together, as if one might be vulnerable but surely two would be invincible. That comfort also died away over the years.

In turn, Carrie had her own visions and mystical experiences, "dreams" as she described them to Mac, many upsetting to both of them. She struggled to interpret the messages, relying on her intuition to know where her spiritual guides were leading her. Mac could not understand or even tolerate any of this.

"That's conniving with the faeries. Let the netherworld be. We will get there soon enough," he'd say. Tonight his pain intermingled with hers in an endless drama as old as human existence—mythical, preposterous, but real to the dreamers. It meant a sleepless night and tired, nagging moods the next day.

Carrie shivered in the cool air coming through their partially opened window. Mac's tossing and sweating dampened the flannel blankets and soaked her nightgown, as well as his nightshirt. She rose to change the bedding, padding over the wood floor in her bare feet. Enough moonlight filtered into the room that she did not need a lamp, the routine so familiar she could have done it in the dark.

Mac stepped out the back door a short distance to the outhouse, then hurried back, his lean body chilled, to climb into the half-made bed. Carrie slipped into another gown and folded herself around him.

When morning eased over the knobby buttes and sifted into the kitchen windows, even the aromatic black coffee failed to refresh the couple. They did not talk about the nightmares. The small boy, again turned rancher, downed his bacon, eggs, and pancakes while he planned the day's chores. He went out without acknowledging Carrie and Julianna who made breakfast for the crew in the bunkhouse.

Julianna kept a low profile when her employers were stressed or in a mood. "I'll clean up, Mrs. Tarynton, if you want to get on with something else," she offered.

Carrie nodded gratefully and rushed through the rest of the house tidying up and remaking the bed. With a fierce determination to see the Shoshoni medicine woman once and for all about these nightmares, she changed into her riding outfit and put on Mac's old hat.

"I'm going to see Eugenia," she lied to the cook before fleeing out the door to get her horse. Duggan and Pete vied for the privilege of catching and saddling the mount for her. Antonio had gone with Mac and the men to check the lower grazing land and condition of the water.

The distance to Natalya's tipi could easily be walked in an hour, but today Carrie rode fast, skirting the quarry to avoid raising the concern of her friends, the Finnegans. She arrived early and noticed that Natalya had gathered seasonal plants from near and far for her year-long supplies. Nettle stalks for cordage were bundled outside the doorway, and inside the saturated scent of herbs and roots filled the room. Woven reed bags held cattail roots for flour, and peppermint and blue violet leaves for tea were stored in old jars. Nettle leaves for tea were drying on a small rack.

"I had to see you," Carrie murmured. "I have not been able to sleep. Mac thrashes all night and he does not sleep either. It is his dreams, and I don't know where they come from or what they mean."

Natalya's penetrating glance told Carrie she had not forgotten that Carrie had spoken of her husband's anger the last time she was there.

"He was angry when he mistakenly thought I was with child, but this anger is much deeper and he directs it at himself. He has not slept well in all his adult life that I know of. I have failed to help him."

"You are here, Mountain Woman, and your husband is not."

"You are very wise. True, my own visions and dreams are confusing. I came to you for help."

This time Natalya dispensed with the usual tea ritual while Carrie slipped into her accustomed place on the buffalo hide rug. Natalya's husband was not there. The older woman moved slowly, her gray hair thin on top of her head. A heavy, green wool tunic trimmed in rawhide lacing and elk teeth overlay her baggy skirts, worn one over the other. Deer hide moccasins beneath white rabbit fur leggings covered her feet. She seated herself, soon crooning strange words that made no more sense to Carrie than her dreams.

The crooning gradually rose in volume and tempo, sweeping Carrie from the limits of time and space, allowing her to enter upon a faraway plane that made no demands, that refused to listen to her feelings of failure to heal Mac or herself. Fatigue overwhelmed her defenses and she lay against a woven willow backrest. The song became lively, calling her to dance, yet Carrie felt drained and in a deep state between the known world and the world of voices, images, and rainbow colors where fantastical creatures circled. The song merged into sharp, unintelligible words in Shahaptian, but the pleading merged with that of her own heart toward some end, she knew not what.

Natalya's worn hands pulsed with the beat, the pleas punctuated with her fists. After a time, she rose and, breathing deeply, she began a song that washed over Carrie like a gentle breeze. Natalya pointed to the sky, to the fire, to the supplies of herbs and dried foods, and to each of their hearts, thanking and invoking blessings, while her moccasin-clad feet turned about until the thanksgiving came to a quiet end.

Carrie realized that she rediscovered a realm she had half forgotten, where the sense of order in the Universe bid the oceans stay within their coastlines, the moon ruled the heaving tides and women's cycles in a predictable sequence, and life was inexplicably preserved on land between these forces. Her eyes squinted in the light, though her body felt as if it were sound asleep. Surely this order affects all of us—especially women susceptible to lunar changes—at least it inspires confidence in our worthiness to be so honored.

Natalya took up a small, tanned hide drum to maintain the vibrations in the room, a low counterpart to her high-pitched singing voice. The fire burned to embers that snapped and broke, leaving red glowing eyes in the dim light. Carrie's eyelids closed unbidden, while visions of past nights dared cross her mind, indeed, of past years and lives. Haunting symbols appeared— urgent, demanding, belittling her so-called powers, defying her healing.

I am safe here, Carrie told herself, echoing Natalya's unspoken message through the drumming ceremony. The dreams cannot hurt me, and they cannot disturb Mac. With this mostly unconscious realization, she felt compelled to let the dark forces enter, to come into her presence and show themselves. Why go away with the burdens of yesterday if I can let them go today— she purposely stopped bracing against the path ahead, relaxed her tight, jutting jaw, and emptied her chest of life-sustaining air—then she began falling. She tumbled into shadows only to catch herself and stare wildly about. Natalya's crooning became progressively faint, the drumbeat a hollow echo from a distance until Carrie heard neither.

In total silence, time passed uncharted, moments seemed like hours, and sensations became lost in the swirling blackness amid outcries of a creature—no, the wails of a child, the terror of a child encountering real or imagined objects in the dark. Frantically, Carrie reached forth to grasp the child, her arms exploring empty space, her fingers kneading the air, threading past intervening forces, at last touching the soft hair of a baby, a

251

toddler whose flailing arms and hands clung to hers. An image appeared, as clear as if sunlight illuminated the darkness, slanting its rays upon a child—a child with curly brown hair—it was Mac. Sounds issued forth from the back of Carrie's throat like the cry of a wounded animal; her screams rent the air in the tipi and brought her to her feet.

She stumbled, grasping for something to hold on to, to right herself, to find her way out of the depths—she found herself reaching for the light, for a steadying hand—one that felt painfully slow in coming. Carrie existed for a time between her inner and outer worlds, until Natalya appeared at her side. The spell was broken. Carrie's teeth chattered as if all the blood had left her body.

"I am so hungry. I wonder if I've not eaten for days," Carrie said, a startling thought—why that after what I experienced?

But the hunger disconnected her from the stark reality of the dream, the mysterious vision of a child that had trailed her relentlessly until she gave it her full attention. It had revealed itself at last, yet Carrie had to be entirely sure. But for now, she breathed in relief, retrieving a sense of rejoining her body wrapped in her old riding skirt. Hunger, a mundane part of living, told her she had removed herself from the trance, from the mystical.

Natalya lifted the door flap to freshen the room; cold air circulated, clearing away spirits seen and unseen by the people within. Soon a pot of water steamed on the fire and Medicine Woman offered tea smelling of minty wintergreen to Carrie, who cradled a cup in her two hands. Before long she dragged herself out to her horse. Unable to mount without assistance, she found Natalya's husband had appeared in time to help her. She rode home, neither her nor Natalya having spoken a word about the experience.

Sure of what she had seen, but still wanting to deny it, even in her weakened state, Carrie created a story to tell Julianna—

she felt chilled, she had worked too hard lately, she did not feel well—excuses Julianna would correctly guess were related to her mystical experiences. The cook helped Carrie into bed, tending her as she would one of her own children, and wrapped hot rocks in towels for her feet.

17

Night after night these terrors harass him—and his young life becomes miserable, looking forward with dread to the approach of darkness. Prudence B. Saur, M.D.

The men came in later that day after they shot an elk, field dressed it, and packed it back to the ranch. Julianna carved the backstrap for steaks and threw the choice cuts on a hot griddle. She and Carrie grated an oversize fry pan of potatoes for hash browns to feed the crew, as well as those in the house. By the time they carried a hot meal to the bunkhouse, a few snorts from a wrangler's bottle had warmed up the rowdy hunters.

"They're ready for a few nights on the town," Mac said.

Julianna had made thick minestrone soup with extra diced potatoes and macaroni before the men brought in the elk meat. Carrie contented herself with bowl after bowl of easy-to-eat soup to calm her nerves. She slowly savored its herb-laden scent, its chunky consistency that stuck to her stomach and empowered her limbs. The kitchen chatter and clatter continued as usual beyond Carrie's preoccupation with the meal, her visit to Natalya, and her startling experience. Evolving for her was a confidence, a surety that clarified what she already knew—the images that had haunted her for so long were real. The dreams she had fought so strenuously were messages alerting her rather than working against her. The vision of a child she had related to Eugenia and

254

Roxanna, that even she did not want to recognize—indeed she had avoided with every ounce of will she could summon, had appeared again when she allowed it.

I cannot put this off forever, Carrie thought, when the cook went home for the night. I must talk with Mac—he will be angry, but maybe one of us can sleep afterward—so be it.

Mac was dozing in his chair by the fireplace when she moved a stool next to him. Breathing deeply, she stroked his arm that rested across his chest, absorbing the strength of the long straight bone and hard muscles for what she had to do, for what she must say to clear herself of the welcome yet unwelcome vision. And if it helped Mac, who knew? She would find out.

"Mac, did you ever fall? Did you have a bad fall when you were a small child?" She spoke casually, knowing he would be even angrier if she approached the nightmares directly.

"Hmm, I must have, lots of times. Every child does. Why?" His eyes were hollow, face haggard with a scraggly, rust-colored beard.

"I saw you falling—in a vision—," Carrie whispered, summoning all her courage to utter the words, hoping dear God, his fall occurred in the past and was not a symbolic premonition of a future tragedy.

"You know I don't like the visions, Carrie. Why do you do this to me?" Mac flared, his half-closed eyes watching sparks fly from burning embers in the fireplace. After a moment, he added, "I did fall, yes. My folks said I fell into a well."

The two figures in the room stiffened; Carrie's hand ceased stroking his arm. Silence melded around them, stopped up their lips, brought a chill despite the fire, and left each listening to their own quickened heartbeats.

"It was a dry, half-filled well by the old horse barn. They covered it over after that. I don't remember—I was too young. They didn't find me for quite awhile."

Fully awake now, Mac stared hard at Carrie, his eyes searching, uncertain, obviously doubting his wife's visions that he had no use for. A scowl creased the tanned lines of his brow. He swore and turned away.

Carrie drew short breaths that she tried to hide, not wanting to disturb Mac's recall, unwilling to let her feelings infringe on those he struggled to deny— had denied, possibly all of his life.

Mac swore again. "Hell, Carrie, I'm tired. Do we have to keep coming back to these foolish notions of yours? You hound me with superstitions and faerie stories that embarrass and harass a man to death." His toes wriggled in his socks.

In a hyper-alert state, Carrie missed nothing. She could not help smiling to herself. The toes wriggling like a small child's helped confirm her vision infinitely more than Mac's admission, more than her own suspicions. Images circled and began to clear in her mind—the vision of a child she had shared with Eugenia and Roxanna was not her lost child Christina, nor a surprise new baby coming in their middle years, though her sides heaved as if she were indeed giving birth to a baby.

Despite his anger, Mac evidently stayed with his reflections, scowling even more, reaching for cigarette makings, but dropping the Durham and papers back on the end table.

"It was a childish thing really. It meant nothing."

"Or did it?" Carrie asked, wondering that he hadn't noticed a connection while he thrashed for years, falling, desperate to be heard. Yet she, too, had closed off earlier visions, not daring to see him alone in the bottom of a dark well, too afraid to hear him screaming in terror, yet the world beyond consciousness, the world of guides and messages and intuitions had given her no peace. They had nagged and begged—"pay attention Carrie Tarnyton; your husband is suffering. You must help him."

"This occurred in your distant past. You can tell me about it, Mac."

Flames burst from pitch on a log in the fire, creating dancing shadows on the walls of the rustic ranch house. Likewise, Mac's eyes became alive with a flicker of recognition of a time long ago, of a time beyond his memory as a toddler. In the void that now opened between Carrie and Mac, she felt him traveling back in time, struggling with an experience overlain with forty-plus years of night terrors that he had attempted to pack away, never to bother him again, and he had tried to do it alone. Again and again, his manhood demanded he conquer the invading demons. The toddler, bent on an equally threatening journey, begged only survival.

"The story became only a concept, a story that never felt like my own, a dim anecdote related at family events. Grandmother would "tsk-tsk," and Grandfather would cuss," Mac began. "The well was filled in, and the new barn was built over it when water was piped to a horse tank from the spring. I don't remember falling. I don't want to remember now." He edged his chair away from Carrie and reached for but again rejected the cigarette makings.

Buoyed by the clearing images, Carrie felt her "labor pains" draining away, replaced by a profound sense of relief that worked its way into her being, slowed her breathing and eased the tension in her limbs, a tension that also diminished in the ranch house. A trace of the old fatigue passed over Mac's face, and a hint of denial crept onto his lips that tried but failed to formulate objections, until at last a long sigh signaled a token of acknowledgment. His head fell forward on his chest, an attitude of despair Carrie had seen so frequently.

He sat lost in his own ruminations for so long Carrie feared he would go to sleep and slide back into the night terrors, letting the denial assume its former place and power, and losing the connections to his disturbed sleep that they had both just experienced.

"Mac?"

As if she had nudged him, he turned to face Carrie with an entirely new openness, erasing cares she had grown accustomed to seeing. She moved into the circle of his frank, ungrudging acceptance of her, her vision of him, and her presence at his side. Rust-colored curls clung to his brow in heat thrown from the fireplace. He wrapped a long arm around her, their separate worlds colliding, unraveling, and reforming until some sense could be made of the revelation.

In early spring, 1877, a company of Cavalry troops, recognizable by their flat-brimmed campaign hats, brass-buttoned blue coats, and knee-high black boots, traveled towards the Nez Perce conflict in Oregon.

Observations of the movement of troops in Idaho Territory spread on the grapevine and in news out of Washington, D.C. Reinforcements under the command of General Oliver Howard were soon in the Wallowa area of Oregon. Tensions had been escalating, according to other trappers who fled the Clearwater before war broke out. As the military presence increased in Montana Territory, Deer Lodge's *The New North-West*, carried regular front page reports.

"Trappers say they're on the move," Jonathan Duprés told the Finnegans. "I doubt we'll see 'em in Big Butte. If they're from Utah or Wyoming, they'll go straight to Idaho and Oregon through Fort Hall or South Pass. If they come across Montana Territory from Dakota Territory, they'll likely cross the Bitterroot Valley."

"I'm afraid for yer friends, our friends." Roxanna peeped out the cabin window. "It sends chills through my heart. Surely there must be time to avert such a calamity."

"'Tis not for us to solve, my sweet."

"A truce could be made between people of good faith," she urged, but the foreboding news would not abate, keeping her awake night after night. Roxanna reverted to her earlier bouts of anxiety, and Jonathan's efforts to dissuade or console his wife went unheeded.

"What do ye expect, Mum?" she queried repeatedly of her mother. "What do ye feel—what do ye know? Surely the situation for those lovely people cannot be so dire. Why these cavalry reinforcements from afar? Tell me it is not true, Mum."

Eugenia resisted divulging her fears lest her already anxious daughter be taken by hysterics. Roxanna's husband was likewise reticent to voice predictions regarding what appeared to be imminent conflict.

"There be many reasonable-minded chiefs to deal with the matter. Ye let them handle their affairs," he admonished her. "We did all we could, thanks be to God."

Eugenia's rocker spoke more forcefully than words, creaking loudly in answer to the pace she put it through while she prayed, her rosary beads sharply clacking her concern, sometimes for hours each day. Roxanna wandered off to demand that Jonathan tell her of any bad news he may have heard.

"Tell me for my nerves. I cannot bear not knowing. I was a part of the messenger party," she reminded him.

"If ye must know, old Chief Toohoolhoolzote was taken prisoner. Whites charged him with being a Dreamer, one of the Nez Perce medicine men who seek guidance from dreams. The old chief insisted the land must not be divided. General Howard feared young warriors would get fired up, go on a rampage, and be ready for war. Other chiefs—Looking Glass, Joseph's brother Ollokot, and White Bird did not want war.

"What happened to the old chief, the Dreamer?"

"He was let go. There ye have it. That's all I know except the military moved in. It don't look good for my friends." Duprés put on his fur hat and wearily picked up half a dozen muskrat traps from pegs on the cabin wall outside. "I'll check my traps. Maybe somebody'll come by and tell me more."

Roxanna's newly recognized intuition refused to be soothed. Unable to contain her rising apprehension, she hiked up the mountain to see Carrie. Without formalities or sitting down for a cup of coffee, Roxanna released pent-up fears and the scant bit of news she had heard to Carrie's willing ears.

"What does your husband think? Does he expect the worst as you do?"

"Much worse, I am sure. So does Mum, because neither of them will tell me." Roxanna began to sob. "I find the tension, the fear of war, is truly unbearable."

Carrie rummaged through the cupboard for valerian root to calm her friend with a cup of tea.

"I'll get Duggan to come around with the buggy and we will think of something." She hurried over to the bunkhouse.

Duggan uttered a few words she didn't care to hear, and spit a stream of tobacco juice into a foul-smelling bucket. Carrie slammed the door and decided she had better drive the one-horse buggy. Both she and the old codger had heard about her exploits from Mac, who accused them of "galloping around town in places they shouldn't be." He was especially riled that they had done it while he was away.

Duggan can be a pill and Roxanna's energy sets one on edge, Carrie admitted, pausing on the back porch to draw a breath and think for a moment. The first buds climbed up lilac stems, sweet resinous sap had begun to run in the apple trees, and upturned soil in the garden smelled clean, earthy and promising. Carrie breathed in the fragrance of nature's awakening, a momentary hiatus, though she, too, felt a sense of urgency. No good would come of bloodshed for either side. As a woman, it felt like an all too familiar failure to accommodate, one in which women were powerless to intervene yet relied upon later to pick up the pieces.

Roxanna had succumbed to one of Julianna's cinnamon rolls while she waited. Carrie took the opportunity to offer a spur of the moment suggestion.

"Alone, I do not know how we can console ourselves or affect the outcome of these dreadful conflicts, but we might feel better if we gathered together—"

"Oh, yes, let's—" Roxanna enthused.

"I feel helpless myself," Carrie went on, "but I know women of great strength we can turn to."

The two women grasped for a shred of hopefulness to replace their sense of doom, for a sense of shared responsibility rather than individual angst. Both felt the enormity of what was at stake. In silence, they finished their tea and pulled on cloaks for a buggy ride. Duggan glared when Carrie took the reins and breezed past him out of the driveway.

"I bet he's wondering how much trouble I'll get into this time," she laughed, belying any notion of helplessness.

Instead of backtracking to Roxanna's home near the quarry, Carrie turned onto a nearly imperceptible trail leading to the Shoshoni camp by a spring-fed stream that trickled from a hidden draw. Since they did not own a wagon, the road had long ago overgrown. Despite the tribes' seasonal travels, it was uncertain when they had last traveled in anyone's buggy. Carrie asked Roxanna to hold the reins while she rousted the medicine woman with a singular request.

The elder shuffled pots over the fire and stiffly straightened, her eyes deep and sad. Taken aback, Carrie lingered a moment. She must be aware of the battles—victories and defeats—I wonder how much she knows and how much she prophesied. Why am I doing this to her?

"Would you go with us to a Chinese women's circle? It is very important and I will tell you about it on the way." Carrie bit her tongue, but without hesitation, Natalya selected a talisman pouch from among her jumbled belongings and hung it around her neck. With that she walked out the door.

Natalya nodded to Roxanna in the buggy. They had encountered each other many times on trails near the quarry, but they were not well acquainted. Natalya seldom went into town, and then it was primarily to Parker's Apothecary for items not found by foraging, such as ginseng and aloe vera. Carrie angled the buggy uphill while Natalya and Roxanna braced themselves and hung on for a rough, precarious ride. The outfit lurched over low bushes and rocks.

Eugenia heard them coming and met them in front of the cabin. Roxanna jumped down to help her mother gather her things.

"We're going to visit a Chinese women's circle that Carrie knows about. Ye must go, Mum. Here, I have yer coat."

Swept up in the flurry, Eugenia only took time to snatch her rosary, while Roxanna selected the packet of gifts she had received from the Nez Perce women. Any action was preferable to the women than solitary worry. Eugenia's eager face, framed in soft white hair, appeared years younger with the invitation to join Carrie and Roxanna, if not entirely at ease with the medicine woman.

"I know a few Chinese families from crossing paths on my rounds. I especially enjoy their children who quickly learn to speak English and sound just like me," she laughed.

Natalya shifted to the side of the buggy seat to make room for Eugenia, who had also grown quite wide. Roxanna perched on the driver's seat with Carrie, and the fast pacing horse quickly brought them into town. On the way, Carrie encouraged Roxanna to tell of her experiences with the Nez Perce and all that her husband had heard about recent threats. The situation was well known to Natalya, who had her own sources of information and a long-established relationship with the likewise nomadic tribe.

"Many of us are alarmed. It cannot hurt for us women to join together," Carrie ventured, intimidated by the silence of her mentor.

Natalya nodded in assent. "We have pow wows. Our way to talk to Spirits."

"Oh, thank you, my friend. I was unsure how you might feel."

Carrie drove down back streets past numerous Chinese laundries and merchant stalls until she reached the Natural Herb and Apothecary Store. She halted the pacer and went in alone to find Li An, suddenly realizing this visit might be hasty and inconvenient for her. Certainly it was unannounced. A smiling

Li An quickly came in at the sound of Carrie's voice and greeted her like a family member.

"I remember." She bowed and dipped with pleasure, her voice soft and grandmotherly. "You come back and brought friends?" Li An indicated the women in the buggy.

"I want you to meet my good friends, and them to meet you. This is so sudden—without notice. I am sorry." Carrie paused, questioning her own boldness, but resumed, knowing their healing was a bridge between isolated ethnic communities. "We have come because of our concern about our friends, the Nez Perce Indians, who are threatened with death or exile from their homeland in Oregon. Our sorrow is great—their situation is desperate. We do not know what to do but turn to other women."

Li An stepped outside in a light cotton tunic and baggy pants, her feet ill-clad for the cool weather, and motioned a welcome to the women in the buggy, who had been marveling at the flourish of Chinese characters on the signs and displays. They stepped down and Carrie parked the horse out of the way. She returned to find Eugenia and Roxanna inside the store admiring the bundles of leeks, red and green chard, and unknown root vegetables that the frugal gardeners had either saved over winter or grown in sheltered nooks this early in the spring.

Roxanna exclaimed over colorful ginger sweets while Natalya quietly made her way unperturbed around the baskets of shriveled sea urchins or claws of wild beasts. Li An tried to answer Roxanna's endless questions about the unusual imports that "surely came all the way across the ocean." Several men with long black queues and round faces nodded briefly, and shied away from the determined women.

Carrie's momentary concern that she should not have come dissipated in Li An's warm welcome. She remembered she had found solace in her earlier profound experience here at a time of deep personal pain. With that comfort, she felt encouraged to pursue this gathering to its end, what end she dared not guess, resting in her belief in the power and intentions of women, and their sister and brotherhood with those in distant lands.

"I have confidence that whatever happens will be all right," Carrie whispered to Natalya, who made no objection.

The small courtyard was the same this time except it was earlier in spring before plants were in bloom. A young woman in a slim blue tunic hastened to find chairs for the visitors, bringing several down from upstairs. With gracious deference, Li An seated Natalya first in a sheltered spot along the high stone wall. Eugenia and Roxanna seated themselves to her left and Carrie to her right.

"Would it be an imposition if you asked other women to come?" Carrie lowered her voice in recognition of the sacredness of the courtyard. "Like before?"

Li An placed her palms together, bowed slightly to Carrie and her friends, and slipped out. As they waited for her return, the store and town of Big Butte seemed to recede further and further away from the courtyard. The young woman silently entered with small, bowl-like cups of jasmine tea, a ritual that became the new reality, one from which they all emerged in a world of their own. The woman was very shy and did not meet their gaze while she set up stools and boxes to seat other Chinese women, who had been called but had not yet arrived. She stepped lightly to the other side of the courtyard and lifted an upside down wash tub, revealing an altar with a collection of carved figures among articles from nature, twigs, shells, and dried flowers. Natalya squinted to examine the objects.

At last the young woman squatted near the low doorway, obviously waiting for Li An and the others. Long moments passed in which the women drifted into another state, not unlike the one Carrie had experienced by the fire at Natalya's, removing them from everyday life, inviting a higher consciousness to creep into the empty spaces and toy around the edges with pastel hues and notes of a sweet, unfamiliar music. Carrie fully embraced the respite from worry, letting herself sink deeper in order to, paradoxically, rise more freely into higher realms, to soar where, truthfully, she had never gone before.

It seemed almost an afterthought when a few women, mostly elders, filed in behind Li An to take seats in the secluded space along the stone wall. The young woman gently closed the door to the courtyard with a slight click, the only sound within the gathering. Outside, robin chirps mingled with children's high-pitched shouts, the sounds keeping the women anchored in time and space. No one spoke. Several of the women sat lotus style on mats of woven reeds. One of the grandmothers, a thin, drawn woman insufficiently dressed for the chilliness, breathed with a rattle when she exhaled, a worrisome symptom, Carrie thought, but no one seemed to pay attention.

Eventually a low chant began around the circle. Carrie heard Natalya's voice among the others, though the languages, if language were involved, blended in one song, one exultation from many hearts. Roxanna remained notably still. The muffled clicking of beads meant Eugenia prayed her own way, whether to ward off unknown foreign spirits or to join the cascading sound, Carrie did not know.

Carrie felt herself become immersed in the meditation. When she startled and opened her eyes, the talismans Natalya brought were on the ground in front of the medicine woman, and Roxanna had displayed small figures, gifts from the Nez Perce.

As the song gathered strength, pleas emerged from surrounding throats. Natalya kept the rhythm with two shells gently held in one outstretched palm like castanets. Her foot moved to the beat without leaving the earth. An eagle feather floated from her pouch, catching a faint breeze before it settled in their midst.

Tears sprang from behind Carrie's lashes in response to the energy of the group, its peace and beauty in contrast to the threats of war elsewhere. Teardrops fell into her hands, her sobs welling as the song grew more resolute and louder, until it ended with praising and thanksgiving. The last note lilted and faded to drift away and hide among the stones of the wall. Some time elapsed before they all brought their awareness back into the circle.

The elderly grandmother with sparkling eyes pointed to the small figure in front of Roxanna. "Baby?" she asked.

"Oh, so it 'tis!" Roxanna whispered. "I did not know it was a baby." The carved Nez Perce papoose board with painted lacing had appeared like a strange symbol to her.

"You have baby," spoke the elder with a wide toothless smile. Roxanna looked around the circle dumbfounded, only to determine that this whole event was as unimaginable as that of having a baby.

"I—I—sat in a circle with the Nez Perce women," she managed to say. "It was kind of like this. They presented these gifts to me." She ducked her head to gather a few items and hand them to the old woman.

"Su Lin will bring tea and a bite to eat," Li An offered.

Since the young woman was on her way, the visitors did not decline. Li An poured for the guests and a tray went around with tea and delicate sweet rice cakes. The conversation hinged upon Li An interpreting, though Carrie suspected the women knew some English, especially since the grandmother spoke a few words.

At last the cups were gathered on the tray, and among many nods and bows, Carrie and her friends boarded the buggy to go home. Natalya left the eagle feather where it had come to rest in the center of the courtyard.

When Carrie had driven the buggy out of hearing range of the Natural Herb and Apothecary store, Roxanna could contain her herself no longer. "Jesus, Mary and Joseph, I'm going to have a baby!"

Eugenia's shoulders relaxed and laugh lines crinkled around her weary blue eyes as she relinquished the burdens of the outer world for contemplation of that yet to come—things even she had not foreseen.

18

A good wife is heaven's last, best gift to man.　　Jeremy Taylor

The feisty spring weather of 1877 blustered and warmed, then changed its mind and whipped the country with ice-driven rainstorms, thunder and lightning as if competing with the wicked winter just past. Range cows and ranch horses pitted their hindquarters against blasts of east winds until startling sunny days found their way over the Continental Divide.

"Red skies at night, sailors' delight. Red sky in the morning, sailors take warning," Big Butte's newcomers recited, but old-timers admonished, "wind from the east is ner'er good for man nor beast."

Reckless and regardless of Big Butte's hard-working population, Montana Territory inched toward historic events that would forever define it. An empire of Copper Kings spiraled into being after Edison's invention of electricity with its voracious demand for copper. The Nez Perce War stalked southwest Montana Territory day and night, until late in the year remnants of the tribe suffered a tragic defeat at the Battle of Bear Paw, decisively ending their flight. In the East and spreading to the Territories, impassioned speeches by Elizabeth Cady Stanton and Susan B. Anthony inspired a women's movement toward equal rights, including their thus far rejected women's right to vote. In addition, efforts to gain statehood for Montana gained momentum but would languish for another twelve years.

Of these events, that most immediate to Carrie, Roxanna and Jonathan Duprés was the flight of the Nez Perce. The tribe under Chief Joseph and other chiefs had slipped away from their home in Wallowa Valley, bypassing the settlement of Lewiston on the Clearwater, the river they had forever known as their own.

The Nez Perce had defeated the U.S. cavalry the previous fall at White Bird Canyon in Idaho Territory, embittering Washington and arousing a call for reinforcements. The victory proved the tribe's determination to remain a Non-Treaty Nation. *The New North-West* continued to inform Montana Territory's citizens of the raging, ongoing conflict. As predicted, settlers in the Bitterroot Valley had armed themselves against a feared invasion by Chief Joseph and his warriors. The fleeing tribe that called themselves the *Nimíi puu* were especially imperiled because of the massacre of U. S. troops led by General George Custer by a coalition of tribes a year earlier at the Battle of the Little Big Horn near the Yellowstone River. Both defeats of United States troops had fueled the government's goal, right or wrong, to eliminate the Indian threat in the West.

However, Jonathan Duprés understood Joseph's intention to remove his tribe to what the chief had previously experienced as relative safety over the Lolo Mountains, country familiar to them and to him from their past trips to hunt buffalo along Clark's Fork and the Missouri River. Not only had Eugenia and Roxanna's fears for the tribe heightened, but Duprés felt the impending clashes with a particular, penetrating sense of helplessness.

Joseph's plan was daunting even at an optimal time of year, but early spring was still winter in high country with deep snow and freezing temperatures. Yet Joseph and the other chiefs eluded pursuers and led their tribes of up to 800 men, women and children, their supplies, and two thousand head of horses over the Lolo Pass to the east side of the Bitterroot Mountains. At the same time, troops of the United States cavalry advanced from all sides into Montana Territory in anticipation of the fateful September Battle of the Big Hole.

––––––––––––

A hundred miles away as a crow flies events also escalated at the Tarynton ranch, though it enjoyed a hidden niche on the west side of mountains known for their knobby buttes. Tumbleweeds gathered ahead of west winds to bound across open range and fling themselves ingloriously upon settlers' fences. Dried clumps of baby's breath likewise took flight, congregating in windrows along creeks and trails. Juniper-filled gulches sheltered nesting western bluebirds and their kindred songbird, the red-breasted robin. Yet in this seasonal transition, the Tarynton's *TN* ranch took on a somber appearance, too early for the cattle drive to the Elkhorns, and too late to dally over winter.

"Antonio will be leaving us to get his own place," Mac mentioned casually, while he and Carrie sat before the fire late one evening towards the end of May. Usually they discussed plans for moving the herd this time of year, but Mac had been strangely silent about it, and Carrie knew that Antonio had been away.

They had not talked as a couple very often since Carrie had revealed her vision and Mac admitted having fallen into a dry well when he was a toddler. They both slept better; that marked a milestone, however, their lack of personal exchanges hardly registered with her since she was preoccupied by news of the Nez Perce, of whom Roxanna and Jonathan Duprés kept her informed.

"I asked Antonio to get a sense of the land lying along the Ruby and Beaverhead rivers in Madison County, and find out how much of it is already settled. He and Pete spent two weeks over there recently since it's been slack here. According to them, from Beaverhead Rock to the Headwaters of the Missouri there's a lot of open range, there isn't as much snow as we get here, and the grass will be good once it warms up."

Mac rotated his feet, clad in wool socks, on the round wooden footstool his father had given him, his chin sunk part way down on his chest. The old horsehair settee sagged with his weight, and was anything other than comfortable given his lanky size. Carrie sat next to him absently rubbing her toes, her knees pulled up under her long, full skirt, while Mac spoke. Her day had been typical of her routine—assist Julianna cooking meals, ride to town to visit a few favorite patients, talk with Love via distant communication, and spend a few moments stroking and murmuring to Filly, the foal she had vowed to remain unattached to that had won her heart.

"We'll move the cow operation over there as soon as we can. I'm sorry, Carrie, but we'll be leaving the home place here when we get a ranch set up over there."

"Antonio is leaving for his own place? *And we're moving the ranch—away from Big Butte?*" Carrie arched her back as if struck in reaction to the coming upheaval—his flat statement terminated her life here without so much as a preliminary glimpse of what it would be like somewhere else. Without preamble or warning, she had to put flying pieces of a puzzle together out of Mac's foregone plans.

Nodding assent, yet choking down "Oh no, I couldn't possibly do that," she felt herself pulling inward, snatching at impressions, reflecting on scattered memories, sinking into inner and outer realities that caught her off guard, her round brown eyes awakening to find the parameters of her life unhinged, her husband talking like a stranger— no, not a stranger, like the rancher he was—for him a typical day of making decisions, delegating chores, and informing everyone else of plans they would carry out.

But I am his wife, she blinked. How did this happen? He could have told me. We usually discuss upcoming plans over coffee and Julianna's cinnamon rolls.

She shifted her body and stretched her legs, gathering her wildly leaping thoughts. She had been east of the Tobacco Roots once, when she and Mac had attended the graveside service for Kent Berrigan on South Willow Creek near the Madison River. The Jefferson and Beaverhead valleys west of the Tobacco Roots were hearsay as far as she was concerned.

Together, she and Mac had built this home place over the last twelve years. Piece by piece they had constructed the rambling house built to accommodate children, a dream that had not come true, yet the home's hospitality had sheltered and fed many friends and acquaintances over the years, Kent Berrigan and Marion Patton being the two most memorable. The wide-winged barn with a loft, tack and harness room, and indoor storage for the buggy was barely ten years old. Every post and pole of numerous corrals had been hand-hewn. They had lived as newlyweds in the original cabin on Mac's father's old homestead. Later the cabin served as a bunkhouse, and they had built the ranch into a fine spread. The couple had not been idle over the years. The herd of cattle had doubled and tripled from the ranch's earliest days. Saddle and harness horses numbered in the dozens. In a nearby orchard pom-poms of apple blossoms emerged ahead of a hearty growth of leaf buds. A fenced garden tendered minute seeds for early crops of lettuce, onions, and peas she had recently planted with high hopes.

"I've been too busy to sense such a drastic change," Carrie stammered. "Antonio has been with us most of these years. The notion of him moving away is too shocking to contemplate." She found herself unable to acknowledge the imminent need to pull up deep-seated roots. Discussing Antonio's unexpected departure felt like a welcome diversion from leaving her beautiful home, like forcing the move to a distant possibility. The basket of sage, sprigs of lavender and juniper that graced the long dining table now represented her fragile hold on what she had.

Mac continued to narrate recent history of the upheaval unfolding before her. "He saved his money, planning to buy back his folks' place in New Mexico that had been confiscated by the government, but there's trouble there, too. Since he has lived here so long enjoying the streams and rivers he wanted to stay—they don't have a lot of water in the Southwest. I offered to sell him two hundred head of my heifers so he can get a good start. We'll cut back, Carrie. We don't need to be as big as we are now. It'll be easier on us."

Mac still toyed with all the new ideas and the opportunities that change would bring, a preoccupation that distanced him from Carrie's growing disbelief. "When Antonio met that sister of Genevieve Sayles, the tall dark one, he got more innerested, I think," Mac chuckled, sounding entirely at ease with himself and his world.

"The surprises keep coming," Carrie breathed, uncertainty soaring. She had only glanced at Danielle Hartman during the memorial service, but she recalled a tall dark woman from Missouri, who appeared to be of Spanish-Cherokee blood.

"Me, I decided we needed to move from here for my peace of mind and the health of my stock. We are seeing cattle in Deer Lodge Valley with runny eyes and coughs caused by smoke from the smelters. It's a new problem that I think is going to get worse. Duprés told me that if the miners clean up the tailings, the muskrats will come back and the criks will clear. But I guess I'm one of the rats that's leaving."

But what about me? Carrie was barely aware of Mac's voice droning on and on, far removed from the two of them, a steady hum in the background of crashes Carrie experienced happening around her—but what about me? She sensed he was moving, he had moved, his words severing her from early sunrises and late sunsets viewed from the mountain, from the kitchen where she canned her garden produce and made applesauce from their own apples, from the family plot where Christina was buried next to her grandparents.

About to strike back in distress and anger, Carrie stopped herself—maybe this fixation on moving is his way of avoiding me—I intruded upon his dreams—in fact, I brought his night terrors to light. He may have felt I came too close, threatening a secret world he might have been ashamed of, a feeling of short-comings that would have undermined Mac's view of himself, a view he refused to share with me.

"No, Mac. You can't think of your leaving that way," Carrie blurted, saying it just in time to catch herself from saying something he would take as being hurtful. She was unable to see Mac's eyes directly, but she knew full well the admission of being driven out ran against every bit of grit and manhood he had in him, and then some.

He went on. "I'll go over with Antonio to make arrangements. We will head for the Jefferson River and find property above or below Beaverhead Rock. We'll camp like we do on the cattle drives, and scope it out when we get there." His voice lowered and trailed off while he further pondered the sketchily made plans, his chin dropping lower on his chest.

This is weighing heavily upon him, Carrie knew, and she did not interfere. Mac had always felt responsible for saving the ranch he had inherited from his father. She sensed the wrenching decisions he must have gone through to decide he would leave. She envisioned his father as she had known him when he was alive, white-haired, stern and weather beaten. Mac tried to be like him, make him proud and do justice to the ranch. This is tearing him up, she guessed, and he is trying to hold it and himself together.

"We will locate on the other side of the mountains that run behind the Berrigan place. Who knows, we may spread over to the Upper Madison, but I assure you I am not planning on ranching anywhere near where Kent lived. That's connected to bad memories."

Knowing he was still spooked by the assassination that remained an unsolved case, Carrie did not further question where they would resettle. She admitted that the adverse changes had occurred almost overnight, threatening Mac, the ranch, and those downstream. She felt her anger, fear, and tension of a few moments ago subsiding. Mac had his mind made up, plans had been made, what was new?

Only that her deep losses encompassed her home, her friends Eugenia and Roxanna, and her patients in the homes of what was now called Butte City or simply Butte. And what about Natalya, medicine woman, my friend and mentor to whom I owe so much? Carrie yearned to throw herself onto Natalya's buffalo rug and burst into the tears she now withheld.

Instead, she forced herself to accept the notion of moving the entire *TN* operation. Images already reeled through her mind of their growing herd of over three thousand head of cows and calves strung out over miles, crossing the mountains east of Butte near Highland City, and straggling up the narrow Cedar Ridge road past the stage stop, wranglers whooping and hollering from sunup to sundown. A wide swath of grass trampled by their cloven hooves would record the passage of the rambling, bawling bunch prodded on by the Tarynton crew.

Wagons would follow the rutted, dusty dirt trail on what might be a two-week trip, setting up campsites for the crew, hauling rudiments of a new ranch to a yet to be determined property. The job appeared overwhelming compared to the humble beginnings she and Mac had when they married and took over his parents' homestead, which had been rough but welcoming.

"The cows will be a handful. They don't know that route and it's quite a ways." Carrie found a few noncommittal words to express without cracking open feelings she had not caught up with, let alone sorted out. She only sensed that she could not betray Mac now by any trace of ill will or objection.

"I figure they can walk that far," Mac said of the cattle, finishing Carrie's thought. "Some of the longhorns are old, the ones I bought from Nelson Story years ago. They were young'uns then, but if they can walk all the way from Texas, I guess they can damn well walk over the Continental Divide to good grass."

He scooted himself upright on the sofa, tired but game, to face Carrie. "We'll start over, Carrie. I'm sorry. It will hurt you to leave the mountain."

She leaned over, slowly letting her body settle beside his, slipping under his arm which fell over her shoulders.

Mac's voice dropped, became unsteady, and begged for understanding.

"Sure 'n all, Carrie, looks to me like even with all the wrong turns and downturns of our lives this filly has again chosen me."

Prudence B. Saur's Useful Recipes, 1889

The author accepts no responsibility for treatments or uses of the following mid-19th century recipes, or for Mrs. Saur's recommended uses.

Toast Water

Toast slightly a piece of bread, add to it boiling water; if preferred, sweeten. May flavor with lemon or orange peel.

Flaxseed Tea

Take an ounce of flaxseed and Little pounded licorice root; pour on a pint of boiling water; place vessel near a fire for four hours; strain through linen or cotton cloth.

Barley Coffee

Roast barley until well brown, boil a tablespoonful in a pint of water for five minutes; strain and add a little sugar, if desired. A nourishing drink toward the close of fever and during convalescence.

Beef Tea

Take a pound of lean beef, cut it fine, put it in a bottle corked tightly, and put bottle into a kettle of warm water; boil for a considerable time; remove bottle and pour contents out. Tea may be salted a little, and a teaspoon given each time.

Arrow Root Tea

Add a teaspoonful of arrow root to half a pint of boiling water; mix well, add half a pint of milk, boil together for two or three minutes; sweeten to taste.

Indian Meal Mush

Take fine meal of Northern corn, a little salt; stir slowly in boiling water until it is as thick as can be stirred easily. Stand it on back of stove and cook slowly one hour. Is better cooked in a milk boiler.

Sago Gruel

Sago, two tablespoonsful; water, one pint; boil until it thickens, frequently stirring. May add sugar and nutmeg.

Gum Arabic Mixture

Dissolve four ounces of gum Arabic in three teacups of boing water; sweeten and flavor as desired. Useful in cases of inflammation of the stomach and bowels.

Historical Novels Set in Montana Territory
by Jan Elpel

Berrigan's Ride

Kent Berrigan never expected to settle in remote, raw Montana Territory, 1866, when he fled the South after the Civil War to avoid facing his brother—and his own conscience. He identifies with the wild horses in the mountains in Madison County, unsure of who he is and his future until he encounters Marion Patton, a woman from California gold country. When tragedy strikes Norwegian Creek, he pursues Miss Patton who has a vision of the future of the country if not her own destiny.

Healers of Big Butte

Carrie Tarynton saves the life of a prized Irish horse, but she and her intuitive women friends are confronted by the use of modern medical practices in the silver camp of Big Butte, Montana Territory, 1875 – 1877. Carrie faces her greatest challenge trying to save her husband, cattleman Mac Tarynton, and their marriage. The women have visions and intuitions that prompt Carrie to seek her mentor, a Shoshoni wise woman, and bring the ethnic women of Big Butte together in solidarity before the Nez Perce War.

Heirloom China

Patrick Colter marries Shelley Norton in a double wedding in Big Butte, Montana Territory, 1877, and finds his dream job as a law clerk, until his investigation of a murder brings threats against his life. He whisks his family to safety in the East where he attends Harvard, and Shelley becomes a rising star in the women's movement, along with an unlikely friend, Irmgarde Meyer, a prostitute. Shelley and Irmgarde unexpectedly overcome challenges that would keep them in their place, forcing Patrick to make adjustments of his own.

EXCERPTS from HEIRLOOM CHINA
(Sequel to Healers of Big Butte and the third novel in series set in Montana Territory)

Fear flitted across Antonio's eyes. This man of the land who had Mac Tarynton's back, the man willing to sacrifice his life for his boss, looked terrified for an instant. Patrick had called his hand...the TN stockmen sat on their horses on a ridge high above Deer Lodge Valley waiting for cattle to show up below. At mid-day the air was still; only last year's dried yucca pods whispered in the grassland.

At last Antonio let out a long pent-up breath and said, "Maybe I will."

******

"If at one time I entertained the notion of a political career, it appears that I have already been eclipsed by my wife."

"A bit down in the mouth, aye?"

Patrick's expression of the injured party competed with his husbandly duty to control his wife.

******

"... I can reveal to you, Your Honor, that I have heard a sound prediction about the future of Butte—in copper. It is well worth considering in terms of cases and income."

Patrick paused as if reading tea leaves in his coffee cup. He momentarily forgot the judge, the amorphous concept of justice, the thrill of working on a case. Only Shelley Norton Colter filled all the aching, longing, loving recesses of his long lean body... only the need to support her and her disabled sister, Neva, prompted him to lay his ambitions naked in front of so august an individual as Judge H.D. Kirschenbaum.

279

"Perhaps. Perhaps." The judge had lived long enough to see the best of men come and go, their highest aspirations often evaporated into the thin air of the Rocky Mountains.

******

Reuben Bosworth's scowl deepened while he struggled with the many unsavory concepts raised by his son. "Ranchers, Rebels, a drunk trash man, and rumors among the low life. I cannot make a case from what you are telling me."

"You have solved tougher cases, Father." Lucas couldn't resist the jibe.

Thrumming his fingers on the table, Reuben glanced about as if a resolution for compensating a prostitute who saved his son's life would manifest itself.

Lucas let the matter lie.

His father abruptly turned inward, evidently searching his moral compass, ascertaining whether helping her was one he dared countenance. At last his chest heaved with resignation.

"I would agree to help the whole damn District if they had saved you."

The moment held all their unspoken words.

******

Shelley felt the rebuke in her most vulnerable part—the lack of an advanced education. Her husband ruled by his superiority, as well as by the law and Scriptures and a culture of patriarchy. Mrs. Elizabeth Cady Stanton's words spun in her mind: "We suffer daily humiliation of spirit..."

Acknowledgments

Healers of Big Butte was inspired by the encyclopedic handbook, *Maternity, A Book for Every Wife and Mother*, by Prudence B. Saur, M.D., 1889, which I rescued from an old barn in Virginia City, Montana. Sensing it contained a story, I have been thrilled and delighted to discover Mrs. Prudence Saur, whose "excessive mental development" did not impair her health or contribution to the medical literature of the mid-1800s. Her sage advice and observation of human nature illustrates her professional accomplishments and surprisingly modern medical views and practices.

To my daughters, the healers, I am most grateful. Also my mother, Josephine Jewett, and my son, Thomas J. Elpel, for acquainting me with natural and holistic medicine. And to those who preserve Chinese and Native American traditional medicine, now rediscovered in modern medicine, my deep appreciation.

To the meticulous research of Merrill D. Beal on the conflict and ultimate shame of the United States' defeat of the Nez Perce in 1877.

To the Holy Scriptures for the stories of healing that we have known all our lives and may come to understand in a new way.

For *Healers of Big Butte*, and its predecessor, *Berrigan's Ride*, my gratitude to my son, Thomas J. Elpel, publisher, who made both novels a reality; my daughter Jeanne Elpel, Cynthia Logan, Margie Peterson, and others for editing; Ellen Crain, Director of Butte-Silver Bow Archives, and Mitzi Rossillon for their knowledgeable reviews; Crystal Alegria, Director of Extreme History Project of Bozeman for her insights; Linda Griffith for cover design; and my appreciation for invaluable works in the Selected Bibliography, as well as many other books and articles.

Selected Bibliography

Beal, Merrill D. *I Will Fight No More Forever*, 1963

Boettger, Carrie. Essay, "*The Legacy of Butte Mining*," 2001

Crain, Ellen. Butte-Silver Bow Historical Archives' maps and *The New North-West* newspapers.

Documentary. *Butte, America*, DVD, a collection of oral histories of early Butte, 2009

Elpel, Thomas J. *Botany in a Day*, 6th Edition, 2014

Enss, Chris. *The Doctor Wore Petticoats*, 2006

Freeman, Harry, C. *A Brief History of Butte*, Montana 1900

Haines, Francis. *The Nez Perces*, 1955.

Joyce, James. *The Dubliners*, 1914, (a collection of stories), and other J. Joyce books

Kearney, Pat. *Butte Voices, Mining, Neighborhoods, People*, 1998

Leeson, Michael, editor. *History of Montana*, 1739-1885

Lenihan, Eddie. *Meeting the Other Crowd: Fairy Stories of Hidden Ireland*, 2004

Lewis and Clark State College Library, Lewiston, Idaho, Shahaptian Alphabet

MacLane, Mary. *Mary MacLane by Herself*, 1902

McGlashan, Zena Beth. *Buried in Butte*, 2010

McGrath, Jean. *Butte's Heritage Cookbook*, 1984

Madsen, Brigham D. *The Bannock of Idaho*, 1958

Phillips, Paul C. *Medicine in the Making in Montana*, 1962

Potter, Roy, editor. *Medicine, a History of Healing – Ancient Traditions to Modern Practices*, 1997

Robison, Ken. *Montana Territory and the Civil War*, 2013

Safford, Jeffrey J. *The Mechanics of Optimism, Mining Companies, Technology, and the Hot Spring Gold Rush, Montana Territory, 1864 – 1868*, 2004

Saur, Prudence B. *Maternity, A Book for Every Wife and Mother*, 1889

Smith, Phyllis. *Montana's Madison Country: a History*, 2006

Spaulding, Henry H. *Nez Perce's First Book: Designed for Children and New Beginners*, 1839a

Staffanson, Robert. *Witness to Spirit; my Life with Cowboys, Mozart, and Indians*, 2015

Steele, Volney, M.D. *Bleed, Blister and Purge, A History of Medicine on the American Frontier*, 2005

Trenholm, Virginia Cole, and Carly, Maurine. *The Shoshonis, Sentinels of the Rockies*, 1964

Wolfe, Murial. *Montana Pay Dirt*, 1963

Writers Project of Montana. 1943, *Copper Camp, 1970 – 2002*

Yep, Laurence. *Dragonwings*, 1975

About the Author

Jan Elpel, Psy.D, grew up near the Missouri Headwaters in southwest Montana, and that sense of place and time frame the stories she creates set in the mid-nineteenth century. The Jewett family lifestyle among descendents of early immigrants in the 1940s was little different than that of the settlers in **Berrigan's Ride** and its sequel, **Healers of Big Butte,** eighty years earlier. She participated in a Lewis and Clark pageant enacted at the Headwaters, and in 1958, wrote the original John Colter pageant which was produced at the Three Forks rodeo grounds, initiating the town's first Colter's Run.

Her love of Butte began in mid-1980s when she worked at the old St. James Care and Psych Center, and specialized in child and family psychology. She explored much of the north side of Butte, which retains traces of its gold and silver mining days.

CPSIA information can be obtained
at www.ICGtesting.com
Printed in the USA
FSOW03n2328050817
37162FS